THE BRAVE COWBOY

BOOKS BY EDWARD ABBEY

The Brave Cowboy

Fire on the Mountain

Desert Solitaire

Appalachian Wilderness

Black Sun

Slickrock

Cactus Country

The Monkey Wrench Gang

The Journey Home

The Hidden Canyon

Abbey's Road

Desert Images

Good News

Down the River

In Praise of Mountain Lions

Beyond the Wall

The Fool's Progress

One Life at a Time, Please

Hayduke Lives!

A Voice Crying in the Wilderness

THE BRAVE COWBOY

An Old Tale in a New Time

EDWARD ABBEY

HARPER**PERENNIAL** ● MODERN**CLASSICS**

HARPER**PERENNIAL** MODERN**CLASSICS**

HarperCollins books may be purchased for educational, business, or sales promotional use. For information, please e-mail the Special Markets Department at SPsales@harpercollins.com.

First Harper Perennial Modern Classics edition published in 2016.
First Avon Books trade edition published in 1992.
First Avon Books mass market edition published in May 1982.

FIRST EDITION

Designed by Jamie Lynn Kerner

Library of Congress Cataloging-in-Publication Data has been applied for.

ISBN 978-0-06-242996-4

HB 01.08.2024

To the outlaws—
to all of them:
the good and the bad, the ugly
and the pretty, the dead and the live

CONTENTS

It's only a story. None of it really happened. How could it? How could such people be? The prisoner is probably a professor. The sheriff loses the next election. The truck-driver died of emphysema. And as for the cowboy, that character, why nobody even knows where he is anymore. Or even, to be honest, if he ever really was.

THE BRAVE COWBOY

BALLAD OF THE BRAVE COWBOY

Come sit here beside me
and I will relate
the tale of a cowboy
and his terrible fate.

His name it was Burns
and he came from the East;
no more would he say
to man nor beast.

He worked for his wages
on a Magdalene spread:
a dollar a day,
beef, beans and bread.

A tough, dirty life
and death in a ditch;
hard on the kidneys,
bad for the itch;
a man might get suntanned,
he wouldn't get rich.

Like all brave cowboys dead and alive
on riding and wind and stars he could thrive
with a home-made song to keep his heart alive.

Burns was skinny and dark
and he kept most alone;
he had only one friend,
a kid named Bone.

Together they rode
and together they fought
when they got to town
and drank a lot
and bluffed each other
shot after shot.

Like all good cowboys dead and alive
on fighting and grit and blood they thrive
with a little strong whisky to keep hope alive.

One day in the fall
came orders for battle:
twenty-five men against
five thousand cattle.

The sky was yellow
and the sun was red
when the drive started south
for the town of Mordred.

We knew by the signs
we were in for some fun:
the wind screamed high
the dust-devils spun
and five thousand longhorns
started to run.

Like all dumb cowhands alive and dead
on trouble and sand and cactus they fed
and on payday a little brown girl in bed.

It was thunder and hell
when the herd broke loose;
a man was safer
with his head in a noose.

We got them turned
but too strung out,

they kept on running
and came right about.

Young Bone rode the drag
and got lost in the dust,
rode his horse in a hole
and a leg got bust.

He scrambled around
and looked for the fray;
saw 10,000 red eyes
coming his way,
saw 20,000 hooves
coming for pay.

He tried to run
he tried to crawl;
nothing he did
was no help at all.

He liked to have prayed
but could not recollect
the words that his Mother
had tried to inject
and it looked for sure
his career was wrecked.

O all brave cowboys dead and revived
God only knows how you ever survived
or stayed out of Hell with souls unshrived.

Now Burns rode the point
and saw his friend's danger,
came galloping up
like a Texas Ranger.

He hauled the kid up
while his horse danced around
and the herd roared close
on the rumbling ground.

They tried to get clear
but it was too late,
they were surrounded
by bellowing hate
and the panicked horse
completed their fate.

The scream of that horse
was an awful sound
when the crazy herd
rode them all down
and kicked and rolled them
over the ground.

Like many poor cowhands alive and dead
they never had a chance to die in bed
or even get their prayers said.

When the herd was stopped
and the dust blew away
we found their bodies
mixed with the clay.

The kid had a home
in Texas named Blair
where we shipped what was left
of his hide and hair,
but the cowboy Burns
we buried right there.

Like all brave cowboys dead and alive
on riding and wind and stars he thrived
with a home-made song to keep his heart alive
with a song to keep alive.

A PROLOGUE

There is a valley in the West where phantoms come to brood and mourn, pale phantoms dying of nostalgia and bitterness. You can hear them shivering, chattering, among the leaves of the old dry mortal cottonwoods down by the river—whispering and moaning and hissing with the wind over the black cones of the five volcanoes on the west—you can hear them under the red cliffs of the Sangre Mountains on the other side of the valley, whining their past away with the wild dove and the mockingbird—and you may see one, touch one, in the silences and space and mute terror of the desert, if you ride away from the river, which in this barren land is the river of life.

The Rio Bravo comes down from the mountains of Colorado and the mountains of Santa Fe and flows into the valley, passing between the dead volcanoes on the west and the wall of mountains on the east. The river flows past the cornfields and mud villages of the Indians, past thickets of red willow and cane and scrub oak, through the fringe of the white man's city and under the four-lane bridge of his national highway, beyond the city and the bridge and past more mud villages, more cornfields; the river flows beyond Thieves' Mountain far to the south and vanishes at last into the dim violet haze of distance, of history and Mexico and the gulf-sea.

But the river is haunted, the city is haunted, the valley and the mountains and the silent desert are haunted—troubled, vexed, by ghosts, phantoms, and vagrant spirits.

You can hear them—down along the river, shaking and whispering in the leaves of the old cottonwoods; if you go there you must hear them. Or out on the west mesa, around the black craters of the volcanoes—phantoms hissing and moaning with the wind. Or up there among the red cliffs and pinnacles, in those immense gulfs of space under the mountain's rim, where the air is cool and sweet with the odor of juniper and lightning, where the mockingbird and the canyon wren and the mourning dove join with the phantoms in their useless keening. And out on the desert away from the river and the valley, far out beyond the volcanoes, you may see one whirling and whistling like a devil up some dry rocky wash, snapping the brittle lances of the yucca with the violence of its hate—

It was into this valley of ghosts and smoke and unacknowledged sorrows that The Cowboy rode, one morning in October not so many years ago. . . .

PART ONE

THE COWBOY

" . . . Riding in from the desert to the west
coming from God knows where . . ."

CHAPTER 1

He was sitting on his heels in the cold light of the dawn, drawing pale flames through a handful of twigs and dry crushed grass. Beside him was his source of fuel: a degenerate juniper tree, shriveled and twisted, cringing over its bed of lava rock and sand. An underprivileged juniper tree, living not on water and soil but on memory and hope. And almost alone. To the north across the rolling mesa of lava there was a broad scattering of junipers, perhaps two or three to an acre, but here where the man squatted before his fire there was only the one, and south and west of the five volcanoes there were none at all, nothing organic but a rudimentary form of bunch grass and the tough spiny yucca.

The man coaxing his tinder into flame was not much interested in the burnt-out wasteland around him. Occasionally he would glance to the southeast and toward the city several miles away, stretched out like a long gray shadow on the other side of the river, or would take a look at the chestnut mare limping among the black rocks beyond the wash, its forelegs held stiffly together, its iron shoes scraping on the stone. But for the most part he concentrated his attention on his small sprightly fire and when he did look away from it his hands continued their work of breaking and adding sticks of wood.

After a while, when the fire had been built up to about the size of a small fryingpan and a residue of glowing charcoal had accumulated, he lifted a canteen from a branch of the tree, filled a small smoke-blackened pan with water and pushed it lidless halfway into the bed of the fire. He watched it closely for several minutes, waiting for the first globule of superheated air to appear on the bottom of the pan. As he waited he broke a dead stick into short lengths and laid the pieces carefully on the embers.

A cool morning, even in the sunlight. Surfaces exposed to the sun were becoming warm but the air remained chill and sharp, as though the sunlight passed from source to object without heating the intervening medium.

The bubble appeared. The man reached out toward the juniper and pulled a wrinkled beaten old cavalry saddlebag close to his heel, unbuckled its one remaining strap and removed from the interior a black skillet, battered and ancient, then a cylindrical tin labeled Handyman Tube Patching Kit, a can of pork and beans, a punch-type canopener and a slab of salted mutton wrapped in a greasy back copy of the Duke City *Journal.*

The mare on the other side of the wash was staring toward the river, flexing her soft rubbery nostrils, twitching her ears. There was a dim fragrance of tamarisk in the air, and a tension, an electricity, in the old aching silence.

The man wiped his nose once on his sleeve, sniffing a little, then unwrapped the mutton, opened his jackknife and sawed several strips of meat into the skillet, which he set directly on

the fire. A dimple in the bottom of the skillet reversed its cur-
vature with a sudden ping, like a plucked violin string, making
one of the slices jump. He wiped the blade of the knife on his
jeans, closed it and put it back in his pocket, while the meat
sizzled and smoked in the skillet. He opened the can of beans
and poured them over the meat; the gluey mess spread steaming
around the mutton strips, spluttering against the hot metal.

By now the water was simmering in the open pan, its surface beginning to vaporize. The man unscrewed the lid from
the tube patching kit and emptied a certain amount of a brown
granular material into the water, measuring by eye. Instantly
the aroma of hot coffee graced the air and an involuntary smile
appeared on his hungry, lean face.

Within five minutes everything was ready, or ready enough,
and ready almost simultaneously: the coffee cooked and dif-
fused densely through the boiling water, the mutton fried, the
beans hot and smoky. The man began to eat, using his fingers
for the meat, scooping the beans from the skillet with a sawed-
off tablespoon and gulping down the scalding coffee in quick
short draughts direct from the pan.

When he was finished he leaned back against the bole of
the crouching juniper, wiped his mouth on the back of his hand
and sighed contentedly. After a moment he pulled at the yellow
string dangling from his shirtpocket and drew out a small white
cotton sack of tobacco. He reached in the pocket, groping with
thumb and forefinger, and found a packet of wheat-straw cigarette papers. He took one of the papers—thin, brown, not
gummed—and holding it delicately between his thumb and
middle finger, half-rolled to form a trough, he opened the sack
with his other hand and tapped out some of the cheap arid pul-

verized tobacco onto the paper. He tightened the drawstrings of
the sack with a hand and his teeth and put it back in his shirt-
pocket. Then with the thumbs and forefingers of both hands he
rolled the paper around the evenly-distributed tobacco, moist-
ened the edge of the paper with his tongue, sealed it and gave
one end of the somewhat oblate cylinder a half twist. Without
a further glance at his work he stuck the cigarette between his
lips, scratched a match on his bootsole and lit it. Drawing, tasting, releasing the first mouthful of smoke, he stretched out his
long, thin legs, relaxing, and stared at the city beyond the river.

Stared at it from under the brim of his black slouch hat, his
head tilted back against the tree, the hat pushed forward and
almost down over his eyes. The attitude of his head and hat,
the gaze from narrowed eyes down past the flanges of the nose,
the cigarette jutting at an acute angle from his mouth, made his
stare seem disdainful, unconsciously arrogant.

He was a young man, not more than thirty. His neck was
long, scrawny, with a sharp adamsapple and corded muscles; his
nose, protruding from under the decayed brim of the hat, was
thin, red, aquiline and asymmetrical, like the broken beak of
a falcon. He had a small mouth with thin dry lips, and a chin
pointed like a spade, and his skin, bristling with a week's growth
of black whiskers, had the texture of cholla and the hue of an old
gunstock.

The young man smoked on in contemplative silence, staring at the city. He seemed to be thinking as he sat there in the
sun, the juniper growing out of his back and neck. Every line,
fiber, bone and muscle of his body bespoke repose, the assured
unselfconscious tranquillity of a sleeping hound. His hands, big
and long-fingered like those of a flutist or a good plank-stacker,

and hard, brown, leather-skinned, rested like a pair of lifeless tools on his lap, on his groin and genitals. Every now and then a puff of blue smoke drifted out from under the hatbrim, from an apparently immobile mouth and throat. But despite the appearance of a complete somnolence suggested by the relaxation of his body there were indications of an internal activity discernible at two points: the eyes. Deep in the grotto of darkness formed by the tilted hat and the high ridge of the nose the two eyes, like instrument dials of the mind and emotions, registered thought, perplexity, a faint hairline trace of anxiety.

He spat out what was left of the cigarette.

On the other side of the river, miles away, the city lay waiting, stirring faintly but in silence—vague wisps of smoke and dust, glints of reflected light from moving objects, a motion of shadows—not yet fully awake and too far to be heard. In the early morning light, viewed from the west by the man sitting against the juniper, the city appeared as an undifferentiated patch of blue and gray shadow, edges ill-defined, southern and eastern extremities invisible, all blended with the vast wings of the shadow of the Sangre Mountains.

The river, curling beyond and below the edge of the lava flow, was hard to make out from that distance and elevation; here and there he could see strips and sheets of opaque water but mostly nothing except the ragged fringe of vegetation crowding the banks and islands and old channels of the river.

The silence was intense, burning, infinite. He could hear the silence, or what seemed like its music, the singing of the blood through his ears.

Far to the southeast, from the direction of the giant military air base adjoining The Factory, came the shattering roar of a jet engine. The sound rose, drove like an iron wedge through the sky, scoring the air with its transparent vibration. Then retracted, faded, died, and the vast silence closed in again, and sealed its perfect dome over the desert and the river and the valley.

The young man leaned away from the juniper, bending the hinges of his long legs, and stood up. He was over six feet tall, with about two-thirds of that altitude composed of attenuated fuse-like legs. He spread the ashes of the fire with his boot, kicked sand over them, buried the bean can under a rock and scattered the coffee grounds. The skillet and spoon he scoured with a handful of sand, and packed back into the saddlebag. He rolled his light mummy-type sleeping bag into a hard tight bundle, tied it and laid it across the saddle on the ground. Then he looked for the mare.

The mare was watching him now; she stood about fifty yards away in the rocky draw, ears alerted, black tail swiping at a horsefly, shaking her black shaggy mane and watching him. A three-year-old, well-muscled and close-coupled, with slender hocks and a glossy chestnut coat. She had good wide-apart eyes and a stiffly-arched neck and her name was Whisky.

"Whisky," he called, "here girl." The mare's ears went back. "Here girl," he called, and lifted the bridle and reins from a branch of the juniper. The mare eyed him suspiciously, not moving. He reached down into one of the saddlebags and found a small withered yellow apple and held it in the air, baiting the horse. "Come here, Whisky," he called softly, "got something for you." The mare shook her head, watching him, swept a fly from her haunch and stamped at the sand but did not step toward him.

He shrugged his shoulders wearily and walked toward her, eating the apple as he went. He saved the core and when he had advanced to within a few yards of the horse tried again to tempt her. "Whisky," he called gently, proffering the apple core, "here girl. Come here, girl." This time she responded, lurching toward him awkwardly with her hobbled forelegs.

The man smiled and stepped to meet her and fed her the apple core from his palm, holding her head against his chest and whispering into the tense ears. "That's a girl, now you're gettin the idea." He rubbed her face and forehead and patted the strong nervous neck. "You're a good girl, Whisky. You're not so dumb, little girl. No sirree, you're all right." While he was murmuring into her ears he started slowly and stealthily to slip the bridle on; but she resisted, jerked her head up and tried to back away. Quickly he jammed his thumb inside her cheek, forced her mouth open and inserted the bit, pushed the headstall over her ears and fastened the throatlatch. "Easy, girl, easy," he said as the mare laid back her ears again. He caressed her neck and thumped his fist on her powerful shoulder. After a moment he half-knelt to unbuckle the Mormon hobble around her shanks. The mare trembled when the strap slipped off but made no trouble. "That's a girl," he whispered. He straightened up, holding the hobble in one hand, passed the reins over her neck and quickly smoothly pulled himself up and astride her bare back.

For a second the mare stood rigid, frozen in outrage; then before he could put a spur to her she leaped forward as if stung, stopped suddenly, arching her back with convulsive violence, and left the earth in another mighty leap, came back down and hit with braced legs, a sickening bone-jarring shock.

The man on her back gasped through his grin, shook his head and leaned forward and clutched at the mane with one hand, twisting the strong hairs around his fingers and wrist. "Come on, you bitch!" he shouted, and whipped the mare across the flank with the leather hobble.

She sprang forward again, bucked once, twice, then broke and ran; laughing and cursing, the man turned her with a touch of leather on the neck, kept her turning round and round in a tight circle until she began to tire a little, then brought her at an easy canter back to the campsite, stopped her short and slid off. He cradled the mare's head in his arms and talked low-toned soothing nonsense into her quivering ears, while the dust they had raised went drifting by to settle again on different ground.

When she seemed quiet enough he spread a pad on her back and threw on his saddle, an old worn all-purpose outfit with a double rig and rolled cantle. He caught the cinch ring swinging underneath on the other side and pulled it up and passed the latigo through it a half dozen times and jerked it tight. The mare was holding her breath: he deflated her with a pair of good driving punches to the belly, drew the latigo tighter and secured it on the tongue of the ring. After this he hung on the saddlebags and fastened them, tied the bedroll on behind the cantle, and looped his almost-empty government canteen close to the saddlehorn. He had still more gear to attend to, a guitar and a rifle laying on the ground in the shade of the juniper. The rifle, a thirty-two caliber lever-action carbine, went in the scabbard slung under the fender on the right side of the saddle; the guitar he slung across his back by its braided rawhide cord.

All was ready now; the mare waited impatiently under her firm burden of metal and leather, waited for the man's approach and the springy pressure of his long weight on her back. She had to wait; he seemed in no hurry now after completing his preparations. Instead of mounting he stood facing the east and the city, slouching comfortably over his backbone and pelvis, thumbs hooked in the pockets of his jeans, the black hat tilted forward over his eyes.

The sun was now an hour higher in the sky, a good ten feet above the violet crest of the mountains. The shadows contracted, creeping back, and the first miasmic shimmer of heat waves began to obscure the detail of rocks and brush. Between the man and the river a spinning dervish of air and sand, like a translucent tornado, danced across the plain with the weightless bouyant grace of a moving spotlight; at its base the tumbleweeds bounced around and around like figures in a square dance.

The mare pawed at the sand, jerking her head nervously, and the leather gear on her back creaked and rustled—the most reassuring and satisfying of sounds, that agitation of used, worn, familiar leather. The man heard it, turned, caught up the dragging reins, put a hand on the pommel, his foot in the stirrup and swung up into the saddle. The mare was already facing the east, the river; he touched her with his spurs and she started off, breaking almost at once into a trot. He pulled back a little and kept her at a brisk walking gait, heading not for the center of the city but toward the northern tip of its elongated trunk.

Mounted and armed, he rode for the city, the slanting blaze of the sun twinkling on the buttplate of the rifle, the silver buckle, the spurs, touching with fire the brief puffs of dust rising up from each step of the horse, glistening on the smooth hide of the mare's shoulders, thighs, operating muscles. The man himself, in his worn dusty clothing, did not reflect much light; in the full glare of the morning sun there was something shadowy and smoke-like about him, something faded, blurred, remembered.

He gazed straight forward as he rode, apparently indifferent to the vast sweep of desert around him, the sky singing overhead. The five volcanoes to the south, lined up like old ruined tombs, swung slowly around on his wheeling horizon. Riding into the brush of greasewood, live oak, mesquite, he flushed a covey of quail; they rose in unison from the desert floor, shrilling and fluttering, flew ahead for a distance and dropped in unison to the ground again. When he rode up to them they rose into the air again, flew ahead and dropped into the brush, still in front of him. He ignored them, thinking of something else, his eyes under the shadow of the hat fixed intently on the vague complex of the city.

His course brought him to an arroyo, whose sandy bed he followed for a mile or more until it veered too much to the south. Under the arroyo's banks, on the fine drifted sand, he noted the delicate hieroglyphics of field mice, lizards, gophers, jackrabbits, quail and buzzards, but in the light of day only a few lizards appeared, swift and rubbery and insignificant, to watch the passage of man and horse.

When the arroyo turned he rode up out of it and across the lava rock again, through scattered patches of rabbitbrush and tumbleweed, until he came eventually to a barbed-wire fence, gleaming new wire stretched with vibrant tautness between steel stakes driven into the sand and rock, reinforced between stakes with wire staves. The man looked for a gate but could see only the fence itself extended north and south to a pair of vanishing points, an unbroken thin stiff line of geometric exactitude scored with a bizarre, mechanical precision over the face of the rolling earth. He dismounted, taking a pair of fencing pliers from one of the saddlebags, and pushed his way through banked-up tumbleweeds to the fence. He cut the wire—the twisted steel resisting the bite of his pliers for a moment, then yielding with a soft sudden grunt to spring apart in coiled tension, touching the ground only lightly with its barbed points—and returned to the mare, remounted, and rode through the opening, followed by a few stirring tumbleweeds.

He rode on, approaching the rim of the ancient lava flow and the glint of the river beyond it, the willows, the soft yellow-leaved cottonwoods on the banks of the river. The rider relaxed in the saddle, turning in the seat, and lifted one leg and rested it on the mare's neck. After a while he pushed back his hat and unslung the guitar from his back and struck off a few running chords. The mare answered with a twitch of her ears and stepped forward quickly. He strummed a few more chords, tightened one of the strings, and then began to sing, very softly, addressing no one but himself and the mare.

> *I made up my mind . . . to change my way,*
> *And leave my crowd . . . that was so gay . . .*

His hard, wind-honed, sun-dried face softened a little under the influence of the music, became human, almost gentle.

> *To leave my love, who'd promised me her hand,*
> *And head down south . . . of the Rio Grande . . .*

The mare's iron-shod hooves clinked on the black rock; a whisper of wind drifted through the brittle clicking leaves of the greasewood. Beyond the river and ten miles east of the city the Sangre Mountains began to reveal themselves in more detail as the sun rose higher, the rampart of blue shadow dissolving in the light, exposing the fissured red cliffs, the canyons and gorges a thousand feet deep, the towers leaning out from the main wall, the foothills dry and barren as old bones, and above and behind these tumbled ruins the final barrier of granite, the great horizontal crest tilted up a mile high into the frosty blue sky, sparkling with a new fall of snow. The mountains loomed over the valley like a psychical presence, a source and mirror of nervous influences, emotions, subtle and unlabeled aspirations; no man could ignore that presence; in an underground poker game, in the vaults of the First National Bank, in the secret chambers of The Factory, in the backroom of the realtor's office during the composition of an intricate swindle, in the heart of a sexual embrace, the emanations of mountain and sky imprinted some analogue of their nature on the evolution and shape of every soul.

> *It was in the year . . . of eighty-three,*
> *That A. J. Stinson . . . hired me . . .*

The young man rode on, loafing in the saddle and singing to himself and the mare, but with his eyes still sighted on the northern fringe of the city where the houses turned to mud and dried out among cottonwoods and irrigation ditches on the edge of the all-surrounding desert.

He passed within a half mile of a sheep camp: black tarpaper shack, a cardboard housetrailer resting on two flat tires, a brush corral, a flatbed truck with dismantled engine, a watertank and its windmill with motionless vanes, a great glittering heap of tincans; no men or sheep visible. Creeping toward this establishment from the north along the vague scratch of a road was a cloud of dust, moving with what at that distance seemed like agonizing deliberation; at the point of the dustcloud was a minute black object, tremulous in the shimmering light, apparently in motion, disappearing now and then, reappearing, silent and busy and persevering: a truck or car bouncing along at forty miles an hour over a washboard road. The distance and the silence, the grotesque disproportion between the small dark agitated object and its enveloping continuum of space and silence, gave its activity an absurd, pathetic air.

Horse and rider came to another obstacle and a second halt—the black drop-off, the congealed rim of the lava flow, a jumbled mass of rock falling steeply to the plain ninety feet below. The man turned the mare to the north and followed the edge of the cliff until he came to a place where descent was possible. He dismounted then and led the mare down slowly and cautiously, squeezing between the black boulders, switching back and forth across the face of the slope.

Above him, flowing over the dark burnt-out iron of the mesa, the sky turned deep liquid blue, vivid, burning, profound, the bottomless sea of the atmosphere. The young man stopped once and stared up at it, rubbing his jaw, and then went on. The mare followed him reluctantly, eyes rolling and knees trembling, before plunging and sliding down from one ledge to the next. The black rock was sharp-edged, hot, and hard as corundum; it seemed not merely alien but impervious to life. Yet on the southern face of almost every rock the lichens grew, yellow, rusty-brown, yellow-green, like patches of dirty paint daubed on the stone. Horse and man passed other signs and stigmata of life: the petroglyph of a wild turkey chiseled in the stone, a pair of tincans riddled with bullet holes of various caliber, brass cartridge shells, an empty sardine can dissolving in rust. They were nearing civilization.

It took about ten minutes to make the descent. At the bottom, among the scattered slabs of lava, the man swung back in the saddle and went on over the last mile or so of sand and rabbitbrush to the river. He traversed the trails of jeeps and motorcycles, picked his way through a litter of tincans, broken bottles and windblown Kleenex, and came presently to the high western bank of the river. Here he stopped again and rolled another cigarette.

In front of him the sand sloped down an easy fifty feet to the slow brown silt-fat water of the Rio Bravo. At this point the riverbed was about a hundred yards wide, with a fourth of that distance under flowing water and the rest consisting of mud, sand and quicksand drying out under the sun. Twenty-five yards wide, two or three feet deep, except where the heart of the current had gouged out a little more, the greatest river in New Mexico rolled sluggishly south, rippling and gurgling past the willows, the cottonwoods, the wild cane and cattails, toward the desolation of Texas and the consummation of the open sea eight hundred miles away.

He puffed on his cigarette and spurred Whisky down the bank. "Hup," he said, as she tried to resist, "come on, little *puta*." She yielded, crouched down on her hind legs and half-slid, half-fell down and across the deep soft sand to the water, trailing dust and the transparent but powerful flak from a series of startled farts. She splashed for a moment in the swirling water, then jerked violently at the reins, plunging her head to drink.

The rider let her have her way, while the water roiled around his boots. He touched the hot canvas cover of his canteen, lifted it from the saddlehorn and dipped it in the water and let it cool for a while.

Blowing smoke, he watched the blue fumes twist in the downdraft over the water, diffuse and vanish in the cooler air. From where he waited he could see nothing of the city; the heart of it was two or three miles to the south, beyond the trees, fields, ditches and suburbs. On the opposite bank was a solid growth of willows and beyond that a grove of cottonwoods with golden leaves; nothing more was visible. But he had left the zone of silence; though he could not see the city he could hear it; a continuous droning roar, the commingled vibrations of ten thousand automobiles, trucks, tractors, airplanes, locomotives, the hum and whine of fifty thousand radios, telephones, television receivers, the vast murmur of a hundred thousand human voices, the great massive muttering of friction and busyness and mechanical agitation. The rider puffed calmly on his cigarette, waiting for the mare to cool her belly.

When she was satisfied he tossed the butt of his smoke into the river and they started across. The current was stronger than it looked; near the center the mare lost her footing and floundered around, while the man hastily pulled his rifle from its sheath and held it above the water. The mare started to swim back to the west bank and he swore at her, turned her around and kept her going in the right direction until she was wading again, splashing across a submerged sandbar and up onto an island of mud and twelve-foot willows.

They stopped here, while he poured the water out of his boots and out of the saddlebags and out of the soundbox of the guitar. The mare waited for him impatiently, swishing her soggy tail at the flies that swarmed through the bars of light and shade. He finished in a hurry, slapped at a mosquito settling down on his neck, and remounted and rode out of the willows.

Mud lay ahead of them, liquescent oozy mud with the consistency of warm gruel, an unplumbed deposit of fine silt that had once been part of the tilth and topsoil of Colorado and would eventually become the property of the Gulf of Mexico. There was no way around, unless they retreated to the west bank and went five miles south to the highway bridge. Aside from that there was nothing to do but go over or through the mud.

They went through it, the mare sinking in well over her fetlocks, lunging and staggering ahead, every lurching step accompanied by the suction of gasping slime and exploding pockets of air. The rider urged her on with his spurs, soothed her with soft words and caresses, forestalling panic, at the same time scrutinizing the creamy surface that lay ahead for a sign of quicksand.

But there was none; they reached the east bank at last, wet and splattered with mud. The man dismounted, kicked some of the mud from his boots and urinated there on the grass and mushrooms under the cool shelter of the cottonwoods. He remounted after a minute and rode on straight east through the trees until he came to an irrigation ditch. He stopped again here and washed some of the sweat and dust from his face and wet his hair and slicked it back with his hands. He could hear a meadowlark whistling in the alfalfa field beyond the ditch, and the steady rasping of cicada. The sun was high now, approaching noon and very hot.

Without remounting he led the mare on a narrow wooden

bridge across the ditch and through a wire gate in the fence on the other side. After he had closed and fastened the gate he climbed into the saddle and rode up the quiet dusty lane under a nave of cottonwoods squatting fowlwise along the road, their leaves burning, dying slowly, golden and heavy with dust. On each side of the road were fences enclosing pasture and alfalfa, and corn already cut and shocked. The fencerows were almost hidden by jungles of wild sunflowers standing ten feet tall, the rusty brown heads drooping with the weight of their seed. He could smell tamarisk and plowed earth and the smoke of burning cedar. As he rode on a flock of crows took alarm and flapped out of a cottonwood ahead of him, squawking anxiously, and a fine haze of dust filtered down from the trembling leaves.

He passed a man in rubber boots and big straw hat, with a spade in his hands, contemplating the trickle of water that ran through the little ditch beside the road. The rider nodded his head gravely and the man with the spade returned his salute with a cautious handwave.

Dogs began to appear, and children, as he rode past old adobe houses with heavy corroded walls and secret windows. The skinny yapping dogs thronged around the mare, nipping at her heels, and she lashed out at them with her iron hooves and broke into a trot. The rider hauled back on the reins, slowed her to a fast walk. "Easy, girl, easy," he said quietly.

The little dark children of the farmers trotted along beside him in the dust, staring, grinning, making remarks:

"Eh charro, dónde va? Dónde va, meestair cow-*boy*?"

Women came to the doorways in the adobe walls, leaned there casually and scratched at their armpits, watching him ride by with their soft brown animal eyes, curious, appraising, not unfriendly. The rider smiled at them, tipped his hat courteously to each one—dust sliding down from the brim onto his wrist—and some quality or question in his grave smile made the women smile back, uneasily, shyly. There was a silent and tentative exchange of recognition, as though the man on horseback were not a stranger, or something more than a stranger, a figure out of a grandfather's tale heard in childhood, a man thought to be utterly forgotten now returning and riding visibly and audibly down the soft brown dust of the street.

The women touched the medallions lying between their breasts and watched him go.

The children followed him beyond the village, staring at him, trotting beside the horse, asking questions:

"Dónde va, don charro? Eh? Dónde va?"

"Quien sabe?" he answered; "who knows? Who cares?"

The biggest boy, bold and dirty, with a dead cigarette stuck on his lower lip and two gray ropes of snot discharging from his nostrils, was not so deferential: "Eh huesudo, where you come from, huh? What's your name? Barbudo?" Some of the little boys sniggered as they trotted along. "What's your name, huesudo?" the biggest boy said again, grinning at the others. "Barbudo? Viego jodido y reculón? Eh?"

The rider looked down at him. "Watch your manners, mocoso. Quitense."

"Malas cachas!"

The rider stopped his horse. "Come here," he said quietly, detaching his rope from the saddle swell and shaking out the loop. The boy hung back, alarmed. "Venga!" the rider said; "pronto!" He gave the loop an experimental twirl above his head. To the other boys he said: "We'll use that tree there," and pointed to the nearest cottonwood.

The boy with the cigarette turned and ran back down the road toward the village, squealing for his father; after a moment of hesitation all the others turned and ran with him. The rider grinned after them, then pulled the mare about and jogged on toward the city.

He passed between rows of tall golden poplars standing like flaming torches beside the road, past more fields of corn and alfalfa and dead sunflowers, over another irrigation ditch and into the suburban outskirts of the city. The road became a street, with a gravel surface and neat drainage ditches on each side, and the houses were neat and clean and made of cement or brick or cinder blocks with a stucco finish; each house was neatly fenced off from its neighbors. There seemed to be no children in this area, very few dogs, no chickens or geese or crows. The women remained indoors and stared out with pale bleak faces at the strange creature going by on horseback—the rider had occasional glimpses of these isolate housewives, disembodied faces transpiring in the casement windows like potted plants, forlorn, unwatered and unfertilized.

He came at last to the world of gas stations, supermarkets, drugstores, parking meters, and to the first paved street. Whisky stepped onto the hard asphalt, tossed her head and stepped back, fighting the reins.

Automobiles rolled by, the drivers gaping blankly at the horse and man.

The rider watched for an opening in the traffic, while the shopkeepers and motorists stared at him, then spurred the mare sharply forward. She snorted and shook her head, then lunged onto the pavement, her iron-shod hooves slipping and clattering on the hard surface. In the middle of the road she tried to turn and go back. Fat automobiles gleaming like toys came hissing up, horns blaring challenges, white faces staring from behind their glass. The mare spun completely around, a full circle, while the man prodded her with the spurs, flicked her with the loose slack of the reins, talked to her quietly and urgently. She tried to turn again, eyes wild and rolling, nostrils flared, slipped and almost fell, finally leaped forward again and off the road to safety.

While the cars roared past behind them the rider removed his hat, brushed back his black hair, wiped his brow with the back of his hand. He patted the mare's sweating neck, talking quietly into her straining ears. When she had regained a good measure of confidence from his reassurances and the feel of the rough tractional soil of the earth beneath her hooves, he let her go on, following the continuation of the dirt road that led east between hayfields and orchards.

A quarter mile further and they came to a highway, the important north-south highway linking Duke City to Santa Fe and the north—four broad lanes of smooth asphalt quivering under the continual battery of cars, trucks and tractor-trailers. The rider stopped to survey this obstacle, the slippery pavement and the dense moving wall of steel and hard rubber. There was no possibility of outflanking this barricade; though he rode for years he would find no end to it; the track of asphalt and concrete was as continuous and endless as a circle or the walls of a cell. Therefore he sat and waited, hoping for a break in the flow of traffic big enough to sneak a four-legged animal through.

As he was waiting he noticed something strange spread out flat on the surface and near the center of the road: a piece of animal hide, the hairy yellow coat of a dog or coyote. Smeared out and around the hide was the dried blood and glandular juices of this creature which had attempted to jaywalk on Route

85. The big wheels and rubber tires rolled over the corpse with regular and barely perceptible thumps, the faint mechanical recognition of an existence that had not been meant for amalgamation with tar and gravel.

He rested in the saddle and waited and presently an opportunity came, a hundred yards of open space between mutually approaching trucks. He urged the mare forward and again the same thing happened. Whisky recoiled at the touch of pavement, resisted his commands and raking spurs and turned around in circles fighting the bit, sliding and clattering on the unfamiliar and unyielding face of the highway. Yet once more he managed to get her across—spurring, lashing, coaxing the mare until she lunged forward in the right direction, fighting down her attempt to stop and rear, driving her by the violence of his language and the force of his will across the path of the oncoming trucks and past the asphalt onto the good earth beyond. The frightened men in the cabs of the trucks stared at him as they went by, while the squeal and snort of airbrakes vibrated through the air.

They rested again, the man and his horse, savoring and treasuring the sweet sensation of life. After a while they went on, still eastward, following the unpaved street past a big new graveyard laid out like a model housing project, past a big new housing project laid out like a model graveyard, across the tracks of the Atchison, Topeka and Santa Fe Railway, through a grove of cottonwoods and over more irrigation ditches, between more fields of alfalfa and corn and potatoes, past more of the soft melting adobe homes of the Mexican farmers and beyond to the fragmentary, disintegrating edges of the city. Between the man on horseback and the great jagged wall of the mountains there now

remained only a handful of scattered mud houses and the ten
miles of open desert. Toward the last, outermost house, a small
adobe with jutting vigas, unplastered walls and a blue wooden
door he now guided the mare. Smelling green hay and grain she
stepped forward eagerly, tugging at the reins. The rider brushed
some of the dust from his shirt, brushed his hat, wiped his face
with the damp red bandana, checked the buttons on the fly of
his jeans, and then let the mare go, loping down the last half-
mile of the road and trailing a cloud of sun-dazzled dust.

CHAPTER 2

Jerry Bondi was kneading bread dough when she heard the horse coming, the sound of the loping hooves muffled at first by the dust, the distance, then sounding close, coming up the lane by the apricot trees toward the house. For a moment she was startled, unable to think, and then the name and the image of the familiar face flashed through her brain and she gave a little half-giggled cry of pleasure. She rushed to the mirror above the kitchen sink, saw a patch of flour on her nose, white flour in her hair. She was about to rub it off when she realized that her hands were plastered and sticky with wet dough. She moaned in a mild panic, hearing the horse trot by the house and into the backyard, the sudden scraping stop and the light thud and jingle of spurred feet hitting the ground. She started to wash her hands, pouring water from the kettle into a basin. She could hear the man outside talking in low tones to the horse, then his steps approaching and the musical rattle of spurs on the back porch.

A knock on the door. "Jerry," the man said.

"Come on in," she called, wiping her hands hurriedly on a dishtowel; her fingers and palms remained caked with dough.

The door opened and the tall rider stood there, his hands dangling uselessly and a shy white grin on his dark face. "Hi," he said.

Jerry went toward him smiling, her arms open. "Welcome, Jack; it's good to see you." And she reached up and embraced his lean neck and left little smudges of wet dough on the back of his shirt. "I was expecting you," she said; "I had an intuition." She pulled his head down a little, stood up on her toes and kissed him square on the mouth. Then she drew back to look at him. He grinned at her, saying nothing. She said: "You look the same, about. You look pretty good. Maybe a little skinnier but tough as a wild billygoat."

"You got flour on your nose," he said.

"Thank you," she said. "You need a shave. Last time we saw you—was that a year ago?—you needed a shave then too. Why do you always look like you need a shave?"

"I shave pretty seldom." He touched his chin, grinning at her. "Never really learned how to shave right."

She continued to smile helplessly at him, entranced by the thawing and illumination of his leathery face, the little creases of pleasure around his mouth and eyes. "Well I'm sure glad you came," she said, after a short pause; "God only knows I'm glad to see you." She remembered Paul, her husband, and her smile began to fade with the thought. "Well—sit down. I'll fix you something to eat. You look like you haven't eaten for a few weeks. How about some ham and eggs?"

"That sounds mighty good, Jerry."

"Okay. Now you sit down." She indicated a spindlelegged chair in a corner of the kitchen. "Just let me put up this bread and then I'll fix you something." She turned back to the bread dough rolled in a field of white flour on the tabletop.

He stepped beside her, towering above her head, and placed his hands on hers and held them still. "Let me finish it," he said, smiling down at her.

"It's almost finished. My hands are already messed up."

"Let me do it," he said again. "I'm expert at this."

"Well, all right," she said, and went to the sink and washed her hands clean of the dough. He stood beside her, waiting to wash his own hands. "I gotta new horse," he said. "A little mare, part Appaloosa and part plain old range stock. She's a real pretty little critter—you oughta go out and take a look at her."

"Wonderful," she said. "I'll do that." She started to dry her hands while he refilled the basin with cold water from the bucket and rolled up his sleeves. "Jack . . ." she said.

"Yeah?" He wet his hands and began soaping them.

"Why are you here?"

Very slowly he rubbed the cake of soap over his palms and the back of his hands. He stared out the window above the sink. Finally he said: "I read about Paul in the papers. I saw his picture and I read under it and it said he was gettin two years in prison for refusin to register for the draft. Is that right?"

"Yes, that's right." She stood beside him at the sink and stared at her hands. "Two years," she said.

"Well, that's too long." He rinsed the soapsuds from his hands and looked around for a towel. "Too damn long," he said; gently he removed the damp towel from Jerry's unperceptive fingers. "I came to town to see if I could do anything."

She raised her head and looked at him, her eyes widening. "He's already in jail," she said; "there's nothing you can do. There's nothing anyone can do." She stared at him with a dim and irrational hope in her mind, her eyes. "What could you do?" she said.

"I don't know. I ain't thought of anything yet." He finished drying his hands and went to the roll of dough and put his clean fingers on it. "I'll think of something," he said. "Step outside and take a look at Whisky. The prettiest and toughest and orneriest little filly you ever did see." He began to roll and fold the moist dough with expert familiarity; he glanced at Jerry. "Go on," he said; "you want to hurt her feelings?"

Jerry had been staring at the floor and rubbing dried dough from her fingertips. "Of course," she said. "I mean no." She raised her head and smiled at him with a perhaps unconscious wistfulness. "Where is this—animal . . . ?" She stepped to the kitchen door and opened it and looked out at the mare tethered to a pillar of the porch. The mare stepped back a pace, her ears stiffening. "Well, Jack, I declare—she *is* a beauty. Now what do you call her?"

"I told you: Whisky."

"Whisky?" Disapproving, Jerry said: "A *fine* name for a horse."

"Well damnit, she drinks." Burns sprinkled more dry flour over the dough. "She was drunk when I bought her—that's how she fooled me. She acts pretty decent when she's all likkered up."

"I'll unsaddle her."

"Better not; she's still kind of spooky. Doesn't like women, anyway." He patted and shaped the dough into a compact mass. "I'll take care of her in a minute." He look about for lard or butter. "Hey, gimme somethin to grease this dough with."

Jerry shut the door and went to the cupboard and took down a can of lard. "Here," she said, pulling off the lid; "help yourself." Burns stuck his fingers in and then smeared the ball of dough. "Now put it in that basin." He did; she covered it with a clean dish towel and then set the basin on a shelf above the cookstove, feeling his dark gaze on her as she moved through the warmth of the kitchen.

"I've been missin somethin," he said.

"What's that?"

He smiled again. "Home life, I guess." He raised a hand to his hat. "Doggone, it's so long since I been in a house I even forget to take my hat off."

"You've got dough all over your hands."

He removed his hat and hung it on a nail by the door; he looked at his hands. "Yeah, you're right."

She went to the sink and poured a little water into the basin. "Here, wash your hands; then you'd better go out and take care of that mare of yours."

"You think she's gettin jealous?"

"You wash your hands." Jerry felt herself blushing. Unable to look at him, she said: "What would you like to eat?"

"You said you were gonna rassle up some ham and eggs," Burns said softly, rubbing his hands with soap. "I could sure go for some ham and eggs; to tell the truth I'm hungry as an old grizzly in April. My belly's gettin all frayed from rubbin against my backbone."

"We'll have to do something about that," she said—a little formally. She opened the firebox of the stove and stuffed in some paper and kindling. "What have you been doing for the last year or so, anyway?"

"I was afraid you'd ask me that." He dried his hands on a towel hanging over the sink. "I can't lie to you, neither; sure wish I could, it's so downright shameful."

She looked at the sly smile on his lips and guessed. "Don't

tell me you've been herding sheep again!" She struck a match on the stove and lit the paper.

"Jerry, you're absolutely right. Yessir, I've been playing nurse-maid to God's lowliest critters. So help me . . ."

She slammed shut the door of the firebox and opened the damper. "At this rate you'll end up on a dude ranch, Jack."

"You're right; when a man's fallen to herdin sheep he might as well go all the way down." He walked toward the door and as he opened it Jerry Bondi reached out and put her hand on his forearm. He looked down at her.

"Jack . . ." She tried to smile at him; she could find nothing to say. He waited. "You'd better take care of your horse," she said finally. They could hear the mare outside, stamping, shaking her gear.

"That's what I aim to do." He gave her wrist a squeeze. "Don't you worry none about Paul; I'll think of somethin. I sure didn't ride fifty miles just to take the air."

"I'm sure of that," she said. "Now I'll have to worry about you too."

"No need for that." He grinned at her. "Nothin can hurt me; I'm like water: boil me away and I come back in the next thunderhead." He stepped outside. "I'll have about six eggs."

"You'll have to put your horse in the corral with the goats."

"I know," he said, untying the reins from around the post. "That's all right; me and Whisky ain't proud."

"There's a bale of alfalfa in the shed. Help yourself."

"Thank you, Jerry." Burns rubbed the mare's neck. "Say thank you to the lady, Whisky." The mare tossed her head and backed away, snorting; "Easy, girl, easy. Goddamnit," Burns apologized, "she's still a trifle skittish." He cradled the mare's head in his arms and stroked her nose. "Now you take it easy, little girl; nothin to get all excited about. She's gonna break my heart," he said to Jerry; "she's so all-fired pig-headed. Gotta crazy streak in her."

"She takes after her master, then," Jerry said.

Burns grinned. "That might be." He gave the reins a tug. "Come on, you vinegaroon." The mare followed him toward the corral, where two goats waited with their white muzzles thrust out between the poles. The sunlight was dazzling, a white glare on the sand and wood; Jerry squinted, watching the man and horse and their black stark shadows. A pair of finches swooped over the yard, shrilling.

She heard an explosion, dim, muffled, like a shot of dynamite going off underground.

Burns stopped. "What was that?"

"I don't know. I heard it too." They stared at each other. "I think it came from the south," she said. "Towards the city." She shaded her eyes with her hand, gazing toward the smoke and dust of the invisible city. She saw something black, a smoking fragment, float slowly down across the blue dome of the sky, down, down, disappearing below the horizon. "Did you see it?" she cried.

"I saw somethin," he said slowly. "Was it an air plane?"

"I don't know. Yes—I suppose it was. Part of one, maybe." They continued to stare at the southern sky, where nothing moved now, nothing burned or shone; the arc of black smoke lingered on in the windless air like something forgotten. "It must have been a jet plane," Jerry said. "They explode now and then—I don't know why."

The cowboy stared at the smoke trail, rubbing his jaw. "Yeah . . ." he said. "Well . . ." He looked at Jerry.

"There's a bucket out there you can water the horse with," she said. "Hanging on a nail by the feed barrel."

"Okay. Thanks." He went on toward the corral, leading the mare and staring south at the hovering thread of smoke.

Jerry took what was left of a ham from the icebox on the porch, re-entered the kitchen and began preparing a meal. When Burns returned about ten minutes later, carrying sad-dlebags, rifle and guitar, she had the kitchen table set with dark home-baked bread, a pitcher of goat's milk, butter, a salad of let-tuce and tomatoes and cucumbers in a wooden bowl, and a plate heaped with four thick slices of fried ham. Burns dropped his equipment on the floor and looked joyfully at the food. "Hey!— look at all that, will you!"

"Sit down," Jerry said. "The eggs will be ready in a minute."

"Doggone—how'd you get all this on the table so fast?" He pulled up a chair and sat down. "You some kind of witch doctor?" Then he stood up again. "I gotta comb my hair and wash my face for a feed like this."

"Would you like your eggs turned over?"

"What?" He filled the basin and splashed water over his face and hair, and groped around for the soap. "No—sunnyside up, please."

"The salad and bread were left over from lunch," Jerry said. "I hope you don't mind." He made some kind of garbled reply from under the water. "I hope you like goat milk; we've got plenty of it." The eggs were sizzling; she lifted them out of the skillet and onto the plate with the ham. "It's all ready."

"Be right there." Burns was fumbling around by the sink, searching for something with soap-blind eyes. "Jerry . . . ?" She put the towel into his hands. "Thanks . . ."

"What did you think of Abigail and Psyche?"

"Don't think I've had the pleasure." He dug the mud out of his ears with a corner of the towel.

"The goats. The bearded one with the big bulging udder is Abigail and Psyche is her daughter." She tossed the salad a little with a wooden fork and spoon. "Come on, it's getting cold."

Burns smoothed back his long black hair with his fingers and sat down. "Say—where's Seth? I knew somebody was missing around here." He began cutting up a chunk of ham. "Haven't seen him around."

Jerry filled his glass with milk from the clay pitcher. "He's in school."

"What's that stuff?"

"Milk."

"That's a good Mormon drink." Burns paused between mouthfuls of ham and egg to drink some of the milk. "It's all right—smells just like the one that tried to butt me." He wiped the white foam from his upper lip and turned back to his plate. "So the little fella's in school already; that's a damn shame."

"He's six years old now." She sat down at the opposite end of the table. "Have some of the salad, Jack." Vague emotions, formless ideas, were crowding her mind: she could not entirely suppress the foolish notion that this strange wandering friend, riding in like a knight-errant, might have the power through magic or valor or wit to bring back to her, somehow, the man to whom she had dedicated her love. She tried to attend to what he was saying:

" . . . Thought you two was gonna teach him yourselves, bring him up right and proper so's the authorities wouldn't get their old superstitions planted in the bairn's head." Burns wiped up his plate with a slab of the dark bread, ate the bread, and took another hearty drink of goat's milk, leaving a white tideline on his beard. He looked at her. "Well, naturally you can't do that now—what with Paul in trouble and you havin to work, I suppose." She made no answer. He pushed his plate aside and leaned on the table, gazing at her. "Mighty good fixins, Jerry. I'm right proud of you." She said nothing. "Gotta toothpick?" She shook her head slowly, looking down at the table, after a moment he pulled a match from his shirt pocket and the jack-knife from a pocket of his jeans and began to whittle himself a toothpick.

She was having trouble with her thoughts; this man Burns, whose mere physical presence was so reassuring, and whose love and loyalty she could never have doubted, yet made her feel for some reason a shade uncomfortable: in his sombre eyes, in his slow smile and the lines of his face, in the firm rank masculinity of his body, she thought she perceived a challenge. A challenge in his every word, every motion.

"He'll be home pretty soon, I suppose?" Burns said.

She looked up. "Who?"

"Seth." He stared at her, puzzled, and then frowned and looked away.

"You've got milk all over your mouth," she said. He wiped his mouth with the back of his hand. "Yes, in about an hour."

This is ridiculous, she told herself. I am an adult woman, mother of a six-year-old boy, wife to Paul Bondi. I'll not be lured into fantasy by anyone, not even by this smoky-eyed centaur on the other side of the table. And even as she said it another truth flared across her mind with the certainty of lightning.

"Would you like some more milk?" she said.

"No thanks."

"Would you like some coffee?"

"No, don't bother. Let's have some later."

"It's no trouble at all."

"No thanks, Jerry." He rested his chin on his fists, looking at her with his grave, almost melancholy eyes.

She felt suddenly annoyed with him. Was he making some sort of game out of her uneasiness?

"Mrs. Bondi," he said. She glanced at him, startled. "Mrs. Bondi, I came here to see you and Paul and Seth and maybe be of some use. I got some money and a rifle. If there's anything I can do I'll do it. That's what I came for. When I'm finished I'll be movin on, like before."

She was grateful for his slow careful speech. She wanted to thank him but she said, half lying: "You didn't have to say that, Jack. I knew." They faced each other in silence for a few moments, both faintly embarrassed. She said: "And for heaven's sake don't call me Mrs. Bondi. You make me feel like a thoroughly respectable housewife."

He smiled. "Well ain't you?"

"I don't know. Yes I am. But I don't want to feel like one." She stood up and started to clear the table of dirty dishes. "You didn't eat any of the salad," she said reproachfully. He was about to speak but she interrupted: "I don't blame you. It is kind of wilted."

"Let me help you with them dishes."

"Absolutely not. I won't have you washing dishes your first day here." She stacked them in the sink and rinsed them with hot water from the kettle on the stove. "I'll not wash them now anyway."

"That's the best idea yet." Burns drew his materials from his shirt pocket and began to roll a cigarette. While his fingers were busy he strolled into the next room and looked at the paintings on the walls—Jerry's work—huge canvases splashed recklessly with color, thick rich oil paint piled on with a palette knife, representing not ideas or things but nervous sensations. Burns lit his cigarette as he contemplated the work: he was mystified but pleasantly stirred, and felt his fingers itching to reach out, touch, dig into and squeeze the refulgent paint.

He turned away from the pictures and toward the books that were lined up, shelf on shelf, against the east wall. There were far more books there than any one man should own, let alone read; and weighted heavily on the side of professional philosophy: from the *Fragments* of Heraclitus to Wittgenstein's *Tractatus*. Burns felt himself in the presence of the absent husband; he could hear, along the networks of memory, the tone and peculiar timbre of that anxious voice, with its precise affectionate articulation of syllables and phrasing. He went back to the kitchen. "There's one more thing I need," he said to Jerry, who was putting more wood into the stove.

"What's that?"

"I need a bath. I smell like an old ram that ain't been dipped or even rained-on for about five years."

Jerry smiled at him. "I was hoping you would think of that. But it's a big project to take a bath here. You'll have to carry about ten buckets of water to fill the tub, and you'll have to chop some more wood to keep the fire going. Do you feel up to all that?"

"Will you scrub my back for me?"

"No." She shut the door on the firebox and straightened up. "There's the tub; here's the bucket. The axe is outside."

"All right," he said. He reached for the bucket. "Guess I'll fill the tub first. Mind if I track up your kitchen floor?" She was standing in the doorway of the next room now, watching him. He grinned at her. "What're you thinkin about, Jerry?"

"Never you mind. You fill that tub." She brushed back her coppery hair with one hand. "I'll see if I can find you some of Paul's clean underwear to put on. I don't suppose you brought any?"

"Nope, not me. I'd sure be much obliged to you." He opened the kitchen door and stepped outside.

"You might have to prime that pump," she called after him. "The well's getting low."

Burns was drying himself with a big green towel when somebody began to fumble with the knob of the kitchen door. "Who's there?" There was no answer; he wrapped the towel around his middle and opened the door. "Come on in, Seth."

A small boy with red hair and a sticky face walked into the kitchen; he set his tin lunch bucket carefully on the kitchen table and then turned to stare at Burns.

"Howdy, Seth." Burns unwrapped the towel and continued rubbing his legs and arms. "Where you been all day?"

The boy was shy. He stared at Burns with soft blue eyes, intelligent but diffident. At last he said: "I was at school."

Burns began to get into Paul's underwear. The shorts were a little slack around the waist. "Did you see my mare, Seth?"

Jerry called from the next room: "Is that you, Seth?"

"Yes," the boy said to Burns. "Can I ride her, Jack?"

"Well, I don't know; she's kinda mean and hard to handle. You any good with broncs?" He put on a clean white shirt belonging to Paul Bondi. The boy did not answer his question. "I'll take you for a ride on her tomorrow evenin. She's had a long trick today."

"What are you two talking about?" Jerry said from the next room. "Can I come in yet?"

"Just a minute." Burns pulled on his dusty, faded jeans; his legs were about ten inches too long for any of Paul's trousers. "Come on in," he said.

The boy said: "I'm not afraid."

Jerry opened the livingroom door and came into the kitchen. She rubbed the boy's hair, bent down and kissed him on the mouth. "How was it today, Seth? Did you have fun?"

"That's a helluva question to ask a fella that's just got out of school," Burns said. He put on a pair of Bondi's clean socks.

"No," the boy said.

Burns smiled as he removed the spurs from his boots. "What'd I tell you?" He hung the spurs to a nail in the wall and sat down to put on the boots. The boy kept his eyes on the spurs. "They're too big for you, Seth. You grow a few more inches, then you can wear em." He tugged at the boots, muttering. "Always hard to get on over clean socks."

"You've got awfully big feet, Jack," Jerry said.

"I know. If I could grow roots like a cottonwood I wouldn't need such big feet."

"Where are you going?" the boy said.

"Me?" Burns looked at Jerry. "Where's that old beat-up Dodge of yours?"

"Down the road about half a mile, out of gas."

"You sure it's outa gas?"

"I don't know. Anyway, it won't run."

"Well me and Seth'll have to see what we can do about that. You wanta come along, Seth?"

The boy nodded.

"You be sure to get him and yourself back here by supper-time," Jerry said. "I don't want *you* two in trouble."

"We'll be back in plenty of time." Burns stood up and looked around; he found his hat, brushed it with his hand and put it on. "Why don't you come too? I'm just gonna get some feed for the mare, maybe a little groceries."

Jerry shook her head. "You two run along; I've got too much to do."

"I'll do it for you."

"I have to write a letter."

"Oh . . ." Burns paused. "Anything I can get you?"

Jerry sighed faintly, passing her hand over her eyes. "No, I guess not." She watched Burns reach for his sack of tobacco and put it into the pocket of the white shirt; the boy stared at him too. "Yes," she said; "get me a pint of ice cream. Two pints. Three pints."

"What kind?"

"Oh . . . strawberry, chocolate—anything. I don't care. We'll have a party when you get back. And get a bottle of wine. A good dry *vino rojo*. Okay? Or would you rather have gin?"

"I'll get both . . . then we can decide later." Burns stepped to the kitchen door and opened it. "Let's go, Seth. By the way—" He looked at Jerry. "You said the car was half a mile down the road. Which way down the road?"

"Toward town. South."

"Thank you, ma'am." He smiled at her. "We'll be back in half an hour. Come on, Seth." He and the boy went out and the door was closed. Jerry gazed ruefully at the washtub full of dirty gray water that Burns had left behind.

The kitchen door opened again and Burns came in, looking sheepish. "Goddamn, Jerry, I'm sure gettin absent-minded. I clean forgot to empty that there tub."

"You might find a use for the car keys, too," she said.

They found the car where Jerry had left it, a dull and rather haggard automobile parked half off the road. Burns got in and switched on the ignition, watching the fuel gauge. The needle remained pointing at the E. He stepped on the starter but nothing happened; there was no response at all.

"It's dead," the boy said, sitting beside him.

"Sure is." Burns got out and lifted the hood. He checked the battery first and found that the ground cable had shaken loose; the bolt and nut that should have fastened it to the frame were missing. He hunted around inside the car, in the dashboard compartment and under the front seat, until he found what was needed. Afterwards, when he switched on the ignition, the fuel gauge registered a quarter full tank.

They drove to a feed and hardware store first. Burns bought two bales of alfalfa, a half bushel of bran and barley for the mare, some Omalene and calf manna for the goats. After he had loaded the feed into the car he went back into the store and bought a quarter pound of horseshoe nails and two heavy-gauge files; outside, sitting in the car, he put a file in each boot and then pulled his jeans down over the tops of the boots.

"Why are you doing that?" the boy said.

Burns looked at him. "If you were in jail how would you get out?"

The boy looked down at the boots. He smiled, and said: "But it's not that hard to get *in* a jail, is it?"

Burns laughed and started the engine. "I don't have to tell you anything, I reckon. Mind now, this is a secret." He looked at the boy. "You understand? You daren't tell anyone, not even Jerry. Okay?"

The boy nodded, his eyes alert with interest. "I won't tell, Jack."

"Let's shake hands on that." They shook. "Fine; now let's go find us some ice cream and *vino*."

It was a quiet party. The boy Seth, Burns, Jerry Bondi, sat around the kitchen table eating their manufactured ice cream with the solemn devoutness of communicants. A few bars of sunlight slanted into the room from the west window. Outside, in the tamarisk by the pump, a dying locust keened away the long afternoon.

"Some more *vino?*" Jerry held the bottle poised over the cowboy's empty glass.

"I want some more," Seth said. His red hair had fallen over his eyes, his mouth and nose were dappled with ice cream. With his mouth open they could see the purplish stain on his teeth.

"You've had enough," she said. She started to pour into Burns' glass.

"*Bastante*," he said. "No more." He pushed the bottle away, lifted the glass and drank down what was in it. "I gotta get goin," he added, and belched gently.

"I tell you, you can't see him today."

"What?"

"They won't let you."

"Won't let me?"

The boy watched them with his serious eyes; he was still sucking ice cream from the end of a big spoon.

"You can't see him until next Wednesday," she said. "Wednesday is visitors' day. If he's still there."

"He won't be there next Wednesday."

"Well, probably not; his stay in the county jail is supposed to be temporary. They—whoever *they* are—will transfer him to some Federal prison as soon as they can." Jerry stared at the tabletop and squeezed the glass in her hand so hard that her arm began to tremble. "—Or wherever they put political prisoners."

"Lots of folks in the jailhouse these days," Burns said cautiously.

"There always are."

"More than usual, maybe."

"I don't know. I suppose so." She sipped at her wine and relaxed a little. "Anyway they won't let you see him today."

"Well I sure aim to see him today."

She looked up at him. You crazy fool, she thought, you think I wouldn't be there myself this very minute if it were possible? Who are *you*, anyway?—he's *my* man. She bit her lower lip, afraid that she might begin to cry. Goddamnit, she thought. She watched him slide back his chair and stand up. Spare my ceiling, you long-connected—Christ, I'm drunk, she thought, and almost giggled.

"There's always one way or another," Burns said. Carefully he set his black hat on his head. "Well, I sure hate to leave this very entertaining party . . ."

"I'm coming with you."

"I'm coming too," the boy said.

He laughed at them. "Not noways you ain't. Neither one of you. No sir." He looked around the kitchen. "Got a hacksaw?"

"If you can manage to see him today then I can too," she said.

"I doubt that. I doubt that very much. Got a good hacksaw?"

"I don't see why I can't go with you."

"I can. How about a file, then?"

"What are you talking about?" She stared at him. "Jack—just how do you expect to see him?"

"Me?" He gaped stupidly at her, rubbing his dark bristling chin. "Doggone, I forgot to shave."

"Jack, you be careful. If you get in trouble you'll just have to stay there, I won't get you out."

"That's right," he said. "Sure." He blinked at her, then walked slowly to the corner of the kitchen where he had stowed some of his gear—the rifle, the saddlebags, bedroll, dirty clothes. He rummaged through one of the saddlebags, then came back to her with a slim canvas bandoleer, its loops filled with cartridges. "Take this," he said, handing it to her.

She took it and her hands dropped under the unexpected weight. She said: "What on earth am I supposed to do with these? I don't want to shoot anybody. I don't think I do, at least."

"Look," he said. He unzipped a long pocket on the inside of the belt, exposing a packet of rich green Federal currency. "In case somethin goes wrong, I want you to use this *dinero*."

"Use it? What for?" Fascinated, she peeked at the corners of the bills. They seemed to be all ten's and twenties. "Jack—did you—?" She let the question hang fire.

Her eager curiosity made him smile. "No . . . I'm ashamed to say I worked for ever bit of it; that's my wages for six months in a sheep camp you're lookin' at so hard."

"But what do you want me to do with all this?" she said.

"You'll think of somethin if you get hungry enough."

She gazed at the money for a long moment; he reached out and discreetly zipped the pocket shut. "Don't give me a hard time," he said. "There ain't as much there as it looks, anyhow. You keep it for me and use whatever you need."

She looked up at him. "This is very kind of you, Jack. But I don't think I'll need it. I expect to find work."

"That's all right, you keep it for me just the same. I'm afraid I'll lose the dang stuff if I tote it around."

"You could put it in a bank."

"Banks? Don't trust em—bunch of crooks." He turned toward the door. "I'm leavin your car here." The woman and the boy stared at him; he smiled. "I'll be back in a little while." He looked at the boy. "Seth, if I'm not back in the mornin you give my mare a half bale of alfalfa and a peck of feed. Will you do that for me?"

The boy nodded, licking at his spoonful of ice cream.

"Wait a minute," Jerry said. She ran into the other room, returned with a sealed envelope in her hand. "Look," she said, "if you do see Paul—and God only knows how you plan to do it—anyway, if you do see him, give him this letter. Okay?"

"I sure will," he said, and dropped the letter down inside his shirt. "Well . . ." They stared at each other. " . . . Reckon I'll go now."

Jerry smiled uncertainly. She said: "You be careful, Jack."

"I'll be careful." He gave them a little wave, like a half-salute, and went out, closing the door.

Jerry listened to his steps crossing the back porch, fading away over the hard baked mud of the backyard and down the lane to the road. She stood quite still, listening, the heavy bandoleer in her hands, and when she could no longer hear him she went to the window. He had already reached the road; she watched him striding along in the dust through the scalding glare of the sun: black hat, white shirt, shadowed face, dark lean legs moving steadily like a pair of calipers out for a walk. He looks better on a horse, she thought, letting the bandoleer rest on the sill; her fingers caressed the cool brass shells of .32 caliber cartridges.

The boy watched her, saying nothing, the secret in his eyes.

When Burns was gone from sight she went to the cupboard and put the bandoleer deep in the back of the top shelf. Then she went to the shelf above the stove to see how much the bread had risen.

CHAPTER 3

Art Hinton, truckdriver, pulled his tractor-trailer off 66 and onto the gravel lot of the Benson steakhouse. He was not hungry; he needed some coffee to keep his eyelids propped open. This was late in the afternoon, with the sun a vague butter-colored disc floating down through a vapory sky over the green damp hills of Missouri. He had come from St. Louis that day and had a long way to go.

When he stepped down from the cab he heard a chorale of crickets, treefrogs, bullfrogs, katydids and harvest flies singing, shrilling, screaming at the world with the elemental and impregnable monotony of surf. He heard them, flipped a cigarette butt toward the field beyond the parkinglot and stepped inside the chromeplated neonized redbrick restaurant. What he wanted was peace, order, and the reassurance of human voices. Behind him his truck waited, engine idling, one among six similar diesel monsters parked at the far edge of the lot. Hinton's trailer, like most of the others, was brightly painted and lettered. His bore the following superscription in huge red letters against a background of gleaming aluminum:

ANOTHER LOAD OF *ACME* BATHROOM
FIXTURES!
AMERICA BUILDS FOR TOMORROW!

Inside the cafe things were not so bad. The air was cool, conditioned for human consumption and reconsumption by tireless electrical engines pumping ammonia through coils of copper tubing. The light was soft and indirect, and even the somewhat rambunctious music from the jukebox was muted to a comfortable degree by the cork-sheathed walls, the heavy cumulus of cigarette smoke, the fragrant gases from the kitchen, the drone of conversation, the general gloom. Hinton sat down on a red simulated-leather stool at the counter, leaned on his elbows and studied the menu. Near him sat other drivers, some of them talking, some of them eating; behind him at the tables and in the booths sat the insurance salesmen in their impressive suits, lower class tourists with their families, and pleasant young men probably working for the CSI or FBI or SSC or AEC or CIA or CCI.

When the waitress came, a girl pretty and clean in her starched uniform, he ordered black coffee, coconut cream pie, and a glass of milk. A habit of his, coffee and milk together: the latter seemed to him to complement the destructive erosion of the other. The pie was placed before him in a few moments; he ate it slowly, drinking the milk with it, saving the coffee for last. He listened without genuine interest to the conversations around him:

Twenty cents a mile is ridikalus, I tole him, abslootly ridikalus. What did they have on him? The usual stuff. Well hell it all depends; if you're haulin from St. Louie to L.A. it's too much, sure, but from St. Louie to say Tulsa—it might pay. Just might. Not very much: a lot seems to have been well covered up. Robbie, don't spill your food on the floor. Please Robbie. Let him alone Martha. People like him really intrigue me, you know, really intrigue me. Let him alone, Martha, what the devil does it matter now? How do they dream of getting away with talk like that? Well I don't care; I still say it's ridikalus. You might be right.

He sighed, finished his pie and began sipping at the coffee. A good coffee, hot, black, rich with the authentic flavor of the bean, but his enjoyment was modest, almost perfunctory: his palate scalded and corroded by tankcars of boiling lunchroom brew, bitter and brackish, and by vats of cheap whisky, and rotted by tons of soft sweet mediocre food, he had forgotten the delight of hunger, the pleasures of thirst. Forgotten, though he must have known them; he looked across the counter at his image sunk in glass, sipping coffee, staring directly at him from above the glasses, Heinz soups, napkins, pats of butter. A small brooding face foreshortened by time and inbreeding, a middle-aged hillbilly looking at him, reflecting his natural features, his mood, his thoughts.

—Of weariness, boredom, of a path winding through laurel and under pines toward home, the dark cabin on the mountainside with its shingle roof and long front verandah where at this very moment, probably, his father and younger brother were sitting, smoking, not talking, watching the lights come on far below in the valley of the Shenandoah.

The lower eyelid of his left eye quivered, jerked again when he touched it. He made a nervous grimace at himself in the mirror, left a quarter for the waitress, picked up the check and walked toward the cashier in her little fortress of glass, tin, cigarettes, candy, cigars and pocket packages of Kleenex. He gave the woman the slip of paper without looking at it, or at her.

"Forty cents, please."

He gave the woman a dollar bill. "You have any Dexadrine?"

"Yes sir." She leaned under the counter, opened a drawer, came back up and set a small metal box on the glass between them. "That will be forty—fifty—ninety cents all together. Ninety from a dollar." She rang the cash register and gave him a dime. "Haven't you been here before, trucker?"

He looked at her now, picking up his change from the rubber villi on the glass. "Yes," he said; "a few times." He was certain he had never seen the woman before. She was not very attractive. "I guess I'd like one of those chocolate bars, too." He put the dime back on the pad.

"I thought I seen you in here before." She slid open the door of the glass case and reached inside. "Which kind?"

"Any kind, I don't care. They all taste the same."

"I never forget a face," she said. She gave him a Hershey bar, and after recording the sale, a nickel. "Where are you heading for this time?"

"Duke City."

"Duke City, New Mexico?" The woman smiled at him. She was short, dark, and about forty years old; she had a large red wen on her jaw.

"Yes," he said. He picked up the candy and the nickel and glanced toward the door.

"They say Duke City is a nice town."

"I guess so. About the same as any other." He started to leave.

"Come back again."

"Sure." He opened the door and went out.

The sky had cleared a little and the sun seemed much lower now, spinning like a gold coin on the rim of the world: the restaurant, the parked trucks and cars, the beech trees, the fallow fields on the other side of the parkinglot, the cement highway, the slabs and blocks of Joplin to the east, the truckdriver Hinton, everything, everything visible, was washed and blurred and mesmerized by an overwhelming radiance the color of new honey. Hinton walked blindly toward his truck, unwrapping his candybar, while the cicada in the field and the frogs in the swampy ditch sang hosannas to the sky.

PART TWO

THE PRISONER

"There was a Prisoner, dreaming of Liberty . . ."

CHAPTER 4

Jack-SON!

Yay!

Have you seen my ole gray mule?

That I has not.

Has somebody here seen my gray mule? Six feet high and bucks like a fool; likes gingerbread cookies and pampas grass, has a notch in his ear and a star up his ass. Now if you done seen my ole gray mule, I'm tellin you straight don't be a damn fool; but show me where he is and sure as I'm alive, you'll get a pot of honey from the ole beehive.

Greene, ain't you never gonna pipe down?

Never!

You better.

Never!

Timothy, you got the makins?

I got a half sack Bull Durham and not a single goddamn paper.

I got a paper.

It's a deal, son. Save that light, Hoskins, we got two hot

babies comin up. Steady boy and watch her roll, save that tobacco while I get the coal.

Thanks, Timothy.

How long you in for, boy?

Thirty days flat.

Vaggin, pimpin, or hustlin?

Went through a red light with my eyes shut. Judge called it
reckless driving.

Mighty reckless drivin. Now tell me the truth, boy.

I lifted a knife at Monkey Ward's.

Ah hah. You tried to. Good knife?

Seven ninety-five plus tax.

Good, good, son. You shrewd like a chicken.

Butt, Timothy?

Butt me no butts. Already spoken for. Hoskins gets it.
Rev'rend Hoskins on his Flyin Machine, waitin for Peter to
open the door, got hog drunk and hit the floor.

Lay off it, Greene.

Never!

I'm tellin you.

Never!

Paul Bondi smiled as he listened, his hands clasped under
his head, his body stretched out at full length on his steel bunk.
A gray Navy blanket, a pad and a steel bunk for tonight. He lay
watching the stripes of sunlight on the steel ceiling, listening to
the others but thinking his own thoughts:

These fellows have something, he thought, have something
which I lack. The vital impulse, along with their lice and bad-
smelling itches and wino-red eyeballs. They—

Someone flushed a toilet; the powerful gasping explosion

of water sent a wave of reverberations through the steel walls over the cement floor; the entire plumbing system strained and vibrated with the detonating ferocity of a heavy machinegun. Bondi could feel as well as hear the clangor and clamor of outraged steel; the vibrations passed in sine curves through his skull, vertebrae and the bones of his legs.

That plumbing, he thought—like a siege, jazzy and vigorous. Suction strong enough to drown a man. Why? Must be a reason. A reason for everything in the county jail. County jail is a thoroughly rational institution, is it not? What could ever take its place?

Crazy, man!

Crazy is right. See that ole cat there, steppin on his tongue, belly bulgin with beans—?

Fuller'n a tick—

That's right, fuller'n a tick. Ole Hoskins, thass who; ole black-balled sonsabitch. Hoskins!

Ho?

Les hear tell about the man what ate electric eels to give the girls a charge.

Go long, man. You divin for Hell, talk like dat.

Rev'rend Hoskins is now gonna say a prayer for us all, poor sorry sinners like we is.

My butt, Timothy?

Take it and keep it, friend, or pass it on, as you please.

Thanks, Timothy. You can have my oatmeal in the morning.

Keep it, friend, I beg you.

Character or depravity, what does it matter? Under the aspect of eternity, so to speak? Now you're talking like an old balding philosopher, tovarish. Watch that stuff. Keep it screened out. Serenity is for the gods—not becoming in a mortal. Better to be partisan and passionate on this earth; be plenty objective enough when dead.

Again the explosion of a flushing toilet and the barrage of anguish from the pipes; through bone and marrow the vibrations jittered, grinding down delicacy, grace, tact, the arts of sense and human concord. Forty men locked, barred and sealed in a cage of steel and cement. Forty bellies semi-bloated with gas, intestines packed with the residue of half-digested pinto beans. Long conversations lost in the shuddering roar and rattle of plumbing.

Sic transit gloria mundi, he thought.

Think we'll get a break tomorrow?

Quien sabe, cuate?

Well we should. They got men sleepin on the floor downstairs. Hate to think what she'll be like come Saturday night.

Who said Saturday night is the lonesomest night?

They got worse jails. Ever been in the one at Juarez?

Ho, Jackson! Gimme light, man, light.

Oh I'm walkin to the river, gonna jump in, I can't float and I can't swim, but I'm an easy man . . . to drown. Cause my baby done leave me, yes my baby done leave me down. So I'm walkin to the river, gonna jump in and drown. And drown. And drown.

Flush that noise! Pass it on to Texas!

Go fly a kite on the moon, you slew-balled old fart.

Chinga madre! Eh, cabron!

You shut up, Greene.

Never!

I said shut up.

Never!

Who got a match?

I ain't got a match. Ain't nobody got a match. What you want a match for, man?

Gimme a match before I spit in your eye.

Sure, sure. Don't get mad.

Don't get mad, he says. Don't get mad, the man says.

When they gonna let me outa here? Why don't the Judge gimme a break? I ain't no bad boy; just a happy little wino.

You'll get a break all right—right over that thick dumb empty halfbreed skull of yours.

Ah, chinga tu . . .

Greene?

Never!

Where's that little book I give you?

Ain't here, man. All gone, man. I give it to that smooth cat in Cell Number Three. Now that's for a fact, man.

Well I want it back.

Kiss it goodby, friend. Give it a wave, *cuate*. Don't cry.

Goddamnit, Greene.

Never!

Greene—

Never!

Now defiance is all very well (said Bondi to himself: the last thread of sunlight had vanished from the steel ceiling) and very sweet, an ideal tonic for the delectation of the soul. Pure naked sheer defiance—defiance for the sake of defiance—sweet and precious as liberty itself. The act of liberty. Timothy Greene and his perpetual thundering Never. But is there a blind edge to it? Should be tempered, no doubt, with good manners. Also, it might be enslaving. Always defiant, a man would be mad, would

have destroyed his power of choice. And the power of choice—
that is what I am here for.

What are you in for, Rev'rend, anyway?

Me, son? My body's here but the spirit's free as a bluebird.

Okay, then why is your body here?

Well now, the Judge he calls it assault. I done hit a man and
he falls down. Didn't hit him hard but he falls down like a log.
Maybe he wasn't standin very good.

Why'd you hit him, Rev'rend?

Well now, you see it was like this: this here fella and me was
workin together in this barbershop. He was barber, I was porter
and shoeshinin man. One day we have a argument about who
left the soap where. A argument.

Hoskins, you ain't got sense enough to pour piss out of a
boot.

What happened then, Rev'rend?

Well now, we's havin this here argument about who left the
soap where when the boss walks in. The boss. Manager.

What soap, Rev'rend?

This soap we use for washin up our hands and so on. In the
crapper. Both of us usin the same piece of soap. I disremember
what kind of soap it was, exactly. White, that's all, and not very
big. Kinda little.

What happens when the boss walks in, Rev'rend?

Well damned if he doesn't tell me to get my hat and coat and
get out. Just like that. Don't even wanta know what we arguin
about. Well I tell him about the soap and he just gets mad. Like
that. Just gets mad.

What'd you do then, Rev'rend?

Nothin. I get my hat and coat only I ain't got no coat and

starts to leave and then ole boss he thinks I ain't leavin fast enough so he tries to gimme a kick. Don't that beat all? Tries to kick me cause I ain't movin fast enough to suit him. Man musta been crazy.

Is that when you got mad, Rev'rend?

Oh I don't get mad. I never get mad. I'll punish a man, maybe, but I never gets mad. It ain't right for a man to get mad. A man ain't no dog, even if he smell like one. That's the way I feels about it. Yessir. Never get mad.

Well, why'd you hit him, Rev'rend?

Oh I didn't hit him. I hit t'other fella.

The other fella. Which fella?

The barber. The fella I hit. No sir, I don't get mad never. It ain't right. No sir.

Well, which one did you hit, Rev'rend, the barber or the boss?

Well now, the boss he was a barber too. Yes, he barbered there just like t'other fella. Only he owned it too. Owned ever bit of it. Yessir. Only he don't own me. No sir.

You got me kinda mixed up, Rev'rend.

Yessir, thass just the way I felt: kinda mixed up. I weren't mad, no sir, but I hit him and he falls down. Didn't hit him hard but he falls down anyway. Like a dead log. Falls right down.

You kill him, Rev'rend?

No sir, I don't think so. He's all right. Leastways he look all right when he come to court. Not a mark on him, except on his left eye. No sir. He looked fine. I shoulda hit him harder.

Well, Rev'rend, I still can't figure which man you hit.

Well now, I don't remember too good myself but I sure hit one of them. Yessir. Knocked him right down. Right down on the floor. Now I weren't mad but I hit him. Not hard but he falls down. Down like a log. Thass the way it was.

I wish I'd seen that fight, Rev'rend.

Well now, it was really somethin. Sure was.

An aquatic implosion and the rattle of strangled pipes: the steel bars hummed, the steel walls vibrated, the resonance flashed through the recumbent bones of forty living men. Again, from a different cell, another roar of water: again the plumbing shook and groaned and whistled with the intensity and lunacy of impending disaster.

While Bondi wrangled with himself: Oh, that dreary old paradox? The libertine-anarchist choosing himself into prison? That? A little simple conviction would help here. My emotions become ideas, my ideas emotions. But here I lie, a victim of both. Should be home milking the goddamned goat. Minding my own business.

He watched a breath of moisture evaporate from the steel barrier three feet above his face. He sniffed and rubbed his eyes.

Agua!

The word passed with telegraphic speed from one end of the cellblock to the other. *Agua!* Water! Douse your lights, hide your smokes, your weapons, hide your words and thoughts.

Agua, agua, agua!

The five cells occupied about half of the block. They were divided by a narrow corridor from the single rectangular steel cage called the bullpen, where the prisoners spent their daylight hours and ate their meals. The corridor had one entrance, or exit, a steel door heavy and ponderous as the gate of a bank vault, which permitted passage from the cellblock to an adjoining anteroom and the rest of the building. This door was now being opened, screeching on its bearingless hinges, rumbling and grinding and scraping on the cement floor.

The forty men in their five cells became silent, cautious.

The door stopped, fully open, and a man came in, stooping under the lintel. A huge man, shambling like a trained bear, and wearing the khaki uniform and leather harness of a Bernal County deputy. His holster was empty; in his left hand he held a billyclub. Slowly he lumbered down the corridor, stopping for a minute or more in front of each cell, carefully inspecting each man within, then moving on.

No one would look at him; all eyes were turned to the floor under the pressure of his red stare. Only when he had passed to the next cell did some of the men dare to glance at one another with shamed and half-frightened faces.

No one spoke a word; no one whispered. The only sound was the shuffling tread of the huge man in the uniform; when he stopped to examine the inmates of a cell the silence became complete.

He came, this bear, this dark enormous man, to the cell in which Bondi lay. He stared balefully at the seven prisoners crouching on their bunks, studying each one in turn, and then raised his eyes to Bondi. Bondi, who had never seen him before, stared back.

He saw two red eyes, small and intent and without depth, as if made of tin, sunk deep in a welter of corrugations and protected by an overhang of bone and leather and ragged black brows. He saw these two eyes, dangerous and animal and implacable with power and hatred, and could see nothing else. And as he looked and waited he became aware of the challenge passing and growing between them, of the silent instinctive struggle for recognition and submission. Bondi felt the chill of fear on the skin of his neck, at his fingertips, and a deadly dryness in his mouth; he turned his head, looked away and though instantly conscious of shame, even of anger, could not compel himself to return that man's unblinking gaze. Could not, though he hated himself for his cowardice. Instead he lay still and silent on his bunk, watching the black forearm of Timothy Greene braced rigidly against the opposite wall. And until the guard moved away, for a full five minutes he lay fixed and tense in the same position looking at the same object, waiting with a burning face and cold queasy stomach for the enemy to release him from the implied violence of that stare.

Gutierrez the guard tramped the length of the corridor, huge and silent and malevolent, crouched to pass through the doorway and was gone. After him the massive door swung slowly shut, dull gray iron grinding in friction, harsh and cold in its finality.

An instant of silence and then the men remembered their humanity, became unrigid and looked at each other and talked, grinned and laughed uneasily, relit cigarettes and talked.

He's after somebody.

Now that ain't no lie. The Bear is a-lookin for somebody. Somebody is in bad trouble.

He's in for it.

That ain't no lie. He's gonna git it. Yessir.

Glad it ain't me. Brother!

You said it, chum. You done said it.

Bondi sat quiet on his bunk, saying nothing aloud, busy at disemboweling his own soul, examining with an attempt at a sterilized logic the soft glistening blue-veined innards of his spirit. While darkness gathered within and around him and the bad air of the cell settled under its own weight of smoke, sweat, human vapors. The sun was gone—its light was gone. Through the filthy frosted glass of the window beyond the grid of bars he could see the muted glow of evening neon, the swing of automobile lights, the yellow rectangles of lighted windows, all the multiple refractions of the great American night.

And then from far below, from somewhere deep in the heart of the labyrinthine jailhouse, came the sound of a man's voice—singing. As if from far away, muffled by barriers of steel and brick and cement, the thin sound of a man singing, a wild drunken singing with the quality of an Indian's wail and the wind's intoxication, the music that a wolf might make if it could sing like a man.

I'm dreaming, thought Bondi, sitting up suddenly, hearing that old and remembered song, that familiar voice, I'm dreaming like a kid on the night before Christmas, like an angel the day before Easter. He sat upright on his steel bed, listening tensely, straining his senses to hear and feel. I'm dreaming, I'm dreaming, I'm dreaming, he thought.

The sound of a man singing.

CHAPTER 5

Burns did not walk far; he stopped at the first bar he came to, a small *cantina* at the edge of the unpaved road and close outside the official limits of Duke City.

He paused at the door; around him was the brilliance and gold and blue of the light, the sky, the white purifying heat, the withering leaves of the cottonwoods, the dust, and the fragrance of tamarisk along the irrigation ditches. He went in and found a dusky coolness, darkness, the smell of beer, the smell of wine, the smell of Mexicans and dogs and the unemployed. The act of entering the bar was like entering a grotto, leaving the real or perhaps only imaginary world outside in the dust and sun.

The cowboy did not wait for his eyes to adapt themselves to the comparative darkness but followed his nose and intuition straight to the beertaps at the bar. He leaned there, put his booted foot on the rail, and waited.

After a few moments, the parts of a man materialized and became visible in the thick gloom behind the bar. A small man, bald and fat and brown as a bean, with truculent eyes and an itchy little mustache. He said nothing; Burns said nothing. The man waited a moment more and then said: "What'll you have?"

Burns leaned against the bar and gazed thoughtfully at a big painting on the wall above the mirror and the rows of whisky bottles: *The Cowboy's Dream.* "A tall beer," he said, not looking at the bartender. The nude in the painting looked down at him from astride a cloudy horse; her limbs were comely, her flesh inviting, but the vague smile on her face suggested detachment, disinterest, the perils of ennui.

The bartender pushed a schooner of lager toward Burns and picked up his quarter. Burns drank deeply, thirstily, then lowered the vessel, wiped his mouth and looked around.

Three men sat at one table talking quietly in Spanish, sipping at bottled beer, chewing piñon nuts. They were looking at Burns with sullen curiosity, their eyes flat, incommunicative, with the opacity of hard rubber, their faces round and coarse featured and colored like the stubborn earth that fed them. They looked at him for several moments, while he returned their stare, then in unison all three appeared to lose interest and they looked away and at each other, continuing their sibilant low-toned palaver.

Alone at a table near the jukebox sat a young man with closed eyes, a wide-brimmed dark felt hat, tight shirt, boots, one good arm and one empty sleeve; in his one hand he held a pint bottle of whisky, half gone. The empty sleeve was doubled up and fastened to the shoulder of the shirt with a brass safety pin.

No one else was in the bar.

In leisure, with grace and affection, Jack Burns finished his beer, the keen edge already taken from his thirst and the contagion of the afternoon—almost evening now, with the sun lowering on the five volcanoes in the west. He finished his beer,

ordered a second. Requested a second: the bartender was no
man to be commanded. Burns requested a second beer and after
a respectable interval of time had passed he received it. But the
lapse of time was of little concern to him; he held the schooner
in his hands, caressed its cool moist surface, revolved and lifted
and weighed it, set it down and took it up again, playing with it
casually for several minutes before taking the first drink.

Time passed: seconds, minutes, a half hour with the ease
and changelessness of time in dreams and in old cathedrals. The
shaft of sunlight that poured through the window by the door
steadily altered its angle of declination, and as it changed the
small parallelogram of light that fell on the nude behind the bar
rose up from her thighs and lap to the belly and hips. The flies
crawled over her body following the light and warmth.

The young man with one arm sat unchanging in his coma-
tose slump, his eyes still closed and his body motionless. But the
bottle that had been half full was now almost empty.

Burns began his third beer. He had already quite forgotten
the wine and ice cream curdling in his stomach.

The three men at the table had left and been replaced by a
dozen others of the same caliber and brand: laborers on the way
home, mud farmers, men from the railroad shops.

Burns was now sitting at a table near the bar, waiting, patient as a snake in the sun. Between beers he ate peanuts and
piñon nuts, tossing them by the palmful into his mouth, and
dropping the little cellophane bags under the table and around
his feet. He rolled a cigarette, smoked it down, and requested
another beer. The beer came, standing in the big mug with over-
flowing head among the wet rings on his table. He blew off some
of the foam, buried his nose in the mug and drank, deeply and

slowly; a slight yellow glaze began to dull the intensity and conceal the depth of his eyes. Quietly, in a gentlemanly manner, the cowboy was getting drunk.

There was music, occasionally, when someone had a spare nickel for the jukebox; the records with their concentric striations, scratched by a blunt steel needle, produced a proximate musical effect; Mexican voices in a kind of vulpine harmony, guitars, loud trumpets pitched a semitone too sharp, the rhythmic grinding of the machine. No one listened to the music, no one cared, drunk or sober; the noise was not meant for entertainment but for the sustaining of a certain psychological atmosphere, the pervasion of space, the dispersal of unseemly silences. So that a man without anything to say and unable to think could still imagine himself at the vortex of an activity, however meaningless.

The young man with the one arm still had not moved but sat slumped in his chair as if dead; under the big hat his face seemed tense, listening, but the eyes were not open. The whisky bottle was empty, with the fingers of his one hand curled tightly around its neck.

When the light and flies had passed above the breast and reached the neck and shoulders of the nude in the painting, the young man opened his eyes and looked at Jack Burns. Burns felt the weight of that look and set his schooner down on the table, gently. As he turned his head to face the one-armed man the other inverted his grip on the neck of the bottle, brought it back behind his ear and threw it, spinning, at the cowboy's head. Burns ducked, and the bottle smashed to pieces against the adobe wall behind him.

At first nobody stood up. And nobody said anything; the

jukebox ran down a record into oblivion and then there was a short spell of silence. Nobody got up; the cowboy sat where he was, relaxed and a little drunk, staring with no more than a polite interest at the man who had thrown the bottle at him.

When the jukebox had stopped its howling and the room became silent, Burns spoke: "Why'd you throw that bottle at me, *cuate*? Never seen you before in my life." He tossed a handful of peanuts into his mouth, dropped the bag on the floor and waited for a reply. The one-armed man stared bitterly at him and said nothing. "How about it?" Burns said, a bit more loudly.

The one-armed man did not answer, and did not move. Burns glanced once around the room at the silent men, the alert faces and hands. He swallowed his mouthful of chewed peanuts, took a sip from his beer, and waited without visible anxiety for something tangible to happen again.

This time the one-armed man threw his glass; Burns jerked his head aside and the glass bounced off his shoulder and slid and rolled across the wooden floor.

"Now looky here, friend," Burns said, "you sure you got the right man? We ain't even been properly introduced." He sat up more formally in his chair.

The young man with one arm stood up, saying nothing, and walked toward the cowboy. His eyes were half open now, a pair of yellow slots, and his lips moved and twisted though no words came through. He came close to Burns, standing above him; he reached up, took off his hat and swung with it at Burns' face. The cowboy flung himself backwards, his chair going over and sliding out from under, leaving him sprawled on his back on the floor.

The one-armed man stood looking down at him, a sick grin

on his face, his eyes gleaming with derision and triumph, his one fist clenched. He started to talk: "Whatsamatter, cowboy, you afraid to fight? You afraid of a one-armed man?"

Burns raised himself to his elbows and looked up at the man. His face had gone cold, expressionless, his eyes were bleak and suddenly sober. But he said: "I don't want to fight you *cuate*. I'm a peaceable fella, don't like to fight." He started to get up and the one-armed man kicked his legs, and he fell flat on the floor again.

The one-armed man looked down at him, grinning. "Can't stand up, cowboy? Whatsamatter with you? Like a little baby."

Quickly Burns rolled away and over, and when the revolution was completed he was standing on his feet, erect and ready; the one-armed man, who had moved to trip him again, stopped in surprise. "All right," Burns said; "now what were you sayin?"

The one-armed man hesitated, no longer grinning. Then he said: "I ain't afraid of you, cowboy. I don't give a damn how big you are or how many arms you got."

Burns said: "Fella, you'd be a lot better off if you'd stop worryin about that one arm. If you ain't satisfied with one arm you oughta get it chopped off."

The one-armed man spluttered after a reply: "You mind your own goddamn business. I lost my arm at Okinawa. What'd you do? I'm a better man than you are, no matter what."

Burns smiled, though his eyes remained hard and watchful. "Maybe you are," he said; "it's a hard thing to settle. Maybe you are. Why don't we have a drink and talk it over?"

"*Chinga!*" the other said; "you're afraid, you *hijo de puta*."

Swift as a cat Burns stepped forward and slapped the man hard across the mouth, driving him back against the bar. A dislodged glass rolled in a half circle, fell off the bar and rolled again, unbroken. "Never call a man that," Burns said; "just you never call a man that. No matter what, never do it. It's very bad." He spoke quickly and quietly, breathing fast. "I might kill you for callin me that, fella. That's how bad it is. Don't ever do it again."

The bartender got busy at the telephone.

The one-armed man sagged against the bar, stunned and off balance, speechless and shocked and outraged. Around the barroom men had risen and were talking excitedly, staring without sympathy at the cowboy. He looked at them, waiting for the charge from the one-armed man. "Now you fellas stand back," he said. "If this *cabron* wants to fight so bad why by god I'll fight him. Do it with one hand behind my back, too." And he slid his left hand under his belt at the small of his back and kept it there. "So don't nobody interfere or I'll use both hands."

The bartender hung up.

The one-armed man roared out at last like a child coming out of a fit, lowered his head and plowed into Burns, butting, kicking, and flailing away with his one violent arm. It was a poor fight: two one-armed men, they made a sorry spectacle with their wild swings and misses, their awkward lunges and tipsy staggers. And the cowboy was getting the worst of it: without experience in one-arm fighting, he nearly fell on his face every time he swung and seemed unable to defend himself adequately—he received several jarring blows on the face and chest. But he kept on, and being much the taller of the two, with a longer reach, he began after a while to give as much as he took.

The fight went on as the two men staggered around through the barroom clubbing each other with skinned and bloody fists, falling over feet and chairs and spittoons, upsetting tables, spilling drinks, breaking bottles. The onlookers had a difficult time merely keeping out of the way, especially when the combatants began throwing things at each other—beer bottles, glasses, chairs, the steel puck from a shuffleboard table. The bartender, like a goalie in a hockey game, spread his arms and threw his body around to save his precious merchandise from destruction, but was not altogether successful: Scotch, bourbon, tokay and muscatel dripped from his shelves and formed dark pools on the floor.

Finally the fighting became general: Burns, knocked down, was getting back on his feet, forgot that he was supposed to be one-armed and used both hands to raise himself. At once there were cries of objection and someone, a little bowlegged man with a face brown and wrinkled as an old saddlebag, stepped up and kicked the cowboy in the ribs. A few seconds later the little old man was crawling under the table clutching at his mouth, a tooth missing and blood streaming from his nose: his three grown sons took his place.

Eventually and much too late the police arrived: a sheriff's sergeant and two deputies, three men with leather belts, .38 caliber revolvers, boots, badges and leather blackjacks. The bartender pointed out Jack Burns or what could be seen of him—a pair of high-heeled boots, swinging arms, the black hat miraculously still attached to a lean, bony and bleeding head, all somehow entangled on the floor in a cluster of squirming human bodies.

The deputies dragged him out, indiscriminately clubbing any heads that got in the way. Burns tripped one of them, punched the other in the belly, and received a sharp leaden rap on the head in return, and a pair of handcuffs on his wrists. Still conscious, he continued to struggle until the sergeant approached him from behind, blackjack in hand, and tapped him expertly on the base of the skull, blacking out the nerve center of the cerebellum.

Limp and inert as a sackful of old rags, long legs dragging, he was hauled out of the bar and across the golden dust of the road to the car, a bright new Ford with siren, red lights, and Bernal County insignia. The sun was low in the west now, a globe of fire singing between the black cones of two burnt-out volcanoes: an immense wave of light streamed over the desert, flooding the cottonwoods and adobe shacks and the red willows along the ditches, pouring across the mesa and mixing with the iron and granite of the mountain crags ten miles away. The men blinked against the glare as they dumped Burns into the back seat of the car. His hat fell off and flopped softly down in the floury dust of the road; one of the deputies picked it up and dropped it on his face. One of the men said: "Will he be quiet now?" and the sergeant said: "He'll be quiet long enough."

The booking officer, a huge man hulking over a tiny portable typewriter, thumping on its keys with two fingers like Polish sausages, peered across the high desk at the ragged figure cowering before him.

"What's that?" he growled; "what the hell kind of a name is that?"

"Konowalski," the little man repeated—a scarecrow, tattered rags on gray sticks, a sagging ruin of a face scored by hunger, blighted by hopelessness. "John Konowalski," he said again, as if not sure of the name himself. He proffered it timidly, expecting a rejection.

"Spell it, for chrissake."

The gray face seemed lost in reverie; the throat gulped, the eyes wavered.

"Spell it!"

"K—" the little man said; "K-o-n-o—"

"K-o-n-o—?" The booking officer frowned at his typewriter, pronouncing the letters silently as he typed them out. He turned to the deputy standing beside the rags. "Joe, the next time you pick up something with a name like this just run it on out of the County; don't bring it up here." The deputy grinned. The booking officer turned back to Konowalski. "Okay: spell it out."

"K-o-n-o-w-a-l-s-k-i . . ."

"Jesus Christ what a name. With a name like that you *oughta* be in jail. You oughta sue your old man."

"It's my name," the little man said.

"You can have it, fella." The booking officer typed a few more words. Then: "Address!" he barked.

The little man swallowed with difficulty, opened his mouth. His eyes were like a pair of bleared and bloodshot testes; they were focused on nothing. He swallowed again.

"What's your address?"

"Don't have none."

"Don't have none? Where the hell do you live?"

"How can I live anywhere when I can't find a job?"

"Just answer the question, fella." The booking officer hammered on the vibrating typewriter with his two big middle fingers. "What's your occupation?"

"Occupation?"

"That's right; what's your trade?"

"I got no job." The little man shuffled his feet, shrugged his shoulders slightly under the ragged coat. "Can't find none."

"Well, what do you work at when you do, if you ever work?"

"Laborer."

"Okay, okay, that's all I wanted to know." The booking officer attacked the typewriter again. He typed out a few lines, then noticed the old man and the deputy still standing there in front of the desk. He said: "Can him, Joe."

"Where'll I put him?"

"One of the blocks."

"They're all full."

"Well . . ." The booking officer typed out another word on the formsheet in the typewriter, then looked up again. "Throw him in the tank for a while. We'll find a place for him later."

The deputy put a hand on the little man's shoulder. "Come on," he said.

"Wait a minute," the man said. The deputy hesitated. "What you locking me up for?"

The booking officer frowned at the paper in his typewriter, his fingers poised on the keys. "Vagrancy," he said, not looking up. He started to type again.

"I didn't do nothin," the old man said.

"No address, no job, no money—that's vagrancy. Lock him up, Joe." The booking officer typed out another word, his lips silently framing the syllables, then removed the sheet from the typewriter and filed it in a manila folder on the desk. Wearily he turned his head toward the two deputies waiting on the bench, with the long collapsed body of Jack Burns between them. "Okay, boys, what you got there?"

"Wait a minute," the old man said, as the deputy started to pull him away. "I didn't do nothin. I was just walkin through town. So I got no money, no job, is that a crime?"

"That's vagrancy," the booking officer said. "If you don't believe me you can argue with the judge in the morning. He likes to argue. Now for godsake, Joe, get this crumb out of here."

The deputy named Joe unlocked a blank steel door at the far end of the office and pushed the old man inside into a windowless room littered with prone sick bodies under a yellow light. Through the open door came a powerful stench of vomit, urine, animal filth. "In you go," the deputy said, and slammed the door shut. Dimly, through the wall of metal, they could hear the old man talking, protesting: I can't breathe, he seemed to be saying, I can't breathe in here.

"All right," said the booking officer, "what's this?" He was looking down at Burns' inert, bloodstained body, held half erect by the two deputies. "Can it talk?"

"He's all right," one of the deputies said. "He acted kinda feisty for a while and the Sarge had to clip him. He'll come around in a minute."

The booking officer put a new formsheet into his typewriter, rolled it around the drum, clicked off five spaces. "Drunk?" he asked.

"Yes," the first deputy said. "Drunk and disorderly; started a fight in Miera's Bar. Resisted arrest."

The booking officer typed down this information, or part of it. "Where'd you say it was?"

"Miera's Bar, North Highland Road."

"When?"

"Five thirty to six this evening."

The booking officer hammered on the machine, then looked up. "What's his name?"

The deputies looked at each other. The first one said: "Who knows? No one at the bar knew him."

"Well, didn't you search him?"

"Yeah, sure." The deputy was holding his cap, upside down, in his hand; he lifted it and spilled the contents onto the desk: a few dollar bills, some coins, matches, a sack of Bull Durham, a pocket-knife, the black dried shrunken ear of a bull.

The booking officer looked disdainfully at the cowboy's property. "Is that all? Isn't there any identification?"

"No," the deputy said; "that's all he had."

"No draft card?"

"No."

"No driver's license, no social security card, no discharge card, no registration card, no insurance card, no identification at all?"

"Nope. That stuff there is all there was."

The booking officer appeared to be extremely annoyed. "My god, he must have *something* on him! A man can't walk around loose without any I.D. at all!" He gave the unconscious Burns a look of disgust and exasperation. "Didn't he have a billfold?"

"Wasn't none on him," the deputy said.

"Where'd he keep his money?"

"In his pocket."

The booking officer clenched his hands and chewed vigorously on his lower lip. "Jesus!" he said. He stared at Burns' sagging head. "No cards, no papers: who the hell does he think he is?" He turned back to his typewriter, two big fingers poised for action—he had nothing to write. "Goddamn!" he said. And then: "Wake him up. Wake the sonofabitch up."

The two deputies shook the cowboy, and slapped his cheeks, but there was no response.

"Throw some water on him."

One of the deputies filled a paper cup from a water cooler and threw the cold water in Burns' face; he stirred slightly, groaned, then relapsed into darkness again. The booking officer growled, got up from his stool behind the desk and opened a cabinet built into the office wall. He groped around for a moment, muttering to himself, then found a small bottle and passed it over the desk to one of the deputies. "Hold that under his nose." The deputy held the tiny vial under the cowboy's nose. Nothing happened. "Take the stopper out first," the booking officer said, patiently. The deputy obeyed. "Now wave it around under his nose." The sharp fumes of ammonia penetrated the air; the deputies held their heads away from the bottle.

Burns began to struggle feebly, trying to avert his face from the bitter pungent bite of the gas. He moaned a little and pushed at the air with his shackled hands; his eyes were screwed tightly shut. "Hold him still," said the booking officer, "and keep that stuff under his nose till his eyes open and he starts to talk." Burns turned and twisted, straining to free himself from the grip of the two deputies. "Hold him!" the booking officer said; "give him a good strong dose."

The cowboy writhed, kicked, opened his eyes and stared blindly at the ceiling. "Lemme lone," he gasped, "lemme lone, lemme lone, damnit, lemme lone." He fought against the steel chain binding his wrists, the arms holding him down. "Lemme lone, I say, by god lemme lone." His black hat was knocked off again and fell upside down on the floor; the three men, straining stepped on it, tramped all over it. "Lemme lone," and swaying like figures in an intense ritual dance, Burns shouted wildly, "lemme lone, goddamnit!"

"Okay," the booking officer said, "turn him loose. Let go of him, he's awake."

The deputies stepped back, releasing Burns; one of them still held the bottle but it was empty—a dark stain spread over the front of his shirt. Burns stood alone in the middle of the room, sagging, weaving, about to buckle at the knees; he wobbled backwards and hit the wall and leaned against it and managed to stay more or less upright, rubbing at his eyes with both fists, talking angrily to himself: "The bastards, the dirty hogs, the damned dirty rotten bastards, the sonofabitches . . ."

"Okay, cowboy, that's enough. Snap out of it." The booking officer waited; Burns continued to mumble bitterly. The booking officer shouted: "I said that's enough. Shut up!"

"Crawlin snakes," Burns said, "the dogs, the rats, the goddamned disrespectful potato-eaters, the no-good lowdown sneakin coyotes . . ."

The booking officer turned to one of the deputies. "Where's Gutierrez?" he said.

"I don't know," the man answered.

"What?"

"I don't know. How should I know?"

The deputy named Joe now spoke up: "He's upstairs," he said. "Gutierrez is upstairs."

"Call him."

The deputy scurried out of the office and down the hallway past the water cooler and the elevator door and a fire hose coiled in a niche in the wall and stopped at the foot of the stairway. "Gutierrez!" he yelled; "hey, big bear!"

"Slimy sneakin skunks," Burns said, rubbing his eyes, "cowards, rotten crapeatin *cabrones* . . ."

They heard the crash of a steel door from somewhere upstairs, the meshing of locks and then a voice, an animal snarl. The deputy returned to the booking office. "He's comin," he said; he stared at Burns.

Who was still talking: "Bunch of hamstringers," he said, "lyin two-faced two-headed split-tongued dry-gulchin pig's litter, yellow-livered yellow-bellied bitch's sons . . ."

The booking officer ignored him as he made an inventory of Burns' property, stuffing the articles into a manila envelope, sealing it and putting it away in a steel filing cabinet. Then he waited.

"Bastards," Burns said, "absolute bastards . . ."

Something was tramping through the hallway, a dark shape and ponderous heavy-footed body coming toward them over the cement floor through the yellow light of the hallway. The bearman, Gutierrez.

He entered the office. "What d'ya want?" he said sullenly; he was sweating: under each armpit was a crescent stain spreading slowly through the khaki.

"Help this man stand up," the booking officer said, pointing at Burns. "Help him to talk polite."

Gutierrez glanced at the sagging, muttering, indifferent figure of the cowboy. "I was goin out," he said; "I'm off in five minutes. I need somethin to eat."

"I know," the booking officer said; "this won't take but a few minutes. I want to find out this man's name and so on."

Gutierrez shrugged, then reached out and put a huge hand around the back of Burns' neck. "Okay, man, stand up straight and answer the questions." He lifted Burns away from the wall and held him up before the desk.

"Get your dirty paw off me," Burns said; he slashed laterally at Gutierrez with his handcuffed fists. "Get away from me."

Gutierrez snatched at the flying hands, caught them and held them still, pushed tightly into Burns' stomach. "Behave," he said, "or so help me I'll break your backbone." He dug his fingers and thumb into Burns' neck, crushing nerves and blood vessels.

"What's your name?" asked the booking officer.

"I can't talk," Burns said. "This black gorilla is stranglin me." He struggled against the man's grip but could do nothing; Gutierrez held him as if he were a child.

"What's your name?" the booking officer asked again.

"Make this ape let go of me and maybe then I can talk."

"What's your name?"

"John W. Burns. Make this bear loosen up on my neck."

"Loosen up a little," the booking officer said to Gutierrez. To Burns: "Where do you live?"

"Anywhere I feel like."

Gutierrez again pressed his iron-hard fingers into Burns' neck. "What does that mean?" asked the booking officer.

"Figure it out for yourself."

"Help him answer the question," the booking officer said. With one hand Gutierrez forced Burns' head forward and down until his chin was jammed against his chest and the vertebrae of his neck stood out like knobs under the inflamed skin. "What's your address?" said the booking officer.

"I don't have none," Burns mumbled hoarsely.

"You got to have an address."

"I don't. I just wander around wherever I feel like." He

breathed with difficulty and involuntary tears were forced from his eyes. "You bastards," he moaned.

Gutierrez kicked him in the small of the back with his knee. "Where do your folks live?" the booking officer asked.

"Missouri."

"Is that the truth?"

"Yes, goddamnit."

"Let go of his neck." The booking officer recorded the information on the formsheet in his typewriter, while Burns, slowly raising his head, stared at him with malignant intensity. "What's your occupation?" asked the booking officer.

Burns looked at him. "Cowhand," he said; "sheepherder; game poacher."

"Which is it?"

"All of them. What difference does it make?"

The booking officer typed for a minute. "Where's your papers?" he said.

"My what?"

"Your I.D.—draft card, social security, driver's license."

"Don't have none. Don't need none. I already know who I am."

The booking officer frowned heavily. "You're not supposed to run around without any identification," he said. "People like you ought to have to wear dog collars." He stared seriously at Burns. "Now where's your draft card?"

"Don't have none."

"You *got* to have a draft card."

"Never heard of it."

The booking officer sighed gently, half closing his eyes. "You got to have a draft card," he repeated; "you have to carry it with you at all times. It's a Federal offense not to. You understand that?"

Burns smiled. "That's news to me."

"Didn't you ever hear of the Selective Service Act?"

"Yes, I heard of it."

"All right." The booking officer rubbed his nose. "Now we're getting somewhere." He peered sternly at the cowboy. "Now what did you do with your draft card?"

"Never had one."

The booking officer scowled. "Never had one? Didn't you register for the draft in 1948?"

"I'm a veteran."

"All right, you're a veteran. We all are. But you still had to register. Did you?"

"Never heard of it. I was out of town."

The booking officer stared at Burns for a moment, then turned to the clerk sitting at the radio and telephone switchboard behind the desk. "Bill," he said, "you'd better contact the FBI. Tell them it looks like we've picked up another draft dodger." He faced Burns again. "Fella, you seem to be in all kinds of trouble." He added more data to the booking sheet, then ripped it out of the typewriter and filed it in the cabinet. He said to Burns: "You know anybody that'll put up bond for you?"

"No," said Burns.

"Okay. You want to make a phone call before we lock you up?"

"No."

"Okay." The booking officer handed a sheet of paper toward Burns. "There's your receipt. Look it over."

Burns took the paper with his manacled hands and studied it. "What's this?"

"That's a receipt for what we found in your pockets. You'll get your property back when we let you out of here." The booking officer looked at the clock on the wall, then at Burns and Gutierrez and the three deputies. "Well, get him the hell out of here, I want to go home."

Burns looked up from the piece of paper. "I want my tobacco and matches back," he said; "you can keep the rest."

"Lock him up," the booking officer said. Gutierrez released Burns and gave him a shove toward the deputies.

"You take him," he said, and walked out.

"I want my tobacco," Burns said. "Ain't you fellas human?"

"Get him out of here," the booking officer said.

"Where'll we put him?"

"I don't care. Anywhere, for chrissake. The cells are all full?"

"I told you that," the deputy named Joe said. "There's men sleepin on the bullpen floors tonight."

"Throw him in the tank," one of the other deputies said.

"Gimme my tobacco."

"Not this one," the booking officer said; "he's wound up a little too tight: he'll just make trouble all night long if he gets in with those other drunks."

"Well, what'll we do with him?"

The booking officer sighed wearily, glancing at the wall clock again and then at his wristwatch. "All right: put him in the Hole for the time being; we'll find a place for him tomorrow."

"That new judge ain't givin no breaks," one of the deputies said; "I wish we could dump a few of these birds in his kitchen."

"Don't you worry about that," the booking officer said. "Now get this guy out of here, please."

"How about my tobacco?" Burns said. One of the deputies

put a hand on his shoulder. "Goddamnit, I want my tobacco and matches."

"Come on, cowboy," the first deputy said, "you've had enough fun for one day." He took Burns by the arm and gently turned him around; the second deputy took the other arm and together they marched him out of the office and into the hallway.

Going through the door Burns twisted his head and looked back at the booking officer. "I'll remember this," he said. "You and that big gorilla both—I don't aim to forget." The booking officer, putting on his hat and jacket, ignored him.

In the hallway one of the deputies spoke to Burns: "You better be careful, man. You'll get in lotsa trouble talkin like that."

"That's right," the second deputy said. "Specially the Bear. You don't want him to hear you talkin like that; he'll hold it agin you."

"Sure will," the first deputy said. "The Lieutenant is all right, he's a good joe, but that Gutierrez—he's mean."

"He's bad," said the second deputy.

"No joke," the other said; "don't fool with him."

Burns limped along between them, staring straight ahead. "I know you're right, boys," he said. "By the way, which one of you crocked me on the back of the head?"

"That was me," the first deputy said; he grinned sheepishly at Burns through his brown Indian face. "I had to, cowboy; you was swingin and kickin like a scared wildcat. I had to quiet you down so we could bring you in."

"Thanks," said Burns.

They turned down a second corridor and stopped before a celldoor in the gray steel wall—a wall like the bulkhead of a warship, studded with rows of rivet heads. One of the deputies unlocked the door and opened it. "Okay," he said to Burns.

Burns hesitated. Beyond the door was the steel cubicle: bare gray walls, no window, no light, no furnishings but a bare steel bunk and a washbasin and a toilet bowl without a seat. "What's this?" he said in a dull voice.

The first deputy said: "It's not bad. You won't be in here long anyway, prob'ly."

"Well, how about some supper?"

The deputy grinned. "You're about three hours too late for that, cowboy."

Burns shrugged his shoulders. "Okay." He held out his shackled hands. "You can take these damned things off now."

The deputies looked at each other. One of them said: "You better get inside first."

"Inside? How're you gonna take these things off if I'm inside and you're outside?"

The first deputy pointed to a sliding panel in the door, big enough to put a hand through. Burns stared at it for a moment, then stepped inside the cell. At once the heavy door crashed shut behind him: he heard the latch clash and grip, then the intermeshing of tumbler and bolt as the big key was turned in the lock. He stood quite still in the sudden darkness and waited.

There was a grating of steel and the panel in the door slid open. "Stick your hands through," one of the deputies called. Burns put his hands through the narrow opening, the steel chain clanking and rattling on the flange. "Hold on a minute," one of the men outside said. He heard the first deputy say: "You got the key, Sam?" The other mumbled a reply which he could not hear; he waited stolidly in the semi-darkness, trying to breathe as little as possible of the dead musty air in the cell. He felt the suffocating oppression of confinement closing in on him: with great effort he suppressed his desire to cry out, to scream, to throw himself against the door. Then he felt a hand on his hand, the conflict of metal, the release of one cuff and then the other. "There you are, cowboy," one of the deputies said. He started to withdraw his freed hands but one was caught and held from outside; something slick and light touched it. "Take these, cowboy," he heard the first deputy say. He pulled the crumpled package inside; he knew by the feel and weight of it that it contained about five or six cigarettes.

"Much obliged, *cuate*," he said, facing the door. "How about some matches too?"

A brown hand appeared in the opening holding a matchbook. "I thank you," Burns said, taking the matches.

"So long, cowboy," one of the men called from outside. He heard them walking away, their footsteps and voices sounding loud and hollow in the long empty corridor, clashing like echoes in a cavern.

Burns stood motionless for several minutes in the stale gloom of the cell, staring at the rectangle of light in the door. Again he felt the full weight of his steel coffin, and the powerful impulse to rage and bellow and hammer with both fists on the door. He resisted, and the spasm of panic and hatred passed, and he was left feeling dull, desolate, emptied of purpose and meaning. He groped his way to the steel shelf and squatted on it, and lit one of the cigarettes.

The first deep drag made him sick, made him suddenly aware of his throbbing head and the sharp ache in his belly and ribs. Afraid that he was going to vomit, he put the cigarette out and back in the pack. He waited, while his stomach seemed to sink, dank and heavy as a bag of sewage, down into his guts. Gradually a profound depression crept up through his limbs, through his heart, into his mind. He shut his eyes and let his head drop down, lower and lower, between his knees, and let his hands hang like dead things over the edge of the bunk. In this position he sat for a long time, perhaps an hour, in the darkness and silence of his steel cell.

But when this hour had passed he lifted his head and opened his eyes, remembering something; he touched his boots. And it was then that he began to sing.

CHAPTER 6

The men awoke soon after dawn, long before the guard came. The cold air streamed through the half open windows beyond the cellblock and through each grill of iron to the men huddled like fetuses under their single blankets. A man would shiver, groan, and open red swollen eyes to view his world, the cage of bars and the steel walls and the dreary light filtering through the dust and cobwebs and dried spit encrusted on each window. The old vagrant in the next cell then began to cough, hack, choke, sneeze and blubber—dying by inches in a deadfall, dying of cold, heat, loneliness, the world's resignation, a piece of bad luck in 1932—and with a shattering nasal blast voided upon the tail of his shirt the night's accumulation of disgust. In the cell at the end of the block some half-heathen Indian kicked a lever in the wall and the waters roared, the iron conduits of sewage shook and rattled and shuddered like a premonition of war. The men growled in helpless and futile rage, scratched at their itching scalps and necks, examined new bites, sat up one by one and dressed: they put on their shoes.

Paul Bondi awoke slowly, with extreme reluctance and ineffectual resistance; he tried to retain his dream, to wrap it like a blanket around his gray and uncomfortable mind—there in that helmet of ideas and disillusions he had known the silence of sleep, and the surrealistic adventures of a god freed upon a green hill of ferns in Arcadia—but his efforts failed, the idyll in his purling brain became ragged and obscure, faded away in a yellow vapor: he opened his eyes.

He closed them at once. Dear God, he thought, God of our hopes and agonies—not *another* day of this, hard, bleak, ugly as sin and gray as virtue. The prospect of boredom, of a dead man's routine—it turns my stomach, Lord, it scratches on every nerve in my body. Something must *happen* today, an adventure, an explosion of fire, the arrival of our savior . . .

And then he remembered. What he had thought was lost forever in some occasional dream, he now remembered had preceded the dreams, though later mixed with them. That wild and solemn music, that wild singing as familiar to his thoughts and feelings as the image of his own face, had not been a dream at all, or not merely a dream: it was part of the gray world on which his eyes were opened now. That mad man—he had come, he was somewhere down below.

Bondi sat up on his steel bunk, smiling; he smiled at Timothy Greene rolled against the opposite wall, he smiled at his own romantic and improbable conjectures. He put on his shoes, lacing them up with stiff cold fingers, indifferent, almost unconscious of the act. He continued to smile—involuntarily, foolishly, happily—and rubbed the sleep from his irritated eyes; the allergy that had attacked him a month before was waning now but there was still the sensation, under each eyelid, of something like finely ground emery: a delight to rub and inflame, except for the liquid misery that followed. And his nose had been for several weeks not a screen and passage for breathing but rather a solid object, a wedge of moist putty, a damp dripping seep of tender flesh, a heavy and incarnadine weight suspended from his suffering eyes.

But he smiled, grinned happily, buckled his belt and scratched at the corners of his eyes, and thought: What can this mean, if anything? This apparition in the night? this wolf prowling through the streets of the city, howling from a cage? To judge from the sound of him, he must have been drunk as an Indian; Jack, Jack, you crazy fool . . . And why are *you* so gay, tovarish? You think he bears a pardon from the governor, news of a revolution, an amnesty for all political prisoners? Or does it please you to have a friend sharing in this little gray Hell!

But he smiled anyway as he slid to the floor from his upper bunk; he went to the toilet bowl in the corner of the cell, urinated, blew his nose on County paper and then flushed his offering into the river and on to Texas. He bent over the washbasin and splashed cold water on his face and hair, dried himself with more toilet paper, and combed his hair. There was no mirror; he felt his chin and wondered when he would get a chance to shave. The week's growth of beard on his chin and jaw annoyed him considerably, but there was nothing that he could do about it here. He found himself looking forward with some pleasure to the day of his transferral to a Federal prison: it would be a small adventure, a change, perhaps an improvement. He looked for the soap; it was gone.

"Good mornin, gentlemen," said Timothy Greene, smiling down from his enthronement on the upper shelf. His smile twisted sourly, became an exaggerated grimace. "Oatmeal and a

wiener," he said. "One slice of bread and a tin cup of rusty java:
Oh, I got them early-in-the-mornin, knocked-down-and-drug-
out, absolutely lowdown blues . . . Who's got the makins of a
cigarette?"

He was not answered. The other men in the cell, six of them
besides Bondi, sat wearily and miserably on their steel bunks
gaping out the window at nothing, pulling on shoes, scratching
their armpits, spitting and coughing like sick dogs. Men crawling like unhealthy, stunned dogs from an evil night into a hostile
day. Displaced: refugees from foggy dreams.

Bondi's elation began to fade with the sound of the coughing. He went to the bars of the cell, put his hands on the cold
steel, and stared at the window on the other side of the catwalk.
This is no place for a living man, he said to himself. There was
nothing to see through the window. He walked restlessly to the
gate of the cell and looked out and down the long gray empty
corridor to the gray barren door at its end: the tunnel to daylight. Beyond that door and beyond a second door like it and
beyond a barred gate and down stairs and through hallways and
beyond the ceremonial doorway of the courthouse—was freedom. A qualified freedom, he reminded himself. But air and
light and movement and purpose, the possibility of choice: the
essential elements of a man's liberty. Beyond the steel and brick,
on the other side of the wall of eyes.

He thought, at this moment, of his home: past the end of
the pavement, at the city's edge, on the boundary of the desert
and a sea of palpable space, the small adobe house with the blue
door and projecting vigas and battered walls set firmly in the
earth; the silvery greasewood in the backyard, the old rails of
the goat corral, the pump and the well, the apricot trees along

the lane, and the garden: a patch of lettuce, radishes, beans and sweetcorn. A clear and almost agonizing remembrance: Bondi, like any caged animal, felt the impulse to rage and strike, the desire to wrench the rigid bars from their bed of concrete.

I've been here too long, he thought, far far too long. Oh, the days are too long.

To avert any momentary, childish fit of despair he kicked gently at the bars, laughed aloud and thought of Jack Burns. Jack Burns in the county jailhouse: he imagined a wolf pacing round and round a straw-littered cell of the municipal zoo.

A clang and groan of metal: the big door at the end of the corridor ground slowly open and six men came trudging in carrying brooms, mops, mop buckets—the trusties. Beyond the doorway someone turned a key in a locked panel on the wall, opened it and turned the crank that pulled aside the bullpen gate. The six trusties entered the bullpen and at once, in silence, set to sweeping and mopping; in the doorway at the end of the corridor a uniformed guard stood and watched. Paper and dirt were swept in a pile, shoveled into a box and carried out; the men with the mops followed the sweepers, smearing the cement floor with water and disinfectant. The air in the cellblock became dank and depressing with the smell of sodium hypochlorite—the atmosphere of latrines, slaughter houses, county homes, mortuaries, county jails, orphan asylums, insane asylums, reformatories, public schools—a smell calculated to dishearten the free spirit and smother hope: the revenge that old men take upon children.

The trusties came out of the bullpen in single file, carrying their equipment with the air of harried slaves. The guard watched them and when they were all out and out of the corridor and in the room beyond the doorway he turned a second crank in the control box outside of the cellblock: the five grids of steel that served as gates to the cells slid sideways on ungreased runners, screeching and rattling like miniature trolleys. At the same time he slammed shut the heavy door and watched the prisoners through the spyhole; they could see his fat lips, the bulge of his nose as they waited by the open gates. The guard shouted at them through a screen below the glass: "Okay," he said; "good morning, men. It's a beautiful day in Duke City." Nobody laughed. Then he said: "Now I want you all to march into that bullpen like gentlemen. If I catch anybody pushing or running I'm coming in there and knock his block off." The men waited. "All right," the guard said— "March!"

The men filed silently out of their cells one at a time and in order, those in the cell nearest the door leaving first, then those in the second cell, and so on. The guard watched and counted heads as the men went through the bullpen gate. When all forty had left their cells and entered the bullpen he reversed the crank and closed and locked the gate, leaving the cells open. Then the massive cellblock door was opened again, the trusties came in carrying their buckets and mops and brooms and went to work cleaning the cells, the corridor and the catwalk around the cellblock. The guard left the door open, watching for a while, then turned and disappeared. Immediately the trusties and the prisoners clustered together along the bullpen bars, and there was a lively commerce in tobacco, cigarettes, comic books, dope, money and messages:

Timothy Green to Fred Blackburn, trusty: Fred, where the hell is my wife? Hain't she showed up yet? I dunno, Greene, I ain't seen her. But goddamn her, she promised she'd talk to the

Judge, try to get me off with ten days. I ain't seen her, Greene. Well God damn her to the blackest hole in Hell. I hear she's been hangin round with some cat from Dallas, Greene. What? What's that again, man?

Paul Bondi to Mike Sanchez, trusty with mop: Mike, do you know what they've done with a man named Burns? He's downstairs somewhere. Who's that? He's a good friend of mine, his name is Jack Burns. I don't know, boy, I didn't hear nothin about no Burns guy—what's he look like? He's tall, very tall, and skinny as that mop handle; he has black hair and a long crooked nose and is probably wearing an old black Stetson and boots. I didn't see nobody like that, boy; you sure he's here? You bet I'm sure; I heard him singing last night. Was that a man?—I thought it was some crazy Navajo.

The Wetback to Pete Herrera, trusty from Laguna: I gotta get outa here, Pete. Me too. It's drivin me crazy, Pete, I can't take it no more. I know how you feel. I got sixteen acres corn to cut, Pete. Sure, it's bad all right. I wanta go home. They'll let you outa here pretty soon, *cuate*. That's too long, Pete. You shoulda stayed off First Street, Wetback—me too!

The guard appeared in the doorway. "Break it up!" he shouted. "Keep those mops going! You men stand back from the bars or I'll turn the hose on you!"

The men slunk away, settled quietly on the steel tables bolted to the floor of the bullpen or sat on the floor or went to the far corner of the pen and hung on the bars and gazed sadly out the window at the outside world; the intersection of Fourth Street and Fruit Avenue with its milktrucks, police cars, early morning wanderers, newsboys and hotel porters. The window was much too filthy to be transparent, but it was open far enough to permit this fragmentary view of the city, two stories down.

Bondi sat on a tabletop and cleaned his fingernails with a folded piece of cardboard torn from a paper cup. He had to reconsider the possibility that he had been dreaming awake last night, that the sound of Jack Burns singing one of Burns' own songs had been a form of illusion, the actualization of memory and possibly desire rather than a direct perception. He had to prepare himself for the discovery that he had been wringing hope from a rag of a dream. And hope of what? He remembered the invisible inscription above the arch of the Court House entrance: *Lasciate ogni speranza voi ch'entrate.* The last notion made him smile, ruefully.

Chow down!

Chow down! The good word passed along; the men formed a line, a column of ducks, along one side of the cage. At the head of the line, waiting by the slot in the steel wall where the food came in, was the old Indian from Sandia who had been in the County Jail longer than anyone could remember—he claimed to have been born there. While the men waited the last of the trusties marched out of the corridor with their mops and buckets, leaving behind the glistening cement and the soursweet reek of the disinfectant. The guard came into the cellblock then, standing between the bullpen and the cells, and watched the feeding of the beasts.

The panel that covered the slot was opened from the other side and Joe Riddle, another trusty, his face like a map of the Bad Lands, eyes sore and running, peered in. The old Indian spat at him and the face was withdrawn; a moment later a cracked enamel tray appeared containing oatmeal, a slice of bread and a tin cup of coffee. The Indian seized it and hurried to a corner of the bullpen and began scooping up his slop with the greed of a starving hyena. Another tray was shoved into the slot and the man second in line grabbed it and sat down at the nearest table. The ragged column of prisoners shuffled forward, staring at those who were already seated and eating, and mumbling complaints:

What the hell?

No wiener today!

What's comin off around here, anyhow?

They'll be feedin us toasted cow pies next.

Bastards, they don't give a damn whether we live or starve.

I wanta see the manager.

Yeah!

The guard smiled indulgently and said nothing. Within five minutes the last man in line, Paul Bondi, had accepted his breakfast and was looking for a place to sit. The guard yelled at the trusties and the slot was closed; the guard left the cellblock and a moment later the big steel door clanked into place, sealing off the outside world for a few more hours.

Bondi sat down on the floor at the corner window; the tables and benches were already full, jammed with hungry men jostling each other with their elbows, dribbling oatmeal on their shirtfronts, gulping coffee down ragged throats. Bondi held his tray up to the light and examined the offering: much the same as he had received each morning now for almost two weeks— lukewarm watery coffee, a puddle of cold gray mucous oatmeal, a slice of flabby bread, a spoon. Only the customary wiener was absent this morning. He drank the coffee before it became any colder, then forced himself to eat the oatmeal. This required a sustained effort: the stuff had the flavor and consistency of the primeval slime and when swallowed settled heavily to the pit of his belly like a trowel-load of cold putty. But he ate it every bit of it, down to the last viscous gob; then he ate the useless slice of bread and his breaking of the night's fast was complete. He took his tray to the slot in the wall and stacked it with the rest, and then went back to the window and gazed out at the street below and the light of the morning sun glimmering on the leaves of the hedge by the courthouse wall.

The eschatology of the jailed, he remarked to himself—so pure, so deliriously pure: liberation, liberation. The fulfillment of all desires—in liberation. He reached up and clenched his hands around the rigid bars, pulled at them and attempted to stretch the kinks and knots of confinement out of his muscles. Liberation . . .

He watched two armed deputies, broad-shouldered and wide-assed, hustle across the sidewalk and into a Sheriff's-Department car; in ten seconds they were gone, leaving behind only a blue cloud of gases and the smell of combustion. They're after somebody, he thought; someone has been discovered living with a woman he's not married to—in sinlock; someone is in a fight, some poor drunk has assaulted another drunk, somewhere another fire is breaking out. He heard the wail of a siren in the distance. Sirens are always howling, men are constantly running, in this poor sad forsaken city of ours—a dim prelude to the disaster buried in vaults in that hill by the canyon. When the final chain reaction of terror begins . . .

Enough of that, he thought, and withdrew from the window—three men took his place, Indians with hungry eyes gazing down at the little picture of free movement in the air and light outside—backed away, and began walking up and down the length of the bullpen, stepping over prostrate winos and forgers and shoplifters. He paced back and forth, hands in his pockets, shoulders rounded, head slumped forward: a young man, twenty-five years old, with a stocky body, fair skin, bloodshot blue eyes, and close-cut brown hair bleached a little by the sun. Enough, enough, he was thinking.

Agua!

Cigarettes were crushed, comic books hidden, conversations turned off like tap water—

Agua, boys, agua!

With an iron grumble the cellblock door began to open, slowly, heavily, like the portal of a cave. Most of the men stood up to see who or what was coming in. But no one came in. The crank was turned and the bullpen gate slid open. The guard stood in the doorway with a sheet of paper in his hand.

"Court call!" he shouted. The men listened attentively. The guard started to read a list of names. "Abeyta," he said, "Joseph Abeyta." A small dark fellow wriggled through the crowd, through the bullpen gate and out into the corridor. The guard signaled him to stop and wait. "Arnold," the guard said, "Henry Arnold." There was no response to that name. The guard went on. "Burns," he said, "John W. Burns." Again there was no response, except Bondi's smile. "Davila," said the guard, "Jake Davila." A solid, grim-looking man went through the gate. "Good luck, Blackie," someone shouted after him. The guard went on, reading in alphabetical order a list of some thirty names. About a third of those called were present; the others were in different cellblocks. The guard closed the bullpen gate, then motioned to the men waiting in the corridor to follow him. All disappeared, and the big cellblock door rumbled shut.

Bondi went to the window and gazed out at the world, smiling helplessly again, rubbing his itchy eyes. He blew his nose heartily on a sheet of toilet paper and then sat down to wait.

About an hour later the *agua* signal was again flashing through the bullpen. Men stopped to watch the door open, looking for something new or the return of old friends; Bondi was among them.

The door opened and the guard appeared. "Head count!" he shouted. Like trained animals the men in the bullpen lined up against the bars of the opposite wall. The guard stood outside in the corridor and did his counting, pointing a finger at each head and mumbling to himself. After a second count he went out, looking a trifle glum.

Bondi sat down again, picking at his nose. His disappointment was sharp and not merely temporary. He was aware of the fact that there were three other cellblocks in the jail—the odds were three to one against Burns appearing in this one, even if the Hole and the Tank were not considered. He picked disconsolately at his sore, damp nose.

Two hours passed; the men began thinking about beans: dinner. Bondi sat on the bench of the table near the window, looking out at the street life, thinking about Jack Burns facing Judge Alexander Cheroot across the varnished bar of justice. He remembered his own trial weeks before, in a different, greater court, before the District Judge, a long gaunt man with a gray mustache and the gentle unhappy eyes of an ulcerous aristocrat. The prisoner was unhappy too—two unhappy men facing each

other across a slough of law and necessity, convention and courtesy and the complex weeds of politics. A brief, formal arraignment and hearing had taken place later, but the issue of the trial
was decided in the Judge's office one afternoon in September.
They sat in comfortable old chairs upholstered in mohair and
black leather in a cool dark room lined with books—ponderous
unreadable volumes of legal history, statute and precedent,
bound in olive drab linen and lettered in gilt. The Judge—his
name was George Willem van Heest—smoked a black briar
with drooping stem: Bondi would never forget the fragrance of
Old English Shag, nor the creaking sound the chairs made each
time they crossed their legs or the Judge leaned forward to tap
the ashes out of his pipe, nor the sound of the Judge's voice—
pleasant, mellow, and melancholy, like his eyes and face, like his
old-fashioned 1895 office.

They had talked quietly and respectfully and for a long
time—nearly three hours—and had grown to like each other
almost as much as two men can in such a situation, and of such
different ages, backgrounds, income, status, metabolisms. The
Judge had been exceedingly sympathetic, and persuasive, and
wise; so much so that Bondi had felt a little ashamed of himself for putting such a gracious and kindly gentleman in such a
difficult position. But there had seemed to be no compromise
possible, and neither would or could yield on the fundamental
question: respect for and obedience to the written law of the
land. The old man, bound by a thousand hoops of habit and
tradition and profession, held that the law must be obeyed
whatever its social or political or moral significance; the young
man, sustained by the vague but apparently limitless strength of
conviction, could not agree. Therefore, after those nearly three

hours of comfortable and mutually-enriching conversation, together with the rich dark atmosphere of age and smoke that had brought them together in the gloom, like father and son, leaving impressions on the mind and emotions of each that no span of time would ever completely efface, United States District Court Judge George Willem van Heest had found it necessary, in conclusion, to inform the prospective defendant Paul Maynard Bondi that he would certainly be sentenced, under the provisions of the Selective Service Act of 1948, to at least two and possibly five years of imprisonment, to be served in whatever Federal Penitentiary the appropriate officials found most convenient. Bondi shook hands with the Judge and left. Formal proceedings took place one week later; Bondi, pleading *nolo contendere*, was given two years; that is, was deprived of two years.

At this point an awkward if trifling misfire developed in the massive machinery of the law: the United States Marshal was unable to find immediate accommodations for the prisoner in any of the Federal prisons situated in adjoining states. Until the necessary arrangements were completed, then, Bondi was turned over to the Sheriff's Department for temporary incarceration in the Bernal County Jail. The prisoner had shaken hands with three friends down from the University, kissed his wife farewell, and in the custody of a Sheriff's officer disappeared into a brass-doored elevator on the main floor of the County Courthouse.

Never to return, he muttered to himself. He remembered that elevator: the ugliest, most stifling, most slow-moving elevator he had ever known—like a freight elevator in a meatpacking plant. There had been other formalities and courtesies: he was searched, questioned, registered, fingerprinted, numbered and photographed. And finally he had been led down a long yellow corridor, up a flight of stairs, through an iron gate, through a steel door, down another corridor and into the steel cage where he rested now, brooding on his memories.

He stood up and stretched his legs. Miserable dreams, he thought, these wretched . . . Through the open window beyond the bars and below he saw an automobile glide under a yellow traffic light. Police on aluminum-painted motorcycles followed. These wretched dreams, he thought. Stale and unprofitable, barren as a spayed spinster. What I need to fill these gray hours is a plan, a project, a metaphysic of damnation. He noticed that the shadow of the mailbox on the corner had contracted eastward over the sidewalk, uncovering one concrete slab, half covering a second. Time for lunch, he observed. Damnation, beans, coffee . . .

He let his thoughts lapse and mused over nothing, staring vacantly down at the fragments of free life in the air and sun outside.

Chow! someone shouted. *Chow down!* Within seconds the line had formed along the grid of bars. The men waited.

A guard entered and stood in the corridor. On his signal the food slot was opened from the outside and the first tray shoved in. The old man from Laguna grabbed it and sat down in his dark corner. The others filed by rapidly, silently, while the guard counted heads.

Bondi, last in line, picked up his rations and found a seat at the end of a table. Beside him, absorbed in mastication, sat the Reverend Hoskins. Bondi fished a spoon out of the beans and slowly, without enthusiasm, began to eat. Pinto beans without sauce or chili or even much salt; a slice of bread; a tin cup of coffee. Out of loyalty to life and the immortal spirit of man, he ate.

When he had chewed and swallowed the final mouthful of beans, he got up and returned his tray to the stack by the slot. He took his private paper cup out of his shirt pocket and filled it with water from the tap, and had himself a slow thoughtful drink. He thought about Burns, about Jerry, about the last decent meal he had eaten: a steak fry out in the hills—steak, beer, fresh sweet corn baked on the cob. In the evening, with an amber moon edging up over the shoulder of the mountain, another world gigantic and close, with mountains and craters and a strange inner radiance, translucent and cool, like the heart of a ghost. Against the red flare of the west the nighthawks were circling, crying, killing—they plunged toward the earth through invisible swarms of insects, levelled and rose again, wings flitting like those of bats; each dive was accompanied by the soft muted startling roar of air rushing through feathers. Somewhere in the canyon behind them a mockingbird sang: a derisive song beginning on a high clear note and sliding down through a microtonal scale to an awkward, quavering stop. And the odor of burning juniper: three of them around the fire, Jerry, himself and a friend with harmonica. The steaks were crisp and carbonized on the surface, pink and hot toward the interior, the beer cool, the sweet corn smoky and fresh. Red meat and fire, moon, mountain, the music of birds and cicada and man, the great city glittering in the valley, his woman beside him—the compound image was distinctly painful; Bondi tried to think of something else. Of something practical, like war.

He sat down on a bench and buried his face in his hands, closing his eyes. A darkening emotion flooded his heart, drowned his nostalgia in loneliness and helplessness and doubt. So that he scarcely heard and did not care about the opening of the cellblock door, the tramp and shuffle of prisoners, the clang of the bullpen gate, the sudden flurry of talk and laughter among the men. Bondi was conscious of nothing but his own darkness, until he became aware of the light steady pressure of a hand on his shoulder. He did not look up immediately; he uncovered his face, looked at the gray windows beyond the bars and then turned his head, slowly, and saw the cowboy standing beside him, and looking up saw the smile and the lean nose and the eyes of Jack Burns.

CHAPTER 7

TULSA, OKLA.

Hinton stopped for the red light and watched the suburban traffic roll by. Sweat dripped down from his ribs; the air was hot in the cab when the truck was not in motion, despite the buzzing electric fan mounted on the dashboard. Around him the traffic clashed and roared, the smell of hot tar, rubber, oil and metal permeated the air and the blue smoke from the cars and the black smoke from the diesel trucks mounted toward the sky. He watched the women crossing the street—middleaged domesticated cows, long-legged schoolgirls, fat pigs from the reservations—and found nothing worthy of his attention. He puffed nervously and irritably on a cigarette, letting the ashes fall on his T-shirt.

The light changed from red to yellow, from yellow to green: Hinton stepped on the throttle, engaged the clutch and guided his great rumbling truck forward into the glare and haze of the afternoon.

CHAPTER 8

"My God," Bondi said softly. He stood up, staring at Burns. "You really *are* here." He reached out and put a hand on the cowboy's shoulder, and squeezed a little on the tangible skin and bone. "In the flesh—or what there is of it." He began to smile. "You're as skinny as ever—and not a bit prettier."

"*How kola*," Burns said, grinning. "What'd you expect?—a goddamned ghost?"

"No . . . yes . . . I'm not sure." Bondi paused, staring happily at his friend. "I don't know—but I was never so glad to see anyone in my life. Whatever you are."

"Well, I'm the same old Burns." The cowboy returned the scrutiny: "You look pretty good—kinda sleek, like you been in high grass for a while."

"Me? Yes, I guess so . . ." Bondi blinked his eyes. "This is a comfortable little jail. I'm so happy here."

"We'll leave tonight," Burns said, still grinning.

"Sure, we'll break out." Bondi hesitated, staring helplessly at the familiar, homely face of the cowboy. "Well, damnit—shake hands." They shook. "Now sit down. Make yourself at home."

The Reverend Hoskins, who had been watching them, moved over on the bench. "Make yourselves comfortable, boys."

"Thank you, tovarish," Bondi said. He offered a seat to Burns. "Sit down, Jack."

"I've been sittin too long already," Burns said, "but I guess a little more won't hurt me." He sat down and Bondi sat beside him.

"Now," Bondi said, "start talking. Where've you been for the last year or so? What've you been up to? And how'd you get in here?"

Burns grinned and rubbed the back of his neck. "That was easy enough," he said. "No trouble to that."

"You look like you were in a fight."

"I guess I was. I guess you might call it that. I don't recollect too well."

"Wonderful," Bondi said irrationally, as if the other had announced some personal triumph. He could not keep his eyes off Burns' face. "Holy Mary, you're really here."

Burns looked around at their cage of bars. "No doubt about that." He pushed back his trampled black hat. "No sir."

"Well, tell me about yourself. Everything—what you've been doing, where you've been, what you're thinking these days."

The cowboy smiled amiably, looking at Bondi. "Not much to tell, Paul. Specially on that last item. Whenever I get in jail I only think about one thing."

"Getting out?"

"That's right."

"You'll never be a philosopher," Bondi said. "Not at that rate. Only a philosopher can transcend these bars and walls without getting off his actual entity. Or opening his eyes." Even in the surprise and delight of this meeting Bondi was conscious of a third party present, the objective monitor in his brain surveying and appraising the appearance, speech and reactions of his old friend with a certain critical detachment. He seems a little slow, the monitor observed, a trifle dulled by too much wind and sun and animal company—as if not yet fully emerged from the wild wolf's dream of rock and black shadow. The drugged absorption in the natural world.

"Maybe I'll never be a philosopher," Burns agreed. And then he added: "I can only think of one thing worse—you'll always be one."

Bondi laughed. "I'll fool you yet, tovarish: I like that prophecy. I'm flattered." What was I thinking? he said to himself; a kind of wild glaze on his mind? I should know better. Look at those eyes of his—clear and piercing as jets of light. Undimmed by print, the lucky devil.

"You like it?" Burns said. He rubbed his chin, smiling a little. "Well, it takes a mighty wise man to be flattered by insults. I'm beat." He grinned at Bondi. "Why don't you tell me what *you're doin in here?*"

"It was all a mistake. A silly misunderstanding." Bondi squeezed his nose carefully and looked at the floor. "Let's talk about my case later. It's a sad one. I want to hear about yours. You got in a fight, you said. Was it a good fight?"

"No," Burns said; "I lost."

"You look it, all right. But what brought you to Duke City, anyway? I thought you were up in Montana or Wyoming; weren't you going to pan for gold along the Yampa?"

"Never got that far. Never got out of New Mexico. I been herdin sheep for the last six months. Just foolin around before then. Wastin my time."

"You were herding sheep?" Bondi looked more incredulous than he felt. "Were you sick or something?"

"Well, I guess I was. I was sick of starvin to death. Fell in love with a no-good horse, too—a crazy little mare called Whisky." Burns felt his shirtpockets. He grinned. "Also, I thought it might be a good idea to get back in touch with civilization. A sheep camp is a good place for that." Again he felt through his pockets. "You got any smokes, Paul?"

"No, I haven't. But I can get you the materials, maybe." Bondi nudged the Reverend Hoskins. The dark worn face turned toward him. "Reverend, if you'll give my friend here the makings of a cigarette I'll give you my supper coffee."

Hoskins' face wrinkled into a painful smile.

"All of it," Bondi said.

The smile broadened. The Reverend Hoskins had a mouthful of teeth as corroded and awry as the tombstones in an old graveyard. "Well, now, Mister Bondi," he said, "I thought you was a Christian but that ain't no very Christian deal you offers me."

"That's true," Bondi admitted.

"Anyways I don't smoke," Hoskins said. "I don't believe in it. It's sinful."

"You were smoking this morning."

"I was a-backslidin this mornin," Hoskins said; "I'm mendin my ways this afternoon." He looked at the cowboy. "You look like a good man to me," he said. He unbuttoned his greasy coat, pulled a sack of Bull Durham from a vest pocket. "Take this, young man, and enjoy yourself. You look like an honest man to me."

"Much obliged," said Burns, taking the tobacco. "Got any papers?" The sack of tobacco was nearly empty.

"No sir, that I haven't." Hoskins explored his innumerable pockets. "Yes sir, I got this." He drew out a ragged sheet of thin tissue, the wrapping off a roll of toilet paper. "I got this."

"I sure do thank you," said Burns. He folded the paper, tore off a rectangular section and began making himself a cigarette.

"Then you came to town to see me off to Leavenworth?" Bondi asked, turning back to the cowboy. "A lot of trouble for little pleasure, I think."

Burns completed his cigarette and put it in his mouth. "Not exactly, Paul." He looked at Hoskins. "Got a match too?"

Hoskins stirred heavily, his old blue serge whispering. "Match? Well, maybe I do. Now just maybe I do. I won't say for sure, mind, but just maybe. Let's see here . . ." Searching again, every hidden pocket. "Maybe now . . ."

"Not exactly?"

"Not to see you off," Burns said. "To get you outa here."

"Out of here?"

"Might be," Hoskins said, still searching, "just might be now."

"Yes," said the cowboy. "I thought you might need some help. I know a hundred good hidin places."

Bondi finally understood. Liberation, he thought, and smiled. As easy as that. Jack's been to too many Westerns. Too much Zane Grey. "Maybe you don't fully understand why I'm here," he said.

"I think I do," Burns said. "But you can't *stay* here." He looked closely at Bondi, perceptibly anxious. "You want to get outa here, don't you?"

"Here you are, young man." Hoskins proffered one match. "I knowed I had one somewheres."

THE PRISONER 111

"Thanks," Burns said; he struck the match on his teeth and lit his cigarette. "You can't stay in a place like this," he said to Bondi; "you'd go loco."

Stark naked loco, Bondi thought, grinning internally. Maybe I've already sprung my gyroscope. "Well, I won't be here very long," he said, knowing this was the answer Burns did not want. "They'll take me out of here soon enough."

"Wait a minute." Burns hesitated, glancing around: no one was watching them. "Look," he said, drawing one pantleg up over his boot top. "Look in the boot."

Bondi looked and saw the tang and heel of a file gleaming dully against the cowboy's pale hairy shank. "How did you get that in here?"

"Never searched me." Burns lowered his pantleg. "I've got another one in the other boot."

"Then you're not planning to stay for a while?"

"We're gettin outa here tonight."

"This is a serious business, huh?"

"Sure it is. That's why I brought the files."

Bondi considered. Everything was against it, of course, but for a moment he surrendered to fantasy and temptation; to break free, hide in the hills, riding by night . . . He could not conceal from himself his delight in the *idea* of outlawry—the guns and romance. "You amaze me, old man," he said; "and I can see now that you're more or less serious about this . . . practical joke. But after all—I came here voluntarily. What would I prove by escaping a self-imposed sentence?" He smiled wearily. "We martyrs can only choose once."

Burns puffed on his cigarette and stared at the floor.

"The whole thing is crazy," Bondi said. "Suppose we break

out of this place? What then? I'll be an outlaw for life. What about my academic career?"

"How's it comin along in jail?" Burns asked.

Bondi smiled and scratched his scalp. "Well . . . you can see. I had to make a choice. It was either prison or graduate school." He rubbed his eyes; the slightest excitement seemed to aggravate the irritation. "And what about my family? I've got a wife and a kid. I'm a man with responsibilities. I believe you're crazy, old comrade, coming here with a proposition like that."

Burns stared at the floor. "You can't stay in jail for two years," he said; "you'll go crazy."

"You're already crazy."

"You won't be able to take it."

Bondi laughed. "But good lord, Jack—it *is* two years, not a lifetime. If I were in for life your idea would make some sense. But surely two years in prison is better than a whole lifetime as a hunted man."

"Not for me," Burns said. "Anyhow, it won't be like that."

"You've been brooding over lonely campfires too long, my good friend."

Burns smoked his cigarette down to the last pinch of tobacco. "You can't stay two years in jail," he said; "it'll kill you."

"It might at that. I was thinking the same thing this morning."

"And even if you could last out the two years—what then? What'll happen to you then? You'll just get in some kinda trouble all over again. You're that breed."

"Not necessarily."

"Prob'ly. I can see you refusin to pay your income tax because you don't like the way the Government spends your money, or somethin like that." Burns field-stripped the fragmentary butt of his cigarette, dumping the remains into his shirtpocket. "And two years from now, if the big war ain't started yet, things will be a lot tougher than they are now. You might have to wear some kinda uniform by then."

Bondi could not help smiling. "You're so damned eager to get me out of jail because you want me to become an outlaw like you. But I'm not that kind of animal. I have a great deal of respect for law and order and decorum. When I'm sentenced to prison I believe in serving out my term in an obedient, conscientious manner. I think it's only the proper and decent thing to do. And now you come to town, insinuate yourself somehow into the county jail, and begin tempting me with your romantic, outlandish, impossible, nineteenth-century notions. Frankly, Jack, I'm a little shocked."

It was the cowboy's turn to smile. "Hell, Paul, I've gone to a lotta trouble on your account. I came here to rescue you and by God I'm gonna do it."

"But I don't want to be rescued."

"I'm gonna rescue you whether you want it or not."

Bondi sighed and put an arm around the cowboy's shoulders. "Why don't you sing us a song? Write any new songs lately?"

"Sure," said Burns; "I got one called 'Restless Feet Must Roam.' And one I call 'Song of the Timberline.' But I ain't got my guitar with me." He tugged at the bristles on his chin. "And I sure don't feel like singin anyway. I can't understand what's the matter with you."

"With me! You're the one that's all balled up. You outrage my common sense. And what about my principles?"

"You proved your point by comin to jail," Burns said. "The idea now is to break out before they break you."

"They won't break me. I've got a nimble and pliant will, and the powers of a chameleon. I'll conform for a year, or two years if necessary, and when I get out I'll be a wiser man. Maybe a sadder man. Possibly bitter, too—I hope not."

"You didn't look very cheerful when I came in," Burns said.

Bondi rubbed his eyes. "Well, I wasn't. It's the Russian thistle that's breaking my spirit now. One of the reasons I'm so eager to go to prison: I'm anxious to get out of New Mexico."

"Come with me," said Burns; "we'll go high up in the Rockies—maybe the Shoshone Forest in Wyoming. I know where there's a cabin, a good tight windproof cabin, at the foot of a glacier. In winter it's snowbound—no one can get within twenty miles of it. We'll lay in a good supply of venison and elk and pine logs and just sit tight while the snow falls. I'll write songs and you can work on your treatise on whatever you're workin on now."

"A new theory of value," Bondi said; "a general theory of good and evil, beauty and ugliness, progress and regress."

"And Jerry can paint her pictures," Burns went on. "And Seth—we'll educate him, the three of us. We'll learn him to read and write, I suppose, and better things too—how to track deer, how to fish through ice, how to trap the silver fox, how to make things, useful things like bows, arrows, snowshoes, bullets."

"Is he your son or mine? I want him to be a classical scholar."

"All right," Burns said; "you can joke about it but I know you're interested. I can see a peculiar light in your eyes. You're thinkin how much you'd like that kinda life yourself."

"There is a certain primitive attraction in it," Bondi said, "but what about the future? Are we to spend the rest of our lives shooting animals, chewing skins, hiding out from game wardens and county sheriffs?"

"Look," Burns said, "I don't understand why this has to get so consarned complicated. I read in the paper you were in jail so I came to town to get you out. That's all there is to it."

"Keep talking: you may convert me yet. I'm still mildly interested. But remember my wife and kid and my professional standing."

The cowboy fidgeted with his hands. "How can I talk with you when I don't have a cigarette to roll or a guitar to pick on or even a stick to doodle in the sand with? This ain't no place for humans."

"I remember thinking exactly the same thing this morning."

"And when do we eat? I'm mighty hungry. No supper last night, not much of a breakfast this mornin. How about some dinner?"

"You're about an hour late, *compañero*."

"It don't seem right. They lock a man up for practically nothin and then starve him to boot."

"You've got a legitimate complaint."

Burns lowered his voice. "We gotta get outa here, Paul. This place is frazzlin my nerves. We'll file our way out tonight; what do you say?"

"Why go to so much trouble?" Bondi said. "What are you in for—drunk and disorderly conduct? They'll probably let you out in the morning."

"It ain't so simple as that. They're holdin me for investigation, too," Burns said, and he grinned like a schoolboy. "The FBI is gonna investigate me; they think maybe I'm a draftdodger like you."

"Where were you in September, 1948?"

"By God, you sound just like that bookin officer."

"But were you in the States then?"

"Hell, I don't know. I think I was down in old Mexico."

"Then you never registered either?"

"Not me; and even if I'd a-knowed about it at the time I still wouldn't of done it—the Government's never gonna brand a number on me again. Only I had sense enough to keep quiet and not write letters to my draft board."

"But now you're caught."

"That's what *they* think," Burns said.

"And you'll go to prison just like me."

"You know me better than that, Paul."

Bondi blew his nose on a piece of toilet paper and blinked his watery eyes. "Sometimes I think we're both crazy. We don't seem to realize that it's no laughing matter to pull tail feathers out of the American eagle. How'd you get away with it for so long? Didn't your old draft board ever write to you about it?"

"They didn't know where to look for me," Burns answered. "I ain't had a steady mailin address for nearly four years, not since I got outa the Army." He rubbed his knees. "Say, my legs are gettin cold."

"It's the cement floor," Bondi said. "Let's walk around for a while; if you sit still for too long in this dungeon you're sure to get neuralgia or rheumatism or mildew."

They stood up and began pacing the floor along the inner corridor—thirty feet north, thirty feet south, back and forth in the manner customary to all caged animals. "In fact," Bondi was saying, "I've been falling to pieces; my dandruff, always bad, has recently got worse; I've picked up athlete's foot somehow;

my hay fever is still critical; and I've got a dull gnawing ache in one of my wisdom teeth. I hope I get sent to a quiet, clean, well-lighted prison."

"You're gonna light for the hills with me," Burns insisted. "This kind of life is no good. Not even for philosophers."

They neared the steel bulkhead of the cellblock, turned and started back. The bullpen was quiet now, inactive, with most of the prisoners spread out on the tables and benches—the afternoon *siesta*. The cockroach races were over, the stories all told; only the boys at the window, watching the girls pass by, enlivened the air with their comment and disputation.

"Don't step on this gentleman's feet," Bondi warned. The Wetback from Laguna lay in their way, hat over his eyes. "I'm not sure but I think he carries a knife. He's rather truculent for a Pueblo man; bitter about something." Bondi stepped over the Indian. "By the way, Jack, if you're serious about breaking out of here—how can you trust thirty-eight other men? I'm thinking of the noise; everyone in the cellblock will be able to hear you if you try to file one of these bars. What's to stop one of them from calling a guard?"

"That's a chance I'll just have to take," Burns said. "As long as the noise don't go through that steel wall I'll be happy. I won't make much noise, anyway."

"Another thing: how long will it take you to file through one of these bars?" Bondi reached out and put his hand around a bar, pushed and tugged at it for a moment; the bar remained as firm, rigid, immutable as a mathematic abstraction. "You might not be able to get through one in one night; and in that case you'd have to make sure to get back in the same cell the next night, which isn't easy."

"Damned if I'll spend another day in this place," the cowboy muttered. He too wrapped his fingers around one of the bars of the gridded wall. "Are these bars solid?"

"I'm sure I don't know."

"If they ain't we could file through a couple of them in a few hours—three or four hours, maybe. You on one, me on the other."

"Me? Good heavens, I'm no jailbreaker."

Burns studied the pattern of the grid for a few moments: the vertical bars six inches apart, braced by and interlocked with a series of horizontal bars—flat not cylindrical—about eighteen inches apart. "You know," he said, "a man just might be able to crawl through by only cuttin out one bar. That'd give him a hole a foot wide, a foot and a half high. I might be able to do it—go through on my side. One shoulder at a time, maybe; slow and easy-like."

"You'd have to cut out two," Bondi said; "you couldn't squeeze through any other way."

"We'll see," said Burns.

They resumed walking up and down the length of the bullpen. Nobody paid them any attention; in a county jail the privacy of conversation is highly respected. And the guards, the jailer, were elsewhere: upstairs, downstairs, outside—hiding from the smell, the dampness, the tedium, the general dreariness of incarceration.

"Then," Bondi said, "if you do get through the bars you still have the problem of getting through a window and down to the ground."

"The window's nothin," Burns said; "just lift off that screen. Tie two or three blankets together for a rope; climb out, hit the ground, and start walkin. Nothin to it."

"Which window would you prefer?"

"Well . . . what's on the other side? the west side?"

"An alley and the back of a department store. The police cars go through that alley on their way to the parking lot behind City Hall. It's not very dark at night."

"That's the way we'll have to go. We can't go out on the north right by the street. Same for the east—we might land right in the Sheriff's arms."

"I suppose you know there's a penalty for attempted jail-break," Bondi said. "It's not a game; the fact that you're locked up does not give you the legal right to try to break out."

"We'll go out on the alley side, walk up the street away from the courthouse, get to your place, saddle up and head for the hills. We can steal a few horses from that ridin stable place that used to be along North Fourth. Is it still there?"

"I don't know," Bondi said wearily; "I haven't seen a horse prowling around Duke City since the great train robbery."

"Well, if it isn't we can get horses and saddles from that dude ranch out in Scissors Canyon. I know two of the boys that work there. They'll help me out."

Bondi put his hand on the cowboy's shoulder. "Jack, old friend, let's not go on kidding each other all afternoon. We have too many important things to talk about. And I want to hear you sing a few songs—your new ones, the old ones, some of the originals. So please understand me: I'm not leaving with you. I'm staying in jail, this one and the next one, until the authorities are sick of the very sight of me, which I trust may be in less than two years—I might get a parole. Then, when I'm free again, we'll get together, you and I and Jerry and Seth—and your wife: you'll undoubtedly have one by then: and we'll take a little hunting and fishing trip together. Anywhere you like—Canada, the Rockies, Sonora, Baja California. We'll spend a month or more out in the wilds and we'll laugh and sing and forget that this ridiculous nightmare ever happened." Bondi stopped then, and the other stopped with him; Bondi stared at the murky window on the other side of the bars. "Of course this is a nightmare; I loathe every minute of it. I'm sick to the heart of it—but I can't run away. I've got too many commitments to keep, too many weaknesses, too many hopeful ideas." He paused; Burns was silent. "Hopeful?" Bondi continued; "well, not really. I don't see the world getting any better; like you I see it getting worse. I see liberty being strangled like a dog everywhere I look, I see my own country overwhelmed by ugliness and mediocrity and overcrowding, the land smothered under airstrips and super-highways, the natural wealth of a million years squandered on atomic bombs and tin automobiles and television sets and ball-point fountain pens. It's a sorry sight indeed; I can't blame you for wanting no part of it. But I'm not yet ready to withdraw, despite the horror of it. Even if withdrawal is possible, which I doubt."

"But it is possible," Burns said. "It is; I know of places right here in the American West where white men have never been."

Bondi smiled. "You mean Ladies' Rest Rooms?"

"No," Burns said; "I've *been* in all of *them*. I'm thinkin of a few canyons in Utah, a few mountain lakes in Idaho and Wyoming."

"Maybe so," Bondi said; "maybe so. But I'm not ready for that. It's more convenient for me to stick it out for a while, to try to make an honest living introducing a little philosophy into the heads of engineers, druggists, future politicians. Don't think for a moment that I imagine myself as some sort of anarchist hero. I don't intend to fight against Authority, at least not in the open. (I may do a little underground pioneering.) When they tell us to say 'I recant everything' I'll just mumble something out of the corner of my mouth. When they tell us to stand at attention and salute I'll cross the fingers of my left hand. When they install the dictaphones—by the way, is it true that G-Man Hoover's slogan is 'Two Dictaphones in Every Home?'—and the wire-tapping apparatus and the two-way television I'll install defective fuses in the switchbox. When they ask me if I am now or ever have been an Untouchable I'll tell them that I'm just a plain old easy-going no-account Jeffersonian anarchist. That way I should be able to muddle along for a decade or so, maybe long enough to retire on half pay, dig out the old irrigation ditch and raise cucumbers and sweetcorn. Does that sound reasonable to you?"

"Sounds fairly easy," Burns said, smiling; "only I don't think you believe a word of it."

Bondi sighed, picked at his nose and sighed again. "Well, never mind. Call it a working hypothesis."

"If that's really the way you feel why'd the hell you muddle your way into jail?"

Bondi smiled sadly. "Quite right. I was afraid you'd ask me that. It sure was a piece of muddling. I never intended for it to work out this way at all. Here I had thought that since I was a veteran and a sort of scholar and even a gentleman by birth, my old draft board would let me get away with breaking the written law. And as a matter of fact they tried to help me; did all they possibly could for me. Damned nice people—they didn't want any unseemly dealings with the Government any more than I did. The difficulty was they wanted me to register as a conscientious objector. Conscientious objector to what? I asked them. To war, they said. But I love war, I said; my father got rich off the last one canning dogfood for the infantry; all Bondi's love war. Then what do you object to? they said. I object to slavery, I said; compulsory military service is a form of slavery. But there is no provision in the law for such an objection, they said. But it's the law itself that I object to, I said. That is illegal, they informed me. The law is unconstitutional, I replied. Then you had better take up the matter with the courts, they said. I'm a busy man, I said. What are you doing? they asked. I'm constructing a metaphysic based on the theory of unipolar planes of reality, I said. Would you mind repeating that? they said. That would be tautologous, I replied."

"Then they put you in jail," Burns said; "can't say I blame them."

"No, not exactly. They couldn't understand what was wrong with me or what I was complaining about: obedience is such a fundamental habit of the contemporary American mind that any kind of disobedience is regarded as a form of insanity. So they decided I was mentally incompetent and notified my parents; and my father, bless his poor old troubled soul, notified the FBI."

"Your father!"

"Yes, my old man—nobody else. He thought a little shock would do me good—purge me of what he considers immature and pernicious fancies." Bondi rubbed at his eyes. "Don't step on the Indian, Jack. My father, as you know, has a powerful sense of duty—except when reporting his income. But he is patriotic; excessively so, in my opinion. In all things, our country comes first—that's his thesis. As for me . . ."

"Somethin else comes first?"

"Yes," Bondi said. "If I had to choose between my country and my friend I'd choose my friend." He grinned shyly. "You know, my sense of loyalty is getting all twisted around. For example, I find that I feel more loyalty toward immediate concrete things, like my wife and my son and you and myself, than toward the giant abstractions like Democracy and God and The United States of America. I know it's queer—an unhealthy inversion of values. But I can't seem to help it; that's the way I've come to feel. You know what I mean?" Burns nodded. "Well, of course you do; I guess you've felt that way all your life. With me it's come late," Bondi continued. "When it first struck me—must have been about two years ago—I composed a little pledge or prayer to . . . well, sort of formalize it; make it stick in my soul. Would you like to hear it?"

"Yes," Burns said.

"It went like this: 'I shall never sacrifice a friend to an ideal. I shall never desert a friend to save an institution. I shall never betray a friend for the sake of law. Great nations may fall in ruin before I shall sell a friend to preserve them. I pray to the God within me to give me the power to live by this design.'"

They came to the gray wall and stopped. Bondi put his finger on a bolt head fastening one plate of iron to the next. "Pardon my rhetoric," he said, as the cowboy said nothing. "I hope it didn't sound too sententious because in so far as that statement has meaning I intend to abide by it. Perish the contradictions: it's not an ethical system, it's an ethical intuition. A mere emotion, if you wish."

"I'll not argue it," Burns said; "I like it; I think I thought of it before you."

They were silent, gazing at the opaque wall of metal a few inches before them. Then they turned around, and did another turn up the length of the bullpen. "Want to sit down?" Bondi asked.

"Nope, not yet. I still ain't got my legs limbered up. They had me in a little box last night not much bigger'n a telephone booth."

"How'd you like the new judge, A. Cheroot?"

"He's a smart little punk," Burns said; "reminds me of a weasel. I'd sure like to lay a loop over his ears, dally to the horn and take him for a ride down some old rocky wash."

"He's a slick one, all right. But wait till you meet Van Heest. There's an aristocratic old fox; a fine proud old fox."

"I'll never see him," Burns said; "I ain't stayin."

"Of course. I'd almost forgotten." Bondi sneezed into the palm of his hand. "Excuse me. I wish to hell you'd brought your guitar."

"When do we eat?"

"Come here to the window. I'll show you." They went to the corner of the pen nearest the open window and looked out. They could not see much; the window was low on the wall, two feet beyond the grill of bars, opening out from the bottom like a factory window: impossible to see the sky. "See the shadow of that mailbox?" Bondi said. "When it reaches the curb on the other side of Second Street we eat."

"That's a pretty good clock; but I'm hungry now. What can I do about it?"

"You can wait."

Burns clutched at the bars with both hands and stared down into the street. "I couldn't take this," he said; "not again. I'd go crazy in about a week." Cars, trucks, buses clanged through the intersection; arm in arm two highschool girls stepped by, giggling; after them slouched a pair of *pachucos*, round-shouldered, greasy-haired, hands buried deep in the pockets of baggy pants. They heard a long scream of laughter. "This is cruel," Burns said; "it ain't human, keepin a man penned up like a dumb animal. I wouldn't do it to a dumb animal."

"This isn't the first time you've been in a place like this," Bondi said.

"I know it." Burns pulled at the bars; he braced both feet against one of the horizontal members and tugged and strained mightily: a very slight tremor passed through the grid. Burns set his feet back down on the floor and relaxed. "Pretty solid," he said; "a good job." He smiled at Bondi. "Yes sir," he said, "I know what this is like. That's what makes me feel kinda sick and mournful: I can't help thinkin of you in here, or a place like it. It'll make me uncomfortable, itchy, restless, for as long as you're in. I got too good an imagination."

"Thanks for the sympathy, Jack; that'll be something of a comfort to me. But I think I'll make out." Bondi turned his back to the window and contemplated the bullpen, its walls and bare furniture and its thirty-eight other inmates—more now—sprawled like sick or dying men on the floor, on tabletops, on each other. This enormous room has a peculiar and essential horror all its own, he thought, something I shall never forget, shall never forgive—never understand. And it has that old familiar horror common to public institutions everywhere, like that in dim yellow photographs 'exposing conditions' in the county poorhouse or the state mental hospital; the same atmosphere of inertia and hopelessness, the same postures and gestures of utter sickness. "It won't be like this in a Federal pen," he said aloud. I hope not. I hope not.

"What's that?" Burns said, staring out the window.

"I said it can't be like this in a Federal prison. They'll let us outdoors for exercise, there'll be more room and air and light, maybe we'll play baseball now and then." Bondi remembered his days of Spring. "I used to be a passable infielder," he said; "played second base for the Montclair Bandits back in New Jersey."

"New Jersey? What's that?"

"Maybe they'll teach me a trade," Bondi went on. "Carpentry, shoemaking, welding, tree surgery, something like that. I've always wanted to learn to do something really well with my hands. I mean, besides the usual thing. Everyone should be able to do some kind of skilled and useful work with his hands. Even philosophers. Especially philosophers."

"That's just talk," said Burns; "all you really want to do is sit around on your ass and read fat books wrote by cock-eyed old Krauts and lousy Russians."

"I'll not be a slave to my own ideology," Bondi replied. "Why didn't you bring your guitar?"

"Sure—let's go somewhere and have a beer."

"There's better alcohol in a good song."

"Why the hell should I make this easier for you?" Burns scowled as he stared outside, his hands clutching the bars. "I'm too mad to sing. Anyway I don't like to sing when I'm in a cage; —who wants to be a goddamned canary?"

"Well . . . I don't know," Bondi said.

Burns turned away from the window. "Paul," he said, "look—" For a moment he could find no words; in exasperation he lifted one hand and rubbed the back of his neck. "Look," he said, "goddamnit anyhow, I just don't understand you. What's the matter with you? You give me these lectures on how the country's goin to the dogs—you got plenty to bitch about, seems like. You're always bellyachin. And now they got you in jail—two years, like a rat in a cage. And here I am—" He lowered his voice. "Here I am, with files in my boots all ready to get you outa here. And you don't want to go—you say. But still you keep on a-bitchin. I can't figure you out—I think you must be a little loose in the head. If you don't like the way the country's goin why don't you come with me?"

Bondi sighed wearily, leaning against the bars. "So you're back on that," he said. Outside, in the street the shadows were turning from black to purple. He looked up at the cowboy. "I've already explained," he said. "In the first place, I don't believe in your form of escape. It's no good for me, it's no good for my wife and kid, and maybe it won't be any good for you much longer. In the second place, as I said before, I still like the poor ugly world I'm living in even though I don't approve of the long-term trend of things. Did I call myself an anarchist? a Jeffersonian anarchist? Well, that's a metaphor, not a description of my politics. Because if I'm an anarchist I'm not only a Jeffersonian anarchist; I'm an ironical anarchist as well. Why? Because I see clearly enough the utter hopelessness of the anarchist ideal: everything is against it—the massive pressure of overpopulation, industrialization, militarization, the weight of sentiment, the momentum of history. A lost cause—one never found, I should say. Extinguished in America almost as soon as it began: Thoreau, the frontier, the I.W.W. . . . Anyway, Jack, the point is that my anarchism is just a sentimentality; in practical matters I'm a good sound citizen: I serve on committees, vote in elections, will some day run for the local school board."

"Jesus wept!" the cowboy growled; he rubbed the back of his neck, then grinned at Bondi with a glint of sarcasm in his dark eyes. "What a bullshitter you are! I'll bet you almost believe your own talk, the way you carry on. Jesus!" Scornfully he said: "You gonna run for the school board while you're still in jail or wait till you get out?"

Bondi tried not to smile. "I was serious," he said; "I'm always serious. Why the devil didn't you bring your guitar?"

The bullpen came to life; a stir of general excitement: Chow! someone yelled.

Chow down!

Chow! someone called. And the men fumbled their way out of sleep, staggered up, swaying and lurching, shambled into a long ragged line forming behind the Laguna crouched fiercely by the food slot in the gray steel wall. An old man coughed, hawking and spitting on the floor, coughed again and swallowed his torment. The cellblock door clanked and groaned, rolling slowly, heavily, open, and The Bear shuffled in, Gutierrez, and stood in the corridor between bullpen and cells, glaring at the prisoners.

"You pigs!" he bellowed. "*Cabrones!* You swipes, you crumbs, you bloody jag-offs—stay in line there, you dumb pig of an Indian. Stand up straight, goddamnit, or I'll give you the hose."

The men were silent, stiff with anxiety. The food slot opened and Joe Riddle, eyes red and running, shoved in the first tray. The Indian from Laguna took it with trembling hands, crept quietly and quickly to his corner far from The Bear; he studied the floor as he scurried over it. In a dead shuffling scraping silence the others followed, accepting their slop without protest, and went cringing past the red glare of Gutierrez toward a seat at the tables.

With rapid mouths and scraping spoons the men ate—a steady rhythmic sound, a chumping and thudding and snorting, the prolonged concussion of worn teeth and hard pinto beans, fried chips, gristle—accompanied by the muted rattle and clink of tin cups on metal, the slosh of liquids, and a basic passacaglia of grunts, sighs, farts and belches.

"Eat, you pigs!" Gutierrez shouted; "push it down, you lousy bums, you scummy sonsabitches, you twatlappers!"

Last in line were Bondi and Burns. Bondi picked up his tray of beans, his cup of coffee, his slice of bread; The Bear addressed him: "Hello, college boy, how do you like it here, huh? Nice, huh? Like home, huh?"

A wry but apprehensive smile was Bondi's reply. Not looking at Gutierrez, he started toward a table. "Hey!" the guard roared; "you too good to talk to me? You think you're too smart, maybe? Talk to me, college boy."

Bondi stopped, hesitating, looking at his beans. His face was pale, his eyes impatient. "What do you want?" he said.

"What do I want?" Gutierrez screamed; "what do I want! *Santa Maria*, Mother of God! College boy asks me what do I want!" He faced the men sitting nearest him, on the other side of the bars. "You hear that?" he said. The men sniggered obediently. "College boy asks me what do I want!"

Bondi started to move and Gutierrez roared at him again: "Come here, college boy! Come here, you little pink bastard!"

"Take it easy," someone said—the cowboy, Burns.

"Come here!" Gutierrez bellowed. Bondi stared intensely into his tray of beans but found neither solace nor counsel there. He could feel a fiery irritation spreading under his eyelids and the clammy weight of doom in his stomach.

"Come here!" roared The Bear, reaching in through the bars. "You hear me, you dirty little red-nosed shit-eater?"

"Take it easy, fella," Burns said quietly, addressing the guard. He stood in a corner of the bullpen, halfway between the food slot and Bondi, holding his tray in one hand and his coffee in the other, and facing Gutierrez through the bars. "What's the matter with you, anyway? You mad at the world? Take it easy and you'll grow fatter." Gutierrez gaped at him with startled eyes and clutched at the bars, looking more jailed and dangerous than any prisoner there. "Honest," Burns said, talking quietly and with apparent sincerity, "any doctor'll tell you the same thing. Ever time you get mad you take a year off the end of your life. That's for a fact, fella. It raises your blood pressure and that weakens your heart. Or maybe it'll give you an ulcer in the stomach, somethin like that. You gotta be careful." Burns turned away, carrying his tray and cup of coffee. "Where we gonna sit, Paul?"

Bondi was afraid he was going to giggle; he was unable to answer.

"Ain't no seats left," Burns said; "let's sit on the floor, over by the window."

They went toward the corner indicated, while Gutierrez stared at the cowboy's back with red and narrowed eyes, hands clutching the bars above his head. He called after them in a voice more or less normal but taut with a compressed, internal violence: "Hey, you! Cowboy! What's your name?"

"John W. Burns." Burns kicked aside a tattered comic book. "Okay here?" he said to Bondi.

"What?" Gutierrez shouted, his face close to the bars.

"Burns. John W. Burns."

"Okay," said Gutierrez, speaking now in a lower tone; "okay, John W. Burns." He turned, or half-revolved, and lumbered through the cellblock doorway, muttering to himself. Then he crashed the door shut, the latch clashed and coupled, the heavy bolt was slammed home and locked, and nothing more could be heard of Deputy Gutierrez.

They sat down. Bondi ate slowly and carefully; he felt his nerves still tingling, his muscles taut, the roof of his mouth dry and cold. It cost him an effort not to shudder, not to let out the sick laugh caught and half-strangled in his throat. Very slowly and carefully he ate, though he had no appetite now.

The cowboy, chewing systematically on his beans, sopping up the liquid residue with his slice of bread, did not allow the silence to grow too heavy. "These beans shoulda been cooked longer," he said—"hard as bedbugs." Bondi said nothing. After a moment Burns said: "No rocks or burrs in em, though." He gulped down some of the coffee. "Coffee's pretty bad; but you gotta expect that—coffee's always bad in jail." He looked at Bondi's face, still strained and unhappy. "I was hopin it was hot," he said; "I was all set to throw it in that big gorilla's eyes a minute ago."

Bondi crunched on his beans. "I'm glad you didn't," he said. He was brooding again over what he felt to be his incurable cowardice. He wondered if there was any point in speaking of it to Burns.

"I'm glad too," Burns said; "mighty glad." He finished up his beans with the pad of bread. "That fella scares me. Can't figure him out." He drank more coffee. "I thought he was just the regular bully type. Kind you always find workin in a place like this. Stupid as a hog, and afraid inside. But I ain't sure about this here one. He might be different. If I was gonna be here long I'd be scared. I'd feel kinda mournful about my future."

Bondi munched his tasteless mouthful of bread and beans. "I should have stood up to him," he said. Not necessary, he told himself; Jack knows. Why fuss over it?

"Don't talk like a highschool kid," Burns said. "Who's gonna stand up to a man in the fix you're in? You couldn't; nobody could. Not when the other fella's got everything on his side and you ain't got the chance of a crippled prairie dog. That's no way to talk. The thing to do, if you have to take his crap, is to be quiet and wait and when you get outside, lay for him. And not with your fists neither, not if he's big and you're not. And not with a knife—Gutierrez is the kind of ape that's carried a knife all his life; you wouldn't have a chance that way. You can't let the other fella pick the weapons if it gives him all the edge and you ain't got none. The thing to do is use somethin you're handy with. Maybe a piece of lead pipe or a tire tool. Or a gun, if you're mad enough."

"How about a slide rule?" Bondi said. "I could rap his knuckles smartly and then run like hell."

"This is serious business," Burns said. "You know it." He finished his coffee. "You said you played baseball for a while. Well, hell, use a ball bat. And strike first, from behind. Don't give him a chance to take it away from you. You don't want a fight, you want revenge." He grinned a little. "When you just want a fight you can always go home to your wife."

"That's right," Bondi said; "punishment, not a duel, is my aim." He found himself taking refuge in nonsense. "I haven't won a fight in my life," he said, "not since I beat up my best friend back in Montclair, New Jersey. I wasn't mad at him but he was the only kid in the whole school I was sure I could lick. I had to do it."

Both lapsed into silence for a few minutes, straying into retrospection, exhuming old faces and events from some vault in the brain.

"I remember when I was a kid," Burns said. "—I wish I had a smoke, this would come easier." He looked around for Reverend Hoskins, saw him telling a story at the other end of the room. "Well, I'll get one in the mornin. Well, anyway—" He looked at Bondi. "Did I ever tell you about Steve Brock and Charlie Snye?"

"I don't know," Bondi said; "I can't remember."

"Well, when my old man died my mother sent me out here to New Mexico, to my Grandfather's ranch. Sent me Collect, you might say: my Grandfather paid for the shipping. I was only twelve years old at the time, but mean as a bobcat.

"I hated it at first. My Grandfather just had a little place, and everybody had to work hard, includin me. First time in my life I ever did an honest day's work."

"Why didn't your mother come too?" Bondi asked.

"She had another man, back in Joplin."

"Why didn't she keep you then?"

"She had to get rid of me to keep the man."

"Oh . . ." Bondi tried to imagine that distant situation, the horny dilemma. He saw the boy, bitter and unforgiving, and a strange man with certain inflexible opinions, and the mother, undoubtedly bewildered, probably a little desperate: other brats to feed. And young Hamlet scrounging around, sulking and hatching trouble. Dispatch him to England!

"I landed in Socorro one day in September. My Grandfather picked me up in his old Model A at the bus depot. I'll never forget that drive out to the ranch—forty miles over some of the toughest, roughest, rockiest roads you ever saw in your life. You know what Oscura range is like; nothin but lava beds and dry arroyos and mesquite and cholla and yucca. In that country a cow would walk a mile for a mouthful of grass, and ten miles for a drink of muddy water. I thought it was just about the awfulest country I ever seen. And the ranchhouse was even worse— flat top, mud walls, a few dusty cottonwoods standin around. And some fat old Mexican woman in the kitchen—what a mess! Nothin like good old Joplin—no streetcars, no movie houses, no railroads, no drugstores, no factories, no garbage dumps— nothin but those rocky hills and all that cactus and those buildings made outa mud: I thought the place was awful. I thought it was worthless. I thought my Grandfather was crazy to live in a place like that.

"Well, I thought anyway I'd get a horse and saddle right away. But nope, the first thing we did was put a tin roof on the hay barn. And after that we went to a place down by the Rio where my Grandfather had a few acres and we put in about a week makin hay! I like to broke my back, pitchin on to the wagon and trampin down when we got back to the barn. Weren't no hay balers around then—them was Depression days.

"After we got the hay in and done some other foolin round, it was time for the fall roundup. That was a complicated business I got to tell you all about some time. There was me and my Grandfather and Charlie Snye—a real sour old bastard my Grandfather hired for range cook—and there was two other drifters and then there was this young Steve Brock, who worked for my Grandfather all year round. He was kinda wild and rough, and built like a middleweight prizefighter, and he was as tough as he looked. Only my Grandfather was tougher, though I didn't know it then. Anyway, I was crazy about this Steve Brock; I was just a kid and I thought he was everything a cowboy should be. Then we started out; we had about ten sections of open range to cover.

"But I still didn't get to be a cowboy. My Grandfather made me wrangler and cook's helper; I had to take care of about fifteen cow ponies, carry wood and water for the cook, help him wash dishes, help him pack up the chuckwagon—it wasn't a wagon at all, though, just an old Dodge truck with oversize tires to get through the sand. I didn't like my job; I hated it. The only thing I ever roped on that roundup was dead brush, when the cook wanted more wood—and it took me a long time to learn to do that.

"And I didn't get along with the cook, either. He was old and skinny and nasty and hated himself cause his name was Charlie Snye; I thought that was a pretty good reason, too. And Steve Brock didn't like him either; them two was always at each other's throats, arguin about one thing or another. I think Brock woulda killed old Snye if my Grandfather hadn't been around.

"About ten days after we started out we got back to the ranch headquarters with around a hundred fifty head of cattle. I mean beef, market stuff; the calves, bulls and cows was culled as we went along. Most of the hard work was done now; all my Grandfather had to do was wait for the trucker he contracted with to come and pick up the cattle. Well, the day after we got back my Grandfather paid off the hands and invited them all to stick around for a big dinner that evenin. He said there was gonna be a celebration of some kind, only he wouldn't say what. So the boys hung around.

"That evenin we all sat down at the big table in the ranch-house. Seems to me now that there was the best dinner I ever settled down to: there was a whole side of beef from some slick yearlin that wandered into camp lookin for trouble; and there was a brace of wild ducks from down by the river; and there was gravy, turnips, fried beans, tortillas, guacamole, sopapillas— nearly ever damned thing to eat a body could think of. And there was home-brew, too, and a couple gallons of Dago red. I tried everything in sight, and tried my best to keep awake.

"I was just beginnin to wonder where the dessert was when in came old Charlie Snye holdin a great big cake in his hands, one of the fanciest cakes I ever seen—three layers, with white icing and chocolate trimmin and on top of all that a bunch of little candles all lit up and burnin away as pretty as ever could be. I wondered whose birthday it was, and then old Charlie he started to sing *Happy Birthday* to me, just grinnin like a nigger with a watermelon. Was I surprised! You coulda knocked me over with a feather. I'd plumb forgot all about my birthday— but my Grandfather didn't; him and Charlie musta got together and planned the whole thing in advance. I never felt so good in my life.

"And then an awful thing happened. While Charlie was standin at the head of the table with the big cake in his hands and a big grin on his face, this here young Steve Brock fella picked up about a pound of soft country butter that was settin on the table and reared back and heaved the whole mess at Charlie. And hit him, too, right on the side of his head—covered half his face and spread all over his neck. Made the most godawful splatter you ever saw.

"Well, I was just young enough and dumb enough to laugh. But just once—only once. Cause nobody else let out a sound. Not a tick. Old Charlie set the cake down on the table and started to try to get some of the butter off his face. Didn't say a word; just kinda whimpered a little, like a sick hound. And then my Grandfather stood up—God, I'll never forget that look on his face; there was somethin in his eyes that woulda froze the gizzard of a black panther. And did he look big: I thought he never would stop risin up outa that chair. The only sound you could hear was the rattle of his spurs. And then when he stood up the chair fell back with a crash that like to made me jump right outa my skin.

"There was a rifle hung on the wall and a pair of chaps and a coiled rope. I thought my Grandfather would reach for the rifle; but he took the rope instead and didn't unwind it. Young Brock sat there with a kind of silly grin on his face. He was drunk when he threw the butter but he began to look pretty sober now. My Grandfather walked toward him—great big steps—and Brock started to get up. 'What the hell you think you're gonna do?' he says. Still thinks he's pretty tough. My Grandfather don't say a word; he just reaches down, grabs Brock's shirt and yanks him up outa the chair. Brock starts to say somethin but don't get it out cause my Grandfather spins him round and kicks him in the tail so hard he hits the wall six feet away. Kicks him like you'd kick a mean dog, with the toe of his boot. So it really hurts. Then he opens the door to the front verandah and tells Brock to get out *pronto*. But Brock still has some notions about his dignity; he rolls away from the wall and comes at my Grandfather with both fists flyin. So then my Grandfather slugs him with the coil of rope. Brock stayed on the floor for a long time then, thinkin things over; then he crawled out the door and out to the barn and got into his old Chevvie and left for good. Never came back."

Burns was silent for a few minutes. Bondi waited for him to speak. "That was a rough evenin," the cowboy said; "made a big impression on me. Taught me somethin, I think. Sorta reversed all my standards. There was old Snye—bald as a buzzard, pot-bellied, cranky and ugly and generally miserable; and there was Steve Brock—young, strong, smart, good-lookin. I despised old Charlie and powerfully admired Brock. Then all of a sudden, in five minutes or less, my Grandfather changed the whole picture somehow. Not that he made me like old Snye or hate Brock; it's just that then and ever since whenever it's a case of a Snye agin a Brock I feel I gotta help out the Snye. Not for his sake, but for my own, I think. Or for the sake of somethin more important than any Snye or Brock or me. What would you call it?"

Justice? thought Bondi; natural justice? "I don't know," he said aloud: "but I know what you mean." But what the hell, he was thinking, am I a Charlie Snye?

Burns smiled. "You don't know but you know what I mean? What does that mean?"

"You know what I mean," Bondi said. He rubbed the corners of his eyes, and sniffed tenderly. "Have you ever been back to the old ranch—I mean, since the Government took it over?" He thought of the old man, Burns' grandfather, sitting there on the verandah of his ranchhouse waiting for the Law to come and rob him of his home; he must have seen its representatives coming from a long way off and for a long time: far out on the desert a cloud of dust creeping closer, two small dark metallic objects glinting in the pure light of the sun and coming nearer through the flawless silence, nearer, nearer, no power on earth to stop them. "I suppose it's illegal," he added, as Burns failed to answer.

"Illegal?"

"To go back there."

"Back there?" Burns shoved back his hat and scratched his head. "You mean where the ranch used to be? Yeah, you bet your bottom dollar it's illegal. The signs say 'Danger—*Peligroso*—Keep Out—Military Reserve—USAF.' Fence around the whole area and every gate padlocked. I had to cut wire to get in. Nothin but a few lizards. No sign of deer or coyote or wild burro; even the jackrabbits seem to be gone or all dead. That's the saddest, lonesomest place in all New Mexico. A good place to set off atom bombs."

"Anything left of the ranch buildings?"

"Sure—everything smashed flat. Even some of the fence posts broke off. Adobe bricks scattered all to hell. Looked like a herd of wild elephants run over the place. Sure hope there was nobody there when they set that thing off."

"Did you get close to Trinity?"

"No sir, I didn't go close. But I seen it from top of the hill back of the corral. It's about two miles south of where the ranch-house was—a big glassy disc set in the sand, round and shiny and green. Like green glass. It's just a little east of a gap in the hills we used to call Mockingbird Pass. I camped there lots of times when I was a kid. We had a well there, with a big tank; I swum there plenty of times. Nothin left of it now." Burns pulled at the whiskers on his chin. "But I didn't go close to that green glass. No sir, not me. That there's an evil place. It's haunted. I stay away from places like that."

Bondi was silent, pondering, marvelling over the imagined

scene, the emptiness, the names: *Trinity*—Oscura, The Dark Mountains—Mockingbird Pass—Alamagordo . . . Amazing, he thought, and fantastic and beautiful and evil. And haunted, according to Burns. Haunted? Yes, it must be, it must be—great shoals of wailing ghosts must linger there, glowing like radium in the night, the sound of their lamentations like the moan and sigh of the winds through Mockingbird Pass when the sun has gone down. While the great lone sad empty desert waits beyond, listening, listening . . .

The room had grown dark; the evening filtered through the windows and bars and gathered around them in the room. The prisoners talked quietly and listlessly, waiting for something. Waiting for anything. From outside they could hear the muffled roar and blare of motor traffic, the vast compounded murmur of a hundred thousand human voices, the twittering of starlings, the drone of the evening airplanes. The men waited.

Bondi remembered something. "Look," he said, "we'd better get up by the gate."

Burns opened his eyes, looked sleepily at Bondi. "Why?" he said.

"Are you still in earnest about breaking out of here tonight?"

"Sure am."

"Then you'd better make sure you get in a cell tonight. If you're stuck in the bullpen you won't have any privacy at all. Though I'm not convinced it makes much difference."

"You think there'll be some left over?"

"Some? You mean people? Yes, I think so." Bondi stood up, rubbed his eyelids. "There's something else you ought to know. Suppose you can't file through these bars in one night? What then?"

"I'll finish up the next night," Burns said.

"That's it," said Bondi; "you can't be sure you'll get the same cell the next night. Unless—"

"Unless what?"

"Unless you're among the first eight men through that gate each evening."

"I don't see why I got to worry about that?"

"Because," Bondi said; "because it's a stampede out of here. A mad rush. Nobody wants to get left behind in the bullpen for the night. No mattresses here, no blankets; you sleep on the floor or on a table."

"Well," said the cowboy, "let's crowd that gate hard."

"We're a little late," Bondi said, nodding in that direction. A dark knot of little men squatted on their heels by the gate, muttering in each other's faces. Backs jammed against the bars, feet braced against the cement, they squatted and jabbered quietly, hands active, the veterans.

"We'll have to talk with those fellas," Burns said. "That's all. Come on along." He started toward them.

Bondi followed, a little uneasy. The innocent assurance of this child, he was thinking, this ghost from the past.

Burns squatted down among the men guarding the gate. While Bondi watched, standing several feet away, the cowboy spoke quietly and persuasively to his glum, brooding listeners. Bondi was unable to hear what was said; he saw Burns perk a thumb in his direction, saw the dark faces nod in understanding and agreement, and then apparently everything was settled. Quickly and easily.

The cowboy was speaking to him. "Come here," he was saying; "hunker down here." Bondi moved forward and got down beside his friend. "I've explained everything to these boys," Burns said. "They're mighty helpful. Two of em are thinkin about comin out with us." He nodded toward the tough bitter faces of two Indians; one of them smiled faintly at Bondi.

"You told them?" Bondi said. "But of course . . ."

"Sure," Burns said: "it ain't gonna be no secret very long, is it?"

"No it ain't—isn't," Bondi agreed. He thought: Might possibly be wiser for me to lag behind a bit, get jostled accidentally into a different cell from this rugged crew. Traitorous thoughts . . . impossible. This comrade of mine, though, this amiable madman, is capable of thinking of attempting to kidnap me, dragging me out of here by force. A man bent on chivalry can be quite ruthless. Must be on my guard.

"What's the matter?" Burns said: "you look a mite fretful. The hay fever gettin you down?"

"Are you up to something?" asked Bondi.

The cowboy did not seem to understand the question. "Up to somethin?" he said. "Sure I'm up to somethin." He turned to the dark silent group around him. "Any of you boys got the fixins for a smoke?" One of the Indians pulled a small limp greasy sack from his shirt-pocket and without a word offered it to Burns. Together with a packet of papers. "Thanks," Burns said, proceeding at once to manufacture himself a cigarette. "You know," he said to Bondi, "these two fellas—" He indicated the Indians. "—These two fellas are Navajos. They don't like it in here any better'n I do. And they're supposed to be in for ninety days flat. For talkin to a woman while they was drunk—ninety days; you ever hear the like?"

"What did they say to this woman?" Bondi said. He looked at

the two men. They were clearly distinguishable from the Pueblo Indians—taller, thinner, with lean faces and wild slanted Mongolian eyes. Hard customers, he thought . . . Conceived under the moon by the pillars of Monument Valley—weaned on the milk of the wild mare.

Burns lit his soft brown little cigarette. "These boys been in here nearly a week," he said. "They're beginnin to feel kinda randy . . . like you, maybe." He winked at Bondi.

Like me? thought Bondi.

Agua! came the alarm. There was a general movement of men toward the bullpen gate, a lull in conversations. Bondi found himself pressed against the bars, Burns at his side, the Navajos just behind him. He could smell the decaying armpits of an old vagrant crouching against his ribs. An unfamiliar experience; he had always waited before, aloof and solitary, well behind the compressed pack of criminals.

"Damn," muttered Burns, putting out his cigarette with thumb and forefinger, slipping it into his shirt-pocket. "Damn," he said.

"Don't make a noise when the guard comes in," Bondi said. "Not a word; they'll jump down your throat if you open your mouth."

"I know," Burns said; "I understand these fellas. They got a tough job."

The guard opened the panel in the cellblock door and peered in at them. Bondi could see a nose, pale and damp, the mustache, a pair of dull brown bored eyes. "No pushin or runnin," the guard shouted at them; "if I catch anybody shovin or runnin I'll throw him in The Hole for a week." He stared at them, sniffing. "Okay," he said, and cranked open the cellgates on one side of the corridor. The prisoners watched. Then he cranked open the bullpen gate and the men funneled rapidly and silently out. "No runnin!" the guard shouted.

Burns and Bondi were among the first down the corridor, hastening toward the cell on the outside corner of the cellblock, the cell farthest from the cellblock door. Behind them came the Indians. A trusty stood at the end of the corridor counting heads; when eight men had entered the farthest cell he moved down to the next cellgate and counted off eight more, and so on to the fifth cell and fortieth man. As Bondi had expected there were too many prisoners to fit in the cells; five men had to return to the bullpen.

Inside the cell Bondi sat down on a steel bunk, a lower this time, and leaned back against the wall. He felt suddenly and unreasonably safe, secure, comfortable. Much more pleasant in the cells, he thought, than in the bullpen—more privacy, better lighting, more facilities for relaxation. As he thought of it he shifted his position, lay back and stretched out full length on the gray blanket, the pad beneath it, the steel shelf below that. He pushed off his shoes and watched the cowboy prowling around in the little cage, kicking gently at the bars, tapping on them with his knuckles.

"What are you looking for?" Bondi asked. "A secret exit? Sit down for a few minutes. Take it easy."

"Not much music in these bars," Burns said. "I'm afraid the sonsabitches is solid. We better get to work right away."

Bondi worked his feet out of his socks. "You can't start yet, you damned fool. The guard is still hanging around outside. And the trusties will be in any minute now to clean up."

Burns knelt on the floor, examining the intersecting members of the cell. "I reckon we oughta work pretty low," he said. "Might be easier to crawl through if you can put some of your weight on the floor."

"Maybe so," Bondi said, "but just hold back for a few minutes or you'll get us all in trouble."

"I hate to waste any time," Burns said, not looking at Bondi. "I'm a-rarin to go; I can smell them mountains already."

"Which mountains?"

"*The* mountains. Any mountains. The Mountains of the Moon."

"Well, don't get carried away." Bondi wiggled his toes in the gray dusty air. "Just be patient for a few minutes." He thought of the velvet evening outside, the twilight cooling of the sunburnt city, the final soft wash of radiant pink on the mountains east of the city. "Sit down," he said, as Burns continued to search and turn in the narrow cell. "Sit down, for godsake; you're making me nervous."

"Sure," said Burns; "in a minute."

There was a sudden crash of plumbing, the suck and snarl of violent waters, the jarring pipes. Then the cellblock door ground open, screeching on its hinges, and four trusties came in with their mops, buckets, evil-smelling liquids, and sick, sneaky, suspicious faces. Silently and promptly they went to work while the guard watched them from the doorway, remote in his power and authority, immediate in his menace.

Burns sat down on the foot of Bondi's pallet. He said nothing. Bondi watched him, observing with conscious interest his friend's predatory profile, the black hat concealing the eyes in shadow, the black hair grown wild and curly over the nape of the neck. Poor Jack, he thought, poor old Jack—born too late, out of place, out of time. Look at him, the scheming atavist, all wound up in reality looking for a tunnel back to his boy's dream world of space and horses and sunlight.

One of the trusties shuffled by in the corridor past their cell, pushing a broom, followed by a second trusty leaning despondently on the handle of a sopping, rancid mop. The sour disinfectant smell of public institutions poured into the cell, recalling Bondi to his former preoccupations. That ancient legal stink, he growled to himself; the smog of history, the foul stench of the dead but unburied past.

"Awful," Burns mumbled, as if sharing the thought. "Gotta get outa here before we die of pure misery."

But necessary, thought Bondi, given the situation: "What'd you say?" he asked Burns.

"What?" Burns said. He scratched at his bristling chin. "Stop mumblin," he said, scratching his chin and staring at the floor. "We oughta get started right away."

"A few more minutes," Bondi said. "You're the one that's mumbling," he added.

"I'm figurin," said Burns.

"I should hope so. What will you do if and when you chew your way out of here?"

Burns looked at the six other men in the cell—the two Navajos, sombre and motionless, a pair of Pueblo Indians whispering together, the old gray vagrant Konowalski crumpled on his bunk, one adobe-colored Mexican washing his socks in the toilet bowl. "What'll I do?" Burns said. "I ain't sure; guess I'll head for the tracks and hop the first freight outa town. What else?" He stared at Bondi now, his eyes a little stern with reproval.

Bondi understood, remembering suddenly that he and

Burns were not alone. Am I a complete fool? he thought. I'm not taking this affair seriously enough. An alarming lack of native wit. "I suppose that's the only thing you can do," he said aloud. He was thinking, however, that the cowboy would surely go directly to his—Bondi's—house to recover his gear and his horse. And there, if anyone had been perceptive enough to notice the obvious alliance between Bondi and the cowboy, exactly there is where the Law would go first, seeking Burns or news of him.

They heard again the grinding squeal of metal on metal, then the rumble and crash of the cellblock door. They've gone, thought Bondi.

"They all out?" Burns said.

Bondi stood up, went to the gate of the cell and looked down the center corridor. The door was shut—no sign or sound of trusties or guard. "They've gone," he said; "but it might be a good idea to wait a few more minutes. The guard might be hanging around in the hall outside."

"What of it?" Burns said; "he can't see us unless he comes in."

"He might be able to hear the file."

"Hear it? Through all them walls?"

"Well, I don't know," Bondi said; "I said he might. How should I know? How much noise are you planning to make?"

"Not much." Burns stood by the bars, listening. "How can we tell if the guard's gone?"

"We can't," Bondi said; "not from here. You might get one of those lads in the bullpen to check for you."

"All right," Burns said, "that's what we'll do." He went to the front of the cell and looked across the corridor into the yellow gloom of the bullpen, where several shadows in human shape straggled miserably over the cold cement or lay prone on steel tabletops. "Hey!" Burns said; "hey, one of you fellas . . ."

No one made any move to answer him; he was about to speak again but was interrupted by the flushing of the toilet in the adjoining cell. He waited until the clamor had died down, then called again. "Hey! one of you fellas do me a favor?"

One of the men slouching about the pen came close to the bars on the other side of the corridor; he scowled at Burns. "What're we supposed to sleep on?" he said; "they ain't no mattresses or blankets in here."

"Look pardner," Burns said, "I'll give you my blanket if you'll help me out some. Is the guard gone?"

"How about a pad too?" the man said.

"Okay. But you gotta help me. Is the guard gone?"

"Sure he's gone." The fellow sagged against the bars, his hands hanging to the steel above his head. "What would he hang around for?"

"Well, make sure," Burns said; "take a look."

"I don't hafta," the man said; "I know he's gone."

Burns turned to Bondi. "This one ain't much good," he said.

"Maybe I should have stayed in the bullpen," Bondi said. "I could have stood guard for you all night. Maybe you'd better wait until tomorrow night."

Burns smiled. "That's no kinda talk for an anarchist," he said. "We're checkin outa here tonight. And I need you to help with the file work."

"How about that blanket?" the man in the bullpen said.

"Don't give it to him," Bondi said. "He won't look out for you. All he wants to do is sleep."

"I know," Burns said. "Maybe I shoulda asked one of them other cabrones."

"Don't bother. You won't get anyone to stay up all night watching out for the guards just so you can file your way out of here. You can't trust any of those boys, anyway. You'd better forget the whole thing." Bondi rubbed the itchy spot on his shank where something had bitten him during the previous night. "Mark my words," he said.

"You gonna give me that blanket, cowboy?" The man in the bullpen leaned on the bars, now letting his arms dangle through them. The light, coming from behind his head, made it difficult to see his face. Nothing certain but the black shape, the shining bald skull.

Bondi rubbed his itch. Cockroaches, he thought, lice, spiders, ticks, worms, flies, microbes, bacilli . . .

"Kind of a bad-tempered bunch in that bullpen," Burns said; "I shoulda let them alone." He stripped the blanket from his own bunk and passed it through the bars. "Here," he said— "catch." He tossed it, rolled up, through the intervening space; the man in the bullpen failed to catch it but picked it up from the floor and pulled it through to his own side.

"How about the mattress?" he said, gathering the rag of a blanket under his arm. "Huh?"

"You can go to hell," Burns said. He turned his back to the bullpen and the corridor, went to his selected corner nearest the window. "Let's get to work, boys," he said, and pulled the two files out of his boots. Blue dull-gleaming instruments, hard, clean, perfect, fresh from the machine shops. He offered one of them to Bondi. "Take it," he said, a sardonic grin on his face. "Or do you have to think it over first?"

You insolent bastard, Bondi thought; he stepped forward and took the file. "I'd be glad to be of assistance," he said.

Burns squatted down by the latticework of bars. The cell

consisted of one solid steel wall separating it from the next cell and three barriers of intersecting bars reaching from floor to ceiling which divided it from the corridor and the catwalk surrounding the cellblock: the cell was not a room but a cage. "I'll start here," Burns said, indicating a right angle of iron about eighteen inches above the floor.

Bondi went down on one knee beside him. "What shall I do?" he said. "Keep time?"

"Let's both work on the same bar," the cowboy said: "you on one side, me on the other. We'll cut it through here at the bottom and then bend it up—if we can—and maybe that'll do the trick. That might be all we need."

The Indians watched them, and said nothing. The old vagrant slept, the Mexican twisted his socks, dripping water on the floor: he saw the glimmering files then and his eyes widened, his mouth sagged open.

Burns winked at Bondi, spat on his palms, rubbed them together, picked up his file and ground it against the iron bar—a grating sound, low-pitched and dull. Once, twice, he scraped the file across the bar, then stopped to listen. From beyond their wall came the sound of Greene singing, of Hoskins preaching, the coughs and groans and chatter of the others, an explosion of activity in the plumbing system. "Not so bad," Burns said; he paused. "But they'll hear us in a minute, ever one of them."

"What can we do about it?" Bondi said.

"Nothing." Burns went to work again, grinding his file edge into the iron bar. "We could sing . . . but that ain't gonna cover it up neither. Besides, this is gonna take a mighty long time." He filed steadily, with quick short strokes; within a few moments a small shining notch appeared on the side of the bar, and on the cement below the bright hot silvery dust began to accumulate, to glisten—iron sweat, the jewels of freedom.

Madness, thought Bondi, this is madness. He drew his file across the bitter iron—God! He was afraid he might burst out laughing—or weeping. A spell of vertigo clouded his vision; it passed but left his nerves vibrating like violin strings. He kept on; he applied the heavy file to the bar with all the free weight of his body. Here we go, he thought, here we go—God knows where!

"Jeez!" the Mexican said, coming close to them, "what you guys doin?"

The cowboy laughed. "We're workin our way through college," he said; "we're goin home. Wanta come along?" Already his forehead was shining with sweat, his black hair dangling over one eye. "How about it, *cuate?*"

"This is bad," the Mexican said. "Lots of trouble. Not for me, no thanks. I get out in a week."

"A week's too long for me," Burns said, filing steadily on. "No more of this jailhouse stink for me . . ."

While Bondi, furious and amazed at his own audacity, wondered what had happened to himself: I'm in league with a fanatic, he thought, a libertine maniac. Suppose I were caught at this criminal occupation? He filed deeper into the iron. This is a criminal activity, he reminded himself, a felonious enterprise; complicity in a jailbreak. Aiding and abetting; quite serious: almost as bad as actually escaping. The Law giveth and the Law taketh away, but retaliation is forbidden and evasion of punishment itself is a crime. He felt his soft, academic muscles relenting before the resisting iron, his thoughts hesitating before the awful magnificence of Authority. But he continued to gnaw at the bar with his slender weapon; particle by particle, grain by metal grain, with painful drudging slowness, the disintegration of the bar proceeded.

Burns, in rhythm with his labor, began to sing:

> *By yon bonny banks*
> *And by yon bonny braes . . .*

A comic, Bondi said to himself, at a time like this he reveals himself: a bloody comic! He ground at the bar and when the refrain came, joined in:

> *O you take the high road*
> *And I'll take the low road . . .*

They grinned at each other through their sweat and the smoky gloom of the air; they toiled and sang and grinned like exceedingly foolish children, while the whole cellblock listened. A pang of pleasure, like an illumination, shot through Bondi's nerves; for a few brief irrational moments he was deliriously happy. Then he, then both of them, became aware of the enveloping silence: not a complete absence of noise—somewhere an old man was coughing his lungs out, somebody was snoring in the next cell, an Indian chanted softly over his clasped hands—but a sudden and striking lapse in the gabble, shouting and mutter of jailhouse conversations.

Bondi and the cowboy stopped their work for a moment to listen. Neither said a word; they waited for the sound of the cellblock door, the voice of a guard. But there was nothing.

Then came the saxophone tones of Timothy Greene, speaking from the adjoining cell. He said: "What you boys cookin up in there? You-all sharpening up your toenails, maybe? You brushin your teeth?"

Bondi did not know what to say. He left it up to Burns. The cowboy squatted there, head tilted to one side, eyes half closed; his right hand and the file rested lightly on his left knee.

"You boys hopin maybe to leave us?" said Greene.

Burns answered this. "Yeah," he said; "we're hopin. And we'll be pretty busy for a while. Don't you worry none about us."

"Sure ain't gonna worry about you, man."

"If you hear anything give us the word."

"Sure will, man," said Greene; "that I'll do."

"Much obliged," Burns said, and he returned to his work: Zing! Zing! went the stroking file.

Bondi sighed, crossed himself, and went back to work.

CHAPTER 9

OKLAHOMA CITY, OKLA.

Blue, red, yellow, flashing and dancing—crash of machinery and a soaring wall of gray tombs, monuments, cathedrals of power ... while the blue red yellow shrieks of neon—frantic, eyeball-clutching—splashed, blared in his face, blinding, inviting catastrophe: a woman, a child, a pride of young men, sightless, skin-seared, moved in agonizing slow motion across the asphalt path of his machine—forty tons of steel, iron, rubber, glass, oil, a cargo of metal and the mere thing of flesh that drove and was driven by it—himself ...

He was sick, miserably and suddenly and inhumanly sick; greased convulsions of nausea in his stomach and throat, a stinging glitter of fire and glass behind his eyes, exploding his skull ...

I've got to stop, he repeated to himself, got to find a place to park this brute, have to get that sewage out of my stomach ...

He went through a yellow light while human figures scuttled past his fenders; he blinked his watering eyes, wiped sweat and dust from his forehead, and turned at a narrow sidestreet between a warehouse—SLOAN'S MOVING AND STOR-AGE DON'T MAKE A MOVE—and a used-car lot and followed the dark alleyway past parked cars, back lots, garbage cans, warehouses, barbed wire, cyclone fences, telephone poles . . . He steered his tractor and his freight trailer into the vacant space over the black cinders of a feedmill loading lot, parked askew, slantwise, across the entrance and half the interior, shut off the engine, leaned on the door-handle and sagged with closed eyes, nearly falling, out and onto his knees on the ground and was sick at once, without preliminaries . . .

About ten minutes of satisfying agony was sufficient. He then pulled himself up and crawled, a sad empty stricken animal, into the cab of his truck and stretched out across the leather seat and closed his eyes, invoking sleep; which did not come immediately: he had time to savor the corrosion of his bile and liver, the deadly metallic residue of his sunken, clystered stomach: he had time to speculate—what was it? he thought, what's wrong with me? Never before . . . never before quite so bad, so quick, as this.

He heard the scream of the city soaring over him, felt the yellow dusty night falling on his steel shell, the weight of his eyelids growing under it; never like this, he thought. I'll drive no more tonight. Sleep tonight, maybe see a doctor in the morning. Maybe it was just something I ate. God, it has to be . . .

I need some rest, sleep, a change of rhythm; my kidneys are cracking under the jar and pressure . . . When I finish this trip, soon as I finish this trip . . . see a doctor, knock off for a while, maybe go home for a couple of weeks . . .

Sleep came at last, vague fumbling sleep, and his mind rolled in it, pushed and drawn and split in dreams, smoky shards of dream, reconstructions, recollections:

. . . On a redstone road, past shagbark hickories and a rail fence—alone, or mostly alone—sometimes accompanied by a familiar but unnameable figure—silent as all dreams, soundless but troubled—and then the splintering of barriers and a scramble, an insane charge of pigs, hogs, monsters with red eyes, horns, gaseous withering breath, fury without purpose, blind maniacal destruction . . .

In this manner, filmed in sweat and riven through the heart and brain by internal, insubstantial and powerful terrors, he passed, slept, endured, fought, lost seven hours.

While the city, new and terrible, rode the night, groaned and triumphed over the night and the rolling earth.

CHAPTER 10

At six o'clock in the evening the cellblock lights went on: one dim yellow glow recessed deep in the ceiling of each cell.

Burns glanced up at the light, then at Bondi. "Will they come in now?" he said; he continued to file as he spoke. Beside him the Navajo, relieving Bondi, worked on without stopping or speaking. The iron bar was solid, heavy, and still intact, but a deep notch had been gouged in on two sides. On the floor between the Indian and the cowboy the metal dust piled up, shining softly in the light. "Is somebody coming?" Burns said again.

Bondi heard him and raised his head from his hands. He was sitting on his bunk watching the labor, not seeing it. "No," he said; "they always turn the lights on about this time. Doesn't mean that anybody's coming."

"Maybe I oughta knock that light out," Burns said.

"They'll turn it off in a few hours. Nobody can see in through those windows anyway."

"It worries me a little."

"You have worse to worry about, in my opinion."

They all worried about it but the work went on; at ten o'clock the lights switched off, except for one light above the cellblock's central corridor.

Bondi and the cowboy lay on their adjoining bunks, the cowboy smoking; behind them the two Navajos hewed with the files at the stubborn iron, chanting a slow sullen dirge as they worked.

We can't go on like this all night, Bondi was thinking. Something unpleasant is bound to happen; they've probably already discovered us and are now waiting outside below the window with submachine guns, having a joke at our expense, ready to blast the first head that shows in that window. Burns' head, of course.

"What're you thinkin about?" Burns said.

"Your head."

"My head?"

"I'm afraid," Bondi said. "I have a queer feeling in my stomach that things aren't right."

"We know that," said Burns.

"I mean that something bad is going to happen to one of us—soon. Maybe tonight."

"Wouldn't be surprised."

"You know," Bondi said, "I've never done this sort of thing before—jailbreaking. It's a novel experience for me. Interesting but not very comfortable. A little frightening, in fact."

"I know how you feel. It's a worrisome business."

"Maybe we've already revealed ourselves," Bondi went on. "Perhaps the bars are wired in some way . . . electrically. I can see a little red light blinking on a switchboard in the booking office."

"That's the sub-jailer's wife callin up," Burns said. "Checkin on the old man."

"But if they already knew," said Bondi, "why would they wait? What are they waiting for?"

"To catch us in the act," Burns said; "the guards prob'ly need some target practice."

"I was wondering about that . . ."

Burns turned toward the Navajos. "You boys ready for some relief?" he said.

It must have been near midnight when the final filestroke was made on the bar; the metal hung rigidly above its own base, severed through. For the first time in six hours there was nearly absolute quiet in the cellblock. Bondi and the cowboy squatted on the cold concrete, facing each other, smiling nervously, listening to the snores, the coughing and groaning, the delirium sounds of the sleeping men around them. For the first time they felt it needful to whisper.

"That's it," Bondi said, whispering; "what now?"

Burns was grinning at him; Bondi could see the white teeth shining in the dark face, a glint of the eyes, the indirect light from the corridor outlining the cowboy's head and hat and his narrow shoulders.

"What do we do now?" whispered Bondi.

In answer Burns wrapped his hand around the lower end, the free end of the bar, and pulled: nothing happened. He put both hands around the bar, braced his feet against the base of the grill, and strained backward with all his weight and strength: slowly, very slightly, the metal yielded, the bar bent inward. About one inch. Burns stood up, gasping, and kneaded the small of his back. "We need a strong man," he said; "we need some gorilla like Gutierrez now."

"Want me to try it?" Bondi said.

"Don't bother."

"What do you mean by that?" Bondi said quickly. "Eh?"

The cowboy laughed. "Go ahead, if you want to. Be careful you don't bust a gut, that's all. Use your legs as much as you can and spare your back."

So Bondi put his hands to the bar, straightened his back, bent his legs, and tugged, heaved, jerked without perceptible result. Burns stood watching him, hands on hips, grinning. Bondi bit his lip and tried a second time, pulling steadily and carefully at the grudging iron. Without success. He gave up then, saying: "To hell with it; this is no office for a gentleman."

Burns laughed again. "No, it ain't," he said. "What we need is about three feet of steel pipe; that would help us some."

The two Navajos were watching; the cessation of the filing had awakened them. One of them stood up and came forward. "I'll do it," he said. He squatted and pulled, the sweat popping from his forehead, and managed to bend the bar another inch or two inward and upward. Then Burns pulled at it a second time and brought it forward another inch and the two of them, alternately straining and resting, succeeded in bending the bar in and up to a position approximately perpendicular to the plane of the grill of bars. This left an opening twelve inches wide and about sixteen inches high, allowing for the bent bar above and the slight rough butt of the bar below.

"You can't get through that," Bondi said.

"I can," Burns said; "I don't know about you, what with all that fat around your middle and them wide hips."

"Never mind; I'm not going anyway."

"This fella can get through," Burns said, indicating the Navajo. "You'd be surprised how flexible the human body is when it has to be. I remember a time up in the Shoshone

Mountains I got caught in a crack in a dead pine tree—I'd been a-chewin jerky all day long and was gettin kinda bloated—"

The lights went on.

The light seemed to intensify the sudden stillness. "Now what the hell . . ." Burns said. "What's up now?"

"I don't know," Bondi said. They listened but could hear nothing—other than the cacophony of sleeping prisoners.

"Well," Burns said, "let's not stand around worryin about it. We gotta rig up some kinda rope now; about three or four of these blankets, maybe." He stooped to pull a blanket off the nearest bunk.

And then they heard the squeal and rumble of the cellblock door rolling open. And the voice of Gutierrez:

"Burns!" the voice said; "John W. Burns!"

They heard the grinding of the crank and saw the cellgate slide open. Open to the corridor, the gaping gray space . . .

"Don't answer," whispered Bondi. "He may not be sure you're in this block. He might look for you in one of the others."

"Are you crazy? He knows damn well I'm in here."

"Burns!" cried the voice beyond the corridor; "you're wanted in the office. Telephone call!"

"A very funny fella," Burns muttered, his eyes taking on the dull glaze of hatred. "The bastard . . ."

"Burns!"

"I'd better go," the cowboy said. "If I don't he'll come stompin in here and see what we done. Hide the files," he said to the Navajo. And to Bondi: "I'll be back in a minute." He smiled briefly, bitterly; and walked out of the cell and down the long corridor. They heard his boots rapping on the cement, a growl from Gutierrez and the closing of the door—a ponderous grumble of steel, the slam and mesh of locks. The cellgate screeched on its trolley, slid shut and locked. Bondi stared, unbelieving, frozen in fear and astonishment. An awakening, it seemed to him, from a bad dream into a nightmare. But he was unable to think beyond that point; stunned and incredulous, he gazed through the wall of bars, into the yellow light in the corridor, the spreading shadows.

The lights were not turned off.

The two Navajos did not wait. One of them was already engaged in trying to twist his body through the opening in the bars. He had his head and one shoulder through but was having difficulty with the other shoulder. His companion squatted beside him, whispering advice and encouragement. The man in the hole squirmed and writhed patiently, delicately, anxious but not in haste.

The other men in the cell, except the old man Konowalski, were now awake. They sat up on their bunks and stared in silent stupefaction at the Navajo wriggling among the bars like an impaled worm. The Mexican giggled nervously, biting his fingernails; the Pueblo Indians smiled and nudged each other with their elbows.

The Navajo seemed unable to get through. After several minutes of wordless struggle, sweating and breathing heavily, he withdrew his shoulder and head, returned his entire body to the cell. He sat on the floor for several minutes, panting and staring gloomily at his fists. The other Navajo, a thinner man, whispered suggestions into his ear and made signs with his hands.

Bondi returned to his bunk after a while, sat down slowly and cautiously, and tried to avoid imagining what was probably happening to the cowboy. His helplessness fed his anger;

he fumed and cursed internally, sick with rage, with surprise, with apprehension. He shut his eyes, lay back and made some pretence at sleep, hoping in that way to induce true sleep, but this was foolish and worthless: his fear made sleep impossible, despite his aching body, his overwhelming weariness.

It's my fault, he decided; if I had stood up to Gutierrez at supper there, like a man should, Burns wouldn't be where he is now. No—I'd be there instead.

The idea made him pause in his thought; he stared up at the bottom of the bunk above his head.

Of course, he went on, that doesn't diminish my moral responsibilities. But then—wife and kid . . . And maybe they'll come and get me anyway, when they're finished with . . . (This possibility, suddenly realized, sent a little hot flash of terror through the core of his body.) That Gutierrez is a clever villain, waiting until God only knows what hour in the morning—one o'clock? two o'clock?—to seize his revenge. We should have expected it; the shrewd brute, waiting till now, till the jailer's gone home or out or is drunk or asleep . . .

And maybe they're coming for me too, he thought again. For me—what do they do? Slaps, kicks, I could take—I'd shut my eyes and relax, try to faint; but suppose they do something more sophisticated—use a rubber hose; ducking in water, steam heating? A man like Gutierrez—capable of anything, I'm sure, any mode of horror . . .

Bondi felt a queasy loosening in his entrails, a sudden need to go to the toilet. But after a few bad moments he managed to get a better grasp on his thoughts and nerves, to make his speculations revolve around the reasonable, the human, the ordinary: What they've done, he argued, undoubtedly what they've done, they've taken him down there for further questioning, investigation. Perhaps some unsolved robbery or adultery is involved; or maybe it's merely the FBI come to inquire about his draft status. He's in some kind of difficulty there, didn't he say? Yes, it's late at night but the FBI has its methods, so I've heard, it's good and sufficient reasons, answerable to nobody . . . Earnest, intelligent, well-trained men, they know what they're doing—best that common citizens not attempt to interfere: would only muddle things unnecessarily . . .

Telephone? But why telephone?

The Navajo removed his shirt; he wore no undershirt. He put his head through the aperture to liberty, then one smooth brown shoulder—his skin and muscles sleek as a skinned cat—and then the second shoulder. This was the difficult part; the flesh became jammed and compressed between bone and iron: neither would yield. But the man continued to tug and gasp, sweat glistening on his animal hide; the other Navajo endeavored to assist him, pushing from inside at the imprisoned limb, gently dislocating the shoulder bone to get it through, shoving with both hands at the slippery meat. The breathing of the struggling Indian filled the cell with its noise, seemed loud enough to be heard throughout the cellblock. A slight tearing sound, like the ripping of tissue, and the man was through—but wounded, a bad laceration welling with blood on his side. He ignored the pain, dragged his hips and legs through and rested for a minute or more on the floor between the bars and the window. The second Navajo passed him his shirt and he put it on.

Could I ever get through there? Bondi wondered—if I had to?

Both men went to work, the one inside twisting and knotting together several blankets, the other—standing in the narrow passageway which surrounded the cellblock—trying to remove the fine-mesh screen from the window. He pushed and shook the screen from a kneeling position, careful not to interpose his body between the window and the pallid light from the cell. The screen would not come off.

"Gimme one of the files," the Navajo said to his companion. "And see if you can put that light out."

Bondi sat still and watched; he wanted to help, to take part, but some dull fear kept him quiet and inert.

The Indian inside the cell slipped one file through the bars to his friend; with the other in his hand he climbed to an upper bunk and jabbed at the light globe sunk in the ceiling, poking the tang of the file through a wire grid. The globe cracked and broke; tiny slips of frosted glass tinkled on the floor. The incandescent bulb inside the globe still shone, undamaged; the man jabbed farther through the grid and the bulb popped out, an inhaling vacuum, and more glass fell and the cell was dark.

Back to the womb, thought Bondi, back to the womb of night, of darkness and—Christ! What are they doing to Jack? How long has he been gone now? Ten minutes? twenty? half an hour?

The taller Navajo was crawling through the hole in the bars; the first one had the screen wedged off the window and was busy tying one end of the blanket-rope to a bar of the cell.

Above, on their steel shelves, the two Pueblo Indians carried on a hasty debate, murmuring in their river language into one another's ears, making circular motions with their hands.

The Mexican watched the proceedings without uttering a sound, picking forlornly at his nose. The ancient vagrant

Konowalski remained indifferent to all activity, lay with his face
to the wall wrapped in his rags and peculiar smells, and sighed
and spluttered in his sleep like a dog with worms. Like an old
dog with old worms.

Moving swiftly and efficiently, the Navajos completed their
preparations. One of them looked out the opened window,
waited for a few seconds, then swung over the sill and down
outside, climbing down the rope. The second Navajo spoke to
Bondi:

"You haul those blankets up when we're gone. Okay?" Bondi
nodded. The Navajo came close to the bars and looked at Bondi
with his slanted Mongolian eyes; he grinned a little, the skin of
his face wrinkling up like aged cowhide. He smelled strongly of
sweat and horses and beer. "Hey," he said—"you say goodby to
your friend for us. Tell him—" He heard a soft call from below
and hesitated, then turned back to Bondi. "—Tell him, if he ever
come to Moenkopi country, you tell him to come see us. All
right for you too, maybe. Okay?"

"Thanks," Bondi said. "I'll tell him."

The Indian smiled. "I gotta go now." He turned away and
after a quick survey of the darkness outside, backed over the
window sill and disappeared. Bondi pulled gently at the taut
twisted blankets; when he felt them go slack he hauled them up,
in through the window, through the bars and let them lay in a
pile on the floor.

He stretched out full length on his unblanketed greasy ver-
minous pad, pillowed his head on his forearms and closed his
eyes. No visions came in that darkness; but he thought that he
could hear, within the sphere of his consciousness, fragments
of a music like spears of light—brief flashes of sound between

intervals of silence—and then an immense babble of human voices, a sea of gulping mouths, red fleshy lips, the pulp of tongues, submerging the fitful music under a smothering wave of noise . . .

The confusion died; he struggled with his doubt and guilt: He remembered Jerry his wife and her face appeared to him in the private gloom: the serious brown eyes, her freckled skin, her crown of coppery hair. Love and regret swelled in his mind: Jerry, he mumbled, forgive me, my darling, forgive me, oh forgive me.

And there was his son.

He had one glimpse of the gulf that surrounded them, the vast deep ether of time that made a solitude of their three interwoven lives. Remorse, anger, fear, shame, loneliness—in his sorrow he knew or thought that he knew them all. I'm too weak, he thought, too weak for the thing I've done.

The cellblock door opened—Bondi heard a grunt, shuffle, and the fall of a body—and slammed shut again. He listened and heard a man coming down the corridor, slowly, dragging his feet. He stood up. The cellgate slid sideways and the cowboy appeared, shambling through the opening; the crank was turned outside, the gate closed and locked.

Burns sank down on the lower bunk, his hands over his face. Bondi sat beside him, put an arm around his shoulders and managed to speak. "What happened?" he said. Burns did not answer. "For godsake what's the matter with you?"

"I'm all right," Burns mumbled. He passed his hands tenderly over his eyes, nose, mouth. "Don't feel too good but I guess I'm all right."

"They beat you," Bondi said.

The cowboy grinned shakily and sadly; his lower lip was torn and bleeding, a front tooth broken off. "Gutierrez did," he said. "Mostly the others just watched. He didn't beat me bad; I tried hard to make things easy for him, not give him any trouble. I tried not to get mad. Kept my head down, kinda took it easy. Wasn't too bad—I've seen worse." He lowered his hands and looked at Bondi; dried clots of blood hung from his nostrils, one eye was purple and swollen, the skin on one cheek was raw, black. In the semi-darkness of the cell these abrasions gave his face a mask-like, almost comical, fixity. The cowboy grinned stiffly through this mask. "I'm might surprised to see you still here," he said. "What're you waitin for?" He looked around in the cell: the two Pueblo Indians, the Mexican, watched him in silent fascination. "Them Navajo fellas left, I see. Good boys."

"But why?" Bondi said, sickened, still unbelieving. "They can't do things like that to people. Even a prisoner . . ."

"Don't get upset," Burns said. "Take it easy. You might be next. And talk kinda quiet—my ears are ringin like banjos."

"Sorry," Bondi said. He paused, trying to comprehend what was happening. "But surely he can't get away with it?"

"Who? Get away with what?"

"This ape-man—Gutierrez."

"I don't know," Burns said. "He prob'ly will. The other guards ain't gonna tell on him. And the jailer ain't even here—who's gonna know about it? Who'd care anyway? This kinda thing happens all the time: it's what people deserve for goin to jail. I think so myself." He looked around again, saw the open window beyond the bars, the blankets laying on the floor. "We better get movin," he said. "Be daylight pretty soon."

"Well, go ahead," Bondi said, staring at the floor.

"What's eatin you now? You still got the crazy notion of stayin here?"

Bondi placed a hand on his aching forehead. "Please," he said, "let's not argue about it anymore. You know I can't go."

Burns was silent for a few moments, then he said: "Paul— you ever have an impulse?"

Bondi made no answer.

"You know what an impulse is?" said Burns.

"Yes," Bondi said.

"You ever have one?"

Again Bondi was silent. The cowboy said: "See that bar, filed clean through and bent outa the way? See that open window? See them blankets tied together on the floor?" Bondi did not answer. Burns said: "Look at that open window again; think about what's out there. It's dark, it's night. The city is asleep. Out on the edge of the city is your adobe house, Jerry and the kid." Burns waited for some response from his friend but there was none. "Beyond the house, ten miles across the mesa, there's the mountains. The mountains go north to Alaska, south to Guatemala."

"Get to the point," said Bondi.

"I want you to come with me," Burns said.

"Do we have to go through all that again? You're wasting valuable time." Bondi felt irritable, frightened, and confused. "If you're going at all you'd better go now."

"You're a peculiar fella," Burns said. "If you wasn't dearer to me than my own brothers I'd sure say you was a damned fool."

"What of it? It's by my own choice." Bondi gazed at the floor, aware of the other men watching him—Burns, the Indians, the Mexican. "I can get out of here whenever I want to," he said.

"Quite simple: all that I have to do is change my mind. Or I should say, make up my mind." He smiled wryly at Burns. "The Judge added an additional torment to my two-year sentence: he said that if I should care to submit to the law after all, he would suspend the remainder of my sentence."

"Suspend it?"

"Yes; set me free."

The cowboy thought that over. "You *are* a damned fool," he said. "Why don't you take him up on his offer?"

"I don't know; I can't; I don't know why. Would you do it?"

"Me?" said Burns. "Well, I wouldn't get myself in such a fix in the first place. I keep clean away from tanglements like that."

"Would you do it if you were me?"

"If I was you I'd do whatever you would do."

"You ought to go," Bondi said; "you don't make me happy."

"I didn't come here to make you happy," Burns said. "I come here to get you outa here."

"Well, I refuse to be rescued, thanks just the same."

From the other side of the steel wall came a plaintive whine, half-human, half-canine: "Will you guys please . . . I gotta sleep . . ."

"What good do you think you're doin yourself or anybody else by stayin here?" Burns asked.

"I'm not sure," Bondi said. "I only know that if I don't do this, if I give in, I'll be haunted by my surrender for the rest of my life."

Burns stood up, touching his bruised and beaten face. "I ain't gonna argue with you no more. Maybe you know what you're doin." He faced Bondi again. "I can't help rememberin what you said this afternoon, though."

"What?" Bondi said. "What do you mean?"

"Somethin you said—maybe it was only talk."

"Tell me what you're talking about, damnit."

Burns looked sadly at his friend, his own face tired and worn in the obscurity, his eyes dark. He took his hat off, pushed the hair back from his brow, replaced the hat. Bondi was waiting for him to speak. Burns said: "You said somethin about you hoped you'd never—what was it?—sacrifice a friend to an ideal . . ."

"Well? Go on."

"How about a wife?" Burns said. "How about her?"

"I know, I know," Bondi answered desperately. "Can you think for a moment that hasn't been on my mind? For months?"

"I know," said Burns. He hesitated. "I'm mighty sorry I said that, Paul. It was downright stupid."

"Somebody had to say it," Bondi replied. He looked at Burns, then at the open window. "God, I wish I were free to go with you."

"Do you mean that?" Burns said. "Really mean it? If you do—"

"No!" Bondi said. "I don't mean it. It's nonsense. Get out of here before somebody spots that missing screen. You haven't got much time."

The cowboy put his hands on Bondi's shoulders. "It sure pains me to leave you behind, *hermano*. Makes me feel like a traitor. But I'll see you again pretty soon, won't I?"

"Of course," Bondi said.

"We'll go on that huntin trip like you said, soon as you're back from wherever they send you."

"Yes," said Bondi.

"Well . . ." The cowboy picked up the blankets, pushed them

through the bars; he removed his battered hat and shoved it through also. "I guess I'll mosey along," he said. He knelt down on the floor by the hole in the bars. "Say, I almost forgot." He fumbled inside his shirt, inside his undershirt, searching for something. "Got a letter somewhere here. Hope I do; it's from Jerry." He found the letter, wrinkled, sweat-soaked, dirty, and gave it to Bondi.

"Thanks," Bondi said. He held it in his hand without looking at it. He knew already what was inside.

The cowboy put his head through the opening, then his arms, and squirmed his way out of the cell. In the passageway outside he stood up, straightened his shirt, put his hat back on.

Bondi stood up and went close to the bars. "Be careful, Jack," he said. He put his hand through the bars. "Good luck to you."

"Much obliged," Burns said, shaking the hand.

"Good hunting."

"I thank you," Burns said. He turned away and looked out the window. "Kinda dark down there. Is that a hedge or somethin by the wall?"

"It should be," Bondi said.

Burns looked long and cautiously in every direction; then he picked up the knotted blankets and lowered the free end of them outside. He came back to the bars. "If you change your mind," he said to Bondi, "Jerry will tell you where to find me. I'll tell her where I'm goin; too many ears around here."

"Have a good time," Bondi said. "And remember me."

Burns smiled again and climbed over the sill of the window. A final wave of the hand and he was gone.

Bondi leaned against the bars, staring out the window at the shadowy, complex pattern of cracks and stains on the wall of the building across the alley. He listened for what he could hear: the footsteps of a man walking away down the street, the sound of an automobile passing, the high thin scream of a jet plane miles away and above, a brief stirring of wind and the dry rustle of leaves, the indistinct words of a conversation somewhere within the cellblock. He waited and listened, gazing dully through the open window.

Presently, after several minutes of this motionless contemplation, his mind registered what his eyes already saw: the blanket tied to the bars and stretched out the window. He reached down and pulled the blanket inside and the others with it and left them, as he had done before, heaped on the floor by the bars. Then he sat down on his bunk and opened the letter. There was not enough light in the cell to read by but he opened the letter anyway.

The two Indians and the Mexican watched him. "You ain't going with your friend?" the Mexican said.

Bondi looked up. "What did you say?"

"You ain't going with your friend?"

"No," Bondi said. "Not tonight."

"You are smart," the Mexican said; he slapped at something crawling down his bare arm. "It is best not to make trouble," he said. He detached a small sticky object from the upper part of his arm and dropped it on the floor.

CHAPTER 11

She came slowly out of sleep, dreaming of the surrealistic past, hearing in the present and not far away the click of a light switch, light footsteps on the kitchen floor, the scraping sounds of a heavy object in motion. Alarmed, she reached out to touch Paul—he was not there. The weary pain of loss and separation swept over her; in the twilight of consciousness between sleep and awakening she felt the full weight of all the fear and sorrow and loneliness that in her waking hours she had partially suppressed beneath a routine of activity and facile optimism. Again she heard the unfamiliar sounds; unwillingly she opened her eyes and turned her head and saw, under the door to the kitchen, a splinter of yellow light. She was startled, then afraid, caught for a moment in the paralysis of the unknown and unexpected. She wanted to get out of bed but was afraid to make any noise; she caught at her breath, swallowed hard and finally forced herself to speak. She called out:

"Who is it?"—a scarcely articulate croak.

Which brought no answer; the sounds of activity in the kitchen continued: she heard something hard and heavy strike the wooden floor. "Who's there?" she said, louder and clearer.

A moment of silence, then the voice of Jack Burns: "It's me, Jerry. It's Jack. You awake?"

She slid out of bed, gave her hair one quick brush with her hand and went to the door and opened it. There was Jack, grinning wanly at her, blinking in the light; he had his saddlebags on one shoulder, his rifle in his right hand. She stared at him and rubbed her eyes. "Where've you been?" she said. "Were you in jail?"

"I was. In and out. How about—"

"Where's Paul? Is he all right? Has anything happened?"

"Everything's fine. Paul's right where he wants to be. How about makin some coffee? I gotta start off in a few minutes."

"What happened to your face?" she said. "You look awful."

"It's nothin much—just a little trouble."

"But good God, Jack . . ." She hesitated, floundering among her fears and impressions, still not fully awake. "What happened, tell me. Did you *break* out of jail?"

"You're shiverin," he said; "why don't you put somethin warm on?" She stared at him. "Go ahead—I'll start a fire in the stove and tell you everything that happened. Hurry up; I can't stay long."

She heard his words, became aware then of the chill in the air, of the taut roughness of her skin. She went back in the bedroom and shuffled into her slippers and put a heavy jacket on over her pajamas. When she re-entered the kitchen she found Jack stuffing paper and kindling-wood into the firebox of the stove. "Matches on the shelf," she said, and in a continuation of that reflex act she went to the cupboard and measured four tablespoonfuls of fresh coffee into the coffeepot. Burns lit the paper under the kindling, set several chunks of juniper on top of that and replaced the stove lid; the fire began to crackle and roar. Jerry dipped about four cupfuls of water out of the bucket, then set the pot on the stove; she closed the damper and the fire settled down to a muted, steady rumble. All of this required no more than a few minutes; they worked quickly and without speaking, conscious of the cold and the approaching dawn.

When she had finished Jerry said: "What are you going to do?" She stood close to the stove, catching the first radiations of heat from the old iron. "You did break out, didn't you?"

"Sure," he said, "what else could I do?" He had one foot on a chair, buckling his spurs to his boots.

"Are the police after you now?"

"I hope not. They'll be scramblin around pretty soon, though. There's a good chance they'll be lookin for me right here, too." He stood up and stretched his arms and yawned mightily. "God, it sure is good to be outa that cage!" He relaxed and smiled awkwardly at Jerry—the condition of his face made normal smiling very difficult. "How's that coffee comin along?"

"What?" she said. Then: "It'll take a few more minutes."

He picked the saddlebags up from the floor. "I'll go out and saddle up." He opened the back door and looked out into the darkness. "Won't be long," he said; "there's a light blue streak above the mountains now." He could see, through the miles of starlit space, a faint sheen of snow on the crest of the range. Jerry, looking out the doorway over his shoulder, saw the white gleam and shivered again. "Wouldn't wanta be up there now with only my spurs on," Burns said. He grinned at her, lifted the saddlebags to his shoulder, ducked under the top of the doorway and walked out; she watched his thin legs and narrow back retreat in the direction of the corral, fading into the purple night. Feeling cold and desolate, she closed the door, hearing a whinny from the mare at the same time, and went back to the stove and moved the coffeepot to what appeared to be the hottest area on the stove. She stared at the black charred handle of the vessel, at the round lid under it, at the yellow glint of fire visible through the crack between stove lid and center section. She roused herself again, set the skillet on the stove and peeled half a dozen strips of bacon into it. She put another skillet on the stove, poured a little bacon grease into it, and cracked five eggs and let them fry. She tossed the cracked eggshells toward the woodbox and missed; she did not bother to pick them up.

Something has happened, she decided; something terrible has happened.

From outside came the sound of hooves beating on the hard earth, the soft coaxing voice of Burns, the mare Whisky's answering nicker. Again she heard, as in a dream, the jingle of spurs and the cowboy's steps across the porch.

"Hey, somethin smells mighty good," he said, coming in; he spotted the bacon and eggs on the stove. "Jerry, you're my angel."

"I'm a damned worried angel," she said, setting a plate, knife, fork, two cups, on the table.

"What's wrong?"

"What's wrong? What's right?" The coffee began to perk and bubble; she flipped the eggs over, forked the strips of bacon out of the skillet and onto a doubled-up paper towel. "Sit down," she said. "Soon as you eat I'm going to put something on that massacred face of yours. What on earth happened to you?"

"Is that all that's frettin you?" Burns sat down at the table and gave the plate a spin; he remembered his hat, took it off and set it on the floor beside his chair. "Huh?"

"You men make me sick," she said. "You act like children. Even Seth or that mare out there would have better sense. Here you are with your face cut up and running away from the police and there Paul is in the county jail waiting to go to a Federal prison for a year or two. What's the matter with you people?" She dished out the eggs and bacon onto his plate and turned back to the stove to rescue the coffee, already beginning to boil over. "I think you're both crazy, that's all."

"You might be right there," Burns agreed. "Question is—what can you do about it?"

"Don't make me angry," Jerry said; she filled his cup with coffee, then her own. "There's plenty I could do," she added.

Burns gazed sombrely into his black coffee. "Maybe so," he said, "maybe so." The vapor rising from the coffee clouded his face, giving him a temporary intangibility.

Jerry sat down. "What kind of extra trouble is Paul in now?" she asked.

"None that I know of." Burns began to eat. "He helped me get out but there's no call for anybody to learn that."

"What are you going to do now?"

Burns spoke between mouthfuls of bacon and egg. " . . . Up to the mountains. Hide—" He gulped down some of the steaming coffee. "—Hide out maybe a few days. Get some meat, make jerky."

"I can give you some things."

"Can't take canned goods—too heavy, too bulky."

"I baked yesterday. I'll give you some bread."

"That'd be fine, Jerry."

"You say you're going to hide for a few days—what does that mean? What then? Where will you go?"

Burns ate heartily; a touch of egg adorned his beard. "I can go north, west or south. Winter's comin so I guess I'll go south: Chihuahua or maybe Sonora, dependin on how things look."

"What will you do down there?"

"I dunno. Just live, I guess." He swabbed his plate with a piece of bread. "I like Mexico—it's a good clean honest sorta country. I have friends there."

"But Jack—" Jerry hesitated. "You'll be back, won't you?"

"Sure. When I'm nothin but a face on the postoffice wall I'll come a-sneakin back. You'll see me comin down across the mesa out there some evening when things are peaceful."

"Don't talk to me like that. You know you can't go on like this—you're in the Twentieth Century now."

"I don't tune my life to the numbers on a calendar."

"That's ridiculous, Jack. You're a social animal, whether you like it or not. You've got to make some concessions—or they'll hunt you down like a . . . like a . . . What do people hunt down nowadays?"

"Coyotes," Burns said. "With cyanide guns." He finished his coffee and wiped his mouth. "I better get a move on."

Jerry gripped her cup tightly, though it burnt her fingers. "Jack—" she said.

He looked at her over his hand. His lean worn face, beaten and discolored, harsh, asymmetrical, homely as a hound, touched her to the heart. She wanted to reach out to him, laugh and weep for him; instead she forced a smile, saying: "Like some more to eat?"

He stared at her for a long moment before answering. "Thanks, Jerry . . . I've had enough."

"I'll fix you something to take with you."

"That'd be mighty nice of you, Jerry." He pushed back his chair, put on his hat and stood up. "I gotta get goin right away, though."

"Won't take me but a minute." She got up too and started to demonstrate her words. Burns was about to interfere, changed his mind and completed his own preparations: slung the guitar across his back, picked up his rifle and bedroll, and went outside. Jerry finished packing a paper sack with a half loaf of rye bread wrapped in tin foil, and with cheese and salami and oranges. She hurried out after him. "Don't run off," she said.

Burns had slipped the rifle into the saddle scabbard and was tying the bedroll on behind the cantle when she came out. "Here," she said, "take this. It's bread."

"Thanks a lot," he said, taking the package and jamming it into the top of the saddlebag. He knotted the last thong, then went to the pump to fill his canteen; she followed him. The air was chill enough to vaporize their exhalations, lending their speech a vague, smoky visibility.

"I want to give you back the money," she said.

Burns unscrewed the cap of the canteen, held it under the spout and began pumping. Jerry picked up a can half full of water and poured the water slowly into the top of the pump. "You have to prime this damn thing," she said. Flecks of ice glittered in the starlight.

"I forgot." He pumped the handle up and down and after much groaning and gasping the pump started to give water, splashing over the cowboy's hand and over the canteen.

"I don't need the money, you know. Not really . . ." She turned to go back to the house. "I'll get it."

"I could use the ammunition," he said at last. "And I'll take back half the money." Jerry started toward the porch. "No more," he said after her.

She went inside; Burns walked to his outfit and hung the canteen on the saddlehorn. He waited; the mare snorted and twitched her ears, pawing the ground, eager for the dawn and the ride. He looked to the east: the mountains seemed darker now, the snow almost blue; above the rim the sky was fading in waves of green and yellow, a hint of the sun burning below the horizon. But far in the west the night still held, deep and brilliant with the ice-blue crackling points of light from the stars.

Jerry hurried out of the house toward him, the bandoleer in her hands. "All right, I kept half the money. Now take it."

He accepted the bandoleer without a word and put it over his head and across his shoulders, hanging it under the guitar.

"I almost forgot," she said. "I want to do something for your face."

"My face is hopeless," he said, trying to grin. "What can you do for it?"

"That broken tooth may give you trouble."

"Broken tooth?"

"You might at least let me wash the blood off your cheek."

"That ain't blood, that's skin. I washed everything off that would come off before I got here."

"Where?"

He smiled painfully. "In an irrigation ditch."

"That's what I thought," she said. "Come on inside; there's warm water on the stove."

He patted the mare on the shoulder and the horse turned nervously and blew some of her foggy breath in his face. "Jerry, I gotta vamoose. Me and Whisky got a long ways to go." Awkwardly he faced the mare. "Ain't that right, girl?" he said, slapping and rubbing the gleaming shoulder.

"Don't start loving up that damned horse in front of me," Jerry said. "Anything else you need?"

Burns put a hand on the pommel, a foot in the stirrup, ready to mount. "No," he said, and stopped to think. "Well I don't have any tobacco. They took it—"

"Wait," she said, "just one more minute!" And shuffled in her slippers as fast as she could back into the kitchen.

"They took it all away from me . . ." Burns concluded, addressing the kitchen door. He surveyed the eastern horizon again, then turned his narrowed and anxious eyes toward the house and past it and looked up the road that led toward the city.

Jerry came out of the kitchen. "Here," she said, a little breathlessly, "here's some of Paul's old pipe tobacco." She gave him a cellophane-wrapped package of London Dock, still fat and fragrant.

"I ain't got a pipe, Jerry," he said softly. "Could you find any cigarette papers?"

"I know, I know," she said. "No, I couldn't find any papers. But here's a pipe he never uses." She gave Burns a handsome briar pipe with a slender stem. "I know he wouldn't miss it," she added, as the cowboy hesitated; "it's one I bought him for his birthday. Please take it, Jack."

"Well . . . okay," he said. "I'm sure obliged to you. To both of you. Just hope this fancy tobacco don't spoil me." He put the pipe and tobacco inside his shirt. "Pockets all fulla junk," he explained sheepishly.

"Jack—"

"Yeah?" Again he prepared to mount, his foot in the stirrup, his back toward her.

"Jack . . ." She stepped forward and touched his shoulder and he faced her again, waiting. "Kiss me," she said.

"I want to," he said. But he made no move. "I want to."

"What are you afraid of?"

"I don't know. Nothin, I guess." He reached out then and embraced her and kissed her gently and quickly on the lips. "What I'm afraid of," he said slowly, "is me. That's all."

"We're both afraid of the same thing, then," Jerry said.

"Maybe everybody is."

Jerry smiled at him while her vision dimmed. "You'd better go," she managed to say.

"What's so funny?" He returned her smile with a stiff, uncertain grin.

"You'd better go, Jack."

"Yes," he said. "I know." He released her and turned and pulled himself up, a little wearily, into the saddle. He adjusted the guitar and bandoleer on his back, tugged at the forebrim of his hat.

"Goodby, Jack."

"Goodby, kid," he said. "Say goodby to Seth for me." He touched Whisky with the reins and she turned, facing the mountains. "Take care of your old man," he said. "When I come back I wanta see you *both* out here." The mare pranced and whinnied and shook her head, impatient, indignant, eager for flight.

"Yes," Jerry said, "I hope so. God, I hope so."

"I'll see you in a year or so. Maybe sooner."

"Yes," she said; she shivered in the keen air, blinking the mist out of her eyes. "Be careful, Jack."

"Adios," he said, and flicked the mare with the leather, and at once she began to trot, then canter, away from the house and corral and toward the mountains. Burns reined in a little and slowed her to a brisk trot. Jerry, watching him turn in the saddle and wave back at her. Weakly she pulled one hand out of a jacket pocket and held it up for him to see, but he had already turned and straightened and was facing the east.

She stood in the bleak gray light, huddled and cold in the jacket and her pajamas, and watched Jack Burns ride away: she saw him cross the embankment by the big irrigation ditch and disappear for several minutes and heard or thought she heard the rattling dance of Whisky's iron shoes across the wooden bridge; she saw horse and rider reappear on the higher ground beyond the ditch, figures already greatly diminished by the perspective of distance; she saw them slowly mount the rise to the edge of the mesa and there, where she knew there was a fence although now it could not be seen—the light obscure and shifting—she saw the cowboy dismount and work at something in front of the horse, then remount and ride on; she saw them, the man and his horse, fade, melt, diminish by subtle gradations of light and dimension into that vast open expanse of stone and sand and space that swept on, mile after mile after mile, toward the dark mountains.

The qualities of light and space deceived her, baffled her— she felt that the figure of man and horse, now one, might recede from her, shrink in magnitude forever and yet not completely and finally disappear—if only she had the power to prevent it. And in that momentary hallucination she felt that it was suddenly terribly important that she stop them—as if the limits of her vision were an abstract, impossible barrier dividing reality from nothingness.

The hallucination passed. She peered into the gloom of the dawn and saw nothing but shadows. The cowboy was gone.

From a cottonwood tree near the ditch came the whirring call of a grouse hen, the cawing of approaching crows. Jerry shivered, urged her cold aching limbs into motion and returned to the kitchen. She had water to carry, she remembered, a breakfast to make ready for Seth, lunches to pack, dishes to wash, a job in the city at nine o'clock—no end of things to do.

CHAPTER 12

OKLAHOMA CITY, OKLA.

Hinton stopped at a diesel station on the western outskirts of the city to refuel. He gave his credit card to the station operator and then walked to the next-door diner—an aluminum-sheeted neon-lighted potted-pine establishment specializing in truck-drivers' disorders—for an attempt at breakfast.

Six-thirty in the morning: he closed his eyes against the swirling dust that blew along the highway, stinging his face with particles of sand. He felt bad, anyway: his stomach was raw, empty, completely wrung-out, the muscles stiff and sore from last night's struggle with nausea; his throat was burning and strained; his mouth—he would have preferred not to think of that at all—was dry, his tongue shriveled, coated with unfamiliar chemicals. He tried not to think of it; he went inside and sat down in a booth by the windows.

The wind-driven sand scratched at the glass as Hinton stared gloomily out, watching the trucks roll by on the road: a train of trucks, westbound, roaring past in the dusty-yellow light of early morning, a racing caravan that seemed to have no end. He speculated idly on the immense expenditure of human labor represented by that flight of tin and cardboard and plastic and men, and groaned inwardly; dejection overcame him—he was sick of the business, sick of his sickness. He opened the menu and tried to imagine a breakfast honest and homely enough for his tired wracked cowering stomach.

"Yes, sir," the waitress said, bending toward him slightly in her white morning-fresh uniform, a tender and all-forgiving smile (it seemed to him) on her face, a thoughtful regard in her young eyes—the nurse and her first patient.

"Hello," he said. For the first time since leaving St. Louis, two days before he felt a reawakening of his essential humanity, an interest—in the case of this girl not merely sexual—in another human being. He found himself looking at a face that did not instantly depress him, that did not turn his own into a sour, sullen reflection of his jangled entrails.

"What would you like?" the girl said. Her hair was glossy and long, the color of mellow applejack, and in her eyes was a dance and glister of light that he had not seen for—how long?— six years? "Would you like some fruit juice?" she said; her teeth were so fine as to be almost translucent. "We have fresh orange juice, sir; I made it myself just a few minutes ago."

"I used to know a girl like you," Hinton said; "—back in Virginia."

"My folks come from Indiana, sir."

"You don't have to call me 'sir.'"

"You don't look like a sir," she said, smiling.

"I'm not." He paused, and looked down at the tabletop: there lay his two hands—wide, short-fingered, a bit soft in the palms, fingernails fairly clean. "I'll have the orange juice," he said.

"Yes sir." She recorded this request on her little green pad—a novice, he thought. New: she won't always be as green and beautiful as she is now—not for long. "What else, sir?" she said.

He sighed and glanced dutifully over the menu. A girl like this, he was thinking, sweet as a wild haw—she must have grown up in the open. Won't last long in this hothouse. He stared at the menu. "I'll have sausage and eggs," he said. But instantly his stomach recoiled before the provocative image of a fried egg. "Change that," he said. The girl scribbled, crossed out, erased. "Make it sausage and wheatcakes. Do you have real maple syrup here?" he said.

"Yes sir." She hesitated. "I think we do."

"The kind that comes out of maple trees?"

"I think so, sir." She looked genuinely concerned, biting her lip and glancing toward the kitchen. "I'll make sure," she said, starting off.

"Wait a minute," he said. She stopped. "Don't worry about it; just bring me whatever you have. I trust you."

"Yes sir." She smiled again, blushing faintly. He admired, from his remote isolation, the utility and structural delicacy of her ears: receptacle for lies. "Are you all right, sir?" she said, looking closely at him.

"What?" His left eyelid was twitching again; he rubbed it, and the other eye too. "I'm all right," he said. "I feel fine."

"Yes sir." She stood there for a moment, watching him; he looked at her and he thought he knew what she was thinking: What a tired, sad, ugly old man he is. But I'm only thirty-four, he wanted to say. He wanted to say: I have bad dreams and there's something wrong with my insides but I come from a good mountain family. But of course he said nothing, and after this moment of questioning and wondering the girl turned away from him and went to order his breakfast.

Afterwards, while she watched him from behind the counter, he tried to eat. He drank the orange juice without difficulty and ate most of the sausage—it was not good but was good enough, despite the haste and lack of pride involved in the making of it—and he even started on the wheatcakes. He wanted very much to eat everything before him, knowing that the girl was there not far away and watching him with some concern. She had had no hand in the cooking, being merely a waitress; he knew that well enough but still felt an urgent if obscure obligation to eat all that she had borne to him, as if it were a moral responsibility.

She brought him coffee and he drank that easily, pouring the fiercely hot brew down his seamed and hardened gullet without even feeling it. He nibbled some more at the wheat-cakes and forced down almost the last of the sausage, and then surrendered and got ready to leave. He looked at the bill she had left on the table: his breakfast came to a dollar ten, including tax. He owed the girl, according to his code and calculation, an eleven-cent tip. He put a dime on the table, considered for a minute or so and then pulled his wallet out of his hip pocket and opened it. Inside was money, a fat wad of the stuff, green and gray and crackling and greasy, with its definite, peculiar odor. He leafed through this material, seeing a few ones, several fives, many tens. He removed a one-dollar bill and slipped it under his plate, then paused again, staring at the money. He put the one back in his wallet and took out a five and placed it under the dish, carefully, and then he got up and went quickly to the cash register on the counter. The cook was there waiting; Hinton looked again for the girl and saw her at a booth, feet apart and firm on the floor, the upper half of her body slightly inclined toward the bald pate and crusty face of another customer. Hinton paid, picked up his change and went out without looking back.

PART THREE

THE SHERIFF

"The Sheriff was a Proud man . . ."

CHAPTER 13

The big room contained the following objects: (1) On the wall, a photographic portrait of Harry S Truman, framed in plastic and shielded from the mortalizing dust by a veneer of glass; a good likeness, healthily tinted—the blue Missouri eyes stared seriously and hopefully into the future, the pink cheeks attested to three squares a day, the pink neck swelled sedately from a clean white collar. (2) Filing cabinets, chairs, telephones, an electric fan, coat hangers and hatracks. (3) A padlocked weapons rack supporting two sawed-off shotguns, four Browning automatic rifles, four Thompson submachineguns, and two teargas guns. (4) A shortwave radio receiver-transmitter complete with operator. (5) A big ugly desk with papers, boxes, calendars, two telephones, an ivory donkey, blotter, ink, pens, rocks, coffeestains, fingerprints and boot scratches. (6) Behind the desk a big plain man, the passive sedentary relaxed two-hundred-pound corpus of Morlin Johnson, duly elected sheriff of Bernal County, New Mexico. Sheriff Johnson held an open package of chewing gum in his right hand.

The man at the radio desk half-turned in his chair, pushed

his earphones above his ears—while red and amber signal lights flickered irritably on the panel—and spoke to Sheriff Johnson: "Gutierrez says they broke out sometime between three and five-thirty this morning."

Johnson unwrapped a stick of gum. "When?"

"Between three and five-thirty."

"Why?"

"Why?" The radio operator shrugged his shoulders. "How the hell should I know?" Then he grinned self-consciously. "Oh balls, Morey," he said.

Johnson placed the stick of gum between his teeth and chewed it mechanically into his mouth, like a stock ticker champing up blank tape.

His ruminations were prolonged, sober, comfortable. "Musta been cold that early in the morning," he said at last. He unwrapped a second stick of gum and inserted it into his chewing machine. "You took care of the routine, I guess?"

"Yeah," the operator said. "Gutierrez did as soon as he discovered the prisoners missing."

"Gutierrez," Johnson said; "Gutierrez . . ." His mouth tightened after he rolled out the name. "That muscle-bound halfwit," he muttered; he spoke to the operator again, not looking at him. "He notified the city police?"

"Yes."

"The state police and the military police and the reservation police and all the rest?"

"Sure."

"Okay . . ." Johnson masticated his wad of gum. He shoved a hand down inside the front of his sagging trousers and scratched his pubic hair. "Two Navajos and a white man, huh?"

"That's right."

"Are they all three going together?"

"They don't know if they are or not."

"Did Gutierrez question the other men in the cell?"

"Sure; they didn't know nothin."

"Gutierrez grilled them, huh?"

"Yeah."

Johnson growled and frowned heavily at the ivory figurine of a donkey set on his desk. The donkey was flanked on one side by a brace of telephones, on the other by an Esquire-girl calendar. He rolled the gum in his mouth and scratched his armpits. "Anybody go out for coffee yet?"

"Glynn and Herrera went."

"Both of em, huh? One man to carry, one man to guard, I suppose?"

The radio operator grinned weakly. "Well I don't know. I guess so. I don't know."

"How am I gonna keep this job when you boys carry on like that, always screwin off in the poolroom or in the cafe?"

"Well hell, Morey," the operator said, "don't we all vote for you? Hasn't my grandmother voted for you every two years since we buried her?"

"All right," Johnson said, "let me think. I'm trying to concentrate." He unwrapped a third stick of gum and put it in his red mouth and then scratched the back of his neck, his scalp; he looked at the scurf under his fingernails. "What's the story on the escaped prisoners?"

"Right," the operator said. He shuffled through the papers on his table. "Here we are: two Navajos, cousins, names Reed and Joe Watahomagie, address given as Tuba City, Arizona, occupation stockmen, convicted of drunk and disorderly conduct and improper approaches to white woman on a bus, Mrs. Florabel Minnebaugh, aged fifty-two. Sentenced—"

"Menopause?"

"Minnebaugh. Sentenced to ninety days flat, six days served before escape. Physical description: Reed W., aged thirty, five foot ten, one hundred forty-five pounds, black hair, brown eyes—"

"Yeah, I know," Johnson said; "Navajos. Now how about the white fella."

"Right. John W. Burns, no address, occupation cattle herder, convicted of drunk and disorderly conduct and resisting arrest, also being held for investigation on suspicion of draft delinquency, sentenced to ten days pending result of investigation, one day served before escape. Physical description: Age twenty-nine, six feet two, one hundred seventy pounds, black hair, gray eyes, dark complexion, nose slightly misshapen as probable result of old injury."

"That kind of a guy," the sheriff said. He readjusted his bulk in the creaking swivel chair, pulled out a lower drawer in the desk and put one booted foot in it. He chewed on his ball of gum. "Draft delinquency . . . ?" He chewed on that for a minute. "Put in a call to the FBI office. See if they've got a dossier on this character." The operator turned toward his radio panel. Johnson said: "Any of those boys have a previous record?"

The operator checked his clipboard. "Not in this state," he said.

"Okay." Johnson swung around in his chair and hoisted himself to his feet. "Go ahead with that call," he said. "I'll be back in a minute." He opened a door marked PRIVATE, stepped inside, closed and locked the door behind him. He belched comfortably, rubbed his nose, unbuckled his belt, unbuttoned and lowered his trousers and sat down on the toilet. He waited, chewing his gum, breathing through his relaxed mouth. He raised his eyes to the calendar on the wall.

When he returned to the office he found the operator dunking a pecan roll in a cup of coffee; beside him sat Deputy Floyd Glynn in a khaki uniform, gun and badge. There was black coffee and a roll on his desk, waiting for him, and the receiver of his private, unlisted telephone lying off the hook.

"Barker wants to talk to you," the operator said.

Johnson sat down, spat his wad into the wastebasket, took a sip of coffee and picked up the phone. "This is Johnson," he said.

The machine buzzed and clicked in his ear. "Look, Morey," it said, "we're all set. I've been down to the Federal Building this morning: the FHA is gonna back up the loan. We can go ahead right away; I've got three subdivisions lined up on the north side of Minolas Boulevard." The machine paused, silent except for a dim metallic static. "Morey?" it said.

"Yes?"

"You're still interested, aren't you?"

"Sure—I guess so. Only I don't understand about the FHA."

"Listen, you dumb Swede, the FHA guarantees the loan. It's simple: we get the money from the bank—we hire a contractor and we build—we pay off the contractor—we keep the difference between the cost and the full amount of the loan and take a trip to the Riviera."

"We still have to pay it all back, don't we?"

"Sure—we get twenty years to pay it back."

"Well . . . where's it come from?"

"The rent, you dumb farmer. The tenants pay it back. The FHA fixes the rent, depending on the type of apartment, and allows so much extra a year for installments on the loan, plus a seven percent net." Johnson made no reply; the machine said: "Look, Morey, meet me for lunch and I'll explain it all to you. With pictures."

"I'm kind of busy today . . ."

"That's all right, this is important. You got to eat anyway, don't you?"

Johnson hesitated. "Okay. Okay—I'll see you then."

"Same place, same time?" said the machine.

"Yeah . . . So long, Bob." Johnson hung up. He drank some coffee and took a big bite from his pecan roll; the radio operator and Deputy Glynn watched him. "What'd you find out?" Johnson said, staring at the blotter on his desk, his cheeks bulging, holding the coffee mug under his chin. He set down the roll and scratched the inside of his left thigh.

"The FBI is interested in this guy Burns," the operator said. He picked up a notepad and read: "John W. Burns, Socorro, New Mexico."

"Socorro?"

"That's what it says here."

"I thought he didn't have an address?"

"They said Socorro."

"Okay, go on."

The operator read: "John W. Burns, Socorro, New Mex. Born 1920, Joplin, Missouri. Moved 1932 to residence of Henry Vogelin, stockman, R.D. #3, Socorro, New Mex. Drafted at Socorro, March 15, 1942. Served five months in U.S. Army Disciplinary Training Center, Pisa, Italy, for striking superior officer, April 22, 1944."

"What happened between March 1942 and April 1944?"

"They didn't say." The operator continued: "Wounded in action, November 4, 1944, discharged February 10, 1945 at Fort Dix, New Jersey."

"What's all that to the FBI?" Johnson said; he put his foot up on the desk drawer again.

"How should I know?" the operator said. "They didn't say."

"All right." Johnson unwrapped a stick of chewing gum. "What else? Is that all?"

"There's more." The operator read: "Admitted to State University, Duke City, New Mex., September 15, 1945. Known to have attended secret meetings of so-called Anarchist group."

"So-called what?"

"So-called Anarchist group." The operator paused.

"What's that?" Deputy Glynn said.

The operator looked at Sheriff Johnson; Johnson said nothing. The operator said: "I don't know. They're against all government, that's all I know."

"They're worse than Communists?"

"I guess so."

"They have red eyes and they throw bombs," Sheriff Johnson said. He yawned and scratched his ribs. "Read on," he said.

The operator read: "In March 1946 was one of five signers of documents posted on University bulletin boards advocating so-called Civil Disobedience to Selective Service and other Federal activities. Left University in mid-term, fall of 1946. Subsequent activities and whereabouts unknown. Failed to register for Selective Service as required in September, 1948, by renewed Selective Service Act. This man is wanted for questioning by FBI." The operator stopped, drank down the last of his coffee. "That's all," he said. "They weren't too happy to hear about him getting away last night."

"I reckon not," Johnson said softly. He chewed his gum, his eyes half closed, unfocused. "Who else signed that so-called document?" he said.

"I don't know. I didn't ask and they didn't tell me."

"Well find out." Johnson slumped back in his chair, scratching his umbilicus, while the operator lowered his earphones and busied himself at the board. The inter-com telephone on his desk rang; slowly he picked it up. "Yes?"

His secretary answered: "Mrs. Johnson, sir."

He scowled. "All right. Put her on."

The receiver crackled a little, then a feminine voice sharp as a parakeet's shot through it: "Morlin? Are you there, Morlin?"

"I'm here." He compressed his lips and ejected the chewing gum violently into the wastebasket; the pellet rattled against the metal and dropped down among the discarded letters, cigarette butts, ashes, old gum wads, crushed paper cups. "What do you want?"

"You don't sound right," his wife said. "What's wrong with you?"

"Nothing's wrong with me. What do you want?"

"I want you to pick Elinor up after school. She's staying late."

"Why?"

"She's got a part in a play. They're having a rehearsal after school. Pick her up at five-thirty."

"Why can't she take a bus?"

"Why should she? It's not very far out of your way. Besides, with these Anarchists and Indian sex-maniacs running around loose—"

"Sex maniacs?"

"Yes. And another thing: I need an extension cord."

"A what?"

"Extension cord. You know. Pick one up on your way home."

"All right."

"Now Morlin, you won't forget, will you? Remember: Elinor, five-thirty, school, extension cord. Repeat after—"

"Yes! Elinor, five-thirty, school, extension cord. Goodby!" Johnson hung up, muttering heavily. The phone rang again. "Jesus!"—he picked it up. "Yes?"

"Mrs. Johnson is still on the line, sir. She—"

"I'm not here." He slammed the receiver down, swearing. After this interruption—he unwrapped a stick of gum, threw the paper at the wastebasket and missed—several minutes passed before he could recover his standard placidity. He scowled and grumbled, simmered down finally to a state of glum torpor, scratching listlessly at his belly.

"Morey . . . ?" The radio operator was speaking to him. "Hey, Morey . . ."

He raised his head and looked at the operator.

The operator stared at him. "Here's the poop on that document business," he said, the notepad in his hand. Johnson made no answer. "You wanta hear it?"

Johnson nodded and turned his head back to his desk, his jaws moving ponderously over the gum.

While Deputy Glynn leafed through an old comic book and the sheriff, huge and relaxed in his swivel chair, gave no sign of attention, the operator read his report: "Document in question carried five signatures, to wit: Paul M. Bondi, Jack Burns, H. D. Thoreau, P. B. Shelley, Emiliano Zapata. Last three signatories suspected of being fictitious, as no students bearing such names were then registered at the University."

Johnson smiled faintly; he reached forward and made a slight adjustment in the position of the ivory donkey.

"Now they've got all kinds of stuff on this Paul M. Bondi," the operator went on. "Paul M. Bondi, Box 424, R.D. 4, Duke City, New Mex. Born 1924, Montclair, New Jersey, son of Lewis P.—"

"Get him," Johnson said.

"Get him?" the operator said. "Get who?"

"This Paul M. Bondi."

The operator smiled. "Well hell Morey, we already got him. He's in the county jail right now. He was one of the guys Gutierrez worked over this morning. He was in the same cell as Burns and the two Navajos when they broke out."

"Gutierrez what—?"

The operator hesitated. "I said he was one of the guys Gutierrez questioned this morning."

"What was Gutierrez doing there this morning?—his shift's supposed to be from four in the afternoon to twelve. Where was Kirk?" Johnson scratched the side of his neck—not so indolently now.

"I don't know, Morey."

"I'm gonna have to have a talk with that fella," Johnson said. He puttered around for a while with the donkey. "What did he find out?"

"I told you—nothin." The operator waited in his chair. "Want me to tell em to bring this Bondi down?" he asked.

Johnson leaned far back in his squeaking chair; he hooked

his thumbs in his belt, let his head hang loosely and closed his eyes. For two or three silent minutes he remained in this contrived but satisfying position. Then he said: "Is that address up to date?"

"What address?"

"This fella's; Paul M.—whatever it is."

"I'll check." The operator went to the filing cabinet, slid out a drawer and rummaged through an index of manila folders. Johnson waited, sleepily scratching his ear. "Yeah," the operator said; "Paul M. Bondi, Box 424, R.D. 4, Duke City. That's the address he had when he was arraigned."

Johnson sat forward, grunting, and eased himself up and out of his chair. He twiddled with the ivory donkey, then walked slowly to a window and looked out. A grimy newspaper, staggering, rising, collapsing like a dying man, went flopping and sliding by on the sidewalk, chased by a whirling twister of wind and sand and dust. The mountains were still visible beyond the city, but vague and remote, detached from the earth and floating on a yellow haze.

Another dirty day, thought Johnson. He watched a dog—small, tarnished, unlicensed—come trotting up to the courthouse steps, saw it cock one leg and piss on the municipal shrubbery; he watched it sniff eagerly at its own urine glistening on the leaves, then turn and make a second pass.

Good boy, said Johnson to himself, good boy. Now the dog trotted by on the sidewalk under his window with an earnest and purposive air, its ragged coat bristling before the wind. Not a care in the world, thought Johnson, just doesn't give a good goddamn—He watched it disappear around the corner, headed south toward Mexico.

He faced about and spoke to Deputy Glynn. "Put that comic

book away, Floyd, and button your fly. I want you to cruise out
to 424, R.D. 4, and see what you can find."

Glynn complained. "It'll soon be lunchtime, Morey."

"That's all right. You've been fattening up all morning. Go
on out there and when you get there radio me on the spot. You
know how to find it?"

"Sure, Morey, I know. Who's goin with me?"

"God's love'll go with you. Now run along."

Glynn went out; the private telephone rang and Johnson
picked it up. "Johnson speaking."

"Hi, Morey, this is Ed."

"Ed?"

"Ed Kimball."

"Oh—how are you, Ed?"

"Fine, Morey. Say, we're wondering if you can go out to Lead
Hill next Saturday afternoon. The Democratic Club is holding
a public picnic and benefit dance for the Miners' Welfare Association. We want somebody out there to represent the County
Committee. Will you go, make a little speech?"

"I don't wanta make any more speeches."

"We got to have somebody out there, Morey: you're the only
one on the Committee that's not booked up for that day."

"Why don't you go?"

"Because I have to go to Santa Fe—I can't be two places at
once."

"You can't get anybody else?"

"Look, Morey, I told you—"

"Okay, okay, I'll go. What do you want me to talk about?"

"I don't care. Anything but Truman." There was a long
pause; then the voice in the telephone said, quietly: "Morey?"

"Yes . . . ?"

"We're having a little poker game Friday night."

"Is Cox gonna come?"

"No."

"I'll be there." Johnson hung up. Time again for meditations: he unfoiled more chewing gum and provided his mouth and jaw with meaningful activity; he rubbed his knee; slumping forward against the desk he lifted the October page of his illustrated calendar and took a peek at November—exaggerated breasts without visible means of support, the commercial smirk, long thighs leading nowhere. He dropped the leaf. Hell . . . There was another calendar on his desk, the memorandum type: he leafed through it until he came to Saturday, unclipped an automatic pencil—semi-automatic—from his jacket pocket and made a note: Lead Hill.

Outside in the street a car backfired; another spasm of wind swished by and dust pattered like rain against the windowglass.

"Gonna be another dirty day," the radio operator said.

"Somebody's trying to get you," Johnson replied. A little red eye was flashing on the radio control board.

The operator pulled one earphone over an ear and flicked a switch on the panel; he spoke into the heavy radial microphone on his table. "This is CS-1," he said, "this is CS-1. Come in, CS-4."

"The speaker," Johnson said.

The operator flipped a second switch and the black round screen on the receiver began to rasp and crackle. "This is Glynn," the screen said; "where the hell is R.D. 4? Repeat: Where the hell is R.D. 4? Over."

"Let me talk to him," Johnson said, as the operator hesitated.

He heaved himself out of his chair, lumbered over to the radio and grabbed the microphone by the neck as if he were strangling a chicken. "That Glynn," he muttered, "—so dumb he doesn't know whether Christ was crucified or kicked by a mule." He growled into the microphone: "This is Johnson. Where are you now, Floyd? Get me?—where are you now? Over."

"I'm on North Guadalupe Road," the voice in the speaker said. "North Guadalupe. Over."

"Listen, Floyd: go north to Coral Street, then east till you hit Highland Road. Follow Highland Road on north. Understand? When you get past the city limits start watching the numbers on the mailboxes until you come to 424. Do you get me? Repeat my message. Over."

The voice from the screen said: "Okay, Morey, I get you. North to Coral Street, east to Highland Road, north on Highland to Box 424. Am I right? Over."

"That's right, you simple Mick. Now get going. Over and out." Johnson returned to his desk and sat down, scratching at his armpit. "Did you notify Socorro?" he said to the operator.

"Socorro?"

"Give them the information on this fella Burns; tell them he may be coming their way." Johnson thought for a moment. "Tell them to check on Mr. Henry Vogelin this evening. Explain why."

"Okay, Morey." The operator reached for his clipboard and notepad.

Johnson put his feet on a desk drawer and allowed himself about five minutes of complete relaxation. Then, idly and without interest, he glanced through his morning mail. There was a letter from the National Sheriffs' Association containing an invitation to a national convention of county sheriffs in Orlando, Florida; also, a wistful reminder to Sheriff Johnson that he was four years behind in his dues; Johnson filed the letter in his wastepaper basket. A letter from the Peerless Prison Equipment Company of Providence, R.I., announcing a revolutionary new device for the immediate detection of prison break-out attempts: an electronic seismograph which, when properly installed, registers, measures and announces, with appropriate alarms and lighting effects, any effort to tamper with any metallic part of the structure of a standard cellblock, or any effort to tamper with the seismograph apparatus itself; at a price any progressive community can afford: $795.50 plus delivery charges. Johnson flipped the letter into his wastebasket. Then there were letters from his public, mostly unsigned, containing accusations and suspicions directed against their neighbors—wife-beating, the starving of children, disturbances of peace. Among the other anonymous letters was one composed in shaky but unequivocal English with words cut out of a newspaper and pasted to a sheet of brown butcher paper: I AM GONE TO KILL YOU SHERIFF JOHNSON. Johnson examined the envelope of this communication, found it addressed with the same technique; he looked for the postmark; there was no postmark.

This letter and the complaints that were signed he placed in a box of papers and letters destined for the desk of his Deputy Sheriff, Richard Hernandez. His official correspondence—requests, reports and inquiries from state and county functionaries, all of it—he filed away in a drawer containing in addition to a confusion of other letters, a U.S. Forest Service canteen, a box of twelve-gauge shotgun shells, a pair of dirty tennis shoes

stuffed with dirty socks, a Smith & Wesson .38 with holster
and belt, several small chunks of carnotite, chewing gum wrap-
pers, apple cores, little photo magazines, crumbs, pennies and
sand. Johnson leaned back, closing his eyes and clasping his
hands together behind his head.

The office phone rang. He let it ring a second time, then
leaned forward and picked it up. "Yeah?" he said.

The voice of his secretary in the outer office: "Mr. Hassler
would like to see you, sir."

Johnson scowled and swung slowly around in his chair,
turning his face to the wall. "I'm busy," he said; "don't let him in."

The door opened and a young man slipped in smoothly,
hardly making a sound. "What's the matter, Morey?" he said;
"you got secrets?" He wore an inconspicuous tan suit, shell-
rimmed glasses and a complexion like fried liver. "I'll only take a
minute. I gotta make a living too, you know." He came forward
and sat on a corner of the sheriff's desk, pushing the In-Out box
aside. Johnson remained in his averted position, eyes half-closed
facing the wall. "About these three jokers that walked out of
your jail this morning," Hassler began; "—is it true that one of
them is an Anarchist?"

Johnson growled. "They didn't walk out, they worked their
way out," he said.

"Is it true," Hassler said, "that the two Indians are sex of-
fenders?"

"No. Who the be-jesus told you that?"

"They attacked a woman on a bus."

"They didn't attack anybody. They were drunk and they
made this old lady a proposition."

"An indecent proposition?"

"Yes, considering her age."

Hassler scribbled in shorthand in his notebook. "About this man Burns," he said: "What kind of an Anarchist is he?"

"How many kinds are there?" Johnson said.

"Is it true he belonged to a secret Anarchist society at the State University?"

"I don't know if it's true or not."

"The FBI says he did."

"You'd better check with them before you print that."

"How about this manifesto advocating civil disobedience? Did Burns sign that?"

"Who told you all this?"

Hassler smiled. "Just guessing," he said. "Burns did sign it, didn't he?"

"It seems so," said Johnson, still facing the wall. He proceeded to unwrap a stick of chewing gum.

Hassler added to his notations. "Do you think these three men are dangerous, Sheriff?"

"No."

"Do you expect any difficulty in re-capturing them?"

"No."

"Where do you think they're probably hiding now?"

"In New Mexico." Johnson put the chewing gum in his mouth and started to chew.

Hassler smiled again. Then he said: "Is it true that this man Burns is kind of a character?"

"Never met him."

"I mean, that he's kind of . . . eccentric? Offbeat? Queer?"

"I don't know anything about him."

"For instance," Hassler said, "we found out that he rides a

horse everywhere he goes. Doesn't own a car. Rides horseback all the time."

Johnson stopped chewing his gum for a moment; after the pause he said: "Who told you that?"

Hassler laughed. "I told you, Morey: I'm telepathic. I got powers. Isn't it true what I said?"

Johnson was silent. After a while he said: "I can't understand why you boys are so curious about this Burns fella—as far as I can make out he's just another dumb cowhand that's fell on his head too often."

"Why?" said Hassler; he closed his notebook and stood up. He grinned. "Human interest," he said. And then he turned and walked out.

Johnson remained facing the wall for several minutes, sombre and ponderous in his ruminations. Finally he swung around and toward the radio operator, who was now reading Glynn's comic book. Johnson squeezed his nose thoughtfully; a faint belch escaped him. The operator looked up. "Any livery stables in this town?" Johnson asked.

"Livery stables?" said the operator; he turned his gaze slowly from Johnson to the window. "Livery stables . . ."

"If you wanted to leave a horse somewhere overnight what would you do with him?"

"If I wanted to leave a horse somewhere I'd just leave him," the operator said: "I can't stand them brutes." He saw Johnson begin to frown and added: "I don't know, Morey . . . I guess I'd take him to one of the riding stables."

"Okay," said Johnson. "Call every riding stable in town or near town, find out if anybody's left a horse there and if they have get the details."

"Okay, Morey." The operator went to work with his telephone.

Johnson sat for a spell chewing his gum, scratching at his belly, then got up and went into his private toilet and urinated. He was beginning to feel hungry; after he had buttoned up and attempted to hoist his trousers up to the height of what was once his waist line—they promptly sagged down again—he pulled out his old pocket watch and looked at it: three-twenty. He grunted and held it up to his ear and found it had run down; he wound the watch and put it back in his vest pocket. Then he washed his hands in cold water and gave his gray hair a quick inefficient combing—using his fingers; he couldn't find the pocketcomb that his daughter had given him just two days before or the one that his wife had given him a few days before that. He scratched briefly between his buttocks and went out.

"I called four places," the operator told him. "Was all I could find in the telephone book. Four places countin the Fairgrounds. Nobody was boardin any horses this week that wasn't regular customers. One of these places told me to try Buddy Mack out in the Canyon so I called Mack and sure enough a man left two horses at his stables just three days ago and picked them up this morning."

Johnson stood by the window watching the wind chase sand and scraps of paper, spin in eddies, raise skirts. "Two horses?" he said.

"Yeah—Tennessee walkin horses, Mack said."

"What was the man like?"

"Mack said he was kinda sawed-off at each end and spread out in the middle, like a knocked-up Shetland pony. He had a red mustache." Johnson said nothing, continued to stare out the window. The operator, allowing this information to soak in, went on: "He was wearin a polo shirt, white shorts, black knee socks and a beret with a red bonbon on top. He hauled his horses in a aluminum trailer and pulled it with a green Cadillac with California plates. Mack said he pulled off in the direction of the Mississippi River."

"Did Mack tell you what he was drinkin last night?"

"No, he didn't." The operator grinned. "But he said that now he did recall that this fella had a kind of sinister look in his eye and that he wouldn't let his two horses associate with Mack's horses. And he sprayed the stalls before he put his horses in. And he had his own nigger with him to groom the horses and shovel shit. Mack said the nigger had a Oxford accent and wore plus four minus shoes."

Johnson brooded over the windy streetscene before him; he stood there for a long time, silent, occasionally scratching himself. The clock in the window of Koeber's Department Store said fifteen minutes till twelve. "Any word from Glynn yet?" Johnson said, staring out the window.

The operator lowered his comic book. "Not a word," he said. "He must've stopped at a bar somewhere to get directions."

Johnson raised the window sash, spat his wad of gum out into the hedge below, closed the window and turned and picked his dust-colored Stetson off the hatrack. "I'll be back in about an hour," he said. "If Glynn calls in while I'm out tell him to stay right where he is till I get back. Unless he's already got our man."

"Okay, Morey." The operator reached for his lunchbag.

"Tell him not to bother anybody till I tell him what to do."

"Sure, Morey." The operator began unwrapping the wax paper from around a ham-and-Swiss-cheese sandwich. When the door closed behind Sheriff Johnson he spread the comic book out on his knees and started to eat. The name of the comic book was TRUE CRIME STORIES.

Johnson did not return in an hour—it was nearly two hours. He came slowly into the office, parked his hat on the rack without looking, and forged heavily, like an abandoned barge, across the room and into his berth behind the desk. There he settled, sinking in thought, obscured in the solemn atmosphere of a man engaged in prolonged, difficult and crucial introspection. The radio operator, whose face revealed signs of a moderate internal agitation, and who obviously contained news, did not dare to interrupt him. But after several minutes had passed, Johnson raised his massive head and quite suddenly fired a question at the operator: "Well?"

The operator almost flinched. "It's Floyd," he said. "He thinks he's on the trail of something."

"Let me talk to him." Johnson rose slowly from his chair and crossed to the radio bench.

The operator, his earphones in place, flicked on a switch and spoke into the microphone: "CS-1 calling CS-4. CS-1 calling CS-4. Come in, CS-4. Over." He flipped the speaker switch.

The black screen vibrated and from the interior of the loudspeaker floated the strangely transmuted voice of Deputy Glynn: "This is CS-4, this is CS-4. When the hell do I get off for lunch? I'm sick of fig newtons. Where's Johnson? Over."

Johnson reached for the microphone. "Floyd," he said, "this is Johnson. Where are you and what've you found? Over."

The voice in the speaker: "Izzat you, Morey? Hi. I'm out at

this Paul M. Bondi's place. I'm parked in his backyard. There's nobody here right now. The house ain't locked; I've searched it. It looks like a woman and a kid is livin in it now—must be Bondi's wife and kid. No sign of the cowboy guy in the house— except there's *three* dirty dishes in the sink and *three* forks and two cups and a glass. But I found somethin outside: bootprints. Somebody's been walkin around here with cowboy boots on. A full-grown man, I mean. Wasn't this Burns guy supposed to be wearin boots? How long do I have to stay out here? Morey? Over."

"Look, Floyd," Johnson said to the microphone, "is there a horse around there? Or any sign of a horse? Or a barn or a pasture? Over."

"I don't see no horse now but I sure stepped in the sign of one not ten minutes ago. You think this guy has a horse?"

"Is there a barn out there?"

"No. Just a little shed full of hay, and a corral with two goats. No place big enough for a horse except the corral or the house. Why, do you think this guy is on a horse? Over."

"Maybe. Are there neighbors around there?"

"Not many but there's some. You think he's hidin in one of the neighbor's houses?"

"No. Now listen, Floyd: go around to those neighbors and ask them if they've seen anything unusual lately. Ask them if they've seen a man on horseback in the last two or three days. Ask everyone within half a mile of the place until you get some information. Do you get me? Over."

"Okay, Morey. Anything else? Over."

"That's all. Over and out."

The radio operator closed the speaker switch and lifted

his earphones. Johnson set the microphone down on the table, sniffed moodily, staring at the blank wall beyond the operator's head, then went back to his chair and sat down to wait. To wait, to scratch, to reflect and trouble himself.

The little red jewel on the receiver panel started to flash. The operator lowered his earphones, knocked down a toggle switch and listened; after a moment he reached for his pencil and started taking notes.

"Is that Glynn?" said Johnson. The operator shook his head. Johnson turned back to his hands and troubles. He heard a jet plane scream by far overhead and felt a twinge of envy. He might have . . . He tried to think of something else. What was it his wife wanted?

The radio operator turned toward him. "Morey?" Johnson did not look up. The operator said: "They got one of the Navajos."

Johnson sighed and rubbed his ear.

"State Police found em," the operator said. "They was chasin this pickup out west of Grants. When they stopped it two squaws jumped out of the back and started running across the boondock. They shot one in the leg and the other got away. These two Navajos was dressed up like squaws."

"Okay," said Johnson.

"Thought you might like to know," the operator said. He waited, opened his mouth again—"One down, two to go." Johnson made no reply. After a moment the operator turned back to his comic book.

They waited for twenty-five minutes. Then the message came from Glynn. "This is CS-1, this is CS-1," the operator was saying; "come in, CS-4. Over." He switched on the speaker, while Johnson rose ponderously and hauled himself toward the microphone.

Through a haze of static came Glynn's voice, sifted and tinny: "Hello CS-1, this is CS-4. I found out somethin. Is Johnson listening? I found out somethin very interesting. Over."

"This is Johnson," the sheriff said. "Go ahead, Floyd. Over."

"None of the people around Bondi's house would tell me anything," the radio voice said, "but a little way down the street there's a little grocery store run by a man named Hedges. He says that the day before yesterday, around noon, he saw a man on a chestnut mare ride around the corner from the west, go down the dirt road and turn into Bondi's lane. He says that about three, four hours later he saw the same man walk past going toward town. And he says that the mare was in the goat corral all day yesterday. He says that he didn't see or hear any horse this morning; he doesn't know what happened to the horse. What'll I do now? Over."

"What did the man look like, Floyd? Over."

"Hedges says the man was tall and skinny, he had an ugly face and he looked vicious and dangerous. Says he wore a black hat. Over."

"I see." Johnson sighed and said nothing for a minute or so. Then: "Floyd—you must be out on the edge of things there, huh? No houses north or east of Bondi's place, are there? How about it?"

"There's nothin at all east of here. No road, no houses. There's a few more houses along the road goin north. Pretty scattered. Over."

"All right, Floyd, you check those houses to the north you haven't already been to and find out if anybody saw or heard a man go by on horseback sometime this morning. Maybe before daylight. And if you don't get any information that way here's what I want you to do: I want you to go back to Bondi's place, get out of your car, go to that corral and see if you can find tracks going off east toward the mountains. How's the dust blowin out there? Over."

"It's pretty windy but there's not too much dust in the air yet."

"Fine. You look for those tracks. You know what hoofprints look like, Floyd. If you don't find a trail right away you keep walkin in half circles, bigger and bigger, until you do. You think you can do that? Over."

"Sure, Morey. If he took that horse anywhere east of the city I'll find the tracks, don't you worry. Okay?"

"That's all, Floyd. Over and out." Johnson set the microphone down on the table and went to the window again and stared out, hands clasped behind his back. There was nothing to see out there, of course, nothing new—the hardware store, the First National Bank on whose barren wall someone had scrawled JESUS SAVES, the office building, the passing cars and human bodies, the streetlights, the street itself—all of this had long ago lost any but the most perfunctory interest for his eyes. He looked at them without seeing them; he looked at the street as into a mirror.

The telephone. The mechanical wrangle of the telephone drilled into his consciousness: grudgingly he turned and went back to his desk. He picked up the receiver: "Yes?"

His secretary said: "U.S. Marshal's office, sir."

"All right, put em on."

"That you, Morey? This is Daugherty. Say, you've got a Federal prisoner in your establishment by the name of Bondi, haven't you? I hope you still have him."

Johnson frowned, then answered slowly: "He's still here. You want him now?"

"That's right. I've got orders to pack him off to Leavenworth. I'm sending a man over in the morning to pick him up. Is he in good shape for shipment?"

"He's all right."

"Fine. I'll have a man over there in the morning, about nine o'clock. You'll have Bondi's papers ready and everything, won't you?"

"Yes."

"Thanks, Morey. I'll be seeing you. So long now."

"So long." Johnson hung up.

The radio operator glanced up from his comic book. "Was that the Marshal?"

Johnson grunted. He stood for a while by his desk, vacant-eyed, scratching his ribs; his shirttail was coming out. Then he spoke to the operator. "You go upstairs," he said: "Tell this fella Bondi if he wants to make any phone calls he can do it this afternoon. Tell him he's leaving in the morning. And tell him he can have visitors this afternoon if he wants any. Between three and four—no earlier, no later. I'll watch the radio."

The operator put down his comic book and slowly, reluctantly, got up out of his chair. "It ain't visitors' day," he mumbled.

"Don't fret over it," Johnson said.

"Sure, Morey. Okay, Morey." The radio operator went out.

Johnson sat down, waiting and scratching. The public telephone rang again. He let it ring several times, then picked it up. "Yes?"

"Mrs. Johnson calling, sir."

He closed his eyes and slid far down into his chair. "Okay," he said.

The brittle, galvanized voice of his wife: "Morlin? Is that you, Morlin?"

"Yes. What do you want?"

"You don't sound right, Morlin. Are you sick?"

"What do you want?"

"I just wanted to remind you to pick up Elinor and to get an extension cord before you come home. You haven't forgotten, have you? Remember: Elinor, five-thirty—"

"—school, extension cord."

"That's right, Morlin. Goodby, dear."

He hung up, sighed deeply and slid farther down in his chair, picking at his nose. He hoisted his feet to the desktop, crossed them, and backed his squawking swivel chair solidly against the wall under the picture of President Harry S Truman. He sat motionless for some time, bulky and noiseless and self-absorbed as a praying monk.

The radio operator returned. "I told him," he said. "They're lettin him make a call now." He resumed his seat by the radio equipment.

"How did he look?" said Johnson.

"How did he *look?*"

"That's right; does he look all right?"

"Oh." The operator considered. "Sure, he looks all right—no marks on him. He walks good enough. Only thing wrong with him was, he didn't look very happy."

"He didn't say anything about Gutierrez? No complaints?"

"He hardly said a word, Morey. He was hardly even polite."

Johnson asked no more questions. He folded his hands on

his stomach and stared at the toes of his boots. His secretary came in and picked up the letters and papers in the box on his desk. "Where's Hernandez?" Johnson said to her: "I haven't seen him all day."

"Mr. Hernandez left early this morning," the girl said. "He's investigating a knife incident. Somebody got it last night."

"Where was this? I didn't even hear about it."

"Lead Hill." The girl returned to her outer office. Johnson stared at his boots and thoughtfully rubbed his nose.

"Did you hear about Old Heavy?" the operator said. "Somebody called him out on a knife job once."

"Who's Old Heavy?"

"Wallis—the coroner they got out in Lead Hill." The operator paused, watching Johnson for a sign of interest. There was none but he went on: "Old Heavy got called out one day to look at this knife job. He drove to the place and there was this dead Mex layin face down in the middle of the street with a knife in his back. Old Heavy didn't even get out of his car: 'Suicide,' he said, and turned around and drove home." The operator smiled eagerly at Johnson but there was no response. "Didn't even get out of the car," the operator repeated, lost in admiration.

Johnson made no answer, relapsing again into the profound state of abstraction which had enveloped him most of the afternoon. He was interrupted several times by telephone calls from indignant citizens wanting to know what he was doing about the escape of the Anarcho-Red and the two Indian sex-fiends; but after each interruption he seemed only to sink deeper into his morose cerebrations. He still scratched himself, but infrequently.

The red eye twinkled on the radio panel. The operator closed his comic book—a new one—and went into action. In a few moments the spectral voice of Deputy Glynn was issuing from the loudspeaker, while Johnson listened gravely, his big red left hand clutching the neck of the microphone. Glynn was saying, in his faltering but earnest manner: ". . . . Nobody saw or heard a horse at all. No sign of a horse along the road. In either direction. So like you said I went back to Bondi's goat corral and looked around. Plenty of hoofprints there. I looked all around like you said, Morey, and pretty soon I found a trail. Goin straight from the back porch of the house toward the big mother ditch. I followed the trail to the ditch and across a little wooden bridge and to a field. The ground's so hard and dry there I couldn't make out much from there on. But I did find where somebody cut a hole in the barbed wire fence at the edge of the mesa. A new cut—no rust on the ends of the wires. I think this must be our man, Morey, if you're sure he's ridin a horse. Whatteya want me to do now? Over."

"What direction do the tracks go in, Floyd? East?"

"Yeah, that's right, they go east."

"Toward the mountains?"

"Yeah . . . straight toward the mountains. Say—you think that's where he's hidin, Morey? Want me to drive out there?"

Johnson scratched his chin; his chin and jaw were gray with the resurgent roots of whiskers. "What time is it?" he said to the operator.

The operator looked at his wristwatch. "Almost four-thirty," he said.

Johnson spoke into the microphone. "Come on home, Floyd, we'll go out there with a search party in the morning. That's too big an area for one man to cover, even you. Come on in and get something to eat. Do you hear me? Over."

"Okay, Morey, I hear you. I'll be there in twenty minutes. Over."

"Over and out." Johnson went back to his desk and sat down. He scratched his neck, while the radio operator waited for him to speak.

The operator waited for several minutes and then, impatient, spoke first himself: "Ain't you gonna send anybody out there to look around, Morey? He might get away."

Johnson did not answer immediately. Then he said: "If Burns has gone out there to the mountains it's because he wants to hide for a few days, which means he'll still be there tomorrow. If he hasn't gone to the mountains there's no use lookin for him there." The operator was silent. Johnson said: "You might put in a few more calls, though. Call the Forest Ranger at El Sangre station and ask him to check on any campfires not burning in an authorized campground. After you do that radio the relay station up on the rim and ask them to tell us if they see a campfire down below in one of the inner canyons. That's about all, I guess." The operator scribbled notes, while Johnson went on: "You might ask the State Police to send a plane out that way this evening, if they get a chance. And tell them we'll need a plane and maybe some other help in the morning. You got all that?"

"Sure, Morey." The operator pulled his telephone close.

Johnson stood up then and stretched his arms toward the ceiling. He lowered his arms and made an attempt to stuff his shirt back into his pants and then forgot about it, wandering instead toward the window.

The wind had died, gone away, blown south to Mexico. The sky was clear now, vivid as wine and deep with a premonition of night. Far beyond the city, reaching for twenty miles north and south in an unbroken five-thousand foot wall of granite, the Sangre Mountains rose up amid their rubble of foothills and crags and canyons, the naked rock luminous and golden in the slanting light.

Johnson stared at the mountains. That's where he is, he thought; there he waits. Out there among the rocks and yellowpine, watching the city. Might just take a run out there after supper.

He knew the time had come to call Barker. His mind was bent on decision, finality. He went slowly to his desk, put his hand on the private telephone: the benign serious wistful face of Harry Truman watched him from the wall. Johnson raised the telephone receiver to his ear and dialed a number—two one two one four ... He waited ...

"Rio Bravo Development Company."

"I'd like to talk with Bob Barker."

"Just a moment, sir ..." The feminine voice faded away, succeeded presently by the cordial, good-humored, sympathetic tones of Barker:

"Howdy. This is Bob Barker. What can I do for you?"

"This is Johnson, Bob. I just wanted to tell you that I'm backing out." Johnson waited for an answer; there was none. He said: "I don't want any part in it, Bob. You'll have to find somebody else."

Still there was no answer; then from the other end of the line came the sound of a small epiglottal explosion: "—Christ, Morey! Jesus! You can't! You can't turn your back on half a million dollars! Have you gone crazy?"

"I've made up my mind," said Johnson. "Good—"

"Hey, wait a minute!"

"Goodby, Bob." And Johnson hung up. He scratched his armpits, frowning soberly to conceal his intense inner satisfaction. He went to the hatrack and put on his Stetson. He said to the radio operator, who had completed his calls and was also getting ready to leave—"How about that airplane?"

"Plane's grounded this evening but they'll work with us tomorrow," the operator said, sticking an arm into his leather jacket.

"Are you going home with Glynn?"

"Yeah, I guess so, if he ever gets here."

"Tell him to be here at six tomorrow morning. That goes for you too. We might have a little manhunt tomorrow."

"Okay, Morey."

Before he left the office Johnson paused again by the window for a final look at the mountains; he scanned the bartizans of rock glowing pink and gold under the evening sun, the frosted rim glittering like a coronet against the dark violet sky. Beyond the city, beyond the plain, miles away. He gazed at the mountains, thinking: So that's where you are, Jack Burns? Out there. A shade of melancholy passed over his mind, a sweet and fragile sadness. Alone, you poor simple bastard—We'll find you . . .

He stepped toward the door, buttoning his coat. "So long," he said to the radio operator.

"So long, Morey." The operator sat down on the edge of his table to wait for Deputy Glynn.

CHAPTER 14

. . . The great cliffs leaned up against the flowing sky, falling through space as the earth revolved, turning amber as whisky in the long-reaching lakes of light from the evening sun. But the light had no power to soften the jagged edges and rough-spalled planes of the granite; in that clear air each angle and crack cast a shadow as harsh, clean, sharp, real, as the rock itself—so that though they had endured as they were for ten million years, the cliffs held the illusion of a terrible violence suddenly arrested, paralyzed in time, latent with power.

At the foot of the cliffs were the little stony hills, the incidental rubble that had fallen and merged as the earth split open and shoved one edge above the other. Around the hills were litters of boulders, the remains of the ancient pulverized landscape, and a complicated but systematic pattern of ditches, gullies, ravines and canyons that conducted whatever water might fall toward the valley and the river below.

Near one of these hills, beside a sandy wash, in the shadow of the cliffs, a man had once built a house, using the materials that destruction and catastrophe had spawned—stone, mud, wood. The house remained, though the man was gone: now the windows were blank and empty like the cavities of a skull, long since stripped of glass, if they had ever held glass, and the doorway, leaning in a curious way to the east—for the house had shifted without moving from its foundation—was without a door; the rain had undercut the slanting walls, and the flat roof, sagging on rotten beams, half open to the sky, functioned now only as a home for finches and spiders and centipedes and for one stray buckhorn cactus that had somehow taken root in the sand and decayed pine above the front doorway.

To the rear of this ruin was the arroyo, sandy and dust-dry except for a thread of water trickling from a tiny seep-like spring near the front of a rock ledge. Three cottonwoods, great towering plants in this arid zone of cactus and greasewood, were huddled together like gossiping old women around the miniature spring, their buried mouths sucking moisture up from the sand and the aquiferous limestone below. The modest overflow from the spring dripped over the lip of the rock and spread along the base of the ledge, soaking through rather than flowing over the sand; for a stretch of about ten yards there was enough water to support a little grass, some watercress and cattails, a few stunted willows. Beyond this patch of green was a delta of damp sand, thoroughly chopped up by the hooves of deer and cattle, where the last of the water disappeared, its long journey from near the mountain's rim five thousand feet above, beginning under a pocket of snow in some pine grove, falling from there down through ravines and gorges to the canyon, from one climate and world to a greatly different one, ending here in silent evaporation and a vague dispersal underground.

The leaves of the cottonwoods, dry and fragile and lemon-yellow, stirred briefly, rattled and rustled together, and several drifted to the ground. A tufted bluejay flew darkly from one tree to the next, lit on a slender branch and shook more of the dead leaves free.

Below the trees, near the red-stemmed willows, a picketed horse grazed industriously on the strip of grass, switching its tail now and then at a few idle, indifferent flies.

The cowboy was not far away. He lay in the sun near a boulder on the far side of the arroyo, away from the abandoned house; his head was propped against his saddle, and the floppy black hat covered most of his face, revealing only the bearded chin and the mouth, the latter relaxed, partly open, emitting at regular intervals the deep prolonged sighs of sleep. His property was close at hand—the saddlebags, the rifle in its scabbard, the bedroll, all still attached to the saddle itself; while the guitar and the bridle hung from handy stubs on a nearby juniper.

A raven circled above the arroyo and the spring, descended and landed with a cumbersome flapping of wings in the top of the highest cottonwood, shattering a few leaves and sending a wave of tremors through all the others. It spread its black wings, wobbling somewhat on its perch, and bent its head to search for lice. The bluejay in the adjoining tree squawked, chattered, and then flew away. After that, except for the routine murmur of a few insects near the spring, the arroyo was allowed to resume its original and fundamental silence.

Burns slept on, his hands across his belly, his legs apart and fully extended over the ground.

Ten miles away and a thousand feet below, the gleaming river wound through the valley and through the dark ragged crawl of the city and beyond the city into the far haze of the south. The

city steamed and glimmered faintly, smoky and alive and obscure, while a few airplanes droned in circles above it like flies
over a poisonous dump. West of the river the volcanoes, black as
obsidian against the light, cast long tapering shadows over the
tawny skin of the plain, and to the southwest, more than sixty
miles away, the jagged peaks of Thieves' Mountain burned into
the southern sky with a strange vaporish flaming purple, as if
illuminated from within by furnaces of radiant energy.

The raven launched itself awkwardly, like a vivified scarecrow, out of the cottonwood tree and flapped up into the static
yawning vacancy of the canyon beyond the arroyo and the
ruined house.

The silence flowed back in the wake of whispering echoes.

A lizard scurried down the face of the big rock near Burns,
stopped for a moment to watch him, pushing itself up and down
on its forelegs like an exercising athlete, and then hurried jerkily
on and disappeared under the edge of the rock.

The long evening shadows crept over the sleeping man,
darkening his boots, his knees, his lean overalled thighs . . .

Something woke him: partly the change in temperature,
partly the sensation of time elapsed and lost, partly fear—he
heard something which was not a normal element in the audi-
tory character of the arroyo—the birdcries, the leaves, the insects, the movements and feeding of his horse, the sound of his
own breathing. He opened his eyes and reached cautiously for
his rifle at the same time; however, he did not immediately pull
the rifle from its case—when his groping fingers contacted the
cool metal and smooth walnut of butt and stock he was satisfied
and let his hand rest there. Rolling over on one side but not getting up, he concentrated his energies on an intensive inspection
of the visible and audible world around him.

Three Virginia deer stood at the head of the arroyo. At first he did not see them; uncertain as to where the sound had come from, he looked west, down the arroyo and toward the dirt road that ran north and south, paralleling the mountains; then swung his gaze around in a slow half-circle—southwest, across the arroyo and toward the city, south, past the old ruin and along the base of the foothills, southeast, where the great looming wall of the canyon blocked his vision at once, and at last up the slope, eastward, up into the arroyo past the cotton-woods and the spring and the tiers of eroded rock to the little saddle in the ridge that separated the arroyo from the main canyon. And there, among the junipers and cactus and boulders, he spotted the three motionless deer.

Three does, less than fifty yards away, looking as insubstantial and ephemereal as shadows, suggesting even in their alert stillness the grace and silence of flight;—Burns stared at them and suddenly realized that they had not seen him—they were watching the horse below the spring. He tightened his grip on the butt of the rifle and slowly, with patience and extreme care, drew it from the scabbard and passed it under his chest and into the crook of his left arm. Now he had to lever a cartridge from the magazine into the firing chamber, an operation that could not be performed without a minimal clicking and mesh of metal parts. Of course the deer heard the noise: their ears stiffened and their heads swung slightly, in perfect unison, toward the man. But Burns was already in position, taking a bead on the foremost of the three, aiming at a certain vital point on the withers, just under the skin, where the spinal column became part of the neck. A difficult target, even at that range: if he hit too low he would destroy good meat and perhaps only cripple the animal; if he fired an inch too high he would miss. Therefore he did not hurry but waited for a perfect alignment of notched read sight, beaded front sight, and the invisible nexus of nerves on the crest of the doe. When it came he settled into it, holding his breath easily, and began very slowly to squeeze the trigger.

The crash never came; before he could fire he heard a shake and whinny from the mare, and the deer were gone, vanishing instantly, fading like ghosts into the golden jumble of boulders and the gold-tinged olivedrab of the chaparral.

Burns let the hammer down with his thumb; he looked reproachfully down into the arroyo at the mare. "Whisky, old girl," he murmured, "where's your hoss sense? You sure let me down this time, you know that?" The mare stared at him, snorted, and shook her mane again. "Don't try to bushwah me," Burns said: "I heard you." He looked sadly up the arroyo toward the saddle over which the deer had disappeared. He decided that he might as well go up there and have a look, however; the deer might not have been badly frightened—besides they were apparently in search of water, which meant that they would not run far. And he needed meat; if he did not get it now he would have to get it tomorrow.

He got to his feet, brushed the sand and ants from his shirt, and looked around again. He saw nothing which should have frightened the deer, and concluded that they must have been startled by Whisky giving a sudden jerk on the picket rope. He pushed his saddle and the gear fastened to it hard up against the overhanging wall of the boulder, then went down into the arroyo to check the stake and rope. He drove the stake in a little farther with his bootheel, had himself a quick drink at the spring, and started up the arroyo with the carbine cradled in his left arm. Pulling himself up over the ledges and shelves of rock that made the arroyo something like a stairway for giants, he was annoyed by the scraping and clashing of his spurs and knelt down to take them off. He left them there on the bare rock, in a place which he felt sure he could find again, and went on up.

After climbing over a stratum of compressed shale near the head and at one side of the arroyo, he found himself among the runty trees where he had seen the deer. Now he proceeded more slowly and carefully, and as he approached the crest of the saddle went down on his hands and knees and crawled the last few feet to the top. There he halted. Below him was the mouth of the canyon, to his right the canyon itself going steeply up, shelf after shelf, toward the main bulk of the mountain, and across from him on the opposite slope, moving slowly upward among the rock and brush, were the three deer. As he had expected, they had not gone far. But they were well out of range, and moving away. He decided to follow and stalk them.

He tested the wind, such as it was, and found it favoring neither him nor his quarry but drifting up the canyon between them. He advanced over the saddle, crouching under the limbs of juniper and pin oak, and moved down onto the slope below, where the growth was denser, this being the northern snow-holding side of the ridge. He did not go very far down but stayed on the slope, moving quietly but swiftly among the small grubby trees in a direction paralleling the progress of the deer.

A near-silent world: he heard nothing but his own breathing, the faint scrape of his boots on stone and gravel, the whispering boughs of the juniper, the rattle of the oak, the vague, distant and intermittent whistle, like a bad flute, of a mourning dove. Over everything, stone and plant and animal, over the canyon wall, over the face of the mountain far above, the sun radiated its patina of warm, rye-golden, evening light.

Burns felt eager, hungry, intensely aware of every shade,

sound, smell and movement in his environment; a keen convergence of his powers and intentions made each step seem vital, made the actions of his limbs consensual with the purpose in his mind. For the first time in nearly two days and nights he felt himself to be a whole and living creature, a man again and not a derelict stumbling through a mechanical world he could not understand.

Something burst into action above him, on his right; he glanced up and saw the blurred gray rump of a jackrabbit bounding over a log to crash and disappear into the snapping brush beyond.

He moved on, crouching a little as he advanced from tree to tree, circling around open areas where the cover was too meagre, making good time on occasional stretches of almost level ground where piñon trees had forced out the juniper and scrub oak. He had gained rapidly on the deer, though they were still out of range, perhaps three hundred yards away. So long as they continued to move he could not hope to get much closer without attracting their attention; only when they stopped would he have time for the slow, painstaking stealth of a stalking approach.

The ground tilted more steeply under his feet as the slope began to merge with the nearly perpendicular wall of the canyon. He had to angle downwards now, toward the rock ledges and sand floor of the canyon. As he worked his way down, going slow and carefully, he watched the deer: they had a similar choice to make—climbing back and up over the crest of the ridge or descending into the canyon. They chose to go down—and Burns smiled gratefully.

But he had another worry: light and time. He knew by the amber richness of the light that the sun was low in its arc; he looked back once to the west and saw the sun was low in its arc; he looked back once to the west and saw the sun about to fall into the crater of a volcano, separated from the black horizon by only a sliver of yellow sky. The river and the city—what he could see of its northern extension—were already caught in a shadow that was now sweeping on a broad front across the mesa, toward him and the shining mountain. While he watched the sun dropped lower, suddenly, like the twitching of the hour hand on a big clock, and the silhouette of the volcano cut a chunk from its blinding gold disc.

He turned and continued his diagonal descent, going forward across the face of the slope as much as the terrain permitted. He saw the deer still going down, headed apparently for a thicket of willows and bear grass that darkened a pocket in the floor of the canyon. Probably another spring or seep of water there, he noted, and good cover for the deer as well. But the place might also be a trap: the pocket of green ended at the base of a twenty foot water-slide of smooth bare polished stone.

He went more slowly than ever now, though the light passed far above his head and the shadow of the horizon surrounded him. He saw the three deer spring onto the sand of the canyon floor and merge, not quite totally disappearing, with the thicket of willows and high grass. He advanced another hundred yards or so on his feet, taking advantage of every bit of cover, and then, being within three hundred yards of his prey, he went down on his hands and knees and crawled forward, taking the most extreme pains to avoid being seen or heard, stopping often to listen and to study the arrangement of the rocks and cactus and trees ahead. He was now well down on the slope of the canyon, not far from the floor, and as he was anxiously aware, upwind from the deer: at any moment they might catch his scent, leave off their grazing and drinking and go leaping upward across the far slope and over the ridge and not stop until the smell of man was left miles behind. But there was nothing Burns could do about it now; hours would be required in climbing up the slope, going around behind the canyon wall and coming down again from above and farther up the canyon. Already the twilight was spreading over the canyon; thousands of feet above, the rim reflected the final rays of the sun. He had to get closer to the deer as quickly as it was strategically possible and when he was close enough, shoot accurately—there would be little chance for a second shot.

He crept ahead over the stony slope, over dead limbs of piñon, under the low boughs of junipers and around the cholla and yucca near the canyon floor. There he sank down flat on his belly and inched his way forward, keeping his head and butt down, pulling the rifle along by his side, until he was within a hundred yards of the deer.

Only then did he estimate that he was close enough for a decent shot—considering the now-treacherous quality of the light. He peered around the righthand corner of a rock and stared into the clump of willows until he could make out clearly and with certainty the outline of two deer—the third was hidden, probably lying down in the grass. Very gently he pulled back the hammer of the rifle, pressing the breech against his chest to muffle the click of the gunlock. Even then one of the does seemed to hear it; she lifted her head quickly and faced toward him. He was not yet ready to aim and fire, the carbine on its side and partly underneath his body; he waited for the doe to forget the sound and lower its head again. He had to wait about five minutes before that happened; then he was able to slide the rifle forward a little more, get the butt into his shoulder and the stock under his cheek. He aimed.

Both deer raised their heads, alert and sniffing, and took a few steps toward the far slope. The third deer sprang up out of the grass and then all three began to move, not fast yet but with the tense electric grace of creatures about to break into sudden motion. Burns cursed in silent despair, unable in that gloom to follow his target over the sights; he rose to his knees, swearing quietly, and just as the deer were about to break and run, he shivered the silence of the canyon with a sharp whistle. Instantly they stopped, all three of them, and stared at him in mild surprise. He aimed at the nearest, at a point just behind its shoulder, and fired. The crash of the discharge rang through the air, shocking in its violence; at the same moment the doe leaped forward with spasmodic energy, going from sight behind a boulder, while the two others danced up the slope and vanished in seconds. Echoes of the shot were falling from every direction as Burns ran forward, rifle in his hands, ejecting the empty shell and reloading as he ran. He crossed the canyon floor near the thicket, panting a little, his boots crunching into the damp sand, and scrambled up among the rocks and cane cactus on the other side.

Behind the big rock, sprawled on its side and quite still, he found the doe—a small tan faded heap of hide and flesh and bone dropped carelessly on the ground. He uncocked the carbine and set it down, pulled the jackknife from his pocket, opened it and stepped close to the deer. Although certain it was dead, he approached it from above, away from the sharp little hooves. He knelt and raised the doe's head with its big glazed bewildered eyes and pressed the point of his blade into the warmth and softness of its throat. There he held it for a moment, not yet pushing through the skin.

"Sleep long, little sister," he said softly, holding the warm head on his lap. "Don't be mad at me—I'm gonna make real good use of you. Yes sir . . ." He forced the blade through the skin and cut straight across the throat; the warm bright blood came gushing out with alacrity, as though meant to spill on that barren ground. Burns placed his hand under the cut and caught a palmful of the blood and drank it; then he lowered the head and raised the hindquarters, speeding the drain.

When the flow of blood began to lessen he rolled the doe on its back and gutted it, making a straight incision from the ribs down to the pelvic bone, taking care not to puncture any of the internal organs. He laid the knife down, spread the cut hide apart, and carefully and tenderly removed the paunch— severing and setting aside the liver—and handling the slippery mass gingerly, like a paper bag bloated with water, he dragged it some distance away and covered it with brush. He went back to the carcass, squatted down, wiped some of the blood and slime from his hands onto the hide, and ate part of the raw, hot, smoking liver. When he had had enough he threw the rest up the hill and looked around for a tree to hang the carcass from. There was nothing around him now but boulders and cactus; he saw that he would have to pack the doe back across the canyon floor and up to one of the piñons on the other slope.

He got up and walked a few steps away and urinated, rubbing the back of his neck with his free hand and listening to the crickets down in the willows. The twilight had deepened into evening; a solution of dense violet light, like an intangible rain, filled the canyon from wall to wall.

Burns went back to the deer, lifted it over his shoulders, picked up his rifle and stumbled down the slope, across the sand and up the other side to the tallest of the nearby piñons. He opened his knife again and cut a stake about two feet long, sharpening each end, then spread apart the doe's hind legs and braced them with the stake, piercing the shanks with the pointed tips. Now he could have used a piece of rope; since he had none he broke a branch from the limb he had chosen and hung the carcass to the stub. The limb bent slightly under the weight and the doe's fore-hooves, swinging a little, grazed the black carpet of needles on the ground.

The cowboy built a small fire next, his mind on supper—he had eaten just enough of the liver to really rouse his appetite. He brushed off a level spot among the rocks, pulled up some dry bunch grass and crushed it into a ball, sprinkled with pine needles and shreds of bark and a handful of broken twigs, and added a flaming match. When the tinder caught fire, crackling brightly and sending up a thin gray fuse of smoke, he got up and prowled around for a while gathering fuel—dead juniper, a few skeletal stalks of cane cactus. He broke these into short lengths, set several on the flames and in a few minutes had a comfortable little squaw fire blazing away.

He was thirsty; for the first time in over an hour he discovered himself with nothing immediate and urgent to do, so he went down to the willow thicket and through it to the rock face. He found water dripping from fissures in the rock, filling a natural stone basin on the first ledge. He put one hand on the rock, still faintly warm from the sunlight, and bent down and drank, sparingly, and then went back to his fire and the deer, brushing drops of water out of his whiskers. As he approached, something black and awkward, like a ragged mop, rose out of the

piñon tree and paddled slowly away down the canyon, each ponderous stroke of its wings accompanied by a swish of air. Burns
cursed himself—tentatively—and hurried forward to examine
the interior of the carcass. He was relieved to find no sign of the
scavenger anywhere on the meat; he had returned in time to save
the deer, not from much actual pillage, of course, but from what
he considered a particularly odious kind of defilement.

The fire had burned down to a hot, incandescent heap of
charcoal; Burns reached into the abdominal cavity of the deer
with both hands and cut away a long tender roll of the loins and
laid it on the fiery coals. While the meat seared and crackled,
gracing the air with its fragrance, he went back to the carcass,
cut out the heart, the lungs and the diaphragm, threw the latter
two organs away and set the heart down on the edge of the fire,
intending to roast it. He cut a chunk from the half-raw half-
burnt sirloin and ate it while considering what to do next.

The evening thickened about him, a lavender fog of gloom;
he began to think that there was not much time or light left
for moving camp—that is, for loading his gear on the mare and
leading her up the canyon. It would be quite dark by the time
he could climb back down to the spring and the cottonwoods
where he had left her; coming back up with only a few stars
for light would be a difficult and exhausting task. On the other
hand, to carry the deer down there was out of the question; he
had no intention of jerking all that meat in a place where the
smoke could be seen from miles away in several directions.

He ate some of the sirloin, leaving most of it still on the
coals, got up off his heels and staggered down to the canyon
floor. Working fast, he cut and broke off a big solid armful of
greasewood, scrambled back up the steep slope to the piñon

and packed his rough materials into the deer's gaping bellycase, making it a firm, thorny, bristling mass that only a fly could penetrate. That done, he went back to the fire, squatted down and ate the rest of the seared meat, feeding himself steadily and seriously but not fast; he took his time.

The fire was low, a flicker and shimmer of red, blue, violet embers; he shoved the tough heart into the center of the fire and with a stick heaped coals over it. He added a few knots of juniper, then lay back on the ground, half-gorged, immensely satisfied, and sleepy. There was only one thing more that he desired: he searched through his pockets for tobacco, found the pipe and tobacco that Jerry had given him, and filled the pipe. He sat up again, leaned toward the fire, picked up a burning coal and dropped it on top of the bowl of the pipe. He puffed slowly, tasting the unfamiliar, highly aromatic tobacco with caution; he decided that he liked it, stretched out on the ground again, and smoked freely.

Looking up at the strip of sky between the canyon walls, he saw a faint blinking formation of stars that looked like the Seven Sisters—the Pleiades—and this reminded him that the night was coming on. He belched, lying on his back, and considered the possibility of not going down after the mare and his equipment. He would miss his sleepingbag a little, if he did not go down, but then it would not be the first time he had slept on the ground and covered himself with nothing but his shirt and his own back. But there were two serious disadvantages in leaving things as they were: first, the possibility that his horse or gear might be discovered by some Ranger or prowling police officer; second, the certainty that if he waited till dawn to get his outfit he would find the deer riddled with blowflies when he came back up the canyon.

Burns puffed again on the pipe, watching the gray smoke drift toward the stars, picked some fragments of meat out of his teeth, and then sat up, grunting. He straightened the hat on his head, picked up his Winchester and hauled himself heavily to his feet; he started down the canyon, weaving a little in the uncertain light, belching again and wiping his greasy mouth on his shirtsleeve. A locust, dry and brittle as glass, rattled out of the brush and struck him on the chest; he slapped at it in surprise, broke it and brushed it off, then shuffled on over the firm sand, following the narrow winding floor of the canyon. He came to the first big rock ledge and climbed, slid and jumped down the face of it, landing in greasewood and sand again; he marched past a stand of pampas grass, silvery and graceful, and around a bend in the canyon, and suddenly, unexpectedly, the view opened wide and the whole western world lay before him: the canyon dropping down step by step like an imperial stairway for gods, the gaunt purple foothills, the mesa rolling out for miles, the faint gleam of the river, the vast undulant spread of the city ten miles away, transformed by the evening dusk into something fantastic and grand and lovely, a rich constellation of jewels glimmering like the embers of a fire—and beyond the city and west mesa and the five volcanoes another spectacle, a garish and far more immense display of clouds and color and dust and light against a bottomless, velvet sky. Burns stopped for a moment to stare and admire, belched gently, and continued his descent.

Half an hour later he entered the deep gloom under the cottonwoods. He felt better: the city was now hidden from him by the banks of the arroyo, the great flare in the west had faded and died, his supper was partly digested—or at least well shaken down—and he could smell and hear his horse. Whisky greeted him with a complaining whinny. He walked close to her and patted her neck, while she nuzzled him in the chest. "Glad to see me, old girl?" he said; "You think I forgot you? No sirree; you just take it easy now." She snorted and tried to lick his face. "Easy, girl, easy; I'll feed you right off." He climbed out of the arroyo toward the slab of rock that sheltered his saddle and other belongings. He put the rifle in the scabbard, slung the guitar on his back, lifted the saddle to his shoulder and went back down to the mare. He filled his hat with a mixture of bran and barley from one of the saddlebags, about a peck, and set it in the sand before the mare. While she fed he threw on the saddlepad and the saddle and cinched the latigo down tight. He checked off his equipment: bedroll, saddlebags, canteen, rifle, rope—only the bridle was missing. He thought of the twenty-five pounds of jerked venison he was going to add to that burden in about three days and reminded himself that he would never get far toward Sonora without a packhorse. Tomorrow night, perhaps, he would go look for one; tonight he was going to get some sleep. He went back to the boulder above the arroyo and looked for the bridle; he could not find it and did not remember where he had left it until he took a second look at the scrubby juniper near the rock.

He was sliding down the loose bank of the arroyo when he heard a noise that stopped him in his tracks: the slam of a car door. He stood frozen, listening, while his muscles tensed with the instinct to flee. He could hear nothing more, nothing but the whine of cicada and from somewhere down the wash the occasional zoom and groan of a striking bullbat. Quickly but carefully he stepped over the stretch of sand that separated him from the mare, put one hand over her nostrils to prevent a possible nicker and with the other, letting the bridle fall, reached up over the saddle and slid the rifle out of its smooth worn case. He laid the barrel across the saddlebow, leaving the action uncocked, and waited.

For what seemed like a long time, perhaps five minutes, he heard nothing unusual. He could see very little, with the high bank of the arroyo directly in front of him, and the night closing in. Although his cover was good there in the darkness under the trees and between the walls of the arroyo, he was also painfully aware that if he should be discovered he would be pretty well boxed in, with escape possible only by a run down the wash toward the mesa. And he had not even had a chance to bridle the mare. Balancing the rifle with his forearm, he started to untie the rope around Whisky's neck that tethered her to the picket.

Then he saw and almost *felt* a beam of light that swung quickly through the air over his head, danced over the leaves of the cottonwoods and disappeared. A few seconds later he heard the crunch and scrape of gravel under heavy, slow feet. He heard no voices, however, and gratefully assumed that he probably had only one man to deal with. The footsteps approached the bank of the arroyo—while Burns stopped breathing, his thumb set firm on the hammer—and then halted, not coming to the edge. Burns listened; he watched the top of the bank but could see only the dark sky and the tall slender black silhouette of a yucca. From down the arroyo he heard the roar of a bullbat again.

Presently, after a minute or so, he heard the author of the footsteps tramping off, this time apparently in the direction of the old house. Listening intently, he heard the steps grow fainter, then the short crash of a dislodged rock, the rattle of a loose board. He lifted the carbine up from its rest on the saddlebow and wedged it between the cantle and the bedroll, and bent down and felt around on the sand for the bridle. He found it without trouble, disentangled the reins from the headstall, forced the bit into the mare's mouth, slipped the stall over her ears, and buckled the throatlatch. He was ready now; he reached for the carbine again and waited and listened, breathing, slowly and quietly.

He heard nothing, nothing human, for another five minutes; then came the second slam of an automobile door and he breathed more freely. When he heard an engine starting he left the mare and struggled up the bank of the arroyo, and saw the car at once, a dull lustre of enamel and chrome backing and turning on the old wagon road below the ruin. He watched the car get turned around, start forward and go bouncing down the rutted, twisting road, rocks clanging on its fenders, brakelights flicking on and off, the headlights sweeping over a forlorn landscape of boulders and cactus and crouching juniper.

When the car was well on its way back to the city, Burns returned to the mare, replaced the rifle in the scabbard, coiled his rope and tied it to the swell, stowed the picket in the bedroll, had one more drink at the spring, and climbed at last into the saddle, a very considerable pleasure which he had been anticipating for the last two or three hours; he forebore to think of the canyon ahead, where he would have to walk and lead over at least half the distance.

"Hup, girl," he said, and touched the mare with his heels. Fresh and eager, she started off as though bent on a free run through woods and green fields, and he had to rein her in at once to keep her to a walk. He rode up and around the ledge behind the spring, recovered his spurs, rode on up to the head of the arroyo and up the bank there, and over the saddle of the hill and into the canyon. Above him leaned the canyon walls, and above them the mountain with its granite cliffs; far above and beyond the mountain the stars began to appear, one by one, the chill blue glittering stars of the autumn.

Burns felt tired, very tired, and cold.

CHAPTER 15

AMARILLO, TEX.

Hinton drank the scalding coffee, gasped, and set the cup down. It had not been a bad night; he had managed to get some sleep, more than he usually did in a truckers' bunkhouse. He drank the rest of the coffee, then sank his chin in his hands and gazed out the window at the vast flat uninspiring desolation of Texas. The wind, rather brisk the day before in Oklahoma, was howling freely here, whipping the over-grazed, over-planted earth into clouds of bitter dust.

Nine-thirty: he should have been on his way three hours ago, with the rising sun and the gas station attendants. He knew that, he remembered it, but he did not move. Yes, he was late—not a mere three hours but nearly twenty-four, practically a whole day behind schedule. Four hundred and fifty miles to Duke City. And he didn't even care; nothing could have interested him less.

The last trip? He only half-believed it, smiling a little at the thought. The same resolve had come and gone a dozen times in the last three years; he was accustomed to it. How did he know? how could he say? There was the money to think of, not only the hills above the Shenandoah, or the interesting condition of his—the word seemed to him to be exactly correct—of his guts.

Speaking of guts, he thought, there was no point in eating breakfast this morning;—not that he was sick: simply didn't feel like it. Wasn't hungry. After all, he had been living for years on coffee, cigarettes, and diesel fumes.

He lit a cigarette.

I can take it, he told himself; I can last for another ten years, if I want to. He thought of the girl back in the aluminum diner on the edge of Oklahoma City, and smiled involuntarily. Twenty years, he said silently.—But why should I?

As a matter of fact he was full of sentimental notions now, indulging himself as he had not done for a long time. For the last day and night he had been haunted by the remembered image of that girl's face and hair, and by a hazy aureole of ambitions, adolescent dreams, memories and sensations surrounding the image. He felt himself suffering from—or being elevated by—an uncomfortable thawing and leavening of the sensibility. A peculiar strain of experience: he was disturbed both by the novelty and the old familiarity of it.

Hinton became aware of an intense irradiation of heat focussed on his lips; he removed the butt of the cigarette and crushed it in the ashtray. Might as well, he thought, might as well shove on. Tonight the haul will be over; I'll have time to think about these things at last. And of other matters I've been putting off for too long.

Getting up, he felt the odd rather interesting crimp somewhere deep in his abdomen: a tough knotted ache, firm and definite and not particularly painful—almost pleasant, in fact. Just a little baby, he thought; an old friend. He paid for his coffee—four cups—and stepped outside.

The wind screamed in his face, clawed at him, sucked his breath away. He staggered back, surprised and laughing, clutching at his cap. Between here and the North Pole, he recalled, nothing but *bob*wire. The wind rushed at him from the north, cold and powerful and thick with dust.... Baaaah! he muttered, spitting and grimacing; he held tightly to his cap and pushed his way through the massive torrent of air, stumbling a little, toward his truck. He squinted, looking for the silver and red—

ANOTHER LOAD OF *ACME* BATHROOM FIXTURES! AMERICA BUILDS FOR . . .

—Saw it, about where he thought he had left it. America builds, he said. The wind pushed and shoved at him, an angry gritty quarreling wind; he lurched forward, his jacket whipping and snapping about him, the collar flicking his mouth. Damnit, he said, staggering sideways. The power of the wind, he thought; he felt slightly ridiculous, fighting and falling his way through this semi-invisible flood. More dust in his teeth—the sharp pleasing alkaline flavor of South Dakota, the old dry horsechips taste of Kansas.

The wind embraced him, drew at his mouth, flayed his skin with its bitter ardor. He was laughing with excitement when he finally reached the truck.

CHAPTER 16

. . . Striding down the courthouse alley, the radio jeep and two dust-tan Chevrolets waiting for them—"Morey!" Six men bearing arms: pistols, shotguns, submachineguns. "Hey Morey!"

Johnson sat down at the wheel of the jeep. The radio operator got in beside him, wearing a pistol. "You fellas aren't coming with us," Johnson said. He loosened his belt a notch, trying to get comfortable in the cramped space between steering wheel and transmitter; Glynn and the three others stared at him.

"Morey!"

Johnson said: "Glynn, I want you and one of these fellas to go on up on the Rim. That's where you two are gonna spend your time. You have the binoculars?"

Glynn nodded. "Yeah—"

"You know how to get up there?"

"Aw Morey, for chrissake—!"

"Hey Morey!"

Johnson unwrapped a stick of chewing gum. "Well take off. Get up there as soon as you can and when you do, radio me. And I don't want you both just sittin in the car readin funny-books: you have to cover about ten miles of trail. Did you bring any lunch with you?"

Glynn shook his head.

"All right, then get some on your way out of town. Fill your canteens and water bags. Don't try to sneak any beer up there—this is no picnic. Don't leave the keys in the car." Johnson turned up the collar of his leather jacket. "Now you know what to do when you get up there?" Glynn nodded. "Okay—take off. And keep your eyes skinned—the sooner we find this *vaquero* the sooner we come home."

"Okay, Morey . . ." Glynn got into one of the cars; another deputy carrying a sawed-off shotgun followed him.

"Hey Morey!" One of the jailguards stood in the alley door, still shouting at him. Johnson turned his head, frowning. "Morey . . . ?" the guard said tentatively.

"No," Johnson said.

"Gutierrez called up, says he wants to go along."

"No," said Johnson. He faced the other two men who stood there watching him. "Now I'd like you boys to run out to the Pueblo and pick up a man named Pete Sandia. He's a tracker. He'll be waiting for you at the postoffice. After that join me out in the mountains. I'll be at the old Brown homestead. You know where it is?"

"You mean me?" one of the men said. "There's two or three old places out there. I don't know which one you mean."

"This place is right near the mouth of Agua Dulce Canyon; there's a spring there with three big cottonwoods. The house is an old wreck with a cholla growing on the roof." The man nodded then. "You know where I mean now?"

"Yeah, I know." He nodded again. "I been there."

"Okay," Johnson said. He started the engine of the jeep. "We'll expect you in about an hour. Don't come without that Indian—he'll probably be drunk but bring him anyway." He let the engine idle at a moderate speed, warming it up. "If he doesn't want to come arrest him for drunkenness and bring him along." The two deputies grinned. "Okay?" said Johnson; they nodded and got into the other automobile. Johnson craned his head around and backed the jeep off the parkinglot and into the alley.

He stopped by the rear door and spoke to the guard standing there: "Has Hernandez come in yet?"

"No . . ."

"When he does ask him to check again with the State Police about that airplane. He'll know what I mean. And tell him the Marshal is picking up the Federal prisoner named Bondi today."

The guard bobbed his head up and down. "Okay, Morey . . ."

Johnson drove on, turned out of the alley and went north on Second Street. Neither he nor the radio operator spoke; the jeep was only partially closed, with a frame and canvas rig, and the cold morning air rushed through it at forty miles an hour. Johnson regretted not having worn gloves.

They drove for two miles north through the gray bleak city, the streets nearly deserted, the sidewalks empty; nobody passed them in the opposite direction except the drivers of a few freight trucks. They turned east on Mountain Road, passing through one of the more substantial sectors of the city:—row on row of brick and glass boxes squatting under a dense thicket of television antennae, housing engineers and Buicks and dentists; not far away, beyond the golf course, was an Episcopal cathedral rising in imitation gothic above the shrubbery and lost balls; beyond the house of God lay an expanse of expensive formal gardens not easily distinguishable from the golf course, a "Memorial Park" so new that it had as yet found few, and these most reluctant, tenants; beneath those luxurious lawns, if all went well, the neighboring dentists and engineers would someday be interred, to enjoy in sub-pastoral elegance a leisurely recreation they had never known in life.

Past the limits of the city proper now, Johnson and the radio operator jounced along in their hard-sprung jeep, watching the inert passage of a few bars and gas stations and small farms on their left and right. Mailboxes presented themselves, flagged and numbered, and when Number 424 appeared the sheriff slowed for an appraising look at the low adobe house among the tamarisk and apricot trees, at its weed-grown corn patch, the jungle of sunflowers, the outhouses, corral, woodpile, backyard.

"Whatcha lookin at?" the radio operator said, breaking the long silence. Johnson gave no answer. "What's here?" the operator said, looking out himself.

Johnson stepped on the gas again. "That's where this fella Bondi lives," he said. Used to live, he meant. He chewed slowly on his gum, speculating.

"Oh . . ." the operator said. "And that's where . . . ?" He twisted his head around to look back. "Yeah . . ." he said softly; he put one hand down on his pistol butt.

On they went, through the rural fringes of the suburbs: small farms, irrigation ditches, yellow cottonwoods and long brown patches of corn stubble, barbed wire fences, more mud houses, old Chevvies blocked up and disembowelled amid a litter of tools and worn parts, red chili peppers and colored maize drying on the walls, small angry dogs yapping under the wheels, Mexicans sagging in off-plumb doorways, pickup trucks parked in wagon sheds, the smell of horse manure, burning cedar, greasewood, sand, rock, the long cool smoky blue dawn . . .

Johnson stepped on the brakes, pulled at the wheel and the jeep skidded around a corner fence post, rattled over a wooden bridge and then rolled east and upward across the desert toward the shadowy, intangible mountains.

"How far out there?" the radio operator asked; he held on to the dashboard with both hands as the jeep swayed and bumped over the seldom-graded road. A flying stone clanged against the muffler. "Huh?"

"About ten miles to where we're going," Johnson said.

"You think you know where this Burns character is out there?"

"I think so."

The jeep nosed suddenly down into a wash, bounced over rocks and potholes, roared up the other side. The operator braced himself against the floorboards, while his stomach rose, shook and sank again. "Ah . . . did you—" The jeep jolted over a ridge of base rock that underlay the road. "—Did you go out there last night, Morey?"

"Yes."

"What makes you so sure he'll still be there this morning?"

"Nothing." Johnson lifted one hand from the wheel and scratched the inside of his thigh.

The road climbed to the edge of the mesa and then straightened out on the long broad plain that rose gradually toward the base of the mountains. Here the road's surface had acquired the character of a washboard, an unbroken succession of lateral corrugations which made the jeep shake and vibrate with such vigor that it seemed certain to fall in pieces before another mile was covered; however, Johnson merely stepped harder on the gas pedal and as the machine's speed increased it achieved a kind of aerodynamic synchronization of velocity and traction with the ribbed road, reducing the bone-and-bolt-shattering vibrations to a steady, rhythmic, dependable rattle.

The radio operator took advantage of the comparative stability and lit himself a cigarette, though not without wasting several matches in the wind. His cheeks distended, his eyes half-closed, he puffed out smoke that shot past his ears like a fleeing soul. "Haven't been up this early since last deer season," he said cheerfully. He looked through the windshield at the long dark horizontal wall of the mountain, which seemed to recede before them as they approached. Las Montañas del Sangre de Cristo. "Been a long time since I watched the sun come up." He looked for this phenomenon in the yellow sky above the mountains and within a minute, as if his words constituted a celestial command, the sun began to appear above the mountain rim, looking dull, reddish and somewhat late. "Must be a lot of dust in the air," the operator commented. But even so the light was strong enough to make him squint.

The jeep raced over the road after the retreating edge of the great shadow. Behind them the dust boiled up and hung in the air along the road like a long limp dirty wind-cone.

"Might be a nice day yet, though," the operator said. "You—" The road fell steeply beneath them, the jeep hurtled down into a deep wash, crashed through a congregation of tumbleweeds, went zooming up the opposite bank spitting fumes, dust and gravel from behind. The road led on, climbing and winding among boulders, cactus and scattered junipers. Johnson shifted into second gear. The operator completed his statement: "You never can tell for sure just by how things happen to look in the morning."

The sun rose higher through the eastern haze; it began to burn and glare, a hot shimmering disc of fire. The operator squinted and grimaced; Johnson pulled the forebrim of his Stetson farther down.

The road followed a fence; here and there were survey stakes, outlining the streets and lots of an imaginary suburb; a big billboard, alone and conspicuous in this wilderness of rock and sand, addressed them in flattering terms: OWN YOUR OWN MOUNTAIN RANCH ESTATE HOME—Barker Realty, Inc. Johnson grunted. The jeep clattered over an old wooden cattleguard, past a National Forest marker and up into the foothills, the dark wall of the mountain rearing above them, shutting off the sun again.

They came to a junction of roads, one going northeast toward the base of the main wall, the other south across the mesa and around the foothills. The sign pointing left and northeast said: Public Campgrounds, 2 miles; Ranger Station, 4 miles;—the other sign said: US 66, 12 miles; Duke City, 22 miles. Johnson turned to the right.

This was a wider, better road, paralleling the face of the mountains; Johnson followed it for about three miles, then turned east at the bottom of a sandy wash, steered between a pair of junipers and up over rocks and sand toward the canyon known as Agua Dulce. The wheels thrashed and spun in the deep sand; Johnson engaged the front wheel drive, shifted into low range, and the jeep ground ahead, whining and shaking and still in second gear. What they drove over now was not a road but a pair of dim tracks, an ancient wagon trail with beds of sand sucking at the wheels, shale and slate to slash the tires, potholes and ledges and fangs of rock ready to break an axle or shear through an oilpan. Juniper boughs whipped across the windshield, cactus clawed at the wheels, dead brush exploded under the bumper and fenders, but Johnson, with a kind of resigned abandon that seemed to evade disaster only through a fatalistic indifference, drove the jeep—property of Bernal County—up, over, into and through every kind of obstacle that a difficult fate and spontaneous nature had ranged in his path.

The wash narrowed and deepened ahead, became an arroyo with vertical banks and overhanging bluffs. Johnson drove on, upward, around a turn—cottonwoods appeared, three giant sear-leafed trees with elephantine trunks, and beneath the trees a patch of grass and reeds and the ledge of limestone that embraced the spring. The sheriff stopped the jeep, shut off the engine and climbed out; the radio operator hauled himself out on the other side, stumbling and nearly falling on his face.

"Jesus, Morey . . ."

They heard a hissing of compressed steam, the chug and burble of water—spontaneous noises coming from under the hood of the jeep. "Jesus, Morey . . ." the operator mumbled again. He wiped his forehead with the sleeve of his jacket.

Johnson, studying the ground under the trees, made no reply; he observed the droppings of a horse near the patch of grass, hoofprints in the damp sand, a sprawl of sliding impressions on both banks of the arroyo. He stared up the arroyo, up the hill beyond it, up into the canyon behind it, up at the remote and tortured face of the mountain towering beyond and far above the canyon. The sensation of awe was perhaps not a part of Sheriff Johnson's repertory of emotions; yet something in those heights of naked, perpendicular crags and cliffs made him halt in his tracks and suspend, at least for a few moments, his chain of guesses, facts, and inferences. He stared upward, unblinking, at that implacable wall.

"Hey, Morey!" The operator had scrambled up the bank and was now standing on its edge. "There's an old house up here—this the old Brown homestead?" He received no answer. He glanced around, looked down, stooped, then knelt for a close scrutiny of something on the ground. "Morey," he said eagerly, "somebody's been walkin around up here! Jesus—the biggest shoe-prints you ever saw in your life. They don't look human . . ."

Johnson did not answer; he scarcely heard. The expression on his face had changed, losing its air of general apprehension, and become tense, concentrated, fixedly attentive. Far up that canyon, twisting slowly up through the dawn air, he had seen or thought he had seen a wisp of smoke. But too frail, too distant—he closed his eyes for a few seconds, then opened them and looked again. He was not mistaken; he saw smoke. A blue thread of smoke, pale and shifting, hovering on the bounds of invisibility, and a long way off.

"How about these feet, Morey? You oughta come up here and have a look. My God, they're gigantic . . ."

Johnson relaxed, scratching his groin; he spat the wad of gum out of his mouth. He turned and went back a few steps and sat down on the fender of the jeep. The radiator was still sizzling and bubbling, though with less agitation than before.

"Morey . . . ?"

Johnson looked up at the operator. "That's all right," he said; "don't worry about them. I made them tracks myself, last night. Come on down here, see if you can contact any of the boys."

"Okay . . ." The operator stared westward, down and toward the north reach of the city. "There's a car comin across the mesa now. The other guys, probably."

Johnson looked in the same direction and saw a funnel of dust creeping toward the mountains, following the long hairline over the plain that marked the road. Ten miles and nearly a half hour away, he estimated. "Come on down," he said to the operator.

The operator slid down the bank, emerged from a cloud of dust and sat down in the jeep. He flipped a switch, put on his earphones, and waited for the transmitter to warm up. "Who you want me to call?" he said. "Glynn?"

"Call Glynn," Johnson said; he tilted back his head and looked up again, up at the rim of the mountain five thousand feet above. A fringe of snow sparkled there, blue and icy; a plume of cloud floating east made the mountain appear to move, like a great ship advancing across the sky. Falling . . . The sun would not clear that wall for another hour.

The operator flicked his switches, twiddled with his dials; the mouth of the loudspeaker began to hum and crackle with static—electrical, strange, with a certain mathematic symmetry, like a message in code from another world. The operator spoke into the microphone: "CS-3 calling CS-4," he said, "this is CS-3 calling CS-4. Can you hear me, CS-4? Over." He waited; the speaker crackled out its pattern of static, gave no intelligible answer. The operator repeated his call, reversed the switch, waited again. Johnson waited, sitting on the jeep's fender, listening. No answer. "They don't get us," the operator said; "they must be on the other side of the mountains now. When they get up on the rim they'll hear us."

Johnson nodded. "Call them other fellas," he said. "See if they're on the way here. Make sure they've got the Indian with them."

"Okay, Morey." The operator performed his routine and was answered at once: the others were coming across the mesa, the Indian was with them, they would be there in half an hour, over and out. The operator removed his earphones and picked at his nostrils with his little finger.

While Johnson gazed soberly and intently up into the canyon, the trace of smoke was so vague and tenuous that he still could not be quite certain that he really saw it. He muttered to himself, a man with a problem, and scratched in vague distraction at his armpits. Finally he eased his rump off the fender and stood up. "I'm going up the canyon," he said to the operator; "you stay here with the radio. When the others get here tell one of them and the Indian to come on up the canyon too; the other man stays here. When you get Glynn on the radio tell him to keep a sharp lookout up there on the rim."

"You think this guy Burns is up in there?"

"He might be," Johnson said. He started off, stopped and turned again. "Say—call them boys again, tell them not to try to bring the car up the wash. Too rough, they won't make it. Tell them to go south another mile, then follow the old fence line road. It'll bring them out pretty close to here."

"Okay, Morey." The operator stared after Johnson's retreating back. "You forgot the shotgun," he shouted. Johnson flapped his hand downward, not looking back. The operator shrugged and went to work with his radio.

***

A long walk: the sun came over the rim of the mountain, a
furious white heat, fanned by the blue winds; below, Johnson
stopped and leaned against the rock, took off his hat and wiped
his brow; he was sweating but his feet, still in the shade, were
cold. While he rested he heard a mockingbird call, a descending
glissando of sweet lilting semitones—faintly derisive. Johnson
removed his leather jacket and draped it over his forearm. He
looked down: already far below, he could see the jeep, a dull gray
object of uncertain dimensions, and the scrubby hills, the road,
the dust trail of an approaching car. He looked up and saw rock,
nothing but rock, walls and slabs and grottoes of rock. He could
see no trace of smoke, from where he stood, and could hear no
sound but a whisper of wind, the periodic drip of unseen water,
at long intervals the mockingbird's cry.

He resumed his climb, scaling rock slides, struggling up
the canyon slopes to outflank the more difficult dams of rock,
trudging up the almost-level stretches of sand between each barrier. Now and then he could make out hoofprints, sometimes
the mark of a shod horse, more often the sharp dainty imprints
of deer.

The climb and the altitude stimulated an unexpected thirst
for water; he began to wish that he had brought a canteen along.

The canyon narrowed and turned, shutting off the view to
the west, reaching up toward the high ridges, the pines, the final
wall of granite. Johnson climbed another smooth water-worn
facing of rock, scored diagonally with a thin feldspar dike, and
stopped on the brink of it, gazing ahead. He saw the willow
thicket at the foot of the gray water-slide, the bear grass and
greasewood, and on the right, a few yards up the slope and about

a hundred yards from where he stood, a glistening, bulky object hanging from the limb of a tree. Nearby, from a tiny mound of sand and charcoal, a faint thread of smoke rose up toward the sky.

Listening intently, Johnson surveyed every visible surface and aspect of the surrounding terrain. He saw rock walls, talus slopes of sand and gravel, the trees, cactus, brush, a pair of ravens hunched on a boulder near the head of the draw—but no man, no horse. He could hear nothing but the thin vibrations of flies somewhere ahead.

He waited for another minute with straining senses, then relaxed a little and walked ahead, hearing his boots crunch loudly in the sand. Even his breathing sounded much louder than normal, as if the pervading stillness of the place and the towering walls amplified every noise. He was aware of slight echoes repeating each sound that he made, following him from all sides; he felt as conspicuous and self-conscious as a tourist tramping into a silent cathedral. But after the first few uncomfortable moments he overcame the sense of being an intruder, and held his attention to his business.

As he approached the hanging object he saw it as it was, the skinned, partially-dismembered carcass of a doe. Going closer he saw the sand-covered heap that had been a campfire, near it a smoothed-out plot of ground about the size of a grave, where a man had evidently slept the night before. Close to the deer was a crude rack made of green willow branches, supported some three feet above the ground by crosspoles resting in the crotches of forked stakes. Beneath this lattice were the remains of another small fire—charred stubs of juniper protruding from the sand.

Johnson noticed a piece of paper, brown and torn, fluttering against the deer. He went toward it; as he did so the limb from which the carcass was suspended suddenly rose a little, quivering, as a big dirty raven launched itself into the air and flopped away down the canyon. Johnson stared after it, startled, his hand on his pistol butt, then stepped on toward the deer. Flies swarmed around the flayed carcass and crawled in battalions over the ripe, glistening flesh. The piece of paper was impaled on a twig, part of the brush still jamming the interior of the animal; with averted face Johnson reached out through the flies, slipped the paper free and backed away to read what was written on it:

I HOPE YOU BOYS HAVE SENSE ENUF TO USE THIS VENISON BEFORE THE BLOWFLIES SPOIL IT ALL. I WAS GOING TO JERK IT BUT YOU RUSHED ME.

Johnson smiled tiredly and dropped the paper to the ground. He examined the ashes of the fire under the rack, found them still warm. He poked around some more, finding plenty of bootprints and hoofprints, the seep of water behind the willow thicket, the place where the deer had died, the scattered remains of its innards surrounded by the tracks of mice, vultures, ravens, and what might have been—he was not certain—the marks of a cougar. But he was unable to find what he wanted to find, the trail of Burns' departure. The ground was too dry, too stony, and everywhere but on the floor of the canyon, too steep. He climbed up around the cliff back of the spring and looked on the sandy glen above for a sign of man or horse, without success. He paced

out a small arc on the canyon's northern slope—the sunny expo-
sure, the side of the cactus—and could find nothing; he did the
same on the southern slope among the piñons and juniper. Here
he discovered what could have been traces of a horse's passage: a
freshly-broken dead branch, an overturned stone, certain faint
depressions in a bank of gravel. These were signs, possibilities,
but so indefinite and scattered as to be almost useless; if they led
anywhere, it appeared to him, it was straight up the slope—and
the slope ended, fifty yards above, in a perpendicular wall of
rock. Johnson paused and stared around him at the emptiness
of the canyon, at the almost mythical remoteness of the cliffs
above, and again became intensely conscious of the exaggerated
uncanny stillness. A notion came to him, an absurdity: impul-
sively he yielded to it, and cupped his hands around his mouth,
inhaled deeply, and shouted out into the dizzy heights and the
gulfs of space surrounding him—

"Burns!"

The echoes rang out, amplified at first and then fading rapidly as they ricocheted from wall to crag to mountain rim—

—BURNS . . . *Burns . . . burns. . . .*

"Come on back!"

And the canyon echoed—

—ON BACK . . . *On Back . . . on back. . . .*

"You can't get away!"

—GET AWAY . . . *Get Away . . . get away. . . .*

"Come back!"

—COME BACK . . . Come . . . come back. . . .

The echoes faded, dying away among the towering cliffs,
farther, farther, like the cries of vanishing ghosts . . .

Johnson stood listening until the last echo of an echo had

sounded back again. Then he sat down on a rock and unwrapped another stick of chewing gum; he waited.

The stillness was emphasized, not broken, by the stark clear sinking notes of the mockingbird.

They came eventually, two sun-washed men toiling up over the quartzite and granite and sand, faces dark under wide-brimmed hats, bodies pale in the scorching glare. One of them saw Johnson and waved—"Hey." They came closer; the deputy was carrying a portable radiotelephone set and a submachinegun, the Indian an old walnut cane. "Hey," the deputy said, grinning at Johnson—"where's the outlaw?"

Johnson munched on his gum, staring across the canyon. "Come on up," he said.

"We heard somebody hollerin a while ago," the deputy said. "Was that you?"

"You heard more than I did," Johnson said.

They came up the slope, sweating a little, and sat down near him. The deputy was panting like a dog in the sun; the tracker breathed easily, as if he had just rolled out of a hammock. The Indian was short and squat, with a face brown as tobacco juice and wrinkled as a dried apple.

The deputy passed cigarettes around, Johnson declining. "I coulda swore I heard someone hollerin," the deputy said. "Sounded a long way off but it was a man. You didn't hear it, Morey?"

"No. What're Glynn and that other fella doing? Any word from them yet?"

"Not yet. That's a long drive, Morey, through the canyon and up to the rim. Nearly forty miles."

Johnson nodded. "And how about the State Police? Are they coming around with that airplane or still stalling?"

"I don't know. He was callin em when we started up here."

Johnson sighed gently, scratching his belly. "Well, you boys might as well get started. Don't know what kind of luck you'll have—I didn't find much, but maybe you can do better." It had better be the man we're looking for, he was thinking. He stood up. "I'll show you what I found."

He led them around, pointing out the signs he had seen on the south slope. The Indian seemed more interested in the half-butchered deer than anything else. He brushed off the flies with a big knife, cut a pair of steaks from flank and brisket, wrapped them in the big dirty bandana from his hip pocket and stowed the bundle inside the front of his shirt. "Good meat," he said; "lunch."

Johnson waited; presently the Indian came over, squatted down near the broken branch, the overturned stone. "Okay," he said, "a horse went up here."

"How long ago?"

"Maybe an hour, maybe a week."

Johnson nodded, frowning; he could smell the whisky on the Indian's breath. "It's all yours," he said; "I'm going back down. You boys do the best you can." He noticed the deputy sagging under his burdens. "Don't drop that Walkie-Talkie; and give me that burp-gun—you're not hunting a nest of Japs."

"This guy's an Anarchist, Morey. And he must have a rifle."

"Then he's already got the drop on you. That thing's just gonna be in your way. You've got a thirty-eight, that's enough."

The deputy stood there pouting, like a cranky child, the submachinegun in his arms, a revolver at his hip, the radio outfit strapped on his back. "I might need this, Morey."

The Indian was already far above them among the trees, poking around with his walnut stick. "Horse piss," he yelled down under his arm, and continued his investigations.

Johnson looked up. "All right." He turned to the deputy. "Well, keep it if it's so dear to you. But don't use it unless you have a good target." He looked up the slope at the dark figure of the Indian limping along at the base of the cliff, headed up the ridge. "And don't let that fella get out of your sight."

"I won't Morey."

"Okay." Johnson picked up his jacket and started down the canyon. He was thinking: Children, my children. The sun burned into a strip of exposed skin on the back of his neck. A bunch of damned children . . . He clambered down over the smooth face of the first ledge, holding on with fingertips and toes. He dropped the last four feet onto the sand below, went trudging on. Damned children, he was thinking—and then he remembered the echoes. He smiled. Those wonderful, magical, vanishing echoes . . .

Half an hour later he reached the arroyo. Another deputy and the radio operator were sitting on the hood of the jeep, drinking Coca-Cola. The patrol car was parked on the old road below the ruin.

The operator saw Johnson coming. "They seen him!" he yelled, then tipped up the bottle again.

"And the General wants to talk to ya," the deputy said, grinning.

Johnson pushed back his hat and rubbed a few drops of sweat out of his eyebrows. "The General?" he said, surprised. "And who's seen him? Seen who? Burns?"

"Yes," the operator said. "I was just talkin with Glynn. He seen him." He tossed the empty bottle back over his shoulder; it hit the bank and rolled, clinking and bouncing, back down to the bottom. "Way up there somewhere." The operator pointed toward the mountain, indicating several square miles of craggy wilderness. "Glynn saw a man leadin a horse through a hole in the rocks, over this ridge, and down into the canyon on the other side. Then he couldn't see him on account of all the big boulders."

"Couldn't he get him?" Johnson asked.

"No, there ain't no way down from where he is. It was too far to shoot. Glynn says it would take him hours to climb down that wall."

"What are they doing now?"

"Glynn is stayin near the car. The other guy's movin along the rim trail to see if he can foller this guy from above."

Johnson thought for a while, staring at the sand and kneading his cheeks. "What's this about a general?" he said.

"That's right," the operator said. "From the Air Base. The C.O. out there—Desalius, his name is. Wants to talk to you."

"What about?"

"Something about a helicopter."

"A helicopter?" Johnson scratched at his ribs. "See if you can contact him now."

"Right." The operator slid off the jeep's hood and went back to his transmitter.

Johnson became aware of the uniformed deputy, idle and indolent in the sunshine. "Our man seems to be heading south," Johnson said. "Why don't you do a little scouting around over in Bear Canyon?"

"Who me?"

"Yes, you."

"Is there a road?"

"There used to be. If it's washed out you can walk. Drive over as far as you can, climb up on the south ridge and sit there for a spell. If you can get there fast enough this cowboy friend of ours might come ridin right up to you. If you don't see anything within say three hours come on back here. If we're not here—well, we'll radio you." He rubbed his nose. "Don't get lost," he added.

"Okay, Morey." The deputy climbed off the jeep and up the arroyo bank. "Shoot on sight?" he said, from up there.

"What?" Johnson had already forgotten him; he was listening to the radio operator and the radio: static, questions, the murmur of Air Force second lieutenants. "Shoot on sight?" Johnson said; the question penetrated his indifference. He looked up at the deputy, annoyed. "What the hell do you mean? We're not after a murderer."

"This guy's supposed to be dangerous, Morey. The papers say he's a Red."

"I don't give a hoot in hell what the papers say. You oughta know better yourself. You just hold your fire—this is no coon hunt. Now get outa here before I get mad."

The deputy grinned; he had a young pleasant face with small pale-blue eyes, like turquoise buttons. "Sure, Morey," he said, and disappeared. From above came the slam of a car door, the sound of an engine starting, stones banging on metal . . .

These bloodthirsty kids, thought Johnson—where do they all come from? Scowling, he turned back to the radio. The operator was saying:

"Yessir, just a minute, sir." He motioned to Johnson. "Here's Sheriff Johnson now, sir." Johnson took the microphone. "General Desalius," the operator said in his ear.

Johnson nodded. "This is Johnson speaking. What can I do for you, General? We're pretty busy right now. Over."

The loudspeaker crackled for a moment. Then a voice, grand and stately and powerful, boomed out of it: "Sheriff Johnson, how are you? This is General Desalius, Kirk Field Air Base. I understand that you are now engaged in a hunt. A *hunt*, am I not correct? For an escaped criminal—some species of Anarchist, I understand. Is that correct, Sheriff?" Without pausing for an answer the magnificent voice rolled on: "Sheriff, I wonder if you would be good enough to allow me to make a modest contribution to your chase? One of my helicopters, for example, and perhaps a brace of my Air Police? With automatic rifles?" The voice seemed to issue from a genial, sly-smiling face. "My men need a bit of field work, and my helicopter, I should imagine, could be very useful to you in that mountainous terrain. I shall instruct the helicopter pilot to operate under your direction, of course. What do you think, Sheriff? Over to you."

Johnson answered at once. "Thank you, General. We don't need the Air Police but a helicopter would certainly be a big help. We are now near the bottom of the west wall, at the mouth of Agua Dulce Canyon, which is about two miles north of Bear Canyon and about ten miles north of the highway. Tell your helicopter crew to look for three bunched cottonwoods, a ruined adobe, and a jeep. I'll give the pilot instructions by radio when he finds us. Over."

A different voice, mild and clerical, replied: "Lieutenant Cole speaking. The helicopter will be there in twenty minutes, sir. General Desalius wishes you 'good hunting!' Over and out."

Johnson set down the microphone, smiling faintly; he scratched his ribs. The operator grinned happily at him. "A character, that General, huh Morey?" The operator's eyes were shining. "Sounds like Almighty God Himself, don't he? Huh? Makes a man wonder if maybe he shouldna gone to church this morning." The operator stared blankly at the bank of the arroyo, smiling, then looked at Johnson again. "Does he look as blowed-up as he sounds?" Johnson was silent. "Do you think he does, Morey?"

"Who?"

"This General guy."

"Couldn't say," Johnson answered, after a moment's hesitation. "I don't know the man." He gazed at his fingernails, then started to clean them with the small blade of his penknife.

"I never heard nobody like that before," the operator said. "Like God Almighty Himself . . ."

Johnson spat into the sand and scraped at his fingernails. Lapsing into a sullen abstraction, he began to brood over things: prestige, loneliness, money and status, flight, boredom . . .

"What do we do now, Morey?"

The sun gulped and glimmered above them—an unknown object at ten o'clock. Far beyond the sun three jet planes, beautiful and vicious, scored the violet sky with long silver vapor trails; they were nearly gone before they were heard. They passed, and in the wake of their passing, as if disturbed by the remote explosions, the leaves of the cottonwoods trembled on their delicately-sprung stems, shedding wisps of pale coma. Up in the canyon the mockingbird called again; then a wild dove, alone and distant, intoned a few solemn notes, and was silent; while nearby, from among the junipers above the spring, a convocation of locusts added a sustained overtone to the stillness with their sullen, monotonous, interminable vibrations.

"Huh, Morey . . . ?"

"What?"

"What do we do now?"

"We wait."

At their backs the mountain rose, forsaken and naked and sheer, an incalculable mass and shape of undetermined significance, a great petrified god towering over the two men on their simple machine, and over the three cottonwoods and the eye of the spring and the willows and over the subsiding ruin of stone, clay and pine that had once been the home of a man named Brown.

They waited twenty-two minutes and then the helicopter appeared, abruptly, surprisingly near, and so close to the ground as to make them involuntarily lower their heads. A fantastic machine, gay and sprightly, a mechanical dragonfly with whirring roaring wings and spinning rotor that danced lightly on the air at an easy roping distance above their heads.

"Get to the radio," Johnson said. He could see faces pressed to the windows and grinning down at him—three men, one with the muzzle of a rifle showing near his chin. One of them, the pilot, waved at him. The machine hovered so near that he could easily read its markings: USAF "RESCUE", Model H-19B, AF Serial 53-7434. "You got em yet?" he shouted at the radio operator.

"Yes, but they're so close I can hardly hear them."

"Give me that mike." Johnson wrapped his hand around it and spoke: "Ground to helicopter. This is Sheriff Johnson speaking. Can you hear me? Over." He saw the pilot grinning at him, nodding, while dust swirled through the air and the roar of the engine drowned out all other sounds.

"They hear you," the operator was shouting at him, earphones in place. "They hear you, Morey."

"All right," he growled. He continued: "Johnson to helicopter. If you boys want to help us out here's what I'd like you to do: cruise up and down Bear Canyon—that's the big canyon to the south of us—and keep an eye out for a lone man on foot or leading or riding a horse. If you don't see anything in Bear Canyon, hop over the ridge and scout the next canyon south. We're pretty sure this man we're looking for is in one of those two canyons. He seems to be headed south, although he might try to climb up to the rim. As soon as you see something let me know. Over."

The speaker crackled out an answer, while Johnson leaned close to it with one ear, plugging the other with a finger. ". . . . to Sheriff Johnson. Pilot to Sheriff Johnson. We got your message, sir. If we find the man do you want us to drop down and pick him up? Over."

Johnson squeezed his nose. "Johnson to helicopter: you can try to if you want to," he said into the microphone. "I don't know that you're likely to find a place big enough to set that machine down on, though. If you find this fella and can't land just stay with him till we can get there. Okay? Over."

"Pilot to Sheriff Johnson. We'll get him. We can pick him out of the top of a tree if we want to. Here we go. Over and out."

The helicopter banked and roared away, shining in the sunlight and chasing its shadow over the rocks and foothills. Johnson watched it diminish and then disappear into the mouth of

Bear Canyon, the sound of its engine fading out at the same time, cut off by the intervening ridge.

Johnson sat down again on the fender of the jeep. He searched through his pockets for chewing gum but could not find any. He scratched his crotch idly, without real interest, and stared up at the mountain. "Oughta hear something from those boys," he muttered.

"Huh, Morey?" The operator pushed up one of his earphones. "What'd you say?" He waited for a minute, getting no answer. "Looks like we'll be goin home real soon," he ventured to say. "Don't you think so, Morey?" No reply. "What with the helicopter and that Indian—what's his name?—and two boys up on the rim and all. Don't you think so? I don't see how he can get away now." The radio operator picked some dirt from his nose, looked at it with habitual affection, then got rid of it— somewhere. "What I'd do if I was that Burns guy," he said, "I'd just give up when I heard that helicopter comin after me. I'd give up right on the spot and save everybody a lot of trouble. Then we could leave this—" The operator looked around at the sun-splashed cottonwoods trembling with golden light, at the twisted junipers and tall spears of yucca on the slopes, at the blue rock beyond the spring, at the mountain and immaculate sky roaring above him. "—This godawful stinkin place. Huh, Morey? We could all go home."

Johnson raised himself from the jeep's fender, fingering his ears as if in pain, and started walking slowly away, toward the trees and the spring.

"Where you goin, Morey?"

"I'll be back in a minute," he said. "Jus want to . . ." He let the sentence die in his mouth, and the thought with it. He walked through the cool shade under the trees, over the grass and clashing dead leaves to the spring. The cicada went silent. He looked down at the little pool of water, the size of a bird bath, with its coronal of hovering gnats. He knelt down and put his face close to the water—a vague reflection of himself, dark and wavering, with the hollow eyesockets of statuary, came staring up to meet him; he looked through himself and saw the slight stirring of white sand on the bottom of the pool that revealed where the water welled up from below. As he watched, a miniature crayfish, pallid, silt-covered, slid backward across the sand under the water and merged with the pebbles and algae on the other side. Johnson stirred the pool gently with his forefinger, dispersing the particles of dust and insects that floated on its surface, put his mouth to it and drank. The water was cool, not cold, and sweet with a faint piney flavor.

He raised his head and wiped his dripping chin. He half-expected to hear a call from the radio operator, but there was none. Above him the trees rustled in a sigh of wind, the sound of their leaves like the tinkle of gold foil; a locust resumed, tentatively, its shrill keening. Johnson remained for several minutes on his knees before the spring and the blue-veined altar of rock behind it, listening, scarcely thinking, surrendering himself to strange and archaic sensations; he remembered his childhood, forty years gone, and a dim sweet exquisite sorrow passed like a cloud over his mind.

The reed quivered before his eyes. He rubbed his nose, looked sheepishly and furtively over his shoulder, then struggled up to a standing position. No one had seen him; he tramped back through the fallen leaves to the jeep. "What's going on?" he said to the operator, who was listening at the radio, earphones in place. He reached for the speaker switch and found it already on: a dull unintelligible murmur issued from the speaker's mouth. "The trackers?" he said.

The operator nodded, adjusting a knob on the receiver. His lips moved, forming words in silent repetition of what he heard. He flipped a switch and looked up at Johnson. "It's them," he said. "He says they're follerin a trail but it's a mighty poor one and the going's pretty slow. He wants to know if they should come down."

"Have they crossed the ridge into Bear Canyon?"

"Yeah. They saw the helicopter a minute ago."

"Tell them to keep at it."

The operator relayed the order into the microphone, then switched off the transmitter.

"No word from Glynn?" Johnson said. "No word from the helicopter?"

"Not yet."

"You'd think we were chasing a ghost," Johnson growled. "An invisible cowboy with an invisible horse." He scratched at his neck, squinting one eye, a grimace that lifted a corner of his upper lip in what looked like a silent snarl. "How about that other fella? I supposed he's dead too?"

"Haven't heard from him yet, Morey."

"For two bits I'd call the whole thing off." He muttered to himself for a few minutes. "Have you heard from the State Police? Are they gonna help us or not?"

"They've got two patrol cars on Scissors Canyon and they're sending the airplane as soon as they can. That's what they said an hour ago."

Johnson scowled and scratched and thought. After a while

he said: "Let's get this jeep out of this goddamned arroyo. I have the feeling we're getting left behind." He climbed into the seat and started the engine; the operator hooked up and secured his equipment and got in beside him. Johnson ground into gear, backed the jeep into the north bank, gunned the engine and roared straight toward the south bank of the arroyo, which rose up from the sand at an angle of about fifty degrees. The front end hit the slope, jolted upward, all four wheels churning in the sand; the jeep climbed halfway up the bank and then hung there, wheels spinning, engine howling, the entire chassis quivering. Johnson backed down to the bottom and made a second try, this time attempting to crawl rather than race up the bank, but the jeep would not do it.

"Get out and push," he said to the radio operator, who stared at him in alarm. Johnson smiled to show that he was joking. He turned the jeep around and drove back down the arroyo until he came to a place where tributary erosion and crumbling banks made an ascent possible. Once out of the arroyo he drove southeast, following the old trail road that led toward Bear Canyon.

After some fifteen or twenty minutes of grinding around boulders, in and out of ravines and over the rocky little hills, they came to a wide draw, thick with greasewood and cane cactus, which led up and far back into the heart of the foothills. A fence with a barbed wire gate blocked their way; Johnson stopped, idling the motor, while the operator climbed out, lifted the wire loops from the end stake and dragged the gate to one side. Johnson drove through, passing a small yellow metal sign, pockmarked with old bullet holes, which said: UNITED STATES GAME REFUGE, DEPT. OF THE INTERIOR. The operator closed the gate and got back in the jeep and they drove on, following the dim tracks in the sand and stone through acres of greasewood, huge thriving shrubs of a silvery green, their tasseled stalks heavy with seed. The road climbed steadily, leaving the greasewood behind and entering a zone dominated by cactus—cholla, yucca, prickly pear, and beyond that into the region of junipers and giant boulders, where the sides of the draw closed in to make a canyon. Finally they saw the tan patrol car ahead, rear wheels sunk in the sand, churned around it and saw another patrol car, also from the Sheriff's Department, and two private cars nearby, on which half a dozen armed men were sitting and talking. Beer cans glinted in the hot sunshine, beer cans and rifle barrels.

Johnson drove roughly up, the engine whining in low gear, stopped and got out, while the cloud of dust he had raised drifted over him and the jeep and the men waiting there. He knew none of them; some of the faces were vaguely familiar but he knew no names. They watched him, lowering their beer cans. "What the be-jesus is this?" Johnson said. "What're you fellas doing here?"

"Hi, Morey," one of them said, a little man with a quick easy grin and an Army .45 holstered on his hip. "We came out here to hep ya. We're deputies. Hernandez deputized us. We're gonna hep ya catch this here jailbreakin Red."

"Is that right?" Johnson said; he scratched at his ribs. "Where's Hernandez?" He glanced at the other County car. "Is he here?"

"Him and Gutierrez is up in there somewhere," the little man said, grinning and jerking a thumb back over his shoulder toward the mountain.

Johnson frowned. He looked up the canyon, saw the red cliffs, small stands of jackpine, the knife-edge north ridge, a circling hawk, but no hint of living men. Then he heard the drone of rotors and saw something slender and silvery turn and flash in the sunlight, far up on the mountainside, floating in space. He turned back to the men leaning against the cars; they were watching him. "You boys might as well go home," he said, "you're not doing anybody any good out here. I don't know what's the matter with Hernandez."

"We're all set to go, Morey," the little man said. "Join in, I mean. We was just havin a beer before startin—a hot day."

"That's right," one of the other men said. "You tell us where to go, Morey, and we'll round up this jailbreaker before you know it."

"Would you like a beer, Morey?"

"I want you all to go home," Johnson said. "There's altogether too many men wanderin around with guns out here now. Worse than the first day of deer season. You boys just better go home." The men stared at him, making no move. "I mean it: clear out."

"Hey, Morey," the radio operator called; "come here!"

The little man grinned. "You can't order us around like that, Morey. We got as much right here as you do."

"Hey, Morey!"

"I'll give you five minutes to get in your cars and get out of sight," Johnson said. "If you're still here by then I'll arrest all of you for interfering with and hindering an officer of the law in the course of his duty." He pulled out his pocket watch, looked at it—it had run down hours ago—and put it back in his pocket. He turned his back to the men and walked to the jeep. The radio operator was busy, receiving a message. He saw Johnson coming and flipped the speaker switch.

"We got him, we got him," said the excited voice of the heli-copter pilot, rasping a little through the radio mechanism. "He's right below us. A man with a black hat leading a horse. Right? He doesn't know what to do. He's got a guitar on his back. He's trying to hide in the rocks." The pilot sounded extraordinarily excited, like a beagle flushing a rabbit. "He can't get away, the poor bastard." There was a long pause; Johnson started up the canyon and saw the helicopter, a tiny speck of silver, hovering in one place on the face of the mountain, up among the tall pines and the granite cliffs. The voice of the pilot again: "Can't land here, there's not room for the prop, but we're lowering a rope ladder. We'll have him in a minute. One of the boys will climb down and get him." Another pause, not so prolonged. "Say—!" The pilot sounded a little puzzled; Johnson could hear nothing for several seconds. "Somebody is shooting at us!" the pilot said. "I believe—yes, this guy is shooting at us, Sheriff. He's shooting at the prop. What'll we do? Sheriff Johnson—? Hey!"

Johnson spoke sharply into the microphone. "Shoot back at him. Keep him covered. For godsake don't let him get away now! Over."

The voice of the pilot, excited and astonished: "He won't stand still—he's running through the . . ." The voice faded out for a few seconds, then came back. "We can't see him, Sheriff; he's crawled under a jumble of rocks. We can see his horse; shall we shoot the horse? Sheriff? Over."

Johnson swore. "Don't be a damn fool. Just keep him holed up until we can get there. Don't take any chances. I didn't think he would—look: can't you get out of his line of fire, let down one of your men, then get back over him? Over."

The pilot answered at once: "That's what we're doing, Sheriff." Another stretch of silence. "Just a minute." Johnson and the operator looked up the canyon and saw the helicopter dropping slowly down across the face of the mountain, gleaming like a fish in the brilliant light. They heard the pilot again: "Something's wrong—the tail rotor. What the hell?" He sounded extremely annoyed. The helicopter continued to sink through the air, falling slowly down, down, down, twisting like a dead leaf. "We seem to be out of control; the tail rotor has been damaged. Damn it anyway . . ." They could hear the pilot muttering and swearing. "We're going to hit hard, Sheriff. Hold on a minute, please." Johnson and the radio operator and the men by the cars all stared up the canyon, watching the helicopter drift down through space, slanting toward the steep north wall of the canyon. They saw it hit a pine tree—dust, bark, and dead limbs exploding in all directions—and then hang for a moment, nose down, the big main rotor still turning, winking light; as they watched the gleaming machine eased down, rolled over and landed belly-up on the rocks. Seconds later came the sound of the crash, a barrage of smashing wood and rolling rocks and clattering, crumpling metal.

"Jesus . . . !" the operator said, his eyes bulging.

Johnson shouted at the six men by the cars. "Get on up there! Hurry up!" He reached inside the jeep and wrenched a big First-Aid kit free of its bracket; he lobbed the heavy metal box at the little man with the .45. "Take that along." The little man caught it and they all started up the canyon at a slow trot, carrying their rifles. "I'll catch up to you in a minute," Johnson shouted after them. He turned back to the operator. "Try to call them."

The operator was already trying: "Ground to helicopter.

Hello, helicopter, anybody there? Can you hear me? Come in, helicopter. Over." He flicked a switch and the loudspeaker buzzed and crackled. They waited. He tried again: "This is Sheriff's party calling helicopter. Hello, helicopter, can you hear me? Come in, helicopter. Over." Again they waited, but there was no answer. "Radio's busted," the operator said.

"All right," Johnson said; he scratched his lip briefly. "Call the Air Base, tell em to rush an ambulance out here or another helicopter if they can—that would be better. With a doctor. After that call our boys and give them the location of the shooting. If they haven't seen it already. If the State Police ever get their plane out here give them the dope too, of course." Unexpectedly, Johnson belched. "Where's those binoculars?" He found them in the back of the jeep, took them out of the case, and looked toward the helicopter. Adjusting the focus, he was able to see two men standing outside the helicopter, apparently admiring the wreckage. He saw a third man crawl on hands and knees out an open hatch on the side of the fuselage, stand up and hobble forward a few steps, then sit down abruptly. There's one casualty, Johnson thought. He continued to watch, saw one man re-enter the fuselage, come out with a rifle in his hands and start up the mountainside. The other two men, after several minutes of discussion, began a slow descent toward the floor of the canyon, the hale-bodied one assisting the other. Johnson lowered the binoculars. "Doesn't seem to be any serious damage," he said, mostly to himself; the operator, busy, did not hear him.

Johnson hesitated, uncertain now whether to go up the canyon to meet the fliers or to stay where he was. He was already beginning to regret having loosed those six vigilantes into the hills; when and if they found the helicopter crew without need of assistance, they would undoubtedly go on after the fugitive: six more nervous, itchy trigger fingers at large. Things were getting out of control; even the wind was beginning to stir and whistle and kick up dust: it looked as if this was going to be a long, busy day.

From somewhere in the yellow sky to the south came the harsh, strained persistent noise of a small airplane. Johnson saw it after a while, a Taylor Cub. The State Police. He glanced toward the radio operator and saw his jaw working industriously under the red nose and the small blue eyes.

I'll wait here, he decided, at least for a while. If the wind gets very bad we might all have to go home anyway.

The operator was in communication with the State Police airplane, directing the crew's attention to the stricken helicopter high on the mountain; the plane banked to the right and climbed through the air, side-slipping a little in a sudden gust of wind, flying toward the helicopter, the granite cliffs, the pine and aspen and vast disorder that sheltered the outlaw and his horse and concealed somewhere in its chaotic depths the dozen or more armed men pursuing him.

The operator pushed up his earphones and lit a cigarette, cupping the match in his hand and turning his back to the wind. "This is a mess," he said. "Huh, Morey?"

"Sure is," Johnson said. Something in his eye—a particle of dust. He pulled at his upper eyelid and tried to blink the eye clean. The irritant, whatever it was, settled firmly in a corner of the eyesocket. "Did you contact the Air Base?"

"They're sendin an ambulance." The operator looked at Johnson. "How about some lunch? I'm starved."

Johnson scratched and rubbed at his eye until he had succeeded in spreading and intensifying the irritation. "There's something in my eye," he said. "See if you can find it." He sat down beside the radio operator in the jeep; the man lifted a grimy thumb and forefinger toward his eye. "I think it's in this corner," Johnson said, pointing. "Under the lower eyelid." The operator's face loomed large before his; he looked serious and concerned and simple and infinitely kind. He spread Johnson's eyelids with his rough scarified fingers; through a film of automatic tears Johnson watched the eye of the operator scanning the surface of his own.

"Look up," the operator said. Johnson looked up. "Look down." Johnson looked down. "Can't see anything . . . . Look to the right," the operator said. Johnson looked to the right. "Look to the left." He looked to the left. "I can't see a thing, Morey," the operator said; "I can't see anything in there."

"All right," the sheriff said. "Thanks for trying. Maybe I blinked it out."

"That's prob'ly what happened. Sometimes when you get rid of a thing it still feels it's in there. For a while."

"Did we bring a lunch?" Johnson said.

"Sure we did. I remember packin it in."

They searched in the back of the jeep for the lunch-bag, found it and the quart thermos bottle full of coffee. They ate cheese and bologna sandwiches and drank hot tan coffee while the wind rolled in from the north and stirred the sand in the arroyo and filled the air with a suspension of fine dust.—The dry almost weightless hulk of a tumbleweed bounced over the sand and rocks, coming toward them.

"They won't find him now," the operator said.

Johnson drank the hot coffee, looking up through the

haze toward the mountain. Above the foothills the air seemed still clear; the sky beyond the mountain's crest was a sharp electric blue. He tried to imagine the activity and the sensations of the solitary man in whose honor he—Johnson—and the others were now waiting in the dust or blundering heavily around in the absurd labyrinth of boulders and canyons and thorny chaparral. Scared as a rabbit, he thought; that's the way he must feel. That's the way *I'd* feel, stumbling through that rocky jungle.

He stared up at the mountain, forgetting Burns again, conscious of a vague annoyance, sharing for a few moments in the general undifferentiated social resentment of this mountain, an impatience with its irrational bulk and complexity, its absurd, exasperating lack of purpose or utility. To the east were the plains, flat and reasonable and cooperative, limited, amenable to man; on this side were similar areas, suitable at least for airstrips, housing projects, graveyards and fraternity picnics; by contrast the mountain appeared as a great ugly eruption of granite, not only meaningless but malignant, and worse than malignant—a piece of sheer insolence.

Thinking about it, Johnson began to smile; he scratched his neck and chuckled aloud. The radio operator looked at him closely.

The tumbleweed had crossed the wash; it bounded lightly before the wind on its tense stems, coming straight at the jeep. It hit a rock and bouncing up was caught fully by the wind and lifted over the hood of the jeep, rustling and cackling aridly, while Johnson and the radio operator shielded their faces. The tumbleweed dropped in the sand again and rolled and bounced toward the opening of the canyon, toward the valley. A dead

mechanism bearing seeds, with a ludicrous semblance of purpose in its hustling, restless movements.

Johnson shined an apple on the sleeve of his jacket. "I'm
going up the canyon," he said. He climbed out of the jeep. "I'm
going up to meet those two aviators. I'll be back in half an hour,
I reckon."

"Okay, Morey." The operator had dribbled a little coffee
on his khaki shirt; he rubbed at the stain with a blue bandana.
"Any message?"

"Message? Message for who?"

"Suppose the General wants to know what happened to his
helicopter?"

"Tell him." The sheriff started off, following the trail in the
sand. This canyon was much like the other one, narrow and
twisting and steeply ascending, with a cactus slope on the north
and a piñon-juniper slope to the south. Again he had to climb
barricades of jammed-up boulders and smooth eroded outcrop-
pings of the underlying granite; between these barriers were the
usual long stretches of sand with their patches of bunch grass,
withered scrub oak, jackpine and cane cactus.

Johnson walked with his eyes down, breathing heavily and
sweating—he removed his jacket, draped it over his forearm—
and watched the procession of tracks in the sand and gravel
before him. Among the footprints, scuffed and overlapping as
if a multitude had passed this way, he was able to recognize the
stamp of a Size 13 boot: Deputy Gutierrez. The bloodhound,
he thought, the murderous bloodhound. He wondered where,
in that hanging wilderness several thousand feet above, the big
man was now, and where the other one—the criminal—was,
and how close they might be to each other, and if either knew.

Especially, if the cowboy knew. The *cowboy!* Johnson spat; his instinctive sympathy for the hunted man was darkened by a scornful pity closer to disgust than compassion. The emotion faded as he climbed on; all emotions and thoughts retreated before the insistent pressure of fatigue and breathing and heat and the problems forced on him by the successive dams and poised cascades of stone.

He was sheltered from the wind now and the air was cleaner. When he stopped to rest and looked back he could see the jeep and the four automobiles at the mouth of the canyon below, and the pattern of erosion spreading over the mesa toward the city. The city, however, had disappeared; where it should have been or had been there was now a boiling shroud of yellow dust. The dust diagrammed the currents and whorls of the winds, smothered and obliterated the ragged crucifix of the city, whirled over river and city and valley to the north and south for as far as Johnson could see. It made an impressive spectacle; Johnson, a man of limited prophetic powers, was faintly troubled by old, obscure, unacknowledged premonitions of suffocation and disaster.

He shrugged his shoulders, glad now to be far above the scene, and turned his back on it and trudged ahead, upward. The holstered pistol weighed uncomfortably against his thigh; he pulled the belt around, shifting the weight to his hip, and tightened the belt by a notch.

A voice hailed him. He looked up and saw the two helicopter crewmen, one supporting the other, limping slowly down the canyon floor. The men were dirty, their green coveralls were torn and dusty, and they both seemed unhappy, sullen, irritable. "Hey!" one of them cried again; "how do we get out of this jungle?"

The sheriff did not reply but sat down on a rock and waited for them to approach. He wiped his brow with his handkerchief and put his jacket back on. The two men came close to him; they looked young, less than twenty; the uninjured one wore sergeant's stripes. The sergeant did not offer to introduce himself or shake hands, but began complaining immediately. "How much farther we gotta go?" he asked. A smudge of grease was spread across his nose and cheek; droplets of sweat glistened under his eyes, on his upper lip. "Hey, man? How do we get outa this goddamned place?"

"You're doing all right," Johnson said, not looking at him. He spoke to the second man, whose face was pale and tense. "What's the matter, son? Sprained ankle?" The young man nodded, standing on one foot, an arm around the sergeant's shoulder. "Sit down and rest yourselves a spell," Johnson said. The young man looked toward the rock on which Johnson had been sitting. "Here," Johnson said, stepping toward him; "let me help you."

"We're in a hurry," the sergeant said.

"That's all right," Johnson said. "You can wait for a few minutes; this fella looks like he could use some rest." He helped the injured man to sit down, while the sergeant stood by frowning and glancing nervously around. "Let me see that ankle," Johnson said, as the young man leaned back, shutting his eyes.

"It's all right," the sergeant said; "I put an elastic bandage on it."

"That's good," Johnson said; he lifted the pantleg of the man's coveralls and began unwrapping the bandage, while the sergeant stood nearby and complained: he was bitter; the affair was supposed to have been a game, good sport, a real man-hunt. No one had suggested the possibility of their being shot down—and in what a jungle! Nothing but rock and cactus; the sergeant was disgusted. And then, worst of all, the goddamned pilot taking off after the guy with his rifle, leaving him to carry a man with a game leg down several miles of cliffs and rock slides;—Christ! Johnson inquired after the men he had dispatched to the scene of the wreck. "Never saw em!" the sergeant said. "Never saw em . . ."

Johnson made a mental note, unwrapping the last of the bandage. He looked at the injury. The ankle was blue and swollen, hot to the touch. "Oughta have splints on this," Johnson said; "it might be broken."

The injured man opened his eyes and smiled weakly at the sergeant. "Didn't I tell ya?" he said; "goddamnit, didn't I tell ya?"

"Bullshit," the sergeant growled; "I know a broken leg when I see one." He scuffed around in the sand, staring down the canyon. "Jesus, what a place . . ." he muttered.

Johnson carried a notebook in his jacket; he pulled it out and broke off the stiff cardboard covers and folded them double. "This'll have to do," he said to the young man; he placed the improvised splints on the sides of the swollen ankle and started to rewrap the bandage.

"And why couldn't they send a 'copter out to pick us up?" the sergeant said. "How can they expect human beings to climb around over this stuff?" He waved a hand at the mountain now surrounding and supporting them. "Why couldn't they send a 'copter?"

"I don't know," the sheriff said. "We asked for one." This here's a cranky case, he was thinking. Parlous upset. I should've known better than to let the Air Corps get into this.

"You're Johnson, aren't you?" the sergeant said; he stared at the sheriff with narrowed, cynical eyes, licking the sweat from his upper lip.

"*Sheriff* Johnson to you." Johnson made the final turn in the bandage and fastened it with the two little metal clips. "That feel all right, son?" The young man nodded.

"You sort of made a mess of things today," the sergeant said, after a short pause. "Isn't that right, *Sheriff* Johnson?"

Johnson slapped on his hat. "Mind your manners," he said, standing up. "And your own business." He put a hand under the armpit of the injured man, who was smiling slyly. "Come on," Johnson said, "let's get this fella down outa here."

"Okay, okay," the sergeant said; "sure. Okay. Yes sir, Mister Sheriff."

Far above them, across the canyon walls, the wind roared through the fiery blue ether of the sky.

When they returned to the foot of the canyon, some three-quarters of an hour later, they found waiting for them—considerably modified by a driving storm of sand and dust and whirling tumbleweeds—an Air Force ambulance with two young Medics huddled in its lee, smoking cigarettes; also, the radio operator, looking flustered and anxious. "The General wants to talk to you," he shouted at Johnson through the yellow current of the wind.

Johnson turned the damaged airman over to the Medics, then struggled through the dust toward the jeep. "What general?" he growled. Sand pattered the metal surfaces of the machine, against the radio, against his leather jacket. "You mean that Air Force fella—what's his name?"

"Yes," the operator said; "him." He pointed to the microphone. "All set. They're waitin for you to call right now."

"All right," Johnson took up the microphone. "This is Sheriff Johnson calling Kirk Field. Come in, Kirk Field. Over." The operator flipped the toggle switches and the loudspeaker crackled and hummed; the operator turned up the volume against the whine of the wind. Suddenly the great voice of General Desalius boomed at them, thundering over the wind and the flapping canvas of the jeep:

"Sheriff, this is General Desalius. Sheriff, what have you done with my helicopter?" Without waiting for an answer the voice roared on, making the speaker screen rattle like a piece of loose tin. "Is this nonsense true that that jailbreaker, that scum, that common vagrant, shot down my helicopter? Eh, Sheriff?" There was a pause; a different voice, startlingly mild and meek, said: "Over."

Johnson replied: "That's right, General. The helicopter was damaged by small-arms fire and forced down. A crash landing. Nobody seriously hurt. Over."

The sergeant and one of the Medics approached, listening.

The rich powerful bellow of General Desalius burst from the speaker again, while the radio operator, with a grimace of pain, removed his earphones and held them on his lap: "Sheriff, don't kid me! That's ridiculous! Impossible! This bandit—why I'll blast him off the face of the earth! Where is the rascal? Why I'll burn him out with napalm, I'll cook him with phosphorus! Where is that vermin? He can't—where is he? By god, I'll drop an atomic bomb on the bastard!"

The two Air Force men were grinning openly, nudging each other. Johnson turned down the volume. The General stormed on:

"Do you know how much my helicopters cost, Sheriff? Do

you? Do you have any notion at all?" Another pause; again the anonymous, meditating voice said: "Over."

Johnson tried to restrain his mounting anger and disgust. "No I don't, General," he said. "Over."

"One hundred and twenty thousand dollars!" the General howled. "Apiece! You hear that, Sheriff? One hundred and twenty thousand dollars, that's what my 'copters cost! One hundred and twenty—"

Johnson switched off the speaker, frowning bitterly. In the comparative silence that followed they could all hear the rasp and rattle of the earphones on the operator's lap, still vibrating with the thunder of the General's anger. But a mechanically reduced thunder, a strange and artificial diminution of what had been so overpowering a moment before. The effect was curious and contradictory—a bellowing in miniature, like the roar of an outraged insect.

Johnson felt a peculiar shame, not for himself but for his kind. The wind and dust assailed him, the sun pale beyond the yellow sky, but he stood motionless, his hand on the radio, his eyes fixed on the ground. He became aware, after a few minutes, of the two Air Force men still watching him. He looked at them and they grinned in a furtive, malicious way. The sergeant said: "The General's real wigged out, huh man? Really flippin his lid, huh?"

Johnson made no answer. "What about the pilot?" the sergeant said.

"What about him?"

"Are you gonna bring him back to the Base?"

"If he ever comes down outa those rocks," Johnson said.

"Well, we're not waiting." The sergeant and the Medic

turned back and climbed into the cab of the ambulance, started the engine, turned noisily in the sand, motor roaring, and drove off down the road. A pair of ragged tumbleweeds went rolling and flopping after them.

"Well?" said the radio operator; the earphones had stopped vibrating on his lap.

"Well what?" Johnson said.

"Are we gonna give up and go home?"

Johnson turned and gazed up the canyon toward the mountain. Fragments of cloud floated across the face of the cliffs, trailing blue shadows over the naked rock. Patches of snow glinted like glass along the crest. Somewhere up there, among those pines and tumbled boulders, under the leaning crags. . . .

"You think they might find him yet?" the operator said.

"We'll wait," Johnson said. "We'll wait till sundown at least." He turned up the collar of his jacket against the singing wind. He looked around. "Let's see if we can't get this jeep a little farther up the wash, close to the wall. I'd like to get out of this wind before the sand chokes us to death." The operator stared at him. Johnson said: "Okay? What's the matter with you? Let's go!"

CHAPTER 17

Burns climbed up the slope, carrying his carbine and leading the mare. His beaten black hat, now sprinkled with pine needles and a few dry juniper berries, was pushed far back on his head, revealing his tangled forelock and a brow smeared with dust and sweat. He was breathing heavily, panting—in the cool shade of the cliff his breath turned to a foggy vapor—but he climbed on at a steady rate, not pausing, his eyes and ears alert, scanning the ridge above him, the slope below, the high rim of the mountain.

The mare slipped and stumbled after him, head and neck drooping, flanks shining with lather. She carried the guitar now, slung to the saddlehorn, and a load of venison stuffed and insulated inside the bedroll behind the cantle.

He kept going until he was within a few yards of topping the ridge. Here, among the concealing yellow pine and piñon he tied the horse and went on alone, crouching a little, to the crest of the ridge. He stopped and made a careful survey in all directions. He saw the airplane to the north, cruising slowly up and down the canyon he had left an hour ago. Above him, on the east, were the red cliffs and the long horizontal strata of sedimentary rock that formed the rim and crest of the mountain: he knew that there was somebody up there looking for him; he had seen the glint of metal, and a flashing mirror communicating in Morse to his pursuers below. Now, however, he could see no one, no sign of man—except the two giant red and white television relay towers perched on the edge of the rim several miles to the northeast.

He looked down into the valley to his south and for a long time could see no man, no enemy. There where the mountain formed a bend, like the inside of an elbow, the forest had crept down and thickened and flourished until the entire valley, or basin, perhaps two miles across at its widest point, was dark and carpeted with the dull drab green of pine and cedar. A man and horse could be tracked but not easily spotted once in there; Burns' eyes were held, his mind and nerves hungering after those trees and that space of security. He removed his hat and pushed back his damp hair; he noticed the blue juniper berries rolling in the crown of the hat and ate them, filling his mouth with the sharp cooling familiar flavor—a little bitter, with the pungency of turpentine.

As he chewed the berries he turned on his heels, squatting, and looked back and down, to the north and northwest and west. He saw two men coming slowly down the slope on the north, less than a mile away; he saw a group of men, five or six, trudging up the floor of the canyon, heads bent to the ground, their rifle barrels shining; he saw, far below at the fanning mouth of the canyon, the dull gleam of automobiles, the minute figures of men moving about; he saw the valley of the river far to the west, though river and city and the five volcanoes were all invisible under the pall of smoke and dust. He looked again at the bright silvery wreckage of the helicopter down on the opposite hillside—all that crumpled metal, that expensive mangled machinery—and wondered now where the third man was, the one with the rifle; the other two he had seen go limping homeward and knew he had nothing to fear from them but a distant ill-will.

Finally he stood up, went back to Whisky and unwrapped the bridle reins from the branch of the piñon. Rubbing her nose, patting her wet flanks, he talked to her: "Okay, little girl, we better get a move on, we still got a few hundred miles to go." He looked up through the black branches of the tree at the towers of granite hanging over them, the remote and silent monuments of an earlier world. "Maybe we'll have to climb that old headwall yet, little girl." He stared up at it while the mare nuzzled his chest, thrusting her snorting nose under his arm. A small fragile white butterfly twinkled within the influence of the tree, dipped and turned in the shafts of sunlight, rose up among the clean branches through the tree toward the bare rock beyond and was suddenly lost, extinguished, in that gulf of light and space and muted thunder. "Come on, girl," Burns said, tugging gently at the reins; Whisky stepped forward and he turned ahead of her and led toward the ridge.

They crossed over under the shade of the pines. Below, the earth fell away steeply, with little cover—boulders and yucca and cholla—toward the valley and the forest. Burns was about to start down when something hot and invisible struck past his cheek with an insane, furious velocity; he heard a metallic twang, the shattering of wood, and as he was falling to the ground, the clear definitive report of a rifle from somewhere down below. He hugged the earth like a lover, his toes digging in, his chin and mouth buried in the dry, fragrant tilth of needles and sand. The first thing he thought, while his gaze searched the brush and rocks below, was: My guitar!—the bastard!—he hit my guitar!

At the moment he could see nothing in the shape of a man; he looked back at the mare, saw her standing alert and uncertain, eyes wide, nostrils flexing, testing the moving air. On the saddle hung the wounded guitar, smashed through bridge and box, a splintered ruin. Burns swore and stared again down the steep hillside, hunting among the boulders and chaparral for a sign of movement, for a shape, a shadow. There was nothing; he became aware of his own hands on the earth before him: brown, leathery, scarred by bark and cholla spines, a pair of complicated tools, impersonal, removed from him—under one hand lay the rifle. He cocked it with his thumb and waited for something to appear below. He waited for ten seconds, thirty, a full minute, while the light wind brushed the trees around him. The stillness was almost complete: he could hear the agitation of the pine boughs, the dry brittle clicking of a dying locust, his own hard breathing, but nothing more. He waited, uncomfortably conscious of his uncertainty, of the men—seven of them? eight?—approaching from the rear, of the restless mare shying back now, ready to drift off: the inevitable thought came, that he might be better off without the horse, might make the crest of the mountain easily, if alone, and lose himself in the forests on the east. He considered the proposition and rejected it.

His senses functioned independently of his brain, still watching and waiting for a trace of the enemy somewhere below. Yet nothing moved but the black shadows of the boulders, the sun edging down through the sky to the yellow horizon of dust on the west. Burns made up his mind to retreat.

He crawled backwards on his belly, groping behind him for the trailing reins of the bridle. He couldn't find them; the mare backed away, slowly, one step at a time. Burns crawled back until the trunk of a pine gave him partial shelter on the front; he rose to his knees, turned and grabbed the dragging reins as Whisky stepped backward again. His nerves tingled, expecting another shot, the hot lash of a bullet in his neck or shoulder or ribs, as he pulled his body around to the safe side of the mare, and then led her back to the northern slope of the ridge. He leaned against her for a moment, resting his shaking limbs, breathing in as a kind of security and strength the warm powerful familiar stench of the sweating horse.

He took a sip of water from the canteen—his mouth seemed painfully dry. He knew quite well that he was taking far too much time, that his pursuers were coming closer with his every pause and delay, that the man who had fired on him—who was down there on the other side?—might even now be stealing up from rock to rock toward the top of the ridge. He had a second swallow of water, screwed the lid back on the canteen and hung it to the saddlehorn.

There was the guitar. He lifted it from the saddle and looked at it and shook his head sadly. He strummed once on the loosened strings and they made a sound so grotesque, so harsh, that the mare jerked up her head and stepped aside, staring at him. Burns broke the back of the instrument over his knee and flung the remains down the hillside. He picked up the rifle and started off, leading the mare up the ridge under the thin screen of the pines toward the great fissured wall of the mountain.

He had no real hope of finding a way up over or through that towering barrier, either with or without the horse; even if he could climb to the rim there would probably be men waiting for him when he got there. Then there was little rationality, anymore than hope, in his choice of direction—upward along the narrowing ridge to the granite cliffs—but he realized now that he had no other way to go, no other way to turn; it was the instinct of the hunted animal, as well as desperation, which drove him upward toward that final wall of rock.

Still far away in terms of time and effort: half a mile above over a rugged jumble of boulders, through jackpine and cactus to the foot of the wall itself and the dessicated pinnacles and cliffs and grottoes that obscured the exact character of the barrier.

Burns marched slowly ahead, leading the mare carefully among the trees and tumbled rocks, around the rigid penetrating husks of yucca, over dusty slabs of sandstone marked delicately with the imprint of lizards. There was no reasonable trail but only a faint and wandering pattering of deer paths leading in all directions and over, through and under obstructions that no horse could negotiate. Once they passed a shelf of rock different in no obvious way from many others; but underneath the overhang, coiled in the sun, was a fat, warm, dust-colored, timber rattler, attentive and annoyed, watching them with its opaque, glittering eyes. The mare did not see it but when she heard the whirr of the rattlesnake's vibrating tail she shied away violently, almost jerking the cowboy off his feet. He swore at her, and quieted her, and led her around through the trees well away from the snake. When they were safely past he left the mare for a moment and went back and lobbed a few small stones at the reptile, not to harm it but only to stir it up a little, in case others should pass this way after him.

They went on, horse and man, stopping infrequently and briefly to rest. Burns was having some difficulty with his feet: the boots he was wearing were old and worn, not designed for walking, quite unsuited for mountain climbing; one heel was loose, tending to give unexpectedly under his full weight. And both feet were swollen, and cold. He was also suffering from an odd, unfamiliar pain in the small of his back, near the kidneys, where Gutierrez had slugged and kicked him the night before last. This pain bothered and worried at him unceasingly, aggravated by the climb and his heavy breathing, and he was compelled to stop more often to ease the sharp ache of it.

Each time he stopped he studied the country behind him, the ridge and its slopes, the canyon on the north, the forested valley on the south. He had glimpses of his pursuers, including a pair on the south slope that must have been those who had nearly ambushed him earlier; he had no doubt that he in turn had been observed and was being followed not merely by trail but by sight. There was little he could do but turn and trudge on.

The ridge ended in a labyrinth of boulders, grottoes, and wrinkled cliffs. Burns and the mare entered a rocky glen, surrounded on three sides by perpendicular walls which effectively hid them from view, and there they stopped again to rest. From somewhere deep in the rocks came the sound of a slow secret drip of water; shrubs of greasewood on the floor of the glen and clinging to its walls spilled their yellow seed into the air, spontaneously it seemed, for the wind could not reach in here. Burns sat down and pushed the sweat from his forehead with a tired hand; he removed his hat, inspected the sweat-sodden band inside, and placed the hat upside down on the ground to dry. He looked up: the sky was blue-golden, a well of space beyond the walls of the mountain. He heard the dripping water, the intermittent uncertain twittering of a Mexican finch. He listened, still looking up at the sky;—the intense blue there seemed to pulsate in his vision, to advance and withdraw in waves with a throbbing rhythm; and strangely, the blue of this sky, despite its cold intensity, seemed less pure, or beyond purity: the blue was suffused with grains of blackness, a quality that deepened as the vision struck farther into the depths of the atmosphere; as though his human eyes were momentarily capable of seeing into the sky and through it to the absolute blackness beyond;—and still listening, heard the bird stop in its dull complaining, and then he heard nothing at all except the muted leak of drops of water. An unnecessary silence, he thought; he picked at his ears and wiped more sweat from his face, though he was already feeling the chill of the heights seep into his blood and bone.

He felt that he was being watched.

Not by human eyes. He sensed no immediate danger in his intuition, but without looking over his shoulder he felt and knew that he and the mare were not alone. For a moment he was troubled, not by fear, but by a sensation of utter desolation and rejection, as if he were alien not only to the cities of men but also to the rocks and trees and spirits of the wilderness. The sensation passed away and he was left with the uncanny awareness of another presence. Skin prickling, he waited for a few moments and then very slowly raised and turned his head. He saw a huge, dark bird perched on the limb of a yellow pine, watching him; two tufts of feathers, like horns, stood up stiffly from the creature's head; the enormous eyes, with lids that rose and fell like curtains, blinked at him once.

Burns smiled wearily and looked away; and then he became

conscious of another one: silhouetted darkly against the sky, a second horned owl watched him from its roost on the top of a boulder near the entrance to the glen. And almost immediately he discovered the third—this one squatting on a ledge high up on the cliff to his left, peering fixedly, idiotically, down at him. The cowboy frowned uneasily and stood up, putting his hat back on. He looked around for more owls but there were only the three, sitting there watching him, eyes blinking and staring from the great horned heads.

Burns heard a man shout, a distant shout, far below; he heard the human voice arch and die, and then a long succession of echoes rolling from cliff to cliff on the mountainside.

He picked up Whisky's reins and led her to the head of the glen, passing below the first silent owl. Expecting a dead end, he found instead a huge cleft in the rock, a natural tunnel formed by the faulting and slipping of a barn-sized block of granite. He took the horse through this opening, glad to leave the haunted glen behind, and came out on a steep talus slope of gravel and fragmented shale. Above the slope rose the sheer wall of the mountain. But it too was incomplete, faulted: a diagonal opening fifty yards wide ran from a corner of the talus slope up through a rift in the main wall to the series of horizontal stratifications that formed the rim of the mountain. Burns saw that he was within a thousand feet of the crest by line of sight, perhaps two or three times that far by foot. The route he would have to take slanted upward at fifty degrees over loose rock, through scrub oak and aspen, and up through the brush to the ledges and the rim and the sky and whatever was waiting for him up there.

This was better than he had thought he had any right to hope for. He stared up that avenue of possible escape, nerve and hope and mental vigor returning to him, and was able to shake off the spell of the cold glen and the three horned owls that brooded like specters over its silence.

There was first the problem of getting across the open area of the talus to the cover of the aspens without getting shot. From the shelter of the leaning rocks Burns surveyed the rim above—he saw no one nor any sparkle of metal or glass—and then the long canyon falling away beneath him. There he could see his pursuers still coming on, crawling it seemed, up that steep complex ascent to the backbone of the ridge: he saw two men far ahead of the rest, one pointing ahead with a stick, the other stooped and lethargic under a burden of some kind on his back; while the other men sat in the sunlight facing the west, one man among them lifting something to his mouth, then throwing it away, a light gleaming object that sailed through the air and down into the depths of the canyon. There were three others to account for but he could not see them—they were the ones he now feared.

But there was little advantage in waiting; fifty yards of target space to cross and then he would reach the comparative safety of the aspen thickets. He stepped forward, clucking at the mare. She followed willingly enough, shivering, eager to get out of the cold shade into the sunlight. He led her at a clumsy trot up and across the sliding broken treacherous rock; twice the mare slipped and fell to her knees, scrambling, snorting, panting after him. He talked quietly to her, urged her on, encouraged her, while the wind came at them, swirling the dust they were raising into their eyes and over their heads, attracting attention. He was halfway across, he and the mare, half-running, when some-body saw them.

Burns heard a wild shout, eager, almost hysterical; it seemed to come from his left, to the north. He didn't look; he tugged at the reins, cursing silently and bitterly—oh you damned pitiful bitch, you simple dumb crazy bitch of a horse, Whisky you stubborn murderous banshee—and kept trying to run to reach those sheltering trees. A bullet swerved toward him through the gulf of sunlit space; it hit and shattered a plate of sandstone a few feet ahead of him, ricocheted off the granite beneath and went whining away toward the south, a hot smashed wad of lead whose fluttering vibrations Burns could feel through the skin of his hands long after the sound was gone. He kept going; the trees were fifty feet away.

He heard the shout again. Stop! someone was shrieking at him—stop! stop!

Burns kept going; this time he felt the bullet coming at him, headed for his chest or belly. He was crouching forward, running and stumbling, the horse lunging after him; he was very much afraid he would be hit but the bullet passed smoothly and swiftly a few inches above his head, streaking by, transparent and innocent, to be lost in the space beyond. A second later he heard the sound of the shot, as futile and harmless as the shouting; he could not help laughing a little.

He was in the trees now, and the mare with him, and both of them alive and excited and eager, intoxicated by danger. He scrambled upward through the small perfect aspens, heedless of the film of sweat clouding his eyes, panting, gasping for breath, half dragging the horse and then nearly being run down as the horse leaped and halted, lunged and scrambled and fell and leaped forward again with him, after him, just behind him, her hot exhalations fanning his neck, her nose shoving at his shoulderblades, her front hooves clipping at his heels. The wind whipped the dust around them—he could smell rock salt and flint, the smoke of rotting fern, the pinetar from below—and lashed at the small trees and spangled them, horse and man, with small dry dead golden aspen leaves.

The slope was too steep to climb without aid; Burns pulled himself up from tree to tree, like climbing a ladder. The mare thrashed and scrambled around behind him, then beside him, snorting and driveling at the lips, her eyes glaring, rolling furiously, mad with panic and fury and the wild happiness of violent effort. She leaped ahead and the cowboy held and belayed her when she stopped and while she struggled for new footing from which to leap again; he kept her from leaving the earth and rolling, falling, down into the canyon beneath them. Somehow he did it, though he knew it was ridiculous and impossible, an outrage of reason and common sense and justice and even natural law. It was all senseless and crazy, but nothing could stop them; both he and the horse were possessed by a mania for ascent.

Five hundred feet to the rim: they kept on going.

They were among and above the great pink cliffs; out of the corner of an eye, through the screen of leaves, Burns saw a hawk soaring over a lake of space a hundred fathoms deep. Yet the hawk was beneath him—he was looking down on it, seeing the stately motionless wings from above. He had a moment of giddiness before he turned his back on the hovering hawk and the blue depths of the canyon; his throat was burning and dry, his eyes tormented by his own dripping sweat, his lungs and heart cracking, expanding, collapsing, as if a vise of iron were closing in around his ribs, stifling his breath, seeming to threaten to break him—but he kept climbing, kept coaxing and dragging the mare and stumbling out of the way when she leaped after him, trampling on his broken heels. He didn't think about what he was doing or why; he kept climbing. He couldn't think: his brain seemed powerless, overwhelmed by the frenzy and passion of his whole body—fiery nerves, quivering muscle, the racing blood.

And then they came, suddenly, to a place where there could be no more climbing.

They stood on the lowest of the great horizontal escarpments, at the base of a sheer ledge forty feet high; the rock here was soft, white and rotten, and overhanging, impossible to climb. For a while Burns would not believe it. He stared angrily up at the rock, trying to see through his unsettled, unfocussed eyes; the mare stood beside him, shaking and jerking as if in a fit, her foamy flanks steaming in the cold air, the wind stirring her black mane and sweeping the ragged burr-tangled disorder of her tail. Burns glared at the powdery white rock, picked off a chunk of it and threw it to the ground.

But at last he gave in and turned south, following the contour of the escarpment, which climbed slightly as he tended south but revealed no opening, ravine or less-than-vertical construction up which he might lead, drag or carry a horse. Gradually he regained his breathing powers, the vise around his chest weakened and faded, the climbing madness evaporated, and he found his senses recovering their alertness, his brain functioning again. They must know, he was thinking, they must know almost exactly where I am now. The ones up above must know. All of them. They're waiting for me—when I climb that last ledge I'll find a rifle bore staring at me.

He heard an airplane; not near yet but coming fast, straight toward him. He stopped where he was, deep in a jungle of harsh dry scrub oak which almost but not quite concealed him and the mare, and waited for the machine to roar over and past.

There was a rush of air, the smell of gasoline and hot metal— Burns saw the plane go by, in its wake the leaves of the scrub oak shaking, twisting, tearing free from their stems. At the same moment the mare whinnied, jerking at the reins, lunging backward, and slid several feet down the slope, dragging the cowboy with her. The overturned stones sparkled with hoarfrost.

"Damn you!" Burns cried; he lashed the mare once across the face with the reins. "Hold still or by God—" The mare stared at him with her brown blood-flecked eyes, shocked, frightened. Burns rose slowly to his feet, rubbing one knee, watching the yellow wings of the plane lift and turn among the crags to the south. "Take it easy, girl," he said; "for chrissake take it easy."

The airplane was coming back. Burns tore off a branch of the scrub oak and jammed the butt of it under the bedroll, partially camouflaging the saddle; he broke a second and laid it over the bedroll and saddlebags. He had no more time; the airplane was boring through the air toward him. He snubbed the bridle reins around the bole of a shrub, crouched down and waited.

Again the machine roared almost directly over him, trailing fumes and turbulent air. Burns brushed away a dead leaf that fell and hung from the brim of his hat. He swore silently, feeling indignant, humiliated, terribly exposed and insecure. He pulled back the hammer of the rifle and waited for the plane to return.

But it didn't; he watched it soar northward, gaining altitude rapidly, then bank to the west, turn and fall away—a shining yellow phantasm now in all that blue space—toward the valley, the river, the dust-hazed obscurity of the city. Burns got to his feet, spitting, hauled at the reins and started himself and the mare on through the chaparral toward the south.

The sky was full of flying objects. He saw something come over the rim of the mountain in utter baffling silence, a flash of silvery metal moving so fast that light and distance betrayed the eye: the thing seemed to move in a series of thrusts, pulses, like a falling star. A jet plane: Burns watched it score westward in its immaculate geometrically-accurate flight; it was nearly gone before he heard the sound of its passage overhead—a thin metallic scream, demoniacal and tortured, like the wail of some Hellbound ghost.

He found himself shivering. He blinked the dust and surprise out of his eyes, wiped his nose, and stepped ahead again on the heavy dull sliding skin of the mountain, forcing his way through the thickets of oak, around yucca and spanish bayonet and the erratic growths of prickly pear spawned by the rocks. He was thirsty again, and hungry, and chilled by his evaporating sweat.

A break in the ledge: here erosion had formed a passageway, a series of gradual setbacks, up through the first ledge to the pines and aspens crowded on the second. Burns led Whisky up this opening, a distance of fifty yards or so, and then continued his traverse on the next shelf of rock, proceeding parallel to and not much more than a hundred feet below the rim of the mountain. He followed the base of the cliff, going south: the rock wall rose up on his left, the slope fell away steeply to his right, ending on the brink of the ledge below. Now and then he paused to listen, to look back and into the canyons below and up to the skyline ahead. He saw no one, heard nothing except the cawing of a magpie somewhere in the pines below, the drone of remote airplanes, the persistent shrill keening of cicada.

His feet hurt him; the heel of one boot was gone, the bent nails gnawing at the hide of his heel. Occasionally something struck him in the small of the back—a hot aching surge of pain, fierce but brief; he learned to anticipate it and each time the pain hit him, was almost ready for it.

He stopped under the sheltering gloom of a yellow pine, letting the reins fall, and took a few swallows of water from the canteen. The water sharpened his hunger: he loosened the rope around the bedroll, reached inside with his knife until he found the meat and sawed off a chunk of the round and ate it as it was, raw and bloody and cool. He wiped his hands clean on Whisky's rump, after he had eaten, lashed the bedroll tight and secure, had another short drink, and was ready to go on. And then he heard a man's voice above him, coming out of the sky:

"Floyd—come here!"

Burns ducked back under the overhanging wall. The mare watched him in surprise, the reins dangling to the ground in front of her. Very slowly and carefully, muffling the operation with his body as best he could, Burns cocked the rifle again. From the ledge above his head he heard a heavy body crashing and struggling through the brush, then a second voice:

"Whaddeya see?"

There was no immediate reply. Burns could imagine the first man putting a finger to his lips, then pointing below. There was silence, then the faint hiss of whispering. Burns strained to hear but could make out nothing but the repeated word "horse." But that was enough. He pressed his body back against the dry, granular rock, waiting, his right forefinger on the trigger.

There was a silence again, the men above also waiting, thinking, planning. Finally, after several dead minutes had passed—the sun was now sinking far down into the sky on the west-southwest—Burns heard the second voice, loud but faintly uncertain:

"All right, you. Burns. We know you're down there. You can't get away. Put your hands up and step beside that horse."

Burns smiled; looking up under his sagging hatbrim he could see the gray rock bending over him, the sky, the top of the pine tree. The mare was still watching him—pointing. She took one tentative step toward him and he scowled savagely at her. She stopped; he noticed for the first time that she was bleeding on the inside of her right foreleg—a dark slow-spreading stain of blood and dust.

The voice from above: "Come on, step out! We know you're down there. Come on or we'll come down after you."

This made Burns smile again. He waited.

The men above went into another whispered consultation; presently one of them tramped away to the south—Burns could hear the popping and exploding of dead twigs and branches. The sounds died away gradually as he waited. Another spell of silence. He began to worry about the men below, the pursuers: they could not be far away now, unless they had given up. He had to doubt that, and yet he did not dare move. He had to wait, find out what these two fellows above were up to. Although it was not difficult to guess: one was waiting above, watching the horse; the second had gone on along the rim looking for him, or looking for a point from which he could see back and under the overhanging rock. This presented no immediate danger because the ledge curved to the east, away from the cowboy. Or perhaps the man was making for a point of descent, so as to be able to approach Burns on his own level. This gave him plenty to think about as he waited there, crouching under the rock and listening, staring below over the brink of the first ledge into the complex of pinnacles and ridges and canyons below.

Beyond the canyon mouths the long broad slope of earth sank toward the river; a yellow haze still obscured the city, and the sun, drifting down into dust and smoke, had assumed the complexion of raw bleeding flesh.

A stone fell, struck rock, shattered and flew into fragments into the branches of the pine. Whisky snorted, reared back a little, her eyes rolling, her breath smoky in the chill air. Burns glanced up and saw the legs and fundament of a man in khaki appearing over the edge of the cliff, a rope dangling below him. Burns stepped out a few feet, holding his rifle lightly and aiming from the hip. The man started to rappell down, letting the rope slide slowly between his legs, across his chest and over one shoulder. He descended about half the distance, a shotgun slung across his back, and then noticed Burns looking up at him.

The man hesitated, licking his lips, swinging slightly on the taut rope. He was twenty feet above the ground, fifty feet from Burns. He licked his lips again and grinned shyly.

"Come on down," Burns said quietly. "And don't let out a whimper or I'll shoot."

Still the man hesitated.

"Come on down," Burns said.

The man came down, slowly, very slowly. He seemed to be having difficulty in handling the rope; several times it got caught among the rocks or in the yucca and greasewood growing in cracks in the wall. At last his feet touched the gravel slope at the base of the cliff. He was facing Burns.

"Put your hands behind your head and turn around," Burns said. The man turned, still grinning foolishly. Burns considered for a moment. "Unsling that shotgun." The man obeyed, lifting the canvas sling over his head and letting the gun fall to the ground. He was wearing a heavy moleskin mackinaw and beneath it, probably, a cartridge belt and holstered revolver. "Keep your hands on the back of your neck," Burns said. He shifted the carbine to his left hand, holding it like a pistol, stepped forward lightly and picked up a short dead stub of pine. Involuntarily the man turned his head and saw Burns approaching him with the rifle in one hand and a club in the other.

"Hey!" he said; "hey—what do you think . . . ?"

Burns swung at his head; the man went down awkwardly, trying to shield his face with his forearms—"Wait a minute, please," he said. The club broke through his guard and smashed solidly onto the side of his skull, above the ear. He groaned and went down slowly, reaching for his head, then collapsing into stillness.

Burns went down with him, jerking open the coat, unbuckling the gun belt. "Goddamnit," he said, "I'm sorry, fella." He felt a little sick, uncertain, nervous. His victim groaned again, stirring feebly, while Burns pulled off the gun belt and fastened it around his own waist. He searched for handcuffs, found them in a pocket of the coat, dragged the man to a tree, put his arms around it and locked his wrists together. The man leaned forward against the trunk of the tree, moaning softly; a few bubbles of spittle oozed from his lips. Burns stared at him. "I'm sorry, fella," he said; "I just can't take any chances now." The deputy had lost his hat; Burns recovered it for him and set it firmly on the blackhaired, sagging head. "There . . . so long." He picked up his rifle and walked to the rope hanging from the cliff.

The mare, Whisky, was browsing among the oak leaves and
pine needles. Burns took the rope in his hand and tugged at
it, testing: it seemed well anchored. The mare raised her head
and looked at him. Burns glared back at her. "You bitch," he
muttered, "you ain't been nothin but trouble to me ever since I
got you." The mare raised her ears alertly, staring at him. "That's
right—nothin but trouble. You're no damn good and you know
it." Burns looked up the rope, up over the gray rock and the
brush, into the sky, into freedom. Above was the rim of the
mountain, and on the other side a thousand miles of forest and
wilderness reaching north into Canada and south into Mexico.
He gave the rope another pull, feeling the eyes of the mare on
him. He cursed again, and thought of his saddle, bedroll, venison, ammunition, all the rest of his gear—and of the horse.
"What the hell." He dropped the rope, went back to the mare,
picked up her reins and led her off.

He started south, stopped, changed his mind and faced
about, and marched northward back the way he had come. This
was painful, retracing his journey—an extravagant waste of
effort, perhaps. Yet it seemed like good tactics.

He fought his way through the clinging brush, making no attempt at stealth, and in less time than he expected—perhaps fifteen minutes—he reached the point where he had ascended from
the ledge below. Here he resumed his usual caution, anticipating a
sudden encounter with his pursuers, but no man appeared.

He did not descend; he left the old route and went on to the
north, looking for another opening that would enable him to get
himself and his horse and baggage up through or over the wall
above him and up to the rim.

There was a tremor, an uncertainty, in the light;—Burns

looked to the west and saw a thin film of cloud, ragged and windblown and ashy-gray, passing across the red sun. The city, the river and the valley remained hidden under a pall of dust; the horizon had disappeared in the general yellow murk. But overhead and to the south and east the sky was still clean and pure, a great dome of primary blue, icy and remote, with the delirious intensity of fire.

Burns stopped for a moment to knead his chilled hands; he craved another drink of water—something in the high piercing air of the mountain intensified his thirst—but he had to consider certain possibilities, ration his needs, conserve his supply. He went on, thinking about water, and in a well-shaded place under a Ponderosa pine he found a patch of glazed snow. He knelt down and scraped part of the surface clean, dug out a handful of the icy stuff and ate it, disregarding the black specks of pine bark distributed through it.

They trudged on, the man and his horse, over the rubble of sliding rock, through thickets of scrub oak, under aspens and scattered pines, until they came to a series of setbacks in the wall above which made it possible to ascend to the rim. Burns led the mare to a point just below the crest, tethered her there among the scrub, and went on up alone to reconnoiter.

He found another world: Instead of canyons, cliffs, boulders, cactus, and radical gulfs of space, he saw an extensive area of meadow and forest sloping gently to the east like the deck of a listing ship, extending for twenty miles downward over rolling foothills to the eastern plains. Here was the old and original surface of the earth, the appalachian country; the tremendous power that had thrust it all a mile into the sky had given it a new climate and different flora but left its basic topographic character unchanged.

Burns stretched out on his belly between buttresses of rock and concentrated his attention on the scene within his purview, searching for the sign or smell of Man. Directly before him was a meadow of grama grass, with a few soft old gray boulders, mellowed by moss and lichens, sunk deeply and comfortably into the earth, each one surrounded by constellations of miniature alpine flowers. Snow lay in patches here and there, preserved in the blue shadows of the rocks. The meadow ended at timberline about fifty yards below, in the stands of slender, white-barked aspens that fringed the dark forest of pine and spruce and fir. A dim trail would out of the trees to the north, passed across the meadow near its center and re-entered the forest to the south, a quarter of a mile off. Burns followed the trail with his eyes: looking north he could see a small cubical structure of stone, a kind of shelter or lookout, set on the edge of the rim about a quarter-mile away. One window, black and empty, like a gunport, faced him from the south wall. He studied that for several minutes. Much farther to the north, five miles or more, he saw the two television relay towers—gigantic red and white skeletons of steel, like a pair of Martian monsters stranded on the brink of the world. There or near there, he knew, was the endpoint of the road that came up the mountain from the east.

He looked to the south: the rim of the mountain curved eastward, then westward, dropping off by easy stages into the dark shadow that was Scissors Canyon, ten miles away. Beyond that were the blue, smoky, pyramidal peaks of the Manzanos and the ranges of mountain wilderness that rolled on for three hundred miles toward Mexico. Burns stared southward, southward, until his eyes began to blur with longing and the ache in his heart crept up into his throat.

He was getting careless already. A man was walking along

the rim toward him, less than a mile away, coming slowly closer, disappearing now and then among the aspens. Something familiar in that shambling gait, the stoop of huge shoulders under the negligible weight of a small, dark, haired-over head—Burns blinked his eyes, narrowed and sharpened his gaze: almost at once he recognized the man as Gutierrez. Naturally, reflexively, the fingers of his right hand tightened around the reassuring heft and shape of the rifle by his side.

Burns plucked a stem of grama and chewed on it for a while, his eyes grave and thoughtful. He waited and watched and presently saw Gutierrez stop at the edge of the rim, looking down. He heard or thought he heard an exchange of shouts—human noises. He waited for Gutierrez to act; he must have found the man that Burns had captured and shackled to the tree. In a moment he would undoubtedly climb down the rope to release him.

He picked a second stem of grass to chew on. He was not particularly comfortable lying there on the hard snow, which was beginning to thaw under the warmth of his body: he could feel a damp coldness pressing into his knees, thighs and elbows. And the westerly was sharp and bitter, a stiff whining persistent wind that penetrated his clothing and chilled his ears and fingers; he could hear it flurry and sough in the forest below, the excitement of the aspen leaves like the sound of falling water or a distant multitudinous applause. Burns listened, his eyes on Gutierrez, his right thumb on the hammer of the carbine.

Gutierrez stood for several minutes looking down over the edge of the cliff. Finally he got into motion again, head bent low as if seeking something on the ground, and lumbered further along the rim toward Burns, a rifle or shotgun cradled in his left arm: the hunter.

Burns stirred on the crusted snow, surprised and alarmed. Below was the forest, dark, warm, deep, charged with secrecy; he looked at it with yearning, then forced his attention back to the left: something had changed in the aspect of the stone shelter on the north. Beside the black aperture in the wall a shadow had appeared, distorted by the stone surface into the shape of a serpent. Burns could see the shadow but not the open eye of a rifle. Five hundred yards.

Gutierrez approached from the south, now within a thousand yards—still far out of range.

The cowboy glanced down at his dried-out hands: on the back of each was a faint encrustation of salt. He felt for a moment the mad temptation of paralysis: to do nothing, nothing at all, to let the end come unresisted. He spat out the chewed-up grass and crawled backward on his knees and elbows, keeping his butt down until he was below the summit of the rise; there he turned and went on down among the chaparral and rocks, crouching nearly double; only when he was definitely below the skyline did he straighten up.

The mare was waiting for him, a sprig of oak leaves hanging from her mouth. He bent down to untie the reins from the base of the shrub, laying his rifle on the crushed dead leaves on the ground. His fingers were stiff with cold and strain; he fumbled uselessly with the knot, then raised his hands to his mouth to blow on them. At that moment he saw the Indian coming around the corner of the ledge below, not more than a hundred yards away; the Indian made a steady dry clashing sound as he walked over the leaves. Burns stared at him; the Indian stopped, looked up and saw him, frozen there on the slope, only half-hidden by the brush. They stared at each other through the

yellowing light and through the sudden ringing silence that followed the Indian's halt.

Burns reached for his rifle, then saw that the Indian was
armed with only a walking stick; he went back to work on the
knot, trying to keep his hands steady. The mare had tightened
the simple overhand by jerking at the reins and for a moment it
seemed to him, in his nerveless desperation, that he could do
nothing. But the knot gave; at the same time he heard the Indian
shout at someone coming up from below, still out of sight. Burns
picked up rifle and reins and started to scramble up the short
slope to the top. For a moment Whisky resisted his lead and he
swore, snarled at her: "You bitch, you whore, you murderin she-
devil—come on! Hup!" and the mare stared back at him with
her lustrous brainless eyes, lifted her right foreleg and followed
him. He heard the Indian shout again but did not look back; he
struggled up over the stones and slippery leaves and the mare
heaved herself up after him, trailing a ruin of mangled leaves,
crushed blades of yucca, a small dusty avalanche of stones.

They reached the top of the rise; Burns glanced back down
and saw a second man appear behind the Indian, awkwardly un-
slinging a submachinegun. Burns kept going, hauling the horse
after him, and as they cleared the high point of the rim and
started into the meadow, he was followed and passed by fragments of exploded rock and the scream of ragged lead butterflies
burning through the air above his head; he heard the barking
stutter of the submachine gun in automatic fire, recoil, refire.

The forest was waiting, fifty yards down across the quiet,
snow-dappled meadow of grama and lupine and mountain vi-
olets. Burns hesitated for a second: he saw Gutierrez running
toward him from the south, saw him stumble, almost fall and
keep on coming; he glanced to the north and saw a tall man in

green military coveralls step out of the stone shelter and aim a rifle at him. There was no more shouting; the only sound, before the man in the coveralls started to fire, was that of the wind in the trees—the excited clashing and rustling of the aspen leaves—and the mare's wild panting for air, and Burns' own heavy breathing.

The man in the coveralls fired offhand, underestimating the range; the bullet cut through grass and plowed into the dirt twenty yards short of the target—Burns scarcely noticed it. But even so he could not deny the clamor of his nerves and blood and senses: *Run!* As Gutierrez was doing—as the man in the green military coveralls began to do. Instead Burns stepped back beside the mare, checked the cinch, slid the rifle into the saddle scabbard and then finally put his foot in the stirrup and pulled himself up into the saddle.

The man in the coveralls stopped running, knelt and fired again; the range was still too great: the lead slug smashed off a rock about a dozen paces north of man and horse. The rifleman raised his rear sight by a millimeter.

Burns turned the trembling mare toward the forest. "Hup," he said, digging his heels into her flanks. Whisky started down, breaking at once into a trot—a little unsteady. She almost buckled at first, but recovered, steadied herself and began to lope. Burns drew her in, keeping her to a good stiff jarring trot. He raised one hand to his hatbrim and pulled the hat down firmly and straight. A matter of pride; the forest was not far away.

The man in the green coveralls fired again from his kneeling position, taking time and care.

Burns, gazing at nothing but the trees ahead, felt the bullet coming; he contracted, shriveling his entire body; at the same time he saw a flake of leather whip off the pommel of the saddle under his hands, and felt and heard the hiss of metal scorching the air. The mare's ears shot up, quivered. They heard the sound of the shot a half-second later. Whisky leaped forward but Burns slowed her again with a pull at the reins.

On the south Gutierrez had stopped running, still too far away for a good shot. Behind Burns, at the crest, the Indian tracker appeared, silhouetted against the sky. He shouted again at the machine-gunner behind him, bent down, picked up a stone and tossed it after the man on horseback. A good try: the stone bounced off the mare's rump and spun to the ground. Whisky snorted, spooked, leaped forward again, cantering over the whispering grass toward the trees. And this time Burns let her go, letting himself go, laughing like a wild fool. Within moments the white slim quaking aspens were all around him, bending in the wind, their yellow leaves chattering frantically, crazily, with the laughing hysteria of old mad women.

The man in the green military coveralls fired once more and missed; he remained on one knee, rubbing his jaw thoughtfully, and watched his target become shadowy, discontinuous, in the maze of the trees. Gutierrez took a random shot from five hundred yards away, aiming north northeast; he heard his bullet ricochet from a rock and go singing into the blue toward Kansas. While on the rim above the meadow the Indian stood, pointing down into the forest. The young man panting and sweating and cursing beside him could see nothing, nothing but light, and insubstantial shadows; nevertheless he pulled and held the trigger of his Browning submachine gun, staggering slightly under its recoil, fighting against the upthrust of the muzzle, and liberally sprayed the grass and rocks and trees with hot shrieking bullets: he wounded several aspens.

CHAPTER 18

"We gonna go home now Morey?" The radio operator looked unhappy, plaintive, like a young lost beagle; his nose and fingers were turning blue with cold. He sniffled through his blue nose.

Johnson explored the inside of his collar. "You say they found Glynn?" He removed a sprig of tumbleweed and dropped it on the ground while the operator answered him. The wind seemed to be dying down now that the sun had gone under; still there was too much fine dust in the air for comfort. "What'd you say?" Johnson said.

"What?" The operator chewed on the dry chapped skin of his lip. "I said yes they found him. He was handcuffed to this tree. Gutierrez saw him and got him loose. He had a bad knock on the head."

"Gutierrez?"

"Floyd—Glynn."

"Yes." Johnson stared up at the mountain: the red veins of iron in the granite which composed those towers and buttresses and cliffs were turning pink now in the last rosy flush of light from the sun that was already below Johnson's horizon. As he watched the pink radiance deepened into lavender, retreating upward before the advance of the blue, violet and purple shadows. The night, he thought—the night is coming: that shade rolling up the face of the mountain, the black night coming from the east—it's dark already in Tucumcari, in Santa Rosa, in Moriarty. Above the rim the eastern sky was changing from blue to a pale cold green—the suggestion of winter.

He turned to the west; the sun had gone down without glory behind a haze of smoke and dust, leaving only a dull yellow stain stretched across the sky, but to the southwest somewhere over Thieves' Mountain a fat star glimmered, flickered, sinking. Venus, said Johnson to himself, Venus—evening star, planet of love . . .

Johnson broke off, abashed by his train of thought. He looked over his shoulder at the radio operator; the radio operator was looking at him.

"Then they're all up there now?" Johnson said.

"Sure—all of them."

"What about the helicopter pilot?"

"Him too." The operator watched him hopefully, sniffing. "You think we still might find this guy tonight, Morey?" he said.

"He'll show up somewhere," Johnson replied. "Sometime."

The operator waited. Johnson scratched at his armpit, staring down at the sand and tangled brush by the jeep: I'm hungry, he thought. It was like a discovery; he freed his mind from the image of the mountain, the star. I'm hungry, he told himself. He heard the radio operator blowing his nose in forlorn desperation.

"All right," Johnson said: "let's go home."

CHAPTER 19

At a bend in the trail and near the beginning of the descent into the canyon, among a group of giant yellowpines, he halted the mare slowly, stiffly, let himself down out of the saddle. He was tired, almost dizzy with fatigue, but still he felt good, satisfied: he had been chewing on raw venison for ten miles and three hours. He sagged against the trunk of a pine, unbuttoned his jeans and urinated, staring at the same time down the mountainside into the purple gloom of the pass. The gloom was far from complete: the four-lane highway that wound through the bottom of the pass was alive, crawling, itching with motor traffic—an endless procession of tiny points of light proceeding like beads on a thread through the darkness, passing and repassing, vanishing, reappearing, fed into the night from apparently inexhaustible sources.

Burns raised his eyes from the monotonous spectacle and gazed across the canyon through miles of space toward the vague looming forms of the Manzano Mountains; there he would rest tonight, among those unknown and velvet hills, lost from the world until . . .

Letting the thought die, he turned back to the mare. Before

getting back in the saddle he examined the wound on her foreleg. The bleeding had stopped hours ago; he could feel the old incrustation of dried blood in the matted hair, and a slight inflammation, but nothing more. The mare nuzzled him with her warm nose as he knelt beside her. He stood up; it seemed that the injury was not serious; at least it had not affected the mare's gait.

He was about to remount when he heard a noise uptrail—the sharp crackle of brush, a clattering stone. Then a silence. He waited, one hand on the pommel, the other on the butt of the rifle. The mare stood frozen, only her uplifted ears twitching, her nose turned into the wind. A wildcat, Burns told himself, maybe a cougar—following us for practice. He waited a minute longer, heard nothing unusual, and hauled himself up into the saddle. "Hup," he said quietly, and Whisky stepped forward, downward, through the darkness under the pines toward the moving lights and the mountains beyond, toward Mexico.

He rode in silence for a while. And then the meter of the mare's walk began to play on his nerves and simplify his thoughts. He breathed deeply, taking in the fragrance of pinetar, cedar, crushed pine needles, the wind from the valley, and softly, gently, to himself and the mare and the trees that passed slowly beside them, he began to sing:

> O I'm a-goin back . . . to old Mexico . . .
> Where the longhorn cows . . . and the cactus grow . . .
> I'm goin back . . . where the bullets fly . . .
> And I'll ride the trail . . . till the day . . . I . . . die . . .

Behind him rose the dark mountain. Far above, remote in time and space, the glittering stars wheeled to the beat of a cosmic drum.

PART FOUR

THE STRANGER

"On the Fourth day cometh Vengeance . . ."

CHAPTER 20

SCISSORS CANYON, N. MEX.

Hinton had had three cups of black powerful coffee at a place called Comb's near the summit of the pass—an illuminated grotto in the night, rich and beautiful with neon, chromium, plastic, red leather, blonde waitresses from places like Lubbock and Little Rock behind the counter, a clean new big outfit with coffee and truckers and comic postcards; somebody kept playing "Haul Off & Love Me One More Time" on the jukebox—but still, despite the coffee and the glare and the jolting music he had come away feeling numb, foggy, sick in the stomach and tired, terribly tired, all broken up inside: he felt like a sackful of old junk. And his eyelids were heavy, drooping, as if someone had already laid pennies on them. He was thinking about that, and about sleep . . .

The cars kept coming toward him, pair after pair of dazzling disembodied lights—no end to them. He was thinking . . .

A faint glow of red appeared suddenly, somehow, just ahead of his left fender. His heart leaped in panic, he jerked at the wheel and swerved around to the left; he had a glimpse of objects floating by on his right—a stack of logs, the pickup, a startled white face looking up from the window of the cab—and then he was past and clear: nothing ahead but a scattering of more red taillights, and the succession of headlights approaching on the left, swishing by like projectiles.

He breathed heavily and passed a trembling hand across his eyes. Too warm, perhaps; he rolled down the window at his side and let the icy night air come blasting in, shocking himself into wakefulness. Effective but too bitterly cold; he closed the window, blinking his eyes and shaking his head. He knew that he should stop and sleep, but with less than twenty miles to go, and a good warm bed waiting for him . . . He'd make it.

He passed another pickup truck, and a car, before he realized that he was going much too fast, his forty tons of iron and steel rolling down a grade that was steeper than it seemed. He glanced at the speedometer: seventy-five. He took his foot off the throttle and pumped on the brakes; the tractor-trailer slowed gradually to seventy, sixty-five, sixty. He blinked his eyes again and checked the pressure of his air brakes: fifty-five pounds—good enough.

He kept trying not to think of her. A useless passion. He was sick enough already—why add to his miseries? No sense in it; stupid. She wasn't even pretty . . . especially. Nice but no glamour girl. He had other things to worry about, more important things. The girl is lost, he argued with himself—lost, you'll never see her again, she's gone now, forget her . . . Tulsa, Oklahoma City, Amarillo . . . Best forget all about her, my unhappy friend . . .

A current of ice lanced through his nerves: he was dreaming. He blinked and shook his head, while his heart pounded up to a climax, hesitated, went down again. The road was still there, unwinding ahead of him, and he was passing cars again, three of them in a row. He swore at himself; the speedometer was reading eighty-five. Eighty-five! He slowed the truck, pumping on the brakes until he was down to sixty.

The highway, four lanes of it, curved grandly around the contours of the mountain; Hinton was dimly aware of vast dark shapes looming above him on either side—that other world, darkness, cold, the wild empty wind howling over rock and cactus and through the colonnades of the forest. He shivered, although the heater under the dashboard was humming, fanning out a constant stream of warm air from the engine.

The cars kept flowing toward him with their glaring lights, hurtling past with the sound of whistling steel and hot hissing rubber.

Another broad curve in the highway: he saw the city. There it lay, miles away beyond the black notch of the canyon, a soft shimmering bed of light surrounded by darkness. Relaxing again, Hinton thought of a fresh warm bed, of rest—he would sleep for days this time, if he felt like it. For days, by God—who would prevent him? His eyelids began to droop. To sleep, he thought, to sleep, sleep, dreaming of the girl . . .

Red brakelights were flashing ahead of him, flashing, pulsating in the blackness. He jerked his head up, his eyes popping open, and pulled at the wheel and roared around the red flashes on the left, on the inner lane. He was dazzled by the headlights of the approaching cars. Dazzled—and then he thought he was dreaming: he saw a horse on the road directly in front of him, turning round and round, and a man or a devil on the creature's back, whipping it with his hat. Hinton's foot plunged for the brakes; at the same time he heaved at the wheel, swerving the truck further to the left and into the lane of the oncoming traffic. He heard a scream, violent and inhuman, and what seemed like a gentle thump on his right fender—he could see nothing but the glare of the lights blossoming in the dark. He pulled the wheel and the truck to the right, back into his own lane, and saw a big automobile sideslipping on his right, plowing up dust and gravel on the shoulder of the road. He was going too fast, too fast; he pushed hard on the brake pedal, hearing his tires screech and shudder on the asphalt pavement. Forty tons, seventy miles an hour: he fought with the giant machine for a thousand feet before he could bring it to a full stop.

He set the parking brake and jumped out, leaving the engine running and all lights shining. He started to run, remembered something, turned back to the cab and groped for the First-Aid kit under the seat. He found it, cradled it in one arm like a football and turned again and ran up the highway, panting, his ribs beginning to ache almost at once. His mind was inert, paralyzed, glazed with shock.

He ran, his shoes pounding loudly on the asphalt; he heard the scream again, long and violent and terrible. Ahead of him he could see lights shining through dust, cars approaching, cars pulling off the highway. He couldn't think; he didn't try; but one noise went through his head, repeatedly, in rhythm with his feet: God, oh God, oh my God, oh God. He kept running.

In the glare of the lights, crumpled strangely in a black sheen of blood, he saw this figure of a man. Hinton was the first to reach him; the man was still alive, breathing convulsively, gasping and trying to talk through a mouthful of blood. Hinton put his hands under his armpits and drew him as gently as he could, not lifting or bending the body, off the pavement onto the gravel shoulder of the road.

A car hissed by, white faces staring; another; another.

Faces, bodies, emerged from the two cars parked nearby. Two men and a woman came up to Hinton and gaped down at the broken body in his arms. From the blackness of the arroyo below the highway came the scream again, wild and struck with terror.

"Blankets," Hinton said. He stared up at the men, the woman. "Please, get some blankets. Quick."

The woman turned and ran back to her car.

"I'll go on and call an ambulance," one of the men said.

"Go ahead," Hinton said. "And for godsake hurry."

The cars roared by on the highway, one after another, endlessly; from each peered a face, or two or three faces, staring blankly.

The woman came back with a pair of woolen rugs; each was woven in the bright, geometric style of the Navajo. Hinton took them and laid them over and tucked them under the body of the man, whose head and shoulders he rested on his lap. Looking down, he saw the face of a young man, white as candlewax, with a week's growth of whiskers, a thin crooked nose, and two vague, stunned eyes staring up at him. "You're gonna be all right, buddy," Hinton said. "Just take it easy." He reached in under the blankets and loosened the man's clothing; he felt the cartridge belt and then the revolver. He left them where they were, hidden by the blanket.

The young man attempted to speak. His lips moved, he swallowed and started to choke.

"Take it easy, friend," Hinton said, lifting his head. He pulled a handkerchief from his hip pocket and wiped some of the blood and sweat and dust from the young man's face.

The horse screamed from below.

"Why don't we put him in my car?" the woman said. She was wearing jeans and a ragged sweater. She had a tough, sun-dried, southwestern face and the kind of voice that often goes with it: soft, slow, gentle.

"We better not try to move him," Hinton said. "I think his back is broke."

A state police car stopped behind them, the red dome of light on its roof revolving, flashing. One man got out, the other stayed inside, speaking into the microphone of the shortwave transmitter.

The first trooper knelt down beside Hinton and looked at the victim's white, sweating face. "We're calling an ambulance," he said. "Is he still alive?"

"Sure," said Hinton. "Of course he's still alive."

The young man opened his mouth again, still trying to talk. "Paul," he said hoarsely—"come on . . ."

"How bad is he hurt?" the trooper asked.

"I don't know for sure. I think his back's broke and maybe worse. He's bleeding inside."

"Yeah? He's in shock, too," the trooper said. "Look at that white face. Maybe you ought to lower his head."

"But he's bleeding too much," Hinton said. "He was almost choking on his own blood when I found him."

"Well . . ." The trooper shrugged his shoulders. "Okay. You might be right." He looked at the smear of blood on the pavement, at the nearby car, at the woman standing above them. "What happened anyway?" he said to Hinton.

Hinton nodded his head dumbly, for a moment unable to speak. He licked at his lips and managed to say: "That's my rig down there."

The trooper glanced down the road toward the gay colored lights that outlined the trailer and tractor. "You hit him?" he said.

Hinton nodded.

From the darkness below the highway came the sound of the heavy body thrashing in agony among the rocks and brush; they heard the ragged, terrorized scream.

"What in God's name is that?" the trooper said.

The woman looked at Hinton. He said: "The horse, I guess. He was riding a horse."

"A horse!" The trooper was silent for a moment. "A horse," he said again, quietly, looking at the man in Hinton's arms. "Well . . . now we know . . ."

"Know what?"

"We been looking for this lad. All over creation."

The stream of automobiles and trucks poured by on the highway, continuously, furiously, roaring through the night . . .

"When's that ambulance gonna get here?" Hinton said.

"It'll take about ten minutes."

"Paul," the young man said. Blood leaked from the corners of his mouth and from his nose. "Paul," he said, breathing hard, "where the hell are you?"

"Easy, pal," Hinton said. "You're gonna be all right." He looked up at the state trooper. "Maybe we ought to take him to the hospital ourselves," he said. "You got a litter in your car?"

"No, we don't." The trooper pulled at his nose, then looked down at his fingers. "I don't know," he said. "You're not supposed to move a man if he's busted up inside."

"I don't think he'll make it," Hinton said.

"We better wait. They'll be here in a few minutes." The trooper readjusted his squatting position, shifting his weight from one leg to the other. "You'll have to make a full report of this," he said to Hinton.

"Sure," Hinton said. "I know. I'll follow you to the station, soon as the ambulance gets here."

Again the horse screamed.

The woman scraped her feet restlessly. "Somebody ought to go down and shoot that horse," she said.

"Where is it?" the trooper asked.

"Down there in the arroyo."

The trooper stood up, pulled a flashlight from his belt and walked to the edge of the highway, drawing his revolver. "I don't see it," he said, aiming his light down into the darkness. "Yes I do," he said and started to descend, slipping a little on the loose gravel.

The young man in Hinton's arms stirred uncomfortably, trying to raise his head. "Paul," he said, staring wildly at Hinton, "you got to come with me." He breathed in short sharp gasps as if in suffocation. "You got to come with me," he said; "Paul," he said, "Paul—" And then his words were cut off in a fit of choking as the dark rich blood gushed out from his mouth and nostrils. The woman knelt down beside him, reaching for his body.

"Don't worry," Hinton was mumbling, touching the young man's hair; "you're gonna be *all right*. Everything's gonna be fine."

From the black arroyo came the scream of the horse, then the sound of the first shot and another scream;—while over the great four-lane highway beside them the traffic roared and whistled and thundered by, steel, rubber, and flesh, dim faces behind glass, beating hearts, cold hands—the fury of men and women immured in engines.

ABOUT THE AUTHOR

Edward Abbey spent most of his life in the American Southwest. He was the author of numerous works of fiction and nonfiction, including the celebrated *Desert Solitaire*, which decried the waste of America's wilderness, and the novel *The Monkey Wrench Gang*, the title of which is still in use today to describe groups that purposefully sabotage projects and entities that degrade the environment. Abbey was also one of the country's foremost defenders of the natural environment. He died in 1989.

BOOKS BY EDWARD ABBEY

BLACK SUN
A Novel
Available in Paperback and eBook

Black Sun is a bittersweet love story involving an iconoclastic forest ranger and a freckle-faced "American princess" half his age. Like Lady Chatterley's lover, he initiates her into the rites of sex. She, in turn, awakens in him the pleasure of love. Then she mysteriously disappears, plunging him into desolation.

THE BRAVE COWBOY
A Novel
Available in Paperback

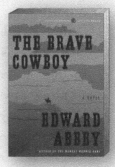

Jack Burns, an "anarchist cowboy," is a loner at odds with modern civilization. He lives by a personal code of ethics that sets him on a collision course with the keepers of law and order. After a prison breakout plan goes awry, he finds himself and his horse, Whisky, pursued across the desert towards the mountains that lead to Mexico, and to freedom.

FIRE ON THE MOUNTAIN
A Novel
Available in Paperback

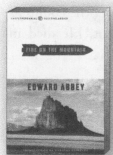

John Vogelin's land is his life—a barren stretch of New Mexican wilderness mercifully bypassed by civilization. Then the government moves in, and suddenly the elderly, mule-stubborn rancher is confronting the combined land-grabbing greed of the county sheriff, the Department of the Interior, the Atomic Energy Commission, and the U.S. Air Force.

THE MONKEY WRENCH GANG
A Novel
Available in Paperback

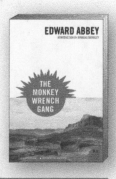

Ex-Green Beret George Hayduke has returned from war to find his beloved southwestern desert threatened by industrial development. Joining with Bronx exile and feminist saboteur Bonnie Abzug, wilderness guide and outcast Mormon Seldom Seen Smith, and libertarian billboard torcher Doc Sarvis, Hayduke is ready to fight the power—taking on the strip miners, clear-cutters, and the highway, dam, and bridge builders who are threatening the natural habitat.